Femme Fatale

Sketch by Wilhelm von Kaulbach

By Carole Nelson Douglas from Tom Doherty Associates

MYSTERY

MIDNIGHT LOUIE MYSTERIES:

Catnap

Pussyfoot *Cat on a Hyacinth Hunt*
Cat on a Blue Monday *Cat in an Indigo Mood*
Cat in a Crimson Haze *Cat in a Jeweled Jumpsuit*
Cat in a Diamond Dazzle *Cat in a Kiwi Con*
Cat with an Emerald Eye *Cat in a Leopard Spot*
Cat in a Flamingo Fedora *Cat in a Midnight Choir*
Cat in a Golden Garland *Cat in a Neon Nightmare*
Midnight Louie's Pet Detectives (editor of anthology)

IRENE ADLER ADVENTURES:
Good Night, Mr. Holmes
The Adventuress* (*Good Morning, Irene*)
A Soul of Steel* (*Irene at Large*)
Another Scandal in Bohemia* (*Irene's Last Waltz*)
Chapel Noir
Castle Rouge
Femme Fatale

Marilyn: Shades of Blonde (editor of anthology)

HISTORICAL ROMANCE
Amberleigh** *Lady Rogue***
Fair Wind, Fiery Star

SCIENCE FICTION
Probe**
Counterprobe**

FANTASY

TALISWOMAN:
Cup of Clay
Seed upon the Wind

SWORD AND CIRCLET:
Six of Swords *Heir of Rengarth*
Exiles of the Rynth *Seven of Swords*
Keepers of Edanvant

*These are the revised editions
**also mystery

Femme Fatale

An Irene Adler Novel

Carole Nelson Douglas

FORGE

A Tom Doherty Associates Book
New York

Dou

FEMME FATALE

Copyright © 2003 by Carole Nelson Douglas

This book is printed on acid-free paper.

Edited by Claire Eddy

Map by Darla Tagrin

Title page art courtesy of California History Room, California State Library, Sacramento, California

A Forge Book
Published by Tom Doherty Associates, LLC
175 Fifth Avenue
New York, NY 10010

www.tor.com

Forge® is a registered trademark of Tom Doherty Associates, LLC.

ISBN 0-765-30682-4

First Edition: October 2003

Printed in the United States of America

0 9 8 7 6 5 4 3 2 1

For Kathy Henderson,
a true blue friend and supporter for more than twenty years,
with deepest thanks

Contents

Acknowledgments

The author is grateful to Don Hobbs and Jim Webb, devoted Texas Sherlockians, for their assistance with matters of the Canon, especially to Don in the area of early editions of the Doyle works, and to Jim for his efforts in helping the Irene Adler series find a wider international audience.

I would give a great deal to know what inevitable stages of incident produced the likes of Irene Adler. Show me a method of forming more women so, and I would show more interest in women.

—SHERLOCK HOLMES, *GOOD NIGHT, MR. HOLMES,*

CAROLE NELSON DOUGLAS

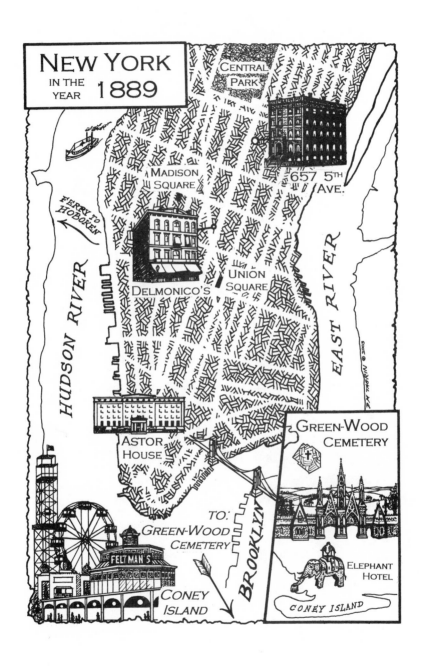

NEW YORK
IN THE YEAR 1889

CENTRAL PARK

657 5TH AVE.

MADISON SQUARE

FERRY TO HOBOKEN

HUDSON RIVER

DELMONICO'S

UNION SQUARE

EAST RIVER

ASTOR HOUSE

GREEN-WOOD CEMETERY

TO: GREEN-WOOD CEMETERY

FELTMAN'S

CONEY ISLAND

BROOKLYN

ELEPHANT HOTEL

CONEY ISLAND

Cast of Continuing Characters

Irene Adler Norton: an American abroad who outwitted the King of Bohemia and Sherlock Holmes in the Conan Doyle story, "A Scandal in Bohemia," reintroduced as the diva-turned-detective protagonist of her own adventures in the novel, *Good Night, Mr. Holmes*

Sherlock Holmes: the London consulting detective building a global reputation for feats of deduction

John H. Watson, M.D.: British medical man and Sherlock Holmes's sometime roommate and frequent companion in crime-solving

Godfrey Norton: the British barrister who married Irene just before they escaped to Paris to elude Holmes and the King

Penelope "Nell" Huxleigh: the orphaned British parson's daughter Irene rescued from poverty in London in 1881; a former governess and "typewriter girl" who lived with Irene and worked for Godfrey before the two met and married, and who now resides with them in Paris

Quentin Stanhope: the uncle of Nell's former charges when she was a London governess; now a British agent in eastern Europe and the Mideast; he reappeared in *A Soul of Steel* (formerly *Irene at Large*)

Nellie Bly, a.k.a. Pink: the journalistic pseudonym and family nick-name of Elizabeth Jane Cochrane, involved in the Continental pursuit of Jack the Ripper in *Chapel Noir* and *Castle Rouge*; a young woman with a nose for the sensational and her own agenda

Oscar Wilde: friend of Irene Adler; a wit and man of fashion about London. He had not yet written any of his classic plays, but his very successful lecture tour of America in the early 1880s included the Wild West

Bram Stoker: theatrical manager of London's finest actor, Henry Irving, and burgeoning writer, who would pen the classic *Dracula*; Irene's ally in the hunt for Jack the Ripper in *Chapel Noir* and *Castle Rouge*

Prelude: The Dead Departed

·◦◦·

*I almost think we're all of us Ghosts.... It's not only what we
have inherited from our father and mother that "walks" in us.*

—MRS. ALVING, *GHOSTS*, ACT II, 1881,

HENRIK IBSEN

◦{ FROM NELLIE BLY'S JOURNAL }◦

This room is darker than a tomb . . .

. . . although I must admit that I have only been in a
tomb once and hope I won't be in another one until I'm
beyond noticing it.

I haven't, however, attended a séance before.

Anyway, the darkness makes it blasted inconvenient for taking
notes, but I guess that when one is awaiting an appearance by the
dead departed a little irritation is small price to pay.

I, of course, no more expect to see or hear the dead tonight
than I'd expect P. T. Barnum to resurrect and turn tent preacher
and start performing baptisms in the East River.

But that's my job: to put myself into situations I don't much
like and then tell everyone about it. That's why I'm more widely
known by a name I wasn't born with: Nellie Bly. Now I have

brought the name of Nellie Bly from the *Pittsburg Dispatch* and women's interest news to the *New York Herald*. Not even feigning madness in the Women's Lunatic Asylum was story enough to earn me respect in Pittsburg, but the sky is the limit in New York, for the new twelve-story buildings going up on Fifth Avenue and for me.

I figure I can take pretty good notes even in the dark, being used to doing it daily. A daredevil reporter lives by her ability to discreetly record what others are doing. That's why my notepad and a pencil are clapped between my knees in a sheltering hammock of skirt.

It is not a posture recommended for ladies, but then who will see me in this gloom?

A woman's low voice suggests that I join hands with my neighbors. This I had expected. Part of the reason is, I suspect, to prove that none of us are the medium's henchmen. Yet it would only take two henchmen (or one of those shopkeeper's wooden display hands covered in a glove) to put the lie to our presumed linkage.

My neighbors, though I can't see them any longer, are decent sorts. One is my mother.

The ladies have kept their gloves on, either for better deception or simply to avoid pressing flesh with anyone who might be unsavory, or, simply, a stranger.

A small tingle works its way from my foot to my shoulder. It could be a cramp . . . or spirit fingers, perhaps?

At the least I expect phenomena. At the most, I anticipate some ghostly voice from the past. Or perhaps suspended musical instruments that play "De Camptown Races." Doo-dah.

Really, mediums should be frank about their trade, sell tickets, and then tell the paying public all their tricks at the end as part of the show.

I do not much believe in the dead returning, anywhere at any time, mainly because I am not much eager to meet my dead again . . . unless it were the judge. No, he is too wise to come back for a return engagement, especially after all that was done with his estate. One would think a judge could protect himself better from the grasping fingers of his nearest and dearest.

Someone sighs. Not me. Not even the thought of all that my mother and I and my brothers and sisters lost at the judge's death can make me sigh for the past. Regret is for lily maids of Astelot, and I am no lily maid . . . in the sense of shrinking violet. I don't commit myself as to my state of virtue. Modern women are much better off being mysterious about that.

Another sigh, deeper.

Now I see. Or hear and understand, rather. This is the overture to the show.

On my left, fingers tighten on mine. This is the aged Mrs. Beale, obviously not a shill with a false hand to palm off . . . unless the squeeze was to allay my suspicions before the hand was substituted. The press is cynical, they say, but we are mostly hard to fool, is all.

There is no movement in the hand on my right, and I would expect none. Mr. Flynn is a nervous reed of a young man who swallows frequently. His thin neck reveals a huge Adam's apple that bobs when he swallows like a homely toad balancing on a reed's swaying end. Having been instructed to join hands and be still, Mr. Flynn will remain absolutely motionless, except for the frequent swallowing of said Adam's apple, which I hear in the darkness as loud as if it were my own nervous gesture. And except for a certain dampness I feel leeching through my cotton gloves, despite their thickness.

Oh, what a pathetic dance partner he would make, although I doubt this modern Ichabod would ever make so bold as to dance!

But I mustn't people the darkness with stories, a weakness for one of my profession. I must be a tireless witness.

The next sigh is louder, extended, almost inhuman.

I suspect some device. Perhaps a sort of bellows?

Whatever the means, it does produce an eerie, shuddering

sound. Of course we all know the bagpipe was invented to instill fear into the Scot's enemies in the fog-shrouded glens. Some natives of Australia, I understand, play a weird keening pipe that is quite unearthly. And even the Swiss mountaineers in their cheerful, comic opera lederhosen send sound echoing eerily across the Alpine peaks.

There are so many ways to buffalo people of any clime and place. I am not about to be alarmed by a series of sighs!

Ah. But this last sigh has become a groan, moving from a contralto to a bottomless basso tone.

I almost feel the table beneath my wrists tremble.

Now that is a nice effect!

Again, the sound. And now the floor beneath my—our—feet vibrates like one of the great bass drums in an orchestra.

The hand on my left jerks in surprise. The right one holds steady, although the grip is tighter and the Adam's apple is held suspended for the moment.

Ah, a faint high keening. A performing flute, I think, this time. Soon some light should trickle into our tomb-dark chamber to show this brassy wand levitating in air, supposedly played by an invisible mouth breathing from dead lungs. Has anyone who attended a séance ever thought why the resurrected dead would want to join a band and what they would really look like?

Rotting, crumbling flesh and all?

Folks like to say my kind have too much imagination, and perhaps they're right. But I'd rather have too much of anything than too little. I am given to understand that this is one of my greatest flaws. And strengths. And that is what brought the name of Nellie Bly from Pittsburg to New York City. I will not remain consigned to women's interest news, but have investigated such topics as child labor and the miserable lot of working girls.

Well, my knees are getting pretty tired of holding my writing implements in place for ready use, and I'm developing a better respect for the trickery of mediums, especially as it involves cracking lower joints as the famous Fox sisters did. Took patience and pain and practice, I bet. More than I have.

So. Let's get on with the show.

Crack!

Our hands spasm in one round of shock and horror.

It was a sound like the snap of a woolly mammoth's shoulder joint, not a woman's; like the thick table legs breaking in unison.

Then more of the reedy flute piping funereally above us.

And we are all still in the dark.

Not all of us, I think.

At this thought, the tabletop proceeds to elevate, lifting our conjoined hands in the mockery of a Maypole dance position.

Soon our wrists are at shoulder level, and my neighbor on the left is moaning softly. Like a ghost. Or a frightened woman.

I do not have time or inclination to be a frightened woman . . . this levitation of my hands is loosening the grip of my knees. My notepad and pencil are about to clatter to the floor.

Luckily a soft, thick rug underlies us all (*and why exactly is it required*, I wonder), and I may not be betrayed by my implements.

Arrrrghhhh.

This is a raw groan, neither instrumental nor human, but something in-between. *Could a penny whistle be so perverted to produce such an outré sound?* I wonder.

I make a very bad audience for a medium, but then a woman who can feign her state of virtue is not one to be taken in, but rather one to take in others.

I smile in the dark as I recall who knows my secret . . . and who does not.

Arrrrghhhh.

This is getting predictable.

But then the dancing flute begins to sway and keen. Then one ever so gradually becomes aware that the gaslight sconces on the wall are warming with light as subtly as the dawn tinting the horizon with rosy fingertips. . . .

All I can see is a faint pale mask in the dark . . . the medium herself, only a face, a luminous oval like a Greek mask of either tragedy or comedy.

Somehow the light, whatever its source, has bleached her skin to parchment, her features to holes torn in such a hide.

Her eyes are pitch-black olives. Her mouth is a black plum, bursting with ripeness into a perfect "O."

And out of that mouth . . . drifts an airy wisp like breath made visible. A snake of smoke and fog. An endless excretion repellent in its implications . . .

I am seeing the spirit substance called ectoplasm.

Yes, I am seeing it. But how?

While I watch, I feel the hands on either side clutch on mine like fleshly manacles that will never release. This visible thread— of breath or life or illusion—weaves like the pipe-enchanted cobra in an Egyptian marketplace, upward and obliquely and never stopping in its motion. It seems that something from our very feet and hands and throats is climbing to the ceiling on the staircase of our conjoined souls.

Enough!

I do not withdraw my hands, or my eyes, but I retract my suddenly childish desire to believe. The judge is dead. I am a woman grown. I will deceive, not *be* deceived.

I feel my knees weaken and my precious pencil and pad slip unheard to the carpet.

My eyes remain fixed on the flute around which the ectoplasm twines like rambling rose over trellis.

The medium's mask of a face still floats on the dark.

"I hear the dead," she intones, her voice as mechanical as one of those heard on Edison's "talking machines." "She is back! The Outcast. The Dancer among the Dead. She will never die!"

And then I notice a strange occurrence in this room dedicated to producing the strange . . . the ectoplasm is weaving back down, as if a thread on a loom were to retrace its path.

A voice without sound executing a glissando of motion, it curls back upon itself, upon its originator. It coils softly around the dark beneath the disembodied face, around the invisible neck.

Then it tightens like a snake quite different from a striking cobra, a boa constrictor made of feathers and fog.

It winds and tightens, tightens and winds . . .

. . . until the face is lost behind its disembodied coils, like a mummy's . . .

. . . until the voice that issues from that disembodied face screams and sighs and sighs and screams.

Finally we stand, screaming as one, drowning out the sound effects, ending the delusion, finally acting not as an audience, but as a sort of demented Greek chorus.

Someone—who knows where? who knows what?—makes the gaslights flare to full brilliance.

The table crashes back to floor. Someone cries in tribute to a wounded toe.

I can hear my fallen pencil snap under the force.

After that dramatic plunge, and the thump of the table creaking back to earth, the room is quiet.

Our medium's face has fallen like a rose blossom too heavy for its stem.

It lies upon the tabletop, open-eyed.

Around its neck is wrapped coil after coil of stringy ectoplasm, now oddly solid and dormant, lifeless.

No one moves.

Then I do.

I approach the dead departed.

I touch the ectoplasmic scarf at her unmoving throat.

It is . . . damp, fragile yet strong, as ropy as an umbilical cord, and I have seen such in my checkered career.

It is also teasingly familiar, this limp, wet rag.

I remember now. Some mediums are regurgitators who can expel yards and yards of consumed cheesecloth at will, like sword-swallowers.

One expects a sword to serve as a weapon.

One does not expect cheesecloth to serve as a garote.

Here it has.

I lift my head. The séance attendees remain assembled, standing, hands still locked, save for mine.

By their faces I can see that they still see spirits.

I see something different.

I see a very clever and puzzling murder.

1.

Duet

~ひᗡこ~

*He was an enthusiastic musician, being himself not only a
very capable performer but a composer of no ordinary merit.*
—DR. JOHN H. WATSON, "THE RED-HEADED LEAGUE," 1891,

SIR ARTHUR CONAN DOYLE

*at Neuilly, near Paris
August, 1889*

"I cannot believe," I told Irene, "that you would agree to such a shocking thing without telling your husband!"

"Which can you not believe, Nell, that I would agree to a 'shocking thing' or that I would not tell Godfrey?"

I had long since learned that my friend Irene Adler Norton was fashioned from an impossible human amalgam resembling iron brocade: apparently decorative but, in truth, nigh impossible to ruffle or bend. I might better exercise my lungs by attempting to blow out the fire in the grate as to move her resolve with the feeble zephyrs of my words.

I shifted ground. "I cannot believe that you would invite That Man to our common home without telling me."

"But I have told you."

"Just now . . . when he could arrive any moment! I am not prepared to receive a guest, even if you are."

I lifted my embroidery hoop from my lap in a gesture of exasperation. The trailing threads immediately attracted the snagging claws of the Persian cat, Lucifer, whose instincts for mayhem were as black as his long, silky coat. In an instant he was tangled in my rainbow skeins.

"Obviously," Irene continued, watching my struggle to unwind embroidery silks from Lucifer's claws with a certain clinical interest, "Sherlock Holmes is not a guest, in your estimation, but an intruder. You must understand that he comes here at my invitation, for a bit of very simple business. I merely have to honor my word and give him the English translation I have had made of the Yellow Book."

"Of course," I said grimly, my shredded threads tugged free of their attacker at last. "It is bad enough that demonic diary fell into our hands at the end of the Ripper affair. I still shudder when I think of the Unholy Trinity that was allied against us then. I doubt that the world will ever be safe from them, however obscurely, and deeply, and securely they are imprisoned. Now you only perpetuate that dreadful time by passing on the demented creature's scribblings to Sherlock Holmes."

"I promised him I would, Nell. And my making the translation allowed me to . . . protect any mention of my dear ones by what you rightly call a 'demented creature.' If Mr. Holmes's presence is so undesirable, you could withdraw upstairs. I don't expect him to remain long."

"How I wish that urgent political depositions in Paris did not keep Godfrey away from home on just this very day! Oh, and I may leave if I don't like the company? Of course! Banish me upstairs to leave you alone with That Man! In Godfrey's absence? I think not. It is my duty to act as chaperon."

Irene sighed, bending to lift the cat free of what was left of my fancy work. "Duty is never pleasant, but I can see that you are determined to make it as unpleasant as possible."

I regarded her with suspicion, but said nothing, though my mind was busy imagining the worst. Was the forthcoming visitor why she had donned her most becoming housedress today? This was a trailing white silk gown with a black net overlay of jet beads and scallops of black lace. The overall effect was of charmingly girlish polka dots, which on closer examination proved far more elegant and sophisticated than that.

Of course, all of Irene's housedresses were becoming, a fact that Godfrey seemed to appreciate. Irene had been an operatic diva, after all, so even her most casual attire displayed inimitable panache. Perhaps that was only because she was extraordinarily comely, as certified by the words of a king: "She has a soul of steel. The face of the most beautiful of women," Wilhelm of Bohemia had observed before adding the unfortunate and equally true afterthought, "and the mind of the most resolute of men."

I had always been taught that masculine resolution belonged to the superior sex. Irene confounded that conviction in me, and in others, including Mr. Sherlock Holmes, the London consulting detective with whom circumstances had recently forced far more acquaintance than I liked.

Irene's own past efforts as a private inquiry agent for the Pinkerton agency in America, even before she descended on England in the early eighties to pursue her operatic career, did not help insure that the likes of Sherlock Holmes and other official and unofficial minions of the law would not darken our cottage doorstep in bucolic Neuilly. At least it was far enough outside of Paris to remain a simple village rather than a crowded and corrupt metropolis.

But now the London "sleuth" was to cross our rural threshold in person.

I glanced down at my striped skirt. And I would be forced to receive him looking like a milkmaid . . . not that a spinster past thirty like myself gave a fig for matters of dress, beauty, or unexpected visitors of the masculine persuasion.

"He will sniff down that sharp London nose of his at our countrified ways," I said. "I am surprised that you are not wearing your favorite Worth."

Irene burst out laughing as she untangled Lucifer's claws from the lace at her elbows. "Sherlock Holmes would as much notice the exquisite couture of Charles Frederick Worth, even though the eminent 'man-milliner' of Paris is a distant relation of his by marriage, as he would Lucifer's savage 'disembowing' of the ribbons along your skirt revers."

"Oh! That dreadful cat! He has indeed managed to undo all my ribbons."

I tossed the embroidery hoop aside and began retying the endless rows just as a knock sounded in the hallway.

I redoubled my efforts. On no account was Mr. Sherlock Holmes to see me with my bows undone, especially since he had witnessed my shockingly irregular attire during the dark events of our previous adventure. I was, after all, an Englishwoman, if not a lady born.

Sophie, our maid of all work and mistress of far too little of it, soon appeared in the parlor door, making what passed for a curtsy. "Where should I place the gentleman's coat and chapeau, *s'il vous plaît.*"

We had so few callers here in the country that no protocol governed their disposition.

"The newel post will do for the coat, Sophie," Irene said airily, "and the hall table for the hat."

At that moment *The* Man himself appeared in the doorway, cloaked in country checks with a plaid hat known as a deerstalker upon his head.

Having only previously seen him in the stripped trousers and top hat of city wear, I straightened red-faced from my bow-tying labors and tried to suppress a snicker. The visitor looked more countrified than ourselves! In fact, I had to admit that his attire was more suitable for a Neuilly visit than city garb. Could it be that Mr. Holmes was less insensitive to the subtle social language of attire than Irene thought?

"Madam," he said with a bow to Irene. "Miss Huxleigh," to me. He handed his coat to Sophie (the poor woman disappeared behind its massive long folds like a mushroom behind a checked mountain) and flung his cap out of sight toward the hall table.

I was irritatingly sure that it had landed where aimed, though I could not see for sure.

With this cavalier gesture, he crossed the threshold into our feminine domain. I saw he wore a brown tweed suit, suitable for travel or shooting holidays.

Irene had risen to extend her hand.

Mr. Holmes took it, hesitated, then shook it in the American fashion.

I could not imagine him kissing it in the Continental fashion, although Quentin Stanhope, or even Godfrey, could no doubt manage that Frenchified sort of salute quite skillfully.

The thought of Quentin kissing a hand, my hand, caused my traitorous heart to skip several beats. I had so stupidly failed both him and myself on the last occasion we had spent time together! Granted, we had both survived great perils and were not ourselves. Yet despite the heightened emotions of the moment, everything severe and cautious from my sheltered Shropshire childhood had risen up to deny him. I could still see the tenderness in his too-truthful hazel eyes fade into such unnecessary apology. I could still hear Nellie Bly, who had accompanied him during the last leg of the rescue mission, calling him "my dear Quentin" not an hour after our disastrous reunion! A reunion that was only disastrous after certain, unforgettable . . . passages between us.

No, no one could hold a candle to Quentin in the hand-kissing department, certainly not a man who considered himself a self-appointed tutor to all humankind!

I clasped my own hands behind my back to avoid any possibility of awkward social contact. If the gesture made me look like a green schoolroom miss, so be it. I knew things about Mr. Sherlock Holmes that even Irene with all her fabled perception could not and would not imagine. It was not that I was especially perceptive, only that I once had occasion to peruse the papers of his associate, Dr. Watson, and had found some thankfully unpublished scribblings about the affair that had first introduced Mr. Holmes into our acquaintance, a manuscript the would-be literary doctor had melodramatically titled "A Scandal in Bohemia."

We were not in Bohemia now, thank the Lord, but France, which was quite another kettle of *poisson*. Odd that the French word for "fish" is so close in spelling to that fatal word in English, poison, but not really odd when you consider how fish taste and smell. That is how I regarded Mr. Sherlock Holmes. As poison to be avoided like the plague. There!

"You are looking better, Miss Huxleigh," *The* Man noted with his usual superior air, "than when last we met."

"I should hope so," I replied. "I have since then been removed from the enforced company of a number of odious persons."

He could not fail to miss that I included him along with the truly heinous villains of our previous adventure.

His smile was private as he turned again to Irene. All men turned again to Irene. She was a magnet whose force could not be denied on the operatic boards or on the more intimate stage of private life.

"I have taken the liberty," she said, returning his smile, "of having a small repast laid out in the parlor window that overlooks the garden. Perhaps you would join us for tea. Meanwhile, I will retrieve the manuscript that is the object of your visit."

"The manuscript that you so fetchingly spirited away from that terrifying castle before I could read it," he pointed out.

"It was in a non-romance language, Mr. Holmes."

"I can read a bit of some non-romance languages, such as the German in *Psychopathia Sexualis*. I must thank you for introducing me to such a rare volume of criminal lore. In fact, I am only now returned from the University of Graz in Austria, where I met with Professor von Krafft-Ebing who heads the Neuro-Psychiatry clinic there, the author of that volume you so kindly . . . lent me."

"It was not a loan, Mr. Holmes, and you need not thank me. It had served my purposes already." Irene had dropped her role of gracious hostess as a man might have cast a gauntlet upon the castle floor. "Do you mean to tell me you have consulted with Baron von Krafft-Ebing? The man himself? Recently?"

"Why else did you think I was abroad again, my dear lady?"

"I assumed another case involving foreign heads of state, of course, my dear sir."

Much as I feared the unwanted secret that I harbored—that Sherlock Holmes was both contemptuous of women's wit in general and enamored of Irene's wit in particular—I realized that I was witnessing a joust, not a tryst. These "my dears" were mere nicks in the verbal fencing match between civilized opponents, not anything personal . . . beyond a keen professional rivalry.

"The book itself," she said, "would seem to be plenty enough food for thought. What more could the author add to his compendium of infamy?"

"There is always more to be learned in the vast arena of crimes of passion around the globe. Professor Krafft-Ebing has achieved something remarkable in the annals of criminal history. He has recorded the acts and particulars of a certain breed of killers he calls lust-murderers as a scientist, not a policeman, would. These are cold and factual case studies, naked of political conclusions and moral confusions. Simple facts. He records the acts, repulsive as they are to any civilized person, without emotion or distortion. And in multiplicity, there is no denying the universality of human wrongdoing. No detail, however debased, escapes his observation and analysis. The book is a classic and the man is a wonder."

"I wonder," said I, "that any civilized person would wish to know more about such grisly matters."

I expected Mr. Holmes to debate me. Instead, he laughed, voicelessly. "Dr. Watson, my esteemed physician friend, would agree with you. He strongly feels that some subjects are not fit knowledge, especially for a woman's sensibility."

"I don't agree with that," Irene said sharply. "What women don't know will hurt them."

Mr. Holmes's expression was both challenged and chagrined. "I said that was Dr. Watson's opinion. I myself do not flinch from the brutal. I have recently been involved in a matter in which a man's thumb was severed as he sought to escape kidnappers."

"Gracious!" I could not help saying, thus unwittingly drawing the man's attention again.

"I am sorry to offend your sensibilities, Miss Huxleigh, though I must admit that I am pleased to see that your thumbs are still attached and busy at household arts, but the world of wrongdoing is full of such deliciously insane events. Professor Krafft-Ebing enlightened me a good deal in that regard."

"Perhaps," Irene said, "the dainty treats of the tea-table are not suitable after such conversation. If you will excuse me, I will fetch the translation." She turned to the hall, then paused and turned back. "Did you find any new evidence in Whitechapel? Anything that would absolve the criminals we captured in the Carpathians earlier this summer?"

Mr. Holmes fingered the small gold sun of a coin that dangled from his watch-fob, a coin that figured, I am sure, in the good doctor's manuscript titled "A Scandal in Bohemia."

"Nothing that would release any of the villains in the case, and nothing that would fully indict them either."

"Nothing?" she asked sharply.

"I did discover more traces of identifiable cork and candle

wax, enough to buttress the case against them, but nothing so conclusive that anyone dare announce a solution. This matter would best be forgotten and buried in the newspaper morgues," he replied.

"A pity. It was so spectacularly grotesque. I imagine the name 'Jack the Ripper' will be used to frighten children into good behavior for some time."

She nodded and turned to leave again, but this time his voice gave her pause, instead of the reverse.

"I do hope, Mrs. Norton, that you are giving me a full translation, with no . . . expurgations."

"My dear Mr. Holmes, if you can read Professor Krafft-Ebing's much despised book on lust-murders and even discuss it with its controversial author, I am sure that I would not be so bold as to Bowdlerize any other volume for your consumption."

"*Hmmm.*" His murmur expressed either satisfaction . . . or doubt.

Irene decided to take it for the former, and smiled again before rustling up our hall staircase.

"Have you read it?"

The question was both abrupt and harsh, and I moved my gaze from Irene's departing skirts to find Mr. Holmes's gimlet gray eyes fixed upon me with the sharpness of a needle point.

"I? Gracious, no. I saw enough of depravity at that Carpathian castle to last me a lifetime. I really cannot understand why you should wish to pursue such matters with the author, and now with that . . . loathsome diary from the hand of a person whose crimes are unimaginable."

"There are no unimaginable crimes, Miss Huxleigh," he said, bending his gaze near my hemline.

I cringed to think that he had noted my unfastened bows, but when I glanced down, I saw that Lucifer, the wretch, had hidden under my skirts and was now thrusting out a suspicious paw, his fat furry foot resembling the toe of a black, ostrich-feather mule.

I stepped back at once to reveal the cat's full form. It was unthinkable that Mr. Sherlock Holmes should believe me capable of wearing anything so frivolous as an ostrich-feather mule!

He made no remark on the cat, instead strolling to where the small round table looked out on the side garden. To do so he had to pass the piano, and his eyes fixed on that instrument with some intensity as he went by it. It was an old-fashioned square piano of rosewood, closed for now and wearing a Spanish shawl. Its lower legs were not swathed in velvet pantaloons, as had been the custom since the days that piano legs were thought too suggestive of women's limbs to reveal.

Mr. Holmes did not appear to direct any licentious glances in their direction, which was a point in his favor.

He clasped his long bony hands behind his back and gazed into the garden, which was entering its autumn stage.

In the parrot cage behind the piano, Casanova edged his gaudy red, green, and yellow plumage down the perch to comment "Good day, Matey," in that odd distant voice of parrots that always sounds like an echo.

The consulting detective ignored the bird's greeting. Indeed, I had the notion that his mind was far removed from this quiet (except for Casanova) parlor in Neuilly outside Paris.

In fact, his entire mien struck me as pensive. (Not the bird's, the man's.) I immediately found my indignation rising on Irene's behalf. Supposedly, the man was secretly besotted with her. Surely he could produce some better reaction to being in her home and her presence than a moody pout!

"The mongoose has slain a snake, I see," he said out of the blue.

"Mongoose!" I dropped my already abused embroidery hoop to the floor as I stood. "Snake! Not a small green one."

"No, a medium black-and-green striped one." He turned, his features tautened with amusement. "Nothing so large and lethal as, say, a cobra, Miss Huxleigh. But then I imagine you have not had an opportunity to see such a fearsome snake in your experience."

I certainly had! More than once. In fact, the mongoose in my care, Messalina, had dispatched more than one when we had occasion to revisit London to save this very man's Boswell, Dr. Watson, from persons with evil intentions toward him.

"A garden snake," I diagnosed with relief. "Messy is fed very well and does not need to eat anything, but at least the victim is not one of Sarah Bernhardt's green snakes that I inherited."

"I imagine the mongoose acts for the sport of the chase, not from hunger. Other creatures than ourselves enjoy the constant game of hunter and hunted."

"I do not, Mr. Holmes. We can all rise above our beastly natures."

"Some of us do not want to," he commented, "which is when I find myself being consulted." He glanced over his shoulder as if eager for Irene's reappearance.

I could only suppose that listening to Casanova, watching the garden, and trying to make awkward conversation with me were not pursuits that suited the man's temperament. He struck me as a strider and a pacer, an indefatigable walker in town and country.

Rapid steps on the hall stair saved us from further attempts at conversation. Irene, as usual, was clattering down the staircase like a schoolgirl.

"Here it is," she announced, a bit breathlessly.

Instead of the producing the small, yellow moiré-bound diary kept by one of the principal villains during our Continental pursuit of Jack the Ripper after Whitechapel, she cradled a sheaf of papers in the crook of one arm, a raw manuscript, written by hand.

Mr. Holmes met her halfway across the room, accepting the untidy sheaf of paper with avidity.

"Excellent! May I ask whom you employed to translate it?"

"An east European actress. I told her it was from a novel."

This was news to me, but while I stared agape, Mr. Holmes nodded. "The tale this tells reads better as fiction, I suspect. A discreet and clever solution to a vexing problem. If the material is unabridged."

He hefted the manuscript, matching his gesture with a lilt of one dark eyebrow. "I should put it in my coat." With that he vanished into the hall, allowing Irene and I to exchange several significant glances, none of which was quite clear to either of us. Consultation after his departure was clearly needed.

He returned so swiftly he was caught in the crossfire of our latest voiceless consultation. His hand still held the manuscript, which was odd.

Then he hefted it up for our inspection and I saw it was a small red-bound book rather. "I offer an exchange of prisoners," he said. "Please accept this small token: my friend Dr. Watson's first foray into authorship."

Irene took it before I could intercept her.

Oh, no! Had that dreadful manuscript called "A Scandal in Bohemia" actually been printed by some penny-dreadful press? And would Sherlock Holmes have the colossal nerve to pass on a fiction that publicly described his fascination with the very woman, the very married woman, who now held the dangerous volume in her hand? Would Godfrey be forced to challenge him to a duel because of it? Godfrey and Sherlock Holmes . . . would it be pistol or sword? Would I risk seeing both of my dear friends distraught and perhaps even destroyed because of this miserable bit of fictioneering?!

I rushed to snatch the small volume from Irene's hands. "Dr. Watson? An author? Oh, I must see! Right now!"

"Nell—!" Irene remonstrated mildly.

One oddity I noticed at once. "It says 'by Conan Doyle.'"

"Watson is modest," Mr. Holmes said, "and doesn't want his medical profession confused with his literary hobby. That is the name of his literary agent."

"Hmmm." The publisher was Ward, Lock and Company, a London house, at least, I observed. I paged through, encounter-

ing some illustrations. In one a lounging gentlemen had ranks of scruffy street Arabs lined up and saluting like some grubby regiment. The caption read: "'TENTION," CRIED HOLMES IN A SHARP TONE.

Although the figure purporting to be Holmes more resembled Oscar Wilde, I could just see him ordering around an array of street Arabs.

"The illustrations are by Mr. Doyle's father, Charles Altamont Doyle, a rather well-known sketcher in his day."

"Hmmmm." I was not about to admit that I found the entire package mystifying as well as disturbing.

I closed the volume. My fingers traced the large elaborate letters of the title, which seemed composed of Oriental slashes. *A Study in Scarlet.*

There was nothing scarlet about Irene's Bohemian adventure, unless you cast her in the role of Scarlet Woman. . . . The villain! That is exactly the sort of lurid character assassination I should expect from a physician who has nothing better to do than scribble stories instead of prescriptions. If Irene was utterly upright in any one area, it was in resisting any temptation to become what the French so coyly term a Grand Horizontal: in other words, a woman who will sleep for her supper.

"I cannot believe you would give us this book!" I said sharply.

"You are right," Mr. Holmes answered. "It speaks of shameless self-advertisement, but, believe me, I offer you this volume, not because it catalogues one of my more interesting cases, but because I believe both of you ladies met one of the principals."

Of course we had "met one of the principals"! The King of Bohemia had been Mr. Holmes's client, Irene's suitor, and my, my mortal . . . enemy, because he was at bottom no friend to Irene's integrity.

Irene was by now eyeing me reprovingly. "One of the principals?" She had no reason to jump to the unhappy conclusion I just had.

"A Mr. Jefferson Hope of the United States," Mr. Holmes went on with relish, surprising me. "The poison-pill killer of the Mormon hypocrites who had forced his innocent beloved into a loveless marriage and spurred her early death in the far-off salt flats of the West. It was among my most satisfying and sensational cases, I might add. The American West produced an avenging angel with a sense of justice as well as of mission. Jefferson Hope was captured in my rooms, answering a trap I had laid in the agony column claiming to have found lost Lucy's ring. He was by then already deadly ill of a heart condition that would claim his noble, if savage, soul soon after. Before that he raved of meeting 'two angels of mercy' who had forgiven him the sins he had committed in order to avenge his dead . . . ah, fiancée. His description of the 'angels' was so physically exact, and indeed memorable, that I realized later that they must have been you and Miss Huxleigh."

By now Irene was freeing the blasted book from my numb fingers, one by one. Jefferson Hope. Yes, we had met that doomed man. That was how we had first learned of the existence of Sherlock Holmes, Dr. Watson, and Baker Street. So had, I imagine, many readers of *Beeton's Christmas Annual* by now. That perfectly respectable publication had first serialized the story that led to this single-volume novel, according to its cover.

I stood confused. This book was certainly not the manuscript relating the Bohemian affair I had seen in the doctor's office. Still, it showed that he not only intended to publish, but had achieved it, which boded ill for that damning manuscript remaining secret. My current relief could not ease my fears for the future.

Even now Irene's palm was caressing the cursed cover. "Jefferson Hope. A most remarkable man. I'm pleased to have this remembrance of him, for he gave me his Lucy's ring and I still treasure it."

"You have the ring! He didn't say that before he died."

Irene regarded him for a moment. "So now that I have solved an old mystery for you, Mr. Holmes, perhaps you can solve one for me."

She moved toward a trunk that served as a side table, its homely origin hidden under another flagrantly figured silk scarf. Belatedly, I recognized it as one of the second-hand trunks she had used to store costume pieces from our early lodgings in London's Saffron Hill district.

As Irene whisked the shawl aside, a wave of nostalgia swept me back to a time seven years ago, before Irene and I had ever met Sherlock Holmes, or Godfrey Norton, for that matter.

Irene knelt to open the ancient trunk and began attacking its contents, shunting crackling pieces of taffeta and limp lengths of lace aside almost as roughly as Lucifer exercising his claws among my embroideries.

Mr. Holmes watched her with an air of puzzled disbelief. It was not the ordinary hostess who fell to her knees to ravage the contents of a trunk on some unknown whim.

I knew Irene and her unknown whims, and I knew that they always had a purpose.

"Here!" She turned and flourished a shabby black case like a magician producing a top hat accoutered with a rabbit. "I knew I still had it. Poor old fellow! He asked me to keep it instead of a pawn shop. The legend of the starving artist is based on all-too-true facts, and Erich was a maestro."

Mr. Holmes actually extended a hand to help her up, but Irene filled it with the handle of the mysterious black case and leaped up as if she were the magical rabbit, with no sense of effort or strain, and certainly no consciousness that a gentleman should assist a woman in all things.

Her face was radiantly pink after the effort of unearthing the black case from her treasure trove of forgotten fabrics. I winced to see her looking so happy and pretty in front of Mr. Holmes.

Yet he had eyes only for the case.

I saw, now that it was unveiled, that it was a pear-shaped violin case.

"Irene!" I couldn't help exclaiming. "I've never seen such a thing in your possession before. Has it always resided in your trunk?"

"I almost forgot about it myself, Nell. The poor old maestro left it in my care as a parting gift, and it soon was lost beneath the flea-market fabrics. I suspect that this old violin is a rather good one. Is it, Mr. Holmes?"

He had laid the object atop the piano and opened the case, almost as slowly as he had explored the poison-bearing cigarette case on an earlier occasion when we had been forced to accept his presence.

Then, he had saved Irene's life.

Now, he attempted to preserve the integrity of an obviously old object.

I glimpsed dusty and flattened rose velvet and flabby leather hinges.

Irene gazed into the case like a child at Christmas, all the actress's artful composure fled, her hand at her mouth as if to hold in excitement, her coiffure trailing loosened tendrils.

"Is it good?" she asked again, clearly unable to wait for a verdict.

Sherlock Holmes was occupying some other place or time. His face lost its habitual hawkish cast. Suddenly I glimpsed the boy in him, the boy at Christmas who did not have many heartfelt presents, and none that spoke to his secret soul. I knew this in my governess's heart, and, as much as I feared the man, even more, for this moment, I pitied the boy. My throat grew suddenly thick.

He neither saw nor noted my reaction, or even Irene's. He lifted the instrument from the case . . . up, up to the light of the window. So a dipsomaniac might hoist of glass of claret, holding it poised on the fingertips of both hands, as if a touch might turn it to powder.

He sighted down its length both front and back like a hunter weighing a field piece. He peered into its recesses, bent to study the faded velvet. Said nothing.

"Perhaps Amati?" Irene prompted.

"No."

"Surely not Stradivarius."

"No."

"Then it is worthless. How sad. I had hoped for the maestro's sake it was not."

"A Guarneri."

I couldn't resist breaking the strange spell that enwrapped them and disquieted me. "Is that a dread disease, pray tell? Like tuberculosis?"

"The Guarneris were a family of violin makers active from the sixteenth into the eighteenth centuries," Mr. Holmes answered me with equanimity. "They were instrumental geniuses of the first water, though their violins are no longer as well known as the Stradivarius or Amati to the general public."

Well, I had never been labeled "the general public" before!

He finally glanced at Irene. I had the oddest feeling that he hadn't dared to do so before.

She awaited his verdict with an annoying air of suspense. Surely there were better appraisers of violins in France than this visiting Englishman! I think what annoyed me most was that she welcomed his verdict, that she was most sincerely interested in it.

"Guarneri," she repeated. "You are right. I am not familiar with that name. Is it . . . playable?"

"It has been abominably neglected."

"I am not a violinist."

"The strings are brittle and the wood weeps for oiling."

"That shall be repaired as soon as possible. I had forgotten it, you see."

"You are a musician. How could you have forgotten an instrument of this rank?"

"I am both a musician and my own instrument. Those strings are my vocal cords. That wooden frame is my sounding board of bone and blood. I maintain myself. I had forgotten the maestro's long-ago gift. Can you play it?"

"I can, but I doubt that I should."

"Just a few passages, perhaps. I should like to hear it again. It had such a sweetness of tone, I remember."

"Madam, really—"

But Irene had dashed around the front of the piano, drawing out the stool and lifting the key cover.

"It is yours, Mr. Holmes, if it is worth having. I will never play the violin, nor anyone else here. I am so glad I remembered it. The maestro would be happy."

"I am an amateur, madam."

"You play. Nell particularly remarked upon it."

He sent me a look sharp enough to debone a trout. I thanked Irene's tact that she did not mention my opinion of the violin-sawing that I had heard emerging from his hotel room on one occasion.

A glissando of notes rippled off of Irene's supple fingers. "Beethoven's 'Für Elise'? Everyone knows that."

"I must tune it." He turned the violin into the crook of a suddenly elegant wrist and then stroked the accompanying bow over the strings.

Lucifer flattened his ears, fluffed his tail, and scampered out of the parlor at the first violently off-tune screech. I had heard that violin strings were fashioned from cat gut, which might account for the wily Lucifer's sudden exit. Then again, the unholy wailing sound the strings emitted under Mr. Holmes's attentions might have accomplished it.

Strangely, the dreadful sound seemed to encourage rather than discourage him. He pressed the instrument to his ear and cheek, his eyes only upon it, turned the tuning pegs, then struck a chord again. And again. Turning and striking and listening with an intensity I have seen in no other living creature than a cat, or a mongoose, waiting to strike prey.

The parlor was forgotten. The piano was forgotten. Irene was, perhaps for the first time in her life . . . forgotten.

She grinned at me in admission of her insignificance compared to a dusty old violin. I realized of a sudden that she had meant to distract him from the issue of how complete the translation of the Yellow Book was, that she had never answered him on that account.

I also recalled Dr. Watson's describing his former living partner's retreat to the seven percent solution of cocaine, and suspected that Mr. Holmes's face and attention must be just so lost and concentrated when he was needling the drug into his hollow veins as when he was drawing sound from the hollow body of a violin.

The process, the intense . . . pitch of it unnerved me. It reminded me of something far closer to home, but I could not quite name it.

Irene ran another introductory glissando up the keys of her piano. Gradually, the tones of the two instruments were growing together, and the teeth-jarring dissonance was muting into melody.

Finally, Mr. Holmes nodded without taking his eyes from the violin, and her hands moved into the familiar lilting notes of "Für Elise."

The violin entered after the first few bars, a sudden low moan of almost-unwanted harmony. And then the two very different instruments rang through their melodic pattern, both in tune and in conflict still, so different and yet so paired. The piano's smooth, bell-like trickling sound ran like clear water. The violin sounded raw, as if each note were wrung from a dry throat. Yet it throbbed with muted feeling, as the veriest beast will whimper for some unknown boon.

I cannot say I have an ear for music. Casanova tilted his head from side to side, yet remained silent. Perhaps if Irene had sung . . . but there were no words to "Für Elise" and the violin was voice enough, the croakings of some abandoned Caliban as it was.

I have always preferred more sprightly instruments like piccolos and flutes to lugubrious bagpipes and the violin.

Yet there is a power in the strings' unspoken longings, in their hoarse straining for expression, and I felt it now, despite myself. I was unhappily reminded of the Gypsy violinists of our last grueling adventure, and of one not-Gypsy violinist.

The piece ended at last, on a piano chord held until the final vibration faded, on a dying rasp of the violin strings that drifted into distance.

I was struck, watching this impromptu recital, by how much physical and mental effort each instrument required, by the emotional vibrato the long-gone composer's score exuded like incense into the room. I thought of dead gardens, and the inexorable march of autumn in the touch of brittle leaves and the reluctant withdrawal of warm sunlight into the cool shadow.

The chamber was silent. The music gone.

It was just Irene gazing sightlessly over the top of the piano, Mr. Holmes lowering the violin and bow together, as if shaking off a spell.

They had collaborated, but separately from one another.

Irene spoke first. "I have no use for it but memory. It is yours if you want it."

"I have a violin."

"Not a Guarneri?"

"No, but what I have is more than sufficient for an amateur. Thank you for the duet, but I am not good enough for you there either."

"You play very well, and that is well enough for even a professional. Surely you can use an extra violin."

"I cannot accept so valuable a gift. On closer examination I have found the initials 'I.H.S.' and the signature of the great

Guiseppe del Gesú of the Guarneri family, an exceptionally devout man who was perhaps second only to Stradivari himself in the construction of exquisite violins."

Irene smiled, played a rivulet of notes. "Small price to pay for Nell's life, which I am most grateful to you for saving. In fact, I am most grateful that you chose to meddle in my affairs in that instance."

"Playing an instrument such as this is reward enough. Who is this maestro you speak of?"

"A person very dear to me, but only informally a 'maestro.' He is probably dead by now."

"What sort of 'informal maestro' would own, and give away, such a masterwork?"

But Irene would say no more of that. "An unplayed instrument of this quality is a sad waste, as its former owner would be the first to tell me."

"No." He laid the instrument and bow back in its shabby box as if interring an old friend only recently rediscovered. "Yet I thank you for the duet and pray you take better care of your Guarneri from now on."

"I owe you my life as well, surely I can spare a violin for it."

"I don't like debts, whichever way they flow. In fact—"

He moved into the hall with giant steps as Irene looked at me and shrugged. She had meant him to have the violin. She had meant to clear the debtor column in her personal ledger. He would have nothing of it.

He returned from rummaging in the deep pockets of his country cloak.

In his hand was a rolled scroll of documents.

"I have, madam, an exchange of documents for you. For the courtesy of your difficult and no doubt costly unabridged translation, I have a small composition."

The word "unabridged" made a mockery of sincerity, but it was not the one that captured her attention.

"Composition?" Irene straightened at the piano bench like a marionette whose strings have been abruptly pulled into a simulacrum of life.

He had surprised her as much as she had surprised him. Irene did not like such parity.

"Why, Mr. Holmes, what have you done?"

"Actually, Bram Stoker and Sir Arthur Sullivan accomplished this." He held out a beribboned bundle.

Irene stepped back and plastered her spread fingers to her throat. "For me? I can't imagine—"

The sad part was, she couldn't. Nor could I imagine what the scrolls contained, only that Irene prided herself on anticipating events, and here she had not a clue.

She delicately eased the ribbon down the scroll's length, then unrolled one sheet to read it, like a page boy in a Shakespearian play.

"Why, this is a libretto, and these other sheaves, the music. I don't recognize the piece."

"Nor should you," Mr. Holmes said. "It is freshly commissioned. After returning to London, I was occupied with reinvestigating and settling the last fragments of the Jack the Ripper matter and putting the proper highly placed persons at peace. I then had a word with your associate in Transylvania, Bram Stoker. Mr. Stoker easily convinced Sir Arthur to compose a chamber opera on the six wives of Henry the Eighth, especially for your vocal range."

"And," I wondered aloud, "who wrote the words?"

"Ah, Miss Huxleigh, an excellent question. I doubt we shall ever know for sure. Stoker himself wrote some of it, but Oscar Wilde had heard of the project and insisted on having a hand in the matter."

"What!" I was appalled. "The vile Wilde?"

"More wily than vile, I would think. This is, by the way, the closet piece on the wives of Henry the Eighth."

"The very work you suggested to me in Paris. I remember, Mr. Holmes," Irene said in obvious surprise, and with perhaps a bit too much pleasure to please me.

"It is one thing to suggest a work of art, another to watch it being born," he admitted, the faintest twinkle of amusement in his gray eyes. "The two librettists did nearly come to blows in my presence concerning the title of the work. Stoker wanted to call the piece 'Brides of the Axe.' Wilde wanted 'Henry the Eighth's Secret Wives.' Sir Arthur settled on a 'A Suite of Queens.'"

"And you, Mr. Holmes," Irene interjected at last, "was there no title you favored? After all, you commissioned the work."

He shook his head and fanned his long fingers in denial. "I suggested the idea. It did not cost me a penny or a pound. That is hardly commissioning a work of art. You were your own benefactress in this case. You have staunch friends in London, madam."

Irene's face glowed at this assurance. I realized that she missed the city and its circle of acquaintants, though she had always made the best of being exiled to Paris by circumstances beyond her control.

"You must have had some hand in this result, Mr. Holmes." She lifted the thick scroll in her right hand as if it were a scepter. Already I could see the mantles of those long-dead queens settling on her artistic soul.

Mr. Holmes shrugged modestly. I could not believe it. "Stoker and Wilde wrote the words," he repeated. "Sullivan the music. I made one minor contribution in suggesting that the violin serve as the model of and counterpoint to the soloist's voice."

Irene hastened to the piano, quickly absorbing the music indicated in the arcane patterns on the parchments.

"'Six Wives, Six Lives,'" she declaimed her version of the title. "And I shall sing of every one of them, and of their deaths."

"Two did not have the grace to die until their own good time," he pointed out.

"I said it was a brilliant concept, but I did not expect—"

Mr. Holmes bowed slightly. "Nor did I expect the Guarneri, madam."

"Apparently," Irene said, "we have managed to exceed each other's expectations equally. Surely now you will take the violin."

He shook his head. "I will take my leave. Urgent matters call in London. This chamber concert was reward enough."

"For Nell's life?" Irene sounded incredulous.

"For the translation, and the introduction to the fascinating Krafft-Ebing and his studies. Adieu, madam. Miss Huxleigh."

He nodded and moved into the hall to redon cape and cap and leave our home.

Moments later the latch fell shut on the front door, followed by the departing hooves of the hired horse-and-trap.

Sophie appeared in the doorway. "So tea will not be served, madam?" she asked in dour tones.

"Of course, it will! Nell and I—and Casanova—will partake royally."

Sophie was no sooner gone than Irene was unrolling the libretto, thumbing papers to grasp both words and music, and humming snatches of melody.

"Written for both English and French. I recognize Oscar's fine Irish hand in the libretto, too. Most intriguing, Nell! Most fascinating."

I was happy to see Irene toying with resuming her singing career, despite the source of the inspiration. The King of Bohemia and Sherlock Holmes both knew now that she was alive, and neither wished her ill. She no longer needed to hide behind the false report of her and Godfrey's deaths in an Alpine train wreck after escaping London more than eighteen months before.

"Nothing would please Godfrey more than your returning to the stage to use your magnificent gift," I noted. "As Mr. Holmes said, it is a crime to conceal such a remarkable instrument. I must admit that I could wish for fewer questionable people to be involved in this project."

"Questionable? You can't mean Bram Stoker! You like him. And Oscar is a remarkable talent in his own right, he has only to find his métier and he will make sparks fly."

"He is a dandy," I said. "And Sir Arthur Sullivan's partner Gilbert is a well-known ladies' man—"

"And Mr. Holmes is quite the opposite, so surely that cancels out Sir Arthur's unsavory professional association."

"Scandal does not work like that, Irene. It is not a matter of mathematics. And who knows what scandalous tendencies a man who answers only to himself, like Sherlock Holmes, might harbor?" I said as darkly as I could without making charges I would have to verify. "He has, after all, given you two gifts today: that ridiculous little book and the libretto."

"It is tit for tat. He knows I could have refused to share the Yellow Book with him, and then, no doubt, he would have been forced to housebreak on his way back from Germany to England, to get it. And he knows I'm rather good at hiding things. Nell! You saw today that he only has eyes for the violin, if you have suspicions otherwise. That man is as close to a monk as any nonbeliever could be, I tell you! Any passions he might have are reserved for his investigations, and, *perhaps*, the occasional musical interlude."

"Which *you* now are."

She laughed, shaking her head. "You are such a romantic, Nell! Really! Besides, nothing could come between Godfrey and myself."

That last I believed.

"What of the violin?" I asked, regarding where it lay on the piano like a dead thing.

"Oh. Yes. Now that I know it is valuable, I will have to take it into Paris to be restored. I had no idea it was in such a sad state. It's just that I haven't thought of my old life in America for years, for some reason . . . or of the maestro." She stroked the violin's crackled surface. "Poor old maestro. I wonder if he's still alive. It would be wonderful to see him again, and he had traveled in Europe in his youth, before I was born. No! He must be dead by now, and if he isn't, too frail to ever return to Europe. How he used to play up storms of pathos on this very instrument. He said I must sing with as much passion as a violin could under the right hands."

"*He* is not an accomplished musician, Mr. Holmes, I mean, it seemed to me."

"Quite passable, actually, yet music is not his profession. Apparently he *is* accomplished at unpredictability and that is more valuable in his line of work than even a Guarneri."

"He may have diagnosed this wrongly. I have never heard of such an instrument," I sniffed.

"Nor have I." Irene hummed a long, lyrical phrase. "How I shall enjoy portraying all of Henry's wives! Henry really didn't know what to do with them when he was alive, but I certainly know what to do with them now that he is dead."

"And what is that?"

"Why, give them the last word, after all."

2.

News from Abroad

Nelly Bly, Nelly Bly,
bring de broom along
We'll sweep de kitchen clean, my dear,
and hab a little song.
—STEPHEN FOSTER, 1850

NELLIE BLY, BYLINE FOR A MUCKRAKING REPORTER, 1885

It was not enough that one unexpected visitor had disturbed our bucolic retreat.

When Godfrey returned from the city late that afternoon, he bore an unexpected message from another person I regarded with as little admiration as I extended to Sherlock Holmes.

As soon as I heard the welcome clatter of his cane and hat being assigned to their domestic resting places in the entryway, I rushed to confirm his arrival.

Seeing him where Sherlock Holmes had stood only hours before, I was struck again by the fact that two men could be much of an age and a height, and even of a coloring, and yet be entirely different. Dr. Watson had reported Sherlock Holmes describing

Godfrey as "a remarkably handsome man, dark, aquiline and mustached" in the mercifully unpublished narrative of our first encounter with the London detective two years earlier. Sherlock Holmes himself was dark, hawk-nosed, and clean-shaven, in some ways similar and in most ways a world apart from Godfrey, for no one would call him "remarkably handsome." The odd thing was that, from his dispassionate yet generous summation of Godfrey's personal attractions, he didn't seem to care a particle about whether anyone did or not. In that small way he resembled myself, who was quite content to be plain despite being publicly paired all my adult life with a great beauty like Irene. Handsome people could no more help their looks than ugly ones, and looks were no sensible reason to judge upon, either way.

I welcomed Godfrey's return not because of his pleasant visage, but for how he always soothed my easily ruffled spirits.

"Godfrey! I was deathly afraid that awful man from London had forgotten his silly cap and was bedeviling our doorstep again."

"Ah, a pity I missed Sherlock Holmes's visit. Apparently you had no such misfortune, Nell," he teased, his light gray eyes glittering with camaraderie, for he was well aware that I regarded the detective as both nosy and annoying.

He went into the parlor to salute Irene with a kiss on the cheek, but had to bend over the piano bench to do it, for she had been picking out the notes of her new chamber opera on the keys ever since *The* Man had left.

"What is this?" Godfrey asked. "Some new lieder from Dvorák? He does favor you with the first glimpse of all his Bohemian folk songs."

"It is new, yes, but from quite a different composer. Sullivan has made a foray from operetta into chamber opera. This is a one-woman solo piece. I will sing the roles of six dead queens."

"That will be a change from consorting with live ones," he observed.

She turned away from the piano. "Oh, it is quite a toothsome sweet of a piece, with words by Bram Stoker and Oscar Wilde. This is the sort of thing I can work up and present anywhere, with any sort of accompaniment."

"What of the wardrobe of six queens, in addition to your own?" Godfrey asked, exchanging a conspiring glance with me. "That does not sound like a very portable endeavor."

"I can make do with a change of headdress for each queen, at the minimum. I assure you, Godfrey, I could tour the wilds of America with this piece and still require only two trunks."

"Only two trunks. Impressive. As for touring the wilds of America, you may be interested in doing so sooner than you think."

This announcement caused Irene to utterly abandon the piano and spin around to face him, and it caused me to drop a stitch.

"Godfrey," Irene said, "the New World is the last place I wish to be at the moment. Nell and I are growing quite accustomed to a quiet life in the country after our recent gruesome hunt across Europe. And you have established an office in Paris that requires running. I thought you would be pleased that I am following your suggestion, and planning to revive my performing career in some manner, however small."

"I am pleased as Punchinello about your plans, Irene, to rephrase a truism, but I received a communication at my new office today that smells of dire news and sudden journeys."

"Oh, Godfrey dearest, do stop sounding like a Prague fortune-teller!—it is most un-English—and let me have this mysterious missive! Surely it has nothing to do with your assignment to untangle the affairs of Bavaria and the late mad King Ludwig? Who is it from? Who has obtained your new office address so swiftly? What is wanted?"

Godfrey withdrew a long narrow sheet of yellow paper from the inner breast pocket of his suit coat. "It arrived at my office because it came first to the Rothschilds' bank and was forwarded to me."

"Unopened, I hope," I put in. I would never trust a banker to leave any piece of paper unturned.

"Unopened, and addressed not to me, but to thee, dear wife."

He held it out, knowing that Irene would leap like a gazelle to any communication not yet read, and therefore mysterious.

Even as she rose to pounce upon the paper, Godfrey pulled it back out of reach. "You have not asked who it is from."

"Who is it from?!" she demanded, reaching for the missive.

"Miss Elizabeth Jane Cochrane."

"Oh!" I cried, dismayed. "Has that forward girl not enough to do on her own uncivil shores that she should bother us again?"

"Bother Irene," Godfrey corrected, ever the barrister and, as such, a bear for accurate details. "We are not among the addressees, you and I, Nell."

"How improper to leave you out, Godfrey. I predict that Miss Elizabeth will never marry with that attitude!"

"Certainly she will never find her name embroidered on a piece of your fancy work."

His comment, however artless, immediately reminded me of a certain gentleman who appeared only last summer to be getting along quite well with the forward American female we discussed, one better known by her quickly-becoming-notorious nom de plume of Nellie Bly, the brash American girl reporter.

While I fell into uneasy silence, Irene was only the more intrigued. "What can Pink have to tell me that is urgent enough to require a transatlantic wire? Give me the thing, Godfrey! You have teased me quite enough to make it interesting."

She snatched at the envelope in his hand, winning a prize she immediately took to the lamp on the piano, the better to read it as twilight stole across our garden and shadowed the interior of the house.

That same shadow fell over my heart.

Pink Cochrane had burst into our lives and enterprises uninvited, and I confess that her energy and astounding cheek, either an American characteristic or a journalistic one, seemed to sap me of will and hope, especially when I discovered that in my absence she had made quite an impression on a special friend of mine, indeed, one of the very few good friends of mine, Quentin Stanhope.

While I stewed with my eyes glued to my embroidery so no one should notice my distraction, Irene was being strangely quiet by the piano.

"Well?" Godfrey asked at last. He was loosening his collar and obviously ached to go upstairs to change into less formal and thus more comfortable clothing for the evening.

Irene said nothing.

She simply sat there, haloed by the lamp that grew brighter behind her as the daylight faded, staring at the folded yellow paper the envelope had contained.

She certainly was well able to read the message, yet her eyes remained fixed on the page. She was deaf to Godfrey's voice, and blind to our presence, though we were growing more mystified by the moment.

"Irene?" I said.

I could have been asking the Guarneri for an answer.

Godfrey leaned forward, peering at her. "Irene? Irene! Good God, what is it?"

I stood, forgetting to set aside my embroidery work. Lucifer dashed from under the piano and immediately snagged it for a plaything. So bizarre had the atmosphere in the room become that Casanova the parrot shifted feet on his perch and began whistling a dirge!

"Irene!" Godfrey repeated, standing as well.

She finally looked up, as if surprised to find that we were still there and then further startled to see us on our feet. Clearly she had heard nothing for the past few minutes.

"Something has happened," Godfrey said.

She looked around, as if seeking an explanation. Her eye fell on the piano top. "That old violin that was left with me. It is a Guarneri. I had no idea."

"Guarneri? What is a Guarneri?" Godfrey glanced at the instrument in its shabby case with true incomprehension. "I didn't know you had a violin. Did it arrive today? With that Holmes fellow? Is that it?"

His tone had definitely become as suspicious as mine would have been when discussing Sherlock Holmes.

While I was pleased to see Godfrey extending the man some of the same animosity I felt toward him, I could not see even he falsely accused.

"The violin is Irene's," I explained. "She'd kept it at the bottom of that old trunk all these years. She merely showed it to Mr. Holmes, who being the expert he is on all minutiae, immediately declared it an apparently rare and valuable Guarneri."

"So it is worth something?" Godfrey asked.

"I suspect a great deal, when it is restored."

His regard fixed on Irene again. "That is not cause for this. Irene adores finding lost treasures. She is as bad as a nine-year-old in her fever to find things. She should be pounding celebratory mazurkas into those old keys, not mooning over a telegram from Nellie Bly." He moved toward his wife. "I must read this for myself."

She snatched it away, not playfully as he had earlier, but with a gesture of unconsidered protectiveness.

"Irene!" I admonished.

I could not help it. The governess instinct becomes ingrained, even though I only held such positions for a year or two. At the moment, my friend and mentor was acting like a sullen child. Although as a former operatic diva she had her share of temperament, this was not a display of that. This was a worrisome state of shock.

Godfrey glanced at me, then lowered his tone into a soothing one. "Irene, we can't . . . help you if you won't share the contents of the message that has so upset you. Please."

At that, the voice of reason, and I must say that Godfrey before the bar was always the most attractive representative of the Voice of Reason in all the Inns of Court, Irene literally shook off her strange state.

"Oh," she said, massaging one temple with her free hand. "I think it must be a bit of mischief engineered by that imp of international interference, Pink." She held the paper out to Godfrey with a rueful smile. "Forgive me, but you will see that the contents are nonsensical enough to strike Casanova mute."

He said nothing as he held the message under the milk-glass globe of the lamp to read.

He still said nothing.

Now *he* simply stood there, frowning down at the paper and reading what was obviously only two or three lines over and over.

Had two such brilliant and independent adults ever behaved so much like schoolroom ninnies? I marched over to Godfrey, snatched the impertinent paper, and read it.

Read it again.

Stared at the typed words as I had once regarded my own work when I had become one of the first typewriter-girls in London.

Well.

What to say?

Something.

Someone must.

I would.

"Irene, this . . . communication—it says that Pink believes that someone is trying to murder your mother. A shocking revelation indeed. Well, if anyone is equipped to deal with such an atrocious situation, who else would it be but a former Pinkerton inquiry agent like yourself?"

"Who else indeed, Nell? Except that I don't *have* a mother. I have never been known to have a mother . . . to murder, or not."

"Oh, Irene! Please! Everyone has a mother."

"You don't."

"I did. She died at my birth. I definitely had one, as she had me."

"Well, I don't," Irene declared with rising animation, as if released from a stage hypnotist's spell. "I have never had a mother, and I don't intend to have one now."

"One's wishes or demands don't have much to do with the facts in such a case," Godfrey said.

"Perhaps not in a court of law," she told him, "but I speak only the truth. I have never had a mother."

"Come, Irene!" Now he was pacing as though in court. "You cannot claim that you were birthed like Athena, the Greek goddess of wisdom and war, as a massive headache emerging from the forehead of her father Zeus! Although I can picture you giving anyone who had the temerity to bear you a migraine or two. You are a remarkable woman, and I agree that wisdom and war are not unknown to you, but not that remarkable."

I couldn't resist adding my twopence. "Oh, I don't know, Godfrey. I can indeed imagine Irene giving the king of the gods a royal headache. She has been known to give a king or two of our day the migraine."

"Most amusing, Nell," she answered. "If you know your classical gods, you would know that 'Irene' is the goddess of peace. I admit that I could use a little peace on this subject. Even those who claim to have mothers may not know them well. You hardly knew your mother yourself," she pointed out—gently—to Godfrey.

"No. I was"—he glanced at me, then steeled himself for the next words—"a bastard."

I gasped, and Casanova mocked me with a perfect imitation.

"But I knew *who* my mother was, if not my father for some time," Godfrey added quickly.

"How?" Irene asked.

I was shocked to realize that they had never discussed this between them. Although I was a permanent member of their household, I should not be present while they explored such painful and personal revelations.

I bent to retrieve my fallen embroidery hoop and steal away when Godfrey spoke again.

"How interesting. That all of us, all three of us, should have never known a mother's care from an early age."

He glanced at me and I glanced at Irene, who stared at him and then turned her gaze on me.

"Nell's mother died," she said at last. "You must have seen a daguerreotype or a photograph of her?"

I nodded.

"And she had a father. You, Godfrey, had a notorious mother who apparently did not acknowledge you publicly, though some-one reared you and paid for your education. You also had a pur-ported father you despised for what he did to your mother, although you never knew him either."

"That's true. Roughly," he admitted. "I will not go into the particulars now, because my past is somewhat known, but yours has always been a cipher from the first."

"Because I never knew a mother or father! I have no names, no photographs. No memories." She lifted and weighed the flimsy cablegram paper on her palms as if it were made of lead. "This assertion must be false. It is impossible. I cannot imagine why Pink would make such an absurd statement, except that she is sadly misled."

"But if she is not," I couldn't help saying. "Murder—"

"Why murder a woman who does not exist?!" Irene's shoul-ders shrugged so violently that her fingers almost tore the message in twain. "And what is it to me if someone does?"

We shared a mutual silence, Godfrey and I. Such callous sen-timents were unlike Irene.

She sat suddenly at the piano and crashed a resounding, atonal chord into the keys.

"It is a fraud," she said, "or a delusion. Let Miss Nellie Bly stew in her suspicions. I will have no part in it."

Godfrey flicked the upsetting message onto my side table.

"You are quite right. One can never trust what independent American wenches may get up to."

Irene laughed over her shoulder at him, her hands sweeping into the lush chords of a Viennese waltz.

The melody, one of Strauss's, was irresistible. Casanova ducked his poly-colored head in time to the notes and swayed from side to side. Lucifer twitched his tail in time like a furry black metronome.

Godfrey bowed before me and swept me into a waltz for the length of time it took us to spin over the threshold into the hall, where he bowed again and left me.

In instants he was thumping up the stairs, undoing his tie, and whistling quite in tune.

I stood by the portal, my head spinning from the sudden turn of events this afternoon.

A Viennese waltz. I had never been to Vienna, but Irene and Godfrey had. After our second unfortunate adventure in Prague, they had packed me home to Paris on a train . . . and left for a second honeymoon in Vienna.

The incessant, thrilling chords of Strauss played on, while my memory waltzed back to that long train trip across most of Europe, with a dashing gentleman my unexpected escort. Quentin. Five days of utter sequestration. Stories, but not waltzes. Moments, not years.

And now . . . I recalled Quentin in a more recent light, part of a rescue party that had saved Godfrey and myself from vile hands in a godforsaken part of the world. Quentin, Irene's trusty ally in finding and saving her husband and her dearest friend, both of them abetted by that American upstart, Nellie Bly!

Quentin, hand-in-glove with that bold young woman who

did not even go in the world under her own rightful name, Elizabeth Jane Cochrane.

And now this miserable girl wanted to draw Irene back to her mother country, all because of fancied danger to a maternal figure Irene had never known.

Nellie Bly.

She was impertinent and shameless. Everything that a proper woman should not be. Yet she had carved inroads into the hearts of everyone I held dear.

Irene pantomimed her carefree moments at the piano, but I was not deceived. Trouble had encroached upon her today . . . in the form of the man from Baker Street, in the wire from the girl from New York City.

We could not allow that, Godfrey and I. We had striven too hard to survive the unthinkable to cede our loved ones to the bold and the beautiful. Well, Nellie Bly was beautiful, somewhat. Sherlock Holmes was not.

Godfrey would know what to do. He had already turned Irene back to her satisfying recent past, from what I could gather had transpired in Vienna and could guess, perhaps a little, from what had happened, and not happened, during my closeting with Quentin for five days in a train compartment from Prague to Paris.

Godfrey and I had been fellow prisoners and now we were fellow conspirators. Our loved one would not succumb to foreign influences!

Our . . . loved ones.

Lucifer attacked my ball of crochet twine and drove it to surrender against the fireplace fender.

Exactly, my feline friend. It shall be tooth and claw to the end.

3.

Foreign Assignment

~⚬⚬~

*A fair young English girl of the past, who is neither bold in
bearing nor masculine in mind.*
—MRS. LYNN LINTON, 1868

"She did not sleep a wink last night."

Godfrey's voice startled me while I was in the garden
the next morning, intermittently throwing Messy the mongoose some grapes that had grown puckered in Casanova's
cage.

The evil bird himself was enjoying the late summer sunlight
on the series of perches André, our coachman and carpenter par
excellence, had made for him. The parrot's multicolored feathers
comprised a blooming garden on their own, though the real flora
was fading as the autumn season advanced. Casanova was teth-
ered by one leg to a long leather leash, so he could do everything
but fly away.

"Off with her head!" he suggested, opening up a rainbow of
wings and beating them on the air, and incidentally mixing up
the snippet of "Royal Wives, Royal Lives" Irene had been playing
with bits of *Alice in Wonderland* that I had read aloud in the past.

Godfrey sat beside me and glanced at the embroidery hoop in my hands. I stopped my busywork. I had not slept a wink last night myself.

"Nell." He said no more.

"You have been thinking," I accused with the accuracy of one who had once been his typewriter-girl.

"Alas, yes. I have been thinking, and I have been doing something even more difficult: endeavoring to find out what Irene is thinking!"

"I thought husbands and wives were utterly frank with each other."

He laughed so delightedly that Casanova tried and failed to mock him. "No, Nell. They should be utterly honest with each other, but frankness is different."

"I cannot see a difference."

"That is because you are not married. Some matters are better to tiptoe around, and the mystery of Irene's American origins are such a matter. She is most protective of them, and Pink's wild cablegram, perhaps coupled with the rediscovery of the violin owned by her former vocal instructor, has stirred up a hornet's nest of conflicting desires in her. She tries to hide it, but it disturbs me to see her so torn in mind and soul."

"I thought she was rather flippant about the entire matter, and most definite that she needed no mother, dead or alive."

"What people are most flippant about is often what galls them the most. I learned that in court. And Irene is a master at pretending to emotions opposite to how she really feels. It was her only defense at one time, I think."

"Before you knew her, you mean?"

"Before I knew her and loved her."

"Before even I knew her?"

"Before even you knew her."

I considered. It seemed as if I had known Irene forever, but we had shared quarters only since 'eighty-one. Eight years. So established was our bond that shortly after Irene and Godfrey married and moved to France, I was invited for a visit that had become a residency. It did not harm anything that I had met and known Godfrey before Irene had, working for him in the Temple as a typewriter-girl. So, it seemed natural that an orphaned spinster like myself should join them at the cottage in Neuilly. Despite the public roles a barrister and an opera singer may play, Godfrey and Irene were very private about themselves. I rarely glimpsed any marital storms, either disagreeable or . . . too personal to share. They were like extremely civilized parents who yet allowed me the exercise of my own will. Godfrey was a brother to me, and I cannot say enough as to how secure I felt with them both. Which is why I was upset at anything that challenged our tranquility.

"You said you had been thinking," I reminded Godfrey.

"Oh. What I thought was that you and Irene should go to New York and find out what Nellie Bly is up to."

"New York? Irene? *I!?*"

"Yes to all three."

"You actually recommend this course?"

"No. I find it ultimately unavoidable, so rush to embrace it before I am forced to by outside elements."

"Not so unavoidable, Godfrey. You heard her. She will not go."

He smiled, ruefully and privately. "She will. And I fear that she needs to, although she won't admit it. Remembering that old violin again has loosed memories and feelings that she may now be ready to face."

"Why now?" I asked.

"Because of us. She is safe now, Nell. She can rely upon us to stand by her no matter what, as we can rely on her. If that old maestro was all she had of a father, perhaps she needs to be sure that there is still not a lost mother somewhere in America."

"Why should anyone need a new mother at this late date?" I grumbled, tossing Messy another grape.

The clever little creature caught the tidbit in her front paws while standing erect on her hind legs. She was better than catlike in her ways, being much less lazy than Lucifer.

"You know Irene. What is her greatest strength, and greatest weakness?"

This time I had to concede. "She cannot leave an incongruity, an unanswered question, a mystery, alone. And, like most people who consider themselves solvers of any of the universe's conundrums, minor or major, she most enjoys *being* mysterious herself. I am amazed by the contradictions in the human character and Irene is not immune to any of them. Yet, Godfrey, if there is one area of inquiry in which she has most violently refused all advances—and I have known her longer than you, if not better—it is in the matter of her origins, her own history, her past. I believe not even Sherlock Holmes could make an accurate deduction on that score, although . . . I should really like to see him try."

This was the first time such an idea had occurred to me and I spent a few happy seconds considering a confrontation of that sort.

"Your wish is too late, Nell, by a day," Godfrey observed. His voice was tart enough that I gathered that he was not entirely happy with Mr. Holmes's visit. Unlike Irene, he did not underestimate her innate ability to charm even the resistant.

"He was too interested in that crackled old violin," I said.

"You sound as if you resent it."

"I suppose I resent anything that implies a bridge between two people who are opponents under the skin, if one of them is Irene."

"You see why you must go with her? You are her shield. She may need one more than ever if there is any truth that a mother remains to be found."

"Godfrey, you talk as if she has reversed course and decided to answer Nellie Bly's impertinent summons. Irene's will is an ocean liner. It will not be diverted from its mission by a . . . cheeky little tugboat."

Godfrey laughed so uproariously that Casanova lofted, squawking and fluttering his wings and Messalina scampered into the rhododendron bushes to hide. The mongoose was valiant when a cobra was in sight, but found the daily domestic hullabaloos of human life annoying.

"Nellie Bly would not appreciate that comparison, Nell," Godfrey observed when he could speak again, "but I do. I wish I could be there, I really do, when these two meet again on Pink's home ground." He sobered. "But the affair in Bavaria is too urgent to abandon."

"As bad as matters have been in Bohemia of late?"

"Worse. I cannot say more, only that these small, so-called fairy-tale kingdoms spawn more intrigue than Sarah Bernhardt."

Mention of my bête noire had me rustling my figurative feathers as violently as Casanova his genuine ones. Godfrey swiftly passed over mention of Irene's friendship with That Awful Actress.

"At least Irene cherishes no deep or deluded affection for Pink," he said, "so she will be skeptical of extravagant claims."

"She does not disapprove of her as much as I do," I warned Godfrey.

"Well, who could?" He smiled beneath his neatly trimmed mustache as a conspirator does. "You are not a person to be taken in by anyone, which is why you must accompany Irene to America. I fear that the matters she may encounter there could . . . impair her judgment."

"Judgment is my bailiwick, that is true, Godfrey. I suppose I can sacrifice my domestic comfort and moral unease to accompany her on yet another foray into foolishness."

"You know, Nell, I was sure that you would see it that way." He seemed pleased.

"We are united in our desire for only the right things for Irene."

"Indeed. As she is determined to desire only the right things for us. I believe I can convince her to go, for she will not be a whole woman again until she has laid this question to rest, and admitted as much to me last night, most reluctantly." He sighed and stared at the fading lilacs. "I wish I could go, too. I'd like to see America, actually. Perhaps another time."

"I sincerely hope not, Godfrey! We will settle this vexing if unspecific matter on this trip and then have no need to set foot on that uncivil continent again."

"As we have put Bohemia behind us, this third and last time."

"Exactly."

Godfrey leaned past me to retrieve a grape and loft it toward the bush that hid Messalina. She darted out, dark and lithe, and captured the treat as if it were prey. "As we put all past matters behind us," he said, "if we are lucky. Permanently."

Once he returned inside I gazed at my remaining companions. Messy had come to my hem, as she was wont when we were alone. Her bright animal eyes watched me, waiting for the next grape, or even a head pat. Casanova settled down on his perch and edged to my side, cocking his head and watching me as vigilantly as Messy.

Lucifer was nowhere in sight, a cause for worry in the wise.

"Well," I said. Their heads lifted at the sound of my voice, a not unpleasant reaction. "There is more to this reversal of course regarding America than anyone is telling me. I imagine that is what married people do: make mysterious decisions behind closed doors. I do think that Godfrey, or even perhaps Irene *and* Godfrey together, also have concluded that an ocean voyage would do me good after the unhappy events of the past spring. Their maneuvering is pathetically transparent. They wish to remove me from my more recent unhappy memories. Will you get on without me for a few weeks, my little friends?"

They did not answer, of course, but their eyes were bright upon me, and I realized that I would miss them, whether they would miss me or not.

At that instant I felt other eyes upon me. I turned to find Irene poised on the stoop, watching me and my menagerie. I couldn't be sure of how much of my monologue to the animal congregation she had overheard.

While I flushed with guilt, trying to recall what I had blathered about, she found her voice.

"I have decided I must go. Godfrey says you have agreed to accompany me."

"Well, yes, certainly. If you must go. Must you?"

"I don't wish to, but I fear I would regret it if I didn't. I am not about to leave my history to explication by the likes of a stunt reporter like Nellie Bly. Consider this a mission of self-defense, Nell."

"I consider that acting in one's self-defense when it comes to Pink's actions is not only necessary, but wise."

"Then we both have reasons to go to America and stop her before she does us harm."

"My cause may be lost," I said, "but I think yours may still be saved."

She came over to me and twined her arm in mine. "Nothing is lost unless we allow it to be."

"Cut the cackle!" Casanova screeched, edging down his perch to bawl the order almost into our very ears.

Irene grinned at the parrot. "Good advice. It's time to act. A pity we cannot import the parrot to America. He would give our forthcoming voyage a piratical flavor. I have always fancied wearing an eyepatch."

"An eyepatch, no! The small cigars and cigarettes are enough!"

"This we can debate on shipboard," Irene said, turning and escorting me back into the house. "A week at sea should do very nicely to settle the matter."

4.

Calling Cards

~◦~

"Let me see," said Holmes, "hum! Born in New Jersey in
the year of 1858. Contralto—hum! La Scala! Prima
Donna Imperial Opera of Warsaw— Yes! Retired from
the operatic stage—ha!"

—SHERLOCK HOLMES, "A SCANDAL IN BOHEMIA," 1891,

THE STRAND

⊰FROM THE DIARIES OF JOHN H. WATSON, M.D.⊱

"There are gentlemen waiting," Mrs. Hudson informed me
when she admitted me to the Baker Street foyer.

"Holmes expected to be back from his Continental
wanderings by now."

"He did, and he is, Doctor, but he is not back from
an errand about town. If you like, you may wait in my
parlor."

"No, I doubt that's necessary. Whatever their business, I can
hold the fort, as they say in America."

I started up the stairs, certain that Holmes would not mind
my entertaining his clients until he arrived.

"Oh, Dr. Watson!"

I paused and looked back. "Yes, Mrs. Hudson?"

"One of them is . . . rather colorful."

Thus forewarned, and mildly intrigued, I made my way to the door at the top and knocked, not wanting to take Holmes's guests by surprise, though these rooms had been my home as well.

A tall, strapping man with a full red beard meticulously trimmed opened what had once been my own door.

A redhead. Was that what Mrs. Hudson had meant by colorful?

"I am Dr. Watson, an associate of Mr. Holmes's. Since I too expected to visit him tonight I thought I might wait with you. I often assisted him on his cases, and it's possible that he intends me to do so again."

"Wonderful to meet you, Dr. Watson," the red-beard said with a hearty handshake. "Come in, of course. We welcome any friend of Mr. Holmes."

"But we are not a 'case,'" came an amused drawl from beyond him in the chamber. "Nor do we require containment. That quite makes us sound rather more precious than any innate value we could ever have, like the family silver."

I stepped over the familiar threshold to behold a sight more exotic than any I had ever before encountered in those rooms.

Mrs. Hudson's "colorful" gentleman also stood over six feet tall, like Red-beard. His long, clean-shaven jaw was emphasized by the middle part in the wavy brown hair that was allowed to fall to either side like spaniel ears.

He wore pale trousers and an olive velveteen vest with a violet cravat. While tall and relatively young, he was already running toward fat in his midsection, which not even his vivid dress could distract from.

"Your doorman," he went on, "is Bram Stoker, the eminent theatrical manager and novice writer. I am Oscar Wilde, the novice eminence and theatrical writer. And what is your specialty, Doctor?"

"I have none. I am a generalist."

"Yet you and Mr. Holmes both take on 'cases.'"

"I suppose you could put it that way."

"Then *I* will! Who, pray, is the patriotic marksman?"

For a moment I was nonplused, then I glimpsed the "V. R." Holmes had etched in bullet holes on the parlor wallpaper. "Holmes."

"I applaud his penmanship and sentiments, but didn't the landlady and neighbors and the horses in the street swoon from fright?"

"I wasn't here, but I suspect he did it very quickly, that being the point of the exercise."

Bram Stoker laughed with delight. "What a scene that would make on stage. I must borrow it for some production."

"I believe Holmes was bored."

Now Oscar Wilde laughed, less heartily. "I had never thought of such an exhilarating cure for boredom. I must try it when my critics are in the room."

"But there are so many of them, Oscar," Stoker responded genially.

"You are right. I would run out of bullets and have to resort to stickpins. But let us not stand on ceremony when there are chairs to be sat on."

With this Stoker settled in the basket chair and left Holmes's velvet-lined easy chair to Wilde. I took my usual seat to the left of the fireplace. Thus we settled into an uneasy conversational lull.

I knew who both men were, of course, but had no idea why they would consult Holmes.

I made so bold as to ask them.

"Consult Holmes?" Stoker asked, blinking his pale carrot-colored eyelashes. "Not at all."

"Quite the reverse is true," Wilde said, crossing his legs to reveal olive silk stockings and shoes that were more slippers than brogues. "Holmes has, in fact, consulted *us*."

"Really?" Politeness would not allow me to probe further, but I couldn't credit that Holmes would ever do any such thing.

He was a man who kept his own counsel. That I had achieved so much of his confidence through our long association was a matter of great pride to me. Wilde's supercilious manner felt sharper than it was probably meant. He had been studying the interior, and I recalled that he edited some magazine involving fashion and interior design and the like.

"I see Holmes and I have a mutual friend."

My eyes went to the photograph of General Gordon on one wall, my sole contribution to the room's bohemian decor.

"The General?" I asked, startled, for he was not only dead but I could not imagine that Wilde had ever met such a military hero, and certainly I had not, despite my years of service in Afghanistan.

"The diva," Oscar said, smiling.

That is when I remembered the photograph of the late Irene Adler that Holmes kept on the mantel along with a Persian slipper filled with pipe shag and his most recent correspondence transfixed with a jackknife.

"That is a fine photograph of her," Stoker said warmly. "Quite the most beautiful woman I ever met, with apologies to Ellen Terry, my own wife Florence, whom you also admired, Oscar, and your own Constance."

"Beautiful, yes," I began, about to explain that she was also very dead, when the door from the stairway opened and there stood Holmes in his usual London garb of top hat and cutaway coat.

He doffed the hat at once and welcomed the assemblage with one of his swift, tight smiles. "Watson! How clever of you to arrive in such a timely fashion to greet my guests."

I had the opposite impression, and stood. "I could see if Mrs. Hudson can offer us some refreshment."

"Capital idea, Watson. I just arrived on the boat train from Paris this morning and would welcome sustenance. Gentlemen?"

Both men shook their heads with a smile. "No," Stoker said. "We both are needed at the theater, and only stopped by to see you beforehand."

"Then Watson and I shall make a picnic of it, eh, old fellow! Do see what Mrs. Hudson can tempt us with. She is a jewel at sudden meals, which my work demands. There's a good chap."

I very much had the impression of a child being sent to bed while the adults begin to discuss the most interesting matters. But off I went, hoping that Holmes would let me know the reason for this astounding visit later.

Mrs. Hudson was the sort of landlady, and cook, who reveled in rising to occasions. I left her happily planning a tasty if impromptu repast, which somewhat made up for my speedy dismissal by Holmes.

Once again I climbed the stairs and wondered at my welcome. The two men were standing, as though taking their leave.

"We were just saying," Wilde noted, "before Dr. Watson went to see to supper, what a splendid likeness of Irene Adler that is. I should have composed an ode to her years ago. She is the female equivalent of a Stradivarius, is she not, Holmes?"

"Watson is the expert on the fair sex," Holmes answered hastily. "I must keep my mind unclouded by such aspects as beauty. I do, in fact, find women as a whole to be clever but unreliable."

"Unreliability is their most charming attribute, my dear Holmes," Wilde said. "The reliable is vastly overrated, far too unpredictable to count upon. Would you ask the wind to blow in four-four time? So, Dr. Watson." Wilde turned to me with a slight smile. "Do you bow with every man of sensibility to the divine beauty of the lovely diva?"

"A fine figure of a woman, no doubt, but—" I said, about to point out that she was dead.

"No 'buts,' Watson!" Holmes interrupted me. "Wilde is the day's supreme connoisseur of beauty. Be flattered that he approves of your taste. A pity you cannot stay," Holmes told our visitors. "I have a rather good claret, but . . . a theater curtain waits for no man. It is interesting that you are beginning to write fiction, Stoker. My friend Watson has had some success in that direction."

"Really?" Wilde sounded so astounded I felt an immediate need to defend my efforts.

"Not pure fiction," I said hastily. "I am minded to write up some of Holmes's most interesting cases, with the actual names and places disguised, of course."

"Of course *not!*" Wilde responded enthusiastically. "My dear doctor, actual names and places are what make for fictional success. So what have you written, or, more to the point, had published?"

"*Beeton's Christmas Annual* featured 'A Study in Scarlet,' which was released last year as a novel."

"The title has an artistic implication I adore, and 'scarlet' is such a divinely lurid word. Was there murder in it?"

"Indeed, and much misbehavior by the Mormons in the American West, which led to a transatlantic quest for vengeance that devoured many years before the villains of the case were found dead in London."

"Mormons! Murder! Vengeance! Corpses in London, dear me. And the American West as well, which I found quite fascinating, and vice versa, during my lecture tours there in early part of the decade. I am currently editor of *The Woman's World*, so if you'd care to offer your work for the glance of my editorial eye, I would be happy to advise. I am always eager to encourage rivals. It gives my constant critics so many more worthy targets."

He aimed a languid forefinger at the wall and sketched an airy pattern. "I make a metaphorical statement. V. O. Either Very Old brandy, or Victorious Oscar. Come, Stoker, let us see what they are up to at the Beefsteak Club. I have a play or two of my own in mind, one involving an earnestly unfortunate fellow who was indeed a 'case,' or rather was found in one in Victoria Station as an infant. Mislaid infants! Possible bastardy! Perfidy in cloak rooms in Victoria Station. I may someday be as acclaimed as Dr. Watson and his sensational fictions. Adieu for now."

On that note the two men left our rooms, or Holmes's rooms now, clattering and chatting together down the stairs.

"Theatrical folk," I commented, surprised by Holmes's high spirits. He was already opening the claret and soon poured two glasses.

"Isn't it odd," I asked, "that those men didn't know Irene Adler was dead?"

"Odd? Not at all, Watson. They live and work in the theater, where anything is possible."

"Why were . . . you consulting them?"

"I was?"

"So they said."

"Ah, did they? Well, Watson, you know how my cases sometimes involve persons of the most elevated rank in the realm, and the most sensitive subjects for the future of the Empire."

"Indeed. Was this latest European jaunt in the service of such eminent persons?"

"Exactly. I soon may be required to go elsewhere as well, in the same service."

"And these two men—?"

"Know everyone who is everyone, and everything about them. I can say no more, save that it is very encouraging that Wilde is willing to assess your work. I would pursue his offer."

"He is the writer of the moment, isn't he? But editor of *The Woman's World* . . . I'm not sure that my sort of thing is his sort of thing."

"Nonsense, Watson! I may immodestly say that my cases, suitably fictionalized and based upon your maiden effort, make most interesting reading."

"I have another manuscript I call 'A Scandal in Bohemia.' "

"I have heard you brandish that annoying little title before and suggest you look farther. That case was much ado about nothing, and I did not exit it in glory, since the lady evaded me."

"But she is dead: perished in that dreadful Alpine train crash while fleeing London with her new husband. She can hardly bring any sort of case against me if I were to present her unhappy history in fiction."

"I sincerely hope not, Watson. Still, I advise you to look farther afield for your second, and perhaps more important effort, for every debut must prove itself with the unquestioned quality of its successor. What about that gruesome affair involving the murder at Pondicherry Lodge and the Agra treasure? It has all that the modern reader yearns for: lost riches, betrayal, a rousing river-borne chase, sudden death, and a charming touch of romance in the stalwart doctor's wooing of the consulting detective's charming young client, Miss Mary Morstan, now Mrs. John H. Watson. That is the sort of thing that appeals to the public."

"Given your praise of Mary, I am surprised that the consulting detective did not rival the doctor for her hand."

"Ah, Watson, the married man! You are speaking to one who can report that the most winning woman I ever knew was hanged for murdering three small children for their insurance money. Women are not entirely to be trusted, not even the best of them."

"I thought you found Irene Adler the most winning of them of all. That is why you call her *'the'* woman and keep her photograph on the mantel, although it seems you would like others to think that *I* am her most fervent admirer. I'm afraid her death has destroyed your sole opportunity to find an admirable woman."

"I am afraid so also, Watson, but I have my diversions."

I knew he referred to the thrice daily seven-percent solution of cocaine he resorted to when life offered no puzzles to challenge his restless intellect. The reference saddened me, for he had as much as admitted that Irene Adler might possibly have been diversion enough for a man and a mind such as his, had she lived, and had she not wed another.

"And I have *my* diversions," I said, hoping that talk of my stories would lure him from the needle case for a while. "You may be right, Holmes, about the Agra treasure affair, but it would require some length."

"So much the better! Substance, that is the thing."

Speaking of substance, Mrs. Hudson knocked on the door with her knuckles, her hands laden with a tray bearing our late-night supper.

"Indeed," Holmes greeted her, whisking the heavy tray into his custody. "And what culinary confabulation have you prepared for us, Mrs. Hudson? No, let us find this undiscovered country for ourselves. Thank you and good night."

After seeing her out, Holmes hovered over the tray, rubbing his hands together in expectation before plucking off a napkin like a stage magician revealing a rabbit. Indeed, the dish beneath was Welsh rarebit, soft and steaming. I quite forgot about Wilde and Stoker and the late Irene Adler and Bohemia in order to apply myself with deserving gusto to the treat before us.

I also chewed on Holmes's literary advice: a longer, bloodier fictional piece that might more likely find an audience than royal scandals and operatic shenanigans in Eastern Europe.

Perhaps he had a point.

5.

Maiden Voyage

DEAR Q.O.—I AM OFF TO NEW YORK. LOOK OUT FOR ME. BLY.

—FAREWELL NOTE TO A COLUMNIST FRIEND ON THE *PITTSBURG DISPATCH*, WHERE SHE FELT HER WORK WAS UNDERVALUED, 1887

From that day in the peaceful garden at Neuilly, I was in short order delivered into the most heinous interim in my life.

I refer to what is called an "Atlantic crossing." It is accomplished by steamship, by a great seven-deck liner as large as a cathedral but far less anchored.

I cannot speak much about the experience, as I spent it confined to our cabin in the depths of *mal de mer*, which is a pretty French phrase for the most unspeakable, relentless nonfatal illness known to man, or woman, or child.

Irene, of course, was as at home on the swaying bosom of Mother Ocean as she was on the stablest stage in Christendom.

She returned frequently to my miserable bunk, both by day

and night, with hot broths and cold compresses, neither of which helped.

Often at night she sang to me, not so much words as lulling syllables, the best palliative for a wracked body and drifting mind. It was criminal, I thought hotly under that tuneful spell, how the King of Bohemia's pursuit had forced Irene to accept the anonymity of presumed death and kept her from the concert stage for almost two years. Sometimes I believed I detected the wretched wailing of a violin behind her voice. Sometimes my heavy eyes saw the shadow of Sherlock Holmes looming behind her. At other times I fancied I saw a wildly white-haired old man sawing away like a Gypsy fiddler in Transylvania. The "maestro" became a malign figure I feared. Hadn't his long-buried instrument resurrected Irene's memories, bringing us both on this miserable journey into her past? Perhaps we would be dreadfully sorry for it. I know I was, already!

"Poor Nell! Darling Nell!" she would croon, then mutter to herself, "It is my fault! I should have considered the effect of an Atlantic crossing on one who has only sailed the Channel between England and the Continent."

I was too weak to agree with her, or even flutter my eyelids in sign that I had heard. And then the soothing trills of her voice mesmerized me, bore me away on a tide of maternal memories . . . not of the dead mother I had never known, but of my own frail attempted lullabies when my schoolroom charges were ill and feverish. I was indeed fortunate to be as sick as a beached seal with a prima donna for a nursemaid.

Smoking was not permitted belowdecks, so even during the night Irene would desert me for a short while. And, often, when she thought me asleep, she paced as she was wont to do only when smoking and puzzling out a conundrum. Now, however, her thoughts rather than tobacco drove her fevered stalking, and she berated herself even more.

"This journey was folly. Folly! Nell is no better for it, but worse, and I . . . my past is checkered, to say the least, and will certainly shock Nell, even though I cannot remember the half of it! Why? *Why!* I can master the libretto of a four-hour score in a foreign language in no time! I am a nine-day's wonder of a quick study. *Why* do I only have fleeting mental pictures of most of my childhood, with familiar but unnamed faces looking on? And something . . . something awful that I almost seem to recall but, maddeningly, cannot quite grasp. What is that mystery looming ever since I unearthed the violin and memories of the maestro! Everything before England is blurred, as through a misted window. Everything after is clear as crystal. Why!"

Her words passed over me like ocean waves, agitated at the onset, but soon drawing away into the shallows of my mind like some ebbing eiderdown quilt.

Later in the voyage, Irene brought back lively reports about that segment of the human race that is impervious to the act of bouncing endlessly in the deep vales and steep hills of saltwater. Somehow she expected that commentary on others' seaboard amusements would cheer me up.

During the day she leaned over me, her expression unnaturally cheerful while she regaled me with tales of promenades on the ladies' deck and her unauthorized excursion to the gentlemen's billiard room, where she won a round and smoked a cigar—Irene would be Irene on Noah's Ark, I swear!

I learned of rattan deck chairs and breezes so lively the women's skirts hoisted like sails. (Our swift and modern steamship only flew a couple of pennants, she explained, and sported two black smokestacks billowing dark clouds.) Of deckside games of shuffleboard and something called "bull," which did not make me pine to be up and about.

She very considerately brought me no reports on the ship's menu. And she emptied my slop pail with the dash of a milkmaid in an operetta performing an entirely quaint and graceful chore, for which I was most grateful. I had never before considered that a gifted actress's dissembling could be an act of charity.

"I have been asked to sing," she told me once, greatly excited. I cannot say when, for there was no night or day for me in my floating bed of pain and disorientation. "At the Captain's gala. He well remembers Buffalo Bill's mind-reading act from a previous crossing. Imagine Buffalo Bill as a mind-reader. It is too amusing."

I muttered something that was not amusing.

"Poor Nell!" She sat beside me glittering like the Diamond Horseshoe of an American opera house in her evening dress, passing a limp cold compress over my hellishly hot forehead. "Had I any idea that you were prone to seasickness I'd have never allowed you to come."

I muttered something not translatable.

"Even toast and tea can't answer. Well, at least you will land with a waist as narrow as Nellie Bly's!"

On that note, she left me. And I felt much better about feeling so bad, as I had once heard the wasp-waisted Nellie Bly so ungrammatically put it in her bold American way, of which I was soon to see much more, unfortunately. . . .

What can I say about our being tugged into New York harbor like a large, dignified matron being dragged somewhere by a determined child?

In this case, Irene was the child, grown, and the mystery of her mother was tugging her back to the land of her birth, and me with her.

What a busy shore that was! Steamships and smaller vessels thronged the harbor, old-fashioned ships with gleaming ranks of sails like seagull wings and flat, ugly ferries conveying immigrants to Ellis Island. All were drifting by the towering figure France had sent America only a few years ago. The Statue of Liberty stood on a pedestal almost as looming as she was, with her sculpted metal robes like a giant curtain opening on Manhattan Island and her torch lifted high. It stood taller than one of the ancient world's Seven Wonders, the male figure of the Colossus of Rhodes. Somehow the gigantic female figure seemed to suit this upstart nation, and it had been commissioned to honor the United States surviving its bitter Civil War.

The scenery beyond the statue loomed as large as Lady Liberty herself did. Buildings did not unfurl in five-story rank and file, but shot up unexpectedly, some perhaps ten or even twelve stories high.

Such metropolitan hubris was unknown to me.

Still green of complexion, I leaned against the deck rail, inhaling air composed of smoke and seagulls and salt and oil.

At least I was standing, now that the Atlantic waves had dwindled into the ripplings of a protected bay and series of inlets.

"The New World," I said.

"The Old World, to me," Irene answered. "I had hoped to put it behind me forever once."

The only things we put behind us now were everything we knew and valued, as we tended to the tasks of getting ourselves and our luggage ashore and to our hotel.

Seagulls shrieked over our heads during the long process of debarking so many hundreds of people. The scent of salt and fish was as overbearing as the press of passengers eager to be on land. I almost became seasick again on the long, canted gangplank.

Luckily, we traveled with one trunk each, a record for Irene, and small ones, too, dictated by the White Star Line to no more than three feet long and a foot or so deep. After two hours we were reunited with the proper trunks and found a four-wheeler waiting at the pier to take us to the Astor House hotel, which Pink had recommended.

This hostelry was not far from the harbor, lying across Broadway from a fine, green park at Barclay Street. It was a four-square, five-story building and remarkable for being an entire fifty-some years old, Irene told me, imagine that. There are peddlers' carts in London older than this!

It was a relief to register in the echoing reception rooms and, after a disquieting ride in an elevator, find ourselves and our trunks installed in a decent enough suite of rooms. Godfrey had insisted that we travel in comfort, and had wired ahead so that American funds should be available to us. Clearly his work on the international front had made him only more thoughtful, able, and useful than ever.

Yet accomplishing all these duties of arrival in a another land ended in no welcome respite, I knew, for Irene had already arranged by telegram to dine with Pink Cochrane this very evening.

If I did manage to swallow a few bites of supper by the evening, I doubted that I could swallow anything our American acquaintance had to offer.

6.

Motherland

My age is 14 years. I live with my mother. I was present when mother was married to J. J. Ford. . . . The first time I seen Ford take hold of mother in an angry manner, he attempted to choke her.

—DIVORCE COURT TESTIMONY OF PINKEY E. J. COCHRANE, 1879

"Now, what is this nonsense about my mother?" Irene asked directly after dinner.

"I do not deal in 'nonsense,'" Pink responded indignantly.

Irene smiled at this forceful reaction. "I only mean that I do not have a mother. I have never been known to have a mother. Thus I am mightily curious exactly whom you are going to produce for this role."

"So you've come all the way across the Atlantic to tell me I've got a cold story?"

I could not resist joining the conversation, now that I could sit upright and nibble at food again. "Oh, you have some story, no doubt, Pink. You 'daredevil girl reporters' are always up to something."

"I did nothing to find this story," Pink replied as hotly as I had hoped. "It came to me, as the best ones always do. It's knowing what's smart to follow up on that counts in the newspaper business."

"And it is a . . . business," Irene noted with a mere jot of British snobbery, which I, as a Briton, could appreciate and applaud. "What right does your 'business' have in meddling in my personal affairs?"

"Because you are news, that's why. Local girl makes good; just as I have."

"Local?" Irene's tone dripped disbelief.

"New Jersey is pretty close to New York City."

"I have never denied that I was born in New Jersey."

"But that's just it. You weren't."

"I ought to know."

"Really? You were a bit young at the time."

At this point it was a match. It struck me that young Pink was holding forth with the same irritating prescience that Mr. Sherlock Holmes employed all too often. Know-it-alls, both of them, though as different from each other as peas from potatoes.

Irene and I, being far from home and our clothing wardrobes, were neatly attired in shirtwaists and skirts and short jackets. Pink, on her own ground, dressed far more grandly. She seemed to indulge in wide-brimmed hats as sweeping as a musketeer's, with silk and velvet flowers nestled along one side instead of the extravagant plume called a panache, which represented the cavalier's honor. I doubted that Miss Pink would wear her honor on her hat, or her heart on her sleeve, for all her admirable reporting of society's wrongs had been done in feigned guise, like a thief or an inquiry agent. I doubted she would ever don men's garb again, as Irene had done in her Pinkerton days and even did today, despite the Paris outing we three had made last spring so scandalously attired.

She was simply too feminine to forgo her charms, a slim young woman with a waist small enough for a garter snake to encompass. She wore her hair in soft curls high on her forehead and pulled close behind her ears, which emphasized the perfect oval of her features. She looked as demure as a schoolroom miss, which was doubtless why her masquerades on the seamy side of life worked so well.

Irene absently rearranged her silverware as one would adjust pawns upon a chessboard. I wondered whether she would respond to Pink's challenge with the olive branch of a teaspoon, the genteel prod of a fork, or the stab of the steak knife.

Irene spoke at last. "It was not mention of a 'mother' that brought me back to these shores. It was mention of murder. And, of course, the utter impossibility of someone attempting to murder my mother. I am, as I'm sure you know, an orphan."

An orphan! I gazed at Irene in dismay.

As hard as it had been for Godfrey to admit that he was . . . well, a word beginning with "b" applied to children "born on the wrong side of the blanket," meaning that he was of, er, illegitimate descent—which meant either that his father was likely a rake like Bertie, or his mother was far worse than she should be— I could only imagine how hard it was for Irene to admit to origins that were the stuff of far too many melodramas. She had been a grand opera diva, and the grand opera regarded itself as far above melodrama even while it purveyed buckets of the same lurid yet sentimental drivel in high-sounding arias.

That is my opinion, anyway.

Irene smiled at Pink's sudden silence. "Even you once signed yourself 'Lonely Orphan Girl,' you told me. That letter and self-deprecating signature interested an editor at the *Pittsburg Dispatch*, and the rest is newspaper history, or will be, if you have your way, Nellie Bly. And you were not ever an 'orphan girl,' by any means, were you?"

"Nor are you! I myself suspect several women of being your mother."

"Ah, now I have a surfeit of mothers! Suspect! Only in your imagination. Perhaps 'lonely orphan girls' develop highly unreliable imaginations."

"I used that signature to let that annoying *Dispatch* columnist know that women work not just to challenge his sense of woman's place, but because they have no man to support them. Many women are 'orphans' in the sense that they must look after themselves and should not be abused for it."

"Hear, hear," Irene rejoined. "A fine speech. I seem to recall that Nell and myself have done just that for some years. Yet by calling yourself an 'orphan' when you weren't one, you undercut your argument that women deserve meaningful work. You make work into an act of charity, not a deserved occupation."

Irene leaned across the table, her voice now as soft as a lullaby, her eyes glittering with sudden sympathy.

"Why did you call yourself an orphan, Pink?"

"I . . . I—Really, Irene, that was so long ago!"

"How long?"

"Oh, four years, but so much has happened since. I had to use a false name. No decent woman allows her true name to appear in print—"

"Unless she is married or buried, didn't someone once say?"

"I don't know, but that's about it. That phrase was simply something I scribbled down on the spur of the moment."

"But you did have a mother, and a father, Pink, and he wasn't that dreadful man Jack Ford you told us about, that brute who forced your mother to seek a divorce when you were fourteen. You want to unearth my mother. Perhaps you owe it to me to tell me about your father. Your real father."

Pink pushed her fork into the candied fruit that comprised our dessert. The gesture was sudden, as if she were stabbing something other than a glazed apricot.

"He was a fine and cultured man, very kind. I often used to sit on his lap and he gave me hard candy. We lived in a town called Apollo, in a beautiful house with four high white pillars and a pediment in front of it. I remember playing and looking up at it and thinking that must be how the mansions in heaven look. . . .

There was no heaven, except for him, if you believe that sort of thing. He . . . what would you say? Collapsed one day. Couldn't move or speak. He was soon dead."

"How old were you, Pink?"

"Six. I had just turned six."

"I'm sorry," Irene said, sitting back. "You must have loved him dearly at that age, and remembered why, more's the pity."

"Indeed. Then the house was gone, and my mother was left with five children and no way to support them. It soon was up to me."

"Had you no older brothers or sisters?"

"My brothers married and started their own families. There was some pittance left, but my 'guardian' seemed to run short of it awfully soon. I had to leave normal school and make my way as best I could. I tutored, played the nanny—"

"Oh, I did, too," I put in at mention of a common fate.

Pink glanced unhappily at me, unencouraged by our shared history. "As soon as I turned twenty-one, I sued that guardian in court."

"Did you win?" Irene asked.

"He was proven to be a very poor accountant, but the case took two years. I guess I exposed him in public, and that's enough."

"So that's what you do now," Irene said, smiling, "you expose other wrongdoers in public. What has made me a target for such a campaign?"

"I mean you no harm! You should be happy to find a lost relative. I defended my mother. I have supported my mother. Even now I live with her. A woman of that generation did not have the choices we have today. We owe them respect and love. I couldn't help running across . . . traces of you as a child, and what a fascinating child you were!"

"How fascinating?" I said, interrupting.

"Not as fascinating as the child Pink," Irene said quickly,

keeping her attention on Nellie Bly. "So you learned where I grew up, and with whom. That still does not presume a mother in the woodwork. Besides, Pink, who cares who my mother was or was not? Not I. Not the public."

"I can't believe you wouldn't care, but I won't argue that. The public will care if someone is trying to kill a woman who is actually your mother, and this may not be the first murder in your former theatrical circle, for all we know. A whole clan of women surrounded you when you were a child."

"Ah. My mother was not absent, but merely incognito. And your claim of maternal danger is merely the opening to the real mystery. Murder. Murders plural, I think, else you would not see the pattern of a 'circle.' You have hooked me, Pink, even though you don't discern the reason why. Let's get down to it, then. Who has been murdered? That is what must be established before anyone supposes who might be murdered next, and to whom the next victim 'might' be related."

"You have taken on a lot of British airs since you have lived abroad, do you know that?"

"I do, and I like it. 'British airs' embody manners and civility, something my former native land and its products could use more of."

My spine straightened as if the Union Jack had been raised over our table. I joined Irene in regarding Pink, christened Elizabeth, presumably by her mother, and renamed Nellie to provide a pseudonym for the newspaper for which she toiled, the *Pittsburg Dispatch*. Even in America in this ultramodern year of 1889 it was recognized that no respectable woman would write under her own name for the public press.

New York was decidedly not the World, in my opinion, or anywhere near the center of it. And Irene was not a motherless lamb to be lured by the *baa*ing of a mythological ewe. Or was I thinking of a Judas goat?

And was that Pink herself?

7.

Domestic Disturbances

∿

Real estate capitalists suddenly discovered that there was plenty of room in the air, and that by doubling the height of its buildings the same result would be reached as if the island had been stretched to twice its present width.

—*BUILDING NEWS*, 1883

What a sad commentary on contemporary mores that I was not surprised when we returned to our hotel rooms after dinner to find a strange and rather unsavory man waiting in our parlor.

He rose as we let ourselves in, and seemed to regard explaining his presence as quite unnecessary. Since Irene had not drawn the little pistol she always carried in even her smallest dress reticules when she traveled, I assumed that she had expected him.

"How kind of your superiors to send you," she said by way of greeting.

"The office," he replied with certain formal wariness, "said I was to spare no effort on your behalf." He blinked at me. "Is this the chit who is blackmailing you?"

Fortunately, the suggestion rendered me speechless, allowing

Irene to create the libretto of her choice. "Not at all. This is Miss Huxleigh, a British . . . inquiry agent who has been working the Continental side of the case."

His glance flicked to me and challenged not a jot of that fairy tale. "Good evening, miss. Ma'am." He nodded at Irene. "I hear you went from an agent to an employer of the Pinkertons on occasion, over in Europe, not that we have many agents working there. Yet."

He was a tall, rather beefy man of the Irish persuasion, with a nose that seemed red, bulbous, and long enough to have regularly inhaled the fumes of ale or even whiskey. Still, his eye was sharp and there was an air about him of a military man, however lowly.

"The case," Irene said, "that called me home is not precisely blackmail, although the young woman you referred to would not stick at a bit of coercion to win her way. No, the real matter in the case seems to be one of murder."

"What case would that be, ma'am?"

"It's a mystery," Irene said roguishly. "The first part of it is that I have been lured to this country by talk of a mother I did not know I had. The second part of it appears to be the notorious stunt reporter, Nellie Bly. Have a seat, Mr.—?"

"Conroy, ma'am."

"And some sherry from the sideboard. Excellent. Then please tell me . . . us, what you have learned."

He immediately accepted the delicate glass Irene offered him, although it posed between his large, callused forefinger and thumb like a crystal thimble, and he sat upon a side chair.

One swallow finished the sipping sherry and then he set the glass on the desk. Next he pulled a cheap and battered notepad and a stubby pencil whose lead had been mutilated by some sort of knife from the side pocket of his jacket.

"She is the cat's meow when it comes to doings of the journalistic sort," he began. "Though she goes by Nellie Bly, her real name is Elizabeth Cochrane, but I figger you know that, ma'am."

"Indeed I do, but hold nothing back. You have had the advantage of investigating her on her own home soil. We first made her acquaintance abroad, where she was herself investigating matters for a sensation story and posing as a prostitute."

His eyebrows rose like grizzled caterpillars about to exchange blows. Not for this blunt American the exquisite, single lofted eyebrow of an Oscar Wilde.

So I was not surprised when blunt words streamed off his tongue. In London, he would have spoken Cockney. Here it was a less accented but no less lowly form of American English. "What? Playing the harlot? And her a judge's daughter?"

"*Judge's* daughter?" Irene rustled forward on the padded ottoman she had chosen to sit upon. "She never mentioned *that.* No wonder she seeks justice so intently."

"I'd guess there were so many of 'em none took it that serious like. He'd had ten children by his first wife. Miss Elizabeth and her four older and younger siblings came along through her mother, a widow named Mary Jane Cummings, who snagged a man of substance in her second marriage. The judge treated the new kids Nellie's mother had after the marriage as well as his first family, and all would have been peaches and cream, except when the judge died, the children of his first wife pretty much got it all, and they sold Mrs. Mary Jane's house right out from under her. She ended up with the furniture, the horse and carriage, the cow, one of the dogs, and no money to keep them."

"Oh, dear me!" I exclaimed. "It sounds so like a situation from a Jane Austen novel. *Sense and Sensibility,* if I recall correctly. I had no idea the laws and customs of America could be so . . . English."

Mr. Conroy frowned at me. "Right." Obviously, he had understood not a word I had uttered. "Thank you, miss," he added with a certain rough, frontier courtesy that I had detected in Buffalo Bill and even Red Tomahawk during our last, er, case. Really, being elevated to an inquiry agent was much more exciting than my former professions of governess, yard-goods clerk, and typewriter-girl.

I subsided.

Mr. Conroy licked the end of his pencil out of habit—a habit that made my governess's soul cringe—and continued. "Put out lock, stock and single milk-cow, they were: the widow and five hungry kids. No wonder that Missus Cochrane soon fetched up married to one Jack Ford."

"Ah." Irene sipped a centimeter of her sherry. She drank spirits as she smoked the small cigars she favored, delicately. She had not produced any smoking paraphernalia tonight. I suspect such an act would have scandalized our crude American colleague, and she didn't wish to distract him. "That is why she remarried so unsuitably."

"You know of the rotter, ma'am?"

"Yes. Some of our research will overlap, but I prefer to hear the whole report entire from you, Mr. Conroy, so please continue."

" 'Rotter' was too good a word for Jack Ford. Drunk. Wifebeater. Debtor would do better. Nasty goods. The kind you like to grind facedown on the cobbles when you finally catch him at his dirty work. Turns out the rampages and such got too much. Missus Cochrane, the late judge's wife, takes the bounder to court for divorce, and little someday-Nellie is her main witness to the man's transgressions. She had spirit. That young Cochrane girl, I mean."

"Still does, Mr. Conroy. Have you any information on how she became a girl reporter?"

"No. That stuff is not on record, as scandalous divorce cases are. Nellie turned up in the columns of the *Dispatch* before she was twenty, and her first story was about divorce."

"Cheeky of her."

"That's for certain! A girl writing about such scandalous stuff. And that was just the beginning. Before you knew it 'Nellie Bly' was taking a train with her mother to Mexico and reporting on distressing conditions there, though I don't expect nothing but distressing conditions across the border. Anyway, it was news to the readers of the *Dispatch*, as was the idea of such a young American girl going down there cool as you please. And there was the stunt after she came to New York when she acted like a madwoman and got the goods on the Blackwell's Island insane asylum, which I would shake in me hobnails before visitin' meself, for fear they'd never let me out.

"There isn't much this gal won't do, and I must say that where she goes and what she sees and tells opens people's eyes. This world is not a fair or just place, but neither was the Old World, which my forebears fled as they would an infestation of fleas, so there you have it. Nellie Bly is a name around New York now, along with her sisterhood, and they are all stirring up things and crying for justice for the poor and mute. Nothing much changes, though, 'cept the daredevil reporters get courted by the rich and famous and the poor and mute pretty much stay that way."

"Mr. Conroy. I didn't expect such an astute and philosophical summary! And what is the state of Miss Bly's private life now?"

"She doesn't much have one. The rival newspapers are arguing the truth in her stories and sending other young ladies to outdo her for daring, which is a bit of a challenge. There's no dirt to dig up on her private life, though you're saying she posed as a woman of ill repute in Paris. That would sully the page a little, but she already got a book out about *Ten Days in a Brothel* here, not to mention a pretty raw novel last year, *The Mystery of Central Park*, based on her story about a stableman who'd pick up naïve girls in Central Park and set them to brothel work. It was supposed to be a series, from the cover, but appears to be a series of one, and not a peep about that French brothel escapade has hit print here. She lives quietly with her mother in a cozy little flat on Thirty-fifth Street, when she is not out scandalizing folk and putting the fear of exposure into the slum landlords and others of that sort who deserve the fear of something more than most."

"Lives with her mother? Apparently the elder woman has never been particularly independent?"

"She has not been a good judge of men's character. Her daughter has benefited from the mother's bad example to the point that there are no men to dig up in her past, save the mostly gray dinosaurs who employ her at the newspaper. If you're looking for dirt on Nellie Bly you are not alone, but you are just as unsuccessful as the girl reporters at the rival papers."

"Well done, Mr. Conroy!" Irene sat back, her sherry still mostly intact. "You make me proud to have been a Pinkerton. Is the Female Department still going strong?"

"No. Mr. Pinkerton was alone in his insistence on such an idea, and once he died in 'eighty-four, no time was lost in abolishing the practice. I admit that I am sorry to see the notion fade, but at least I have had occasion to meet yourself."

He stood, stuffing his homely notepad into his sagging coat pocket. "I take it you had been up to a few stunts in your day, ma'am, that would make Miss Nellie Bly pale to puce by comparison. Mr. Pinkerton spoke of you often, with great regret, in that Europe and the performing stage had stolen away the best female agent he ever had."

Irene stood also. "I am honored to be so remembered. Thank you for your assistance."

"If you need anything more—"

"I will not hesitate to call upon you."

With that our unexpected visitor picked up his sorry derby and departed.

"Ah!" Irene pushed her fists into her whaleboned waist and took a deep breath after he had gone.

"We already knew a good deal of Pink's family history," I pointed out.

"Yes, but from her alone. I find it intriguing that she still lives with—supports—her mother."

"Intriguing? It is only daughterly duty. Had I a mother still living—"

"Yes, I know, Nell. You'd be a paragon of devotion. I can only thank fate that you were orphaned and available to provide such sterling devotion to my causes. Pink, though, is from a different tradition. She is young, modern, notorious, celebrated, and even more impressively, making inroads on her society. Why is she not courted? Why has she not a fistful of suitors? Why does she live, at the ripe old age of twenty-five, with her mother?"

"Not every woman," I pointed out, "is so fortunate as to find a Godfrey."

"But every woman in such a position would have at least found a Crown Prince of Bohemia or two, even if he were only a merchant prince in this most democratic land."

Irene paced, then paused to extract her pistol from the silken evening bag and install it in the desk drawer. Only then did she root in the reticule and withdraw the elegant blue enamel case that held her tiny cigarettes and the lucifers that lit them.

"And why is she so intrigued by the notion of my forgotten mother?"

"Obviously her mother was more important to her than yours was to you."

"For which she does not forgive me. One often requires others to respect the same obligations that oneself is tied to. Yet I must believe that there is more to this matter than a trifling disagreement about the importance of mothers."

"What can we do to discover what it is?"

"For starters, we must meet *her* mother . . . and then I suppose we must contrive to meet mine."

She grinned at me with an insouciance I would be sore put to summon were I about to meet my long-dead and utterly unknown mother.

"You could hardly think, Nell, that I would arrive here on an expedition into the most hidden areas of my past called by Nellie Bly without investigating *her* private affairs. You will recall her impassioned defense of her mother, testifying against her vicious stepfather at the age of fourteen. Perhaps it's not so surprising that she supports and lives with her mother more than ten years later, or that the subjects of her newspaper stunts are the brutal lives of sweatshop girls and fallen women."

"Yet her own life cannot have been that sordid."

"No, but it was sorry enough in parts." Irene gazed at the wallpaper as if it were a painting worth studying. "If you find me odd in not wishing to trace my antecedents, it's because I know that all families have secrets. Family secrets are the most dangerous of all, and we are always the sorrier for finding them out. I don't relish unearthing mine."

I kept silent, meditating upon the one matter I kept from Irene at all costs. I could only be thankful that a dogged investigator like Nellie Bly had not the slightest interest in unveiling my secrets.

8.

Maternal Musings

*You can live as many lives in New York as you have
money to pay for.*
—THE DESTRUCTION OF GOTHAM, 1886

The city of New York was in those days the bustling,
expanding, towering monument to American enterprise
typified by the Statue of Liberty thrusting her torch into
the very vault of Heaven itself.

I reminded myself that it had taken the French to
install so blatant a symbol in New York harbor, and then I was less
intimidated by the city itself. The French are far more intimidating than anybody.

In fact, that city reminded me more of Mother London than
of Grande Dame Paris, for it was crowded, noisy, and noxiously
fumed, while Paris was open, airy, and impossibly French.

The first most distressing impact of New York City life was
the fact that most city streets were numbered rather than named.
And such a hubris of numbers! I understood that humble first
and seventh and twentieth streets soon vaulted into the eighties
and nineties and beyond. The city reminded me of a Scots plaid,

for the north-south avenues that crossed the east-west streets were also numbered, Fifth and Seventh being the most notable.

Pink and her mother resided in "midtown" at 120 West 35th Street.

There Irene and I took ourselves the next afternoon, by horse-drawn tram.

Such noise! Not only the clatter of hooves and wheels, but the yammering of the numerous street vendors, who were not confined to certain areas of the city but poured into all the main streets hawking their dubious wares.

In London one saw essentially two classes on the streets: gentlemen of business and Those Others; in New York everyone poured out of the towering buildings . . . urchins, hucksters, businessmen, and women of all sorts, many of them suspect, as well as others too obviously poor to be suspect of anything but starvation.

I could not guess into which category of women Irene and myself would be assigned by passersby, save that Irene seemed sublimely disinterested in how we would be regarded by others at all.

She had always had this distressful attitude, but in New York City it was more obvious than elsewhere. I reflected that how women on the street were regarded by others—that is, passing gentlemen—was the hallmark of a civilization, and I must admit that the French exceeded the English in this regard.

"I see," Irene remarked, "that Paris is rising in your estimation even as Manhattan Island is sinking like a barge in the East River."

"How can you see anything of the sort?" I demanded.

"Your glances give you away. You have been frowning at the crowds since we left the hotel. And you hold up your hems as if you expect some unknown man in Oriental robes to collapse at your boot toes at any moment, muttering the immortal phrase, 'Miss Huxleigh?'" Irene chuckled. "That Paris street scene smacked of Stanley finding Livingstone in the jungles of darkest Africa: 'Miss Huxleigh, I presume?' "

I would not allow her to trivialize my dramatic encounter with Quentin Stanhope in Paris, that had led us all—Irene, Godfrey, and myself—into serial danger and travels to foreign and ancient lands.

"You cast *me* as Livingstone?"

"Well, like you, he was religious. Stanley was merely a newspaper reporter, a Welsh-born American reporter for the *New York Herald* who did what no man on earth had been able to accomplish: track down the goodly doctor and incidentally confirm the source of the Nile."

"Are you trying to give American newspaper reporters some sort of pedigree?"

"Not at all. I merely point that the historical meeting was when—?"

"In the eighteen-fifties."

"So there is precedence for American reporters combining travel and derring-do and finding impossibly lost persons."

"Miss Pink is an amateur compared to Mr. Stanley. And Dr. Livingstone was a godly missionary. Finding him was worth the effort."

"Whereas finding my mother—?"

"I do not mean to impeach your reputed mother, whose existence even you deny! I merely mention that Nellie Bly has made a reputation purely on injecting herself into lurid situations. If she is interested enough to want to produce a mother for you, I, for one, would be very leery of the result."

Irene smiled while taking my arm and guiding me around a particularly noxious horse dropping.

"I have no high hopes of filling in my family tree all the way back to the Magna Carta," Irene admitted as we stood outside 120 West 35th in what Irene had assured me was the "fashionable"

Murray Hill district. "But I do have expectations of being entertained, at the least. Come. We are expected for tea."

It struck me that only Americans would begin the pursuit of a person's probably scandalous origins over a civilized serving of tea.

The house required us to mount enough stairs to add up to a year, had they been months. Nothing much distinguished this entry, façade, or block of buildings from many others that crowded the walks bracketing New York's cobblestoned streets.

The building stone was dark, not from London's numerous coal-smoke-laden fogs, but due to its very nature. Brownstone, it was called, and it managed to cast a pall on the day without a bit of English fog in the offing.

The entry was narrow and the door was opened by the former associate we had known only as "Pink," an American prostitute in Paris, until her true self had come to light: Nellie Bly, another false persona.

Now we met the girl's no doubt much-put-upon mother, a woman past sixty with her daughter's handsomely regular features. Her iron-gray hair was parted in the middle as in the days of her youth, and she seemed a comfortable sort of person and most cheery.

I must admit that I hoped that such a cozy maternal figure would suit admirably for Irene's lost mother, or for my own dead one.

"Do come in," Mrs. Cochrane urged. "I seldom meet my daughter's associates. And all the way from England."

"Paris," I corrected.

"As high a star over my existence as London, my dear. I am a homebody," said this disinherited widow of a judge, a woman who had subsequently married a monster. I recalled Pink's stories of her stepfather, Jack Ford, breaking the furniture and ruining the laundry simply to make this mother and her children work harder, so he could undo their efforts all over again.

"Miss Huxleigh," she murmured at our introduction. "You do not seem much older than my little Pink . . . nor does Mrs. Norton, yet you are both grand ladies."

"Not I! I am as . . . simple as scones."

"Scones?"

"A Scottish delicacy," Irene explained. "Something like a rather tasteless cookie."

By then we had been ushered into a small but well-accoutered parlor, numerous ferns filtering the daylight beyond the bow window.

"My daughter says that you ladies took her under your wings when she was abroad on newspaper business."

Irene and I accepted our teacups from the woman's hand, so wrinkled and pale she might have been wearing lace gloves.

(I saw all the ironing turned out on the floor, trampled by muddy boots. "Now, do it again!" the ogre thundered. So came heated irons and the re-pressing of every little pleat, sweat and tendrils braiding down a forehead. I recalled the sweatshop poem called "The Song of the Shirt.")

Something made me glance to the archway. Pink stood there making a picture in a frame, wearing a pale summer plaid gown of pink and lavender organdy. She was neat and wasp-waisted, a slip of girl who looked as if she'd never heard of madhouses or sweatshops or most especially brothels.

"How charmingly you are dressed," I couldn't help remarking. I glanced to her beaming mother. "Is that how she earned her childhood nickname? The color pink truly becomes her hazel eyes and brown hair."

Pink flushed at my question, only intensifying the effect I had remarked upon.

"All the other little girls wore dull black stockings and brown calico," Mrs. Cochrane said. "I put Pink in white stockings and starched pink dresses. She was as cute as a button and quite the little attention-getter even then."

Pink's face was now scarlet under a hat of lilac straw festooned with rose satin ribbon.

"Are you ready for our afternoon expedition?" she inquired sharply. Of Irene. At that moment I understood that she wished for both Irene's approval . . . and her downfall.

Mothers and daughters, I thought. Mothers and daughters. I had always been the latter, but I had never been the former. Nor had Irene. Were we . . . missing something, then?

For some reason Godfrey came to mind. I sighed and relaxed. And tensed again. Would we meet a woman who considered herself Irene's "mother" this afternoon, if Pink was not deceiving us?

I considered, as we sat there, sipping tea, that Pink had always been her mother's champion. I saw her then, just over a decade ago, a passionately defensive green girl of fourteen. She had been forced to fight for her family by the merciless laws of inheritance and the eternal tendency of women to seek men for protection even if the men they find are those they need protecting from. I also glimpsed another girl of a decade ago: Irene, perhaps forced to forgo family . . . by what unknowable, unnamable circumstances?

In some way I felt caught in the middle, particularly as that awful word murder hung over all our maternal musings like an executioner's axe.

"My dear child has made me prouder than any mother has a right to feel," Mrs. Cochrane, formerly Ford the madman's wife, said. "And what of *your* mother, Miss Huxleigh?"

"She died, in having me. This happens more often than one would think. My father—"

"Yes?" Irene asked. She knew as little of my family upbringing as I knew of hers.

"My father was a mild and learned man. He taught me more than I—or he—could know. He was both father and mother." I had never said such things before, but now that I did, I knew them for truth.

"The judge," Mrs. Ford said with a hefty sigh.

How could a good man have died and left them nothing to fend with but memory? Of course, when my own father died, what could I do but become a governess? Become "Huxleigh," known by my surname like a servant and yet ministering to the most intimate needs of the family's prized children?

I shook my head and set ignoble memories aside. "Huxleigh" was half a lifetime ago, as my father's death almost was. Seventeen years ago. Father.

I glanced at Irene. If she had never known a mother, had she ever known a father? No. Godfrey was right, in his lawyerly way: Irene came unencumbered—she was there at once, in the here and now, full-grown, full-blown.

There was only one other person who struck me as having such an utterly unrecorded, lonely history.

This was Mr. Sherlock Holmes, a man I both loathed and feared, and also, I discovered to my own surprise, was beginning to pity.

9.

Crime Seen

~ジ~

*We had strong phenomena from the start, and the medium
was always groaning, muttering, or talking.*
SIR ARTHUR CONAN DOYLE, REPORTING ON A SÉANCE

We three patronized the luxury of a carriage for the newest
journey, the lumbering assemblage called a "gurney,"
pulled by two horses, that easily held three people.

Irene had laughed when I remarked that hansom cabs
were not as plentiful in New York as in London or Paris.

"They are much more in evidence than when I was last here,"
she noted.

"And when was that?" Pink was quick to inquire.

"When hansom cabs were not so popular," Irene replied
shortly, then turned to resume her interrupted conversation
with me.

That would teach Miss Pink to respect her elders!

"There was much resistance to hansoms here several years ago,
Nell," Irene went on. "After all, the step-up is a foot and a half,
which makes them difficult for ladies managing skirts. And, I
think, the hansom has become the quintessential English city

transport. They are the water bugs on the great ocean of London, darting hither and yon with speed and agility. New York is a hasty town, but more ponderous."

"That is exactly it, Irene!" I replied. "I've been wondering how I would characterize this city to, say Sarah Bernhardt—"

"How kind of you to consider reporting to Sarah," Irene said.

"Not reporting, but she is the person I can best recall who would require descriptions, as if she is always seeking stage directions. Anyway, the city is indeed ponderous. Thick with buildings and populace, crowded with commerce that flows constant and slow, like molasses. If homely London hansoms are water bugs, practical and swift, Paris equipages are . . . dragonflies over a lily pond, elegant and gliding."

"And New York's transport?" Irene prodded with amused attention.

"New York is humming bumblebees, never silent, always industrious, but . . . ponderous! . . . compared to her British and Continental sisters."

"Oh, pooh!" Pink said. "New York is as light on her feet as any world capital, she just doesn't make a melodrama of it."

I said no more, but felt our cumbersome conveyance itself made my point. It more resembled a dray wagon than a sprightly landau.

"Where are we going?" Irene asked, all practicality again.

"Union Square, near Park and Fifteenth," Pink explained. "The theatrical district."

The phrase divided our party. At those words I recoiled and Irene frowned. Pink beamed.

"You see," she said, "it all started with a most remarkable séance."

"Poppycock," said I.

"Fraud," Irene seconded, surprising me no end. She lived and breathed the theatrical and I could think of no more dramatic bit of stage business than a séance.

"So I thought." Despite our skepticism, Pink remained unruffled . . . except in the charming lavender frills of her shirtwaist. "And, in a sense, you're both right, save that even a fraud and a poppycock shouldn't die for the sin of being suspected."

"Die?" Irene asked.

"Was killed, really, although no one can yet tell why. Or exactly how."

Irene sat forward to plumb her reticule, soon producing her signature blue enamel cigarette case, from which she extracted a dark Egyptian wand of brown paper and tobacco.

She struck me as much relieved by the type of news Pink had for us: the murder of an unknown medium. I had to wonder how our adventurous lives had so upended civility that mention of unnatural death could be a welcome distraction from more sober thoughts.

Clearly, this entire journey disconcerted Irene, and she would tolerate brushing so near her roots only in the name of some greater mayhem than mere childhood.

"So." Irene shook out the flame for the tiny lucifer she had struck against the box's inner lid. "You go amongst the mediums rather than the *filles de joie* now."

"I went to the séance with an ajar, if not open, mind," Pink retorted. "I wish you'd offer me such a crack of credibility, Irene. I truly expected nothing extraordinary . . . none of the atmospheric thrills of an authentic Prague Gypsy fortune-teller, certainly."

"Prague Gypsy fortune-tellers are no more authentic than any others. Apparently you got more than you hoped for here," Irene murmured.

"Oh, indeed, but you must visit the death chamber first. Such an ordinary room. I expect you'll find something extraordinary in it, though."

Irene said nothing, choosing to wait and see before judging. I was not eager to investigate sordid rooms in the city's theatrical district, but I noticed that Irene seemed no more enamored of our destination than I. That was odd, for the theatrical world had always been her home, at least as long as I had known her.

Pink had not exaggerated, for once. (Sometimes she thought as breathlessly as the multiple headlines on a sensational news story.)

Our conveyance came to rest in front of another of those eternal five-story brownstones that line New York streets. This one was no more notable than the rest, and sported the usual middling flight of steps and a single bow window overlooking the street.

Irene paid the driver after we alighted, as the larger gurney had no convenient ceiling trapdoor. We were down upon the city sidewalks again, lifting our skirts so the street filth shouldn't decorate our hems.

Irene looked up to assess the building, perfectly respectable for its kind, save for a crystal ball in one window.

"This was a murder scene. How is that the police have not secured the premises and we can visit it?"

Miss Pink Cochrane snorted like a daintily indignant pony. "First, the police scorn such doings as séances and found the testimony of the witnesses, including myself, 'hysterical.' Second, almost twenty-five thousand people died in the inhumanely overcrowded tenements on the Lower East Side last year alone. Death often seems the rule, not the exception, in New York City. Third, the city police department is as corrupt as the grave. It takes bribes and influence to get them to investigate a crime, which is why we are here doing it instead. And, fourth, if you do not understand the previous whys and wherefores, I can simply tell you that no one cares . . . except landladies who find the superstitious loath to rent such notorious rooms, which is why they are still vacant almost two weeks after the death."

This time when we knocked at a door in New York City it was opened by a stranger, a wizened little woman with a face as leathery as a walnut shell.

She nodded us in.

The odor of some heavy incense hung over the dim hallway like a darkened gasolier, and made me cough.

"I never thought," Irene commented, "to regard my small cigars as perfume. However, here—"

She needed to say no more. Tobacco and match sulphur would smell like French perfume in contrast. Under the cloying Oriental scent I detected the aftermath of boiled cabbage, surely one of the more unfortunate dishes ever prepared in common lodging houses.

That was what we visited, I was sure, a common lodging house. I was especially certain when I glimpsed nicked furniture legs and worn upholstery on the pieces that crowded the hall.

The landlady seemed to recognize Pink, for she took the girl's plump young wrist in one wrinkled hand and pulled her forthwith through a door into the front parlor.

Here the air was mustier even than in the passage, overlaid with a peculiar thick and unpleasant odor.

Our guide bustled out as soon as we were escorted within. Irene went to ensure the door was shut fully behind her . . . and that our landlady wasn't listening. Her silence might have been calculated to disarm us.

The crack of that sturdy oak door hitting the door frame gave me the oddest impression of a coffin lid slamming . . . I had much recent reason to recoil from such a memory!

Irene shed all anxiety and became her brisk, inspecting self at once. "This is the séance chamber, I take it; also the death chamber."

Pink nodded in the dimness.

"How was the furniture arranged? You must show me."

"How do you know that what you see is not the fatal arrangement?"

"Because the carpet bears impressions of the chair and table legs being normally established elsewhere."

"It's too dark to see that," Pink complained.

"But not to feel it." Irene crossed the room again. "My profession, my former profession, accustomed me to making my way onto dark stages. My feet automatically notice any subtle variances in what's beneath them. Can we turn up the lights?"

"Yes. These are gas."

Pink approached a bronze wall sconce and tweaked some part of the fixture I couldn't see. The light within the milk glass globe brightened like a new moon.

"Gas," Irene repeated in a portentous tone I had only heard used in regard to certain intestinal difficulties not suitable for public mention.

In the sudden silence I detected a sibilant *hisssss* from the vaunted gaslights. I understood Irene's skepticism for the new lighting system. Invisible and odorless, gas was unseen and could be deadly, like the subtle serpent hidden in long and rustling grasses.

"The lights were dimmed for the séance." Irene stated as much as asked.

"Of course. Madam Zenobia required complete darkness to work."

"So does a jewel thief," Irene noted.

She was rapidly circling the room, gazing high and low, running her ungloved fingertips over the walls and the furniture. After several swift spirals, she joined Pink and me where we stood gawking in the middle.

"What were this woman's credentials as a medium?" she asked Pink.

"She'd . . . she'd been in all the papers in upstate New York and Connecticut. 'The Nyack Wonder,' she was called. And she was as reputable as a medium could be—"

"Which is nil," Irene interrupted with a brief bark of laughter distressingly like those "Ha!"s employed as emphasis by none other than Sherlock Holmes.

I cringed to hear Irene adopting *The* Man's brusque, high-handed methods, yet I must admit that the chamber's smells did not encourage lingering.

Irene pointed out areas of interest her feet had detected around the chamber. "This central mahogany table has been moved two feet. Observe the indentations on the Turkey carpet there . . . and there. The small occasional tables were of course swept to the room's perimeter in some haste, and recently. Before the police arrived, I assume?"

"The room was prepared for the séance earlier that day."

"And the day before that, and that, and that." Irene strode toward the heavy Empire-style dining table that sat naked of any decorative cloth in the room's center. Above it loomed a huge gas lighting fixture with so many arms it resembled Medusa's serpentine tendrils of hair, had they been cast in bronze.

"There was a cloth over the table during the séance?" Irene remarked. "There always is."

"Yes, but it was a light silken shawl with foot-long fringe."

"Ah, the shawl, an ever-useful accessory whose beauty cannot be allowed to overshadow its . . . practicality. So might we say of women, in general. Weight was not a factor with the cloth employed; obscurity was. Who else was present?"

"Phineas LaMar, known as Professor Marvel, the Walking Encyclopedia. And Timothy Flynn. He's a strapping fellow now, but was a child prodigy called Tiny Tim when he was in baby skirts. Also Gordon Evers, a professional pickpocket of my acquaintance. I wanted someone present who could see if our credulity was being picked."

It struck me that these names and bizarre occupations disturbed Irene, though it was hard to tell what actually did disturb Irene. She was as good at keeping her true reactions hidden as a milliner was at keeping a widow deeply veiled.

"Was that all?" Irene demanded.

"Why do you ask?"

"You have named three people, not including the medium and

yourself. The chair-leg impressions in the carpet beneath the table number six sets."

Pink lived up to her nickname and blushed for her faulty memory, or her deliberate omission. "You forget that my mother came, too. She'd hoped to hear from my dear dead father, the judge."

"So in fact this was both an investigative and a personal expedition?" Irene said.

"I suppose so. I wanted to kill two birds with one stone: end my mother's credulous hope that the judge had wished more for us than penury, and also unmask a fraud who fed people's hopes and starved their pocketbooks."

"I quite approve of the stratagem," Irene said. "Your mother's belief helped hide your less friendly motive."

I could no longer remain silent, and in such situations, I invariably spoke my mind. "Irene, Pink behaved abominably toward her mother! Using her as a . . . gull. A shield. A pretext."

"An accidental ally?" Irene suggested more kindly. "She would have been tempted by the notion of a séance in any case, Nell. Were Godfrey to be snatched from me, I cannot say what measures I would resort to."

This silenced me—for that very instance had happened only weeks before—but it did not silence Pink. Finer feelings never seemed to.

"You yourself resorted to blackmailing all your friends into aiding your recent quest," the young woman accused.

"Not only friends," Irene demurred modestly, as if responding to high praise. "Some enemies as well."

"At any rate," Pink went on, "you provided quite an admirable model of relentless investigation, and so I have called you here, because I believe that what happened in this room requires relentless investigation."

"And because you believe it concerns me in some intimate way you don't understand," Irene said. "You need me to solve your case, so you can have a story for your newspaper."

"I could write up the incident this minute."

"But it has no ending. Even newspaper stories do better with tidy endings." She moved to regard the bare table. "It elevated, I suppose, during the séance?"

"Yes!" Pink sounded surprised.

"Anything else elevate?"

"A flute."

"A flute? Apparently the strongest wires were saved for the table. A flute is a trifle compared to that."

"And the medium's face floated on the dark."

"You mean," Irene corrected, "that only her face was illuminated from some unguessed source." Irene was again pacing the perimeter of the chamber, moving around furniture and occasionally bending to inspect the carpeting as if she were a head housekeeper in search of dereliction of duty by the under-housemaids.

"Ah." Irene stopped near the wall opposite the heavily draped bow window. "Only one chair was set here. Bring me another."

Pink and I glanced at each other. At least we were serving as under-housemaids together.

We seized one of the heavy black walnut side chairs sitting near the naked table and, panting like hod carriers, toted it to where Irene stood by the wall.

She helped us maneuver it . . . into the dents in the carpeting that fit the chair's four legs like a template.

"Hold it steady, ladies!"

Irene grasped the top rail and sprang onto the seat, immediately turning to gaze at the bow window. She balanced herself on the upholstered seat by grasping an arm of the wall sconce.

I was tempted to murmur something about the Lady Liberty posed in New York harbor on her pedestal, lifting her torch, but restrained myself.

"Pink!" Irene sounded very excited indeed. Perhaps it was the altitude. "Drag another chair over by the window draperies and see if there is a slit in the velvet at about the same level as my hat."

I objected immediately. "The chairs are too heavy for one person to move. I'll help her."

"You will not, Nell! I am teetering here as it is. You will hold my chair steady and let Pink manage. I did tell her to 'drag,' not lift, the thing."

"*Hmmmph,*" I sniffed. While I had no reason to spare Pink the wages of her drawing Irene across the Atlantic Ocean on a wild goose chase, I doubted that slip of girl could manage the assigned task.

Perhaps my doubt showed, for she cast me a determined look and began to wrestle the chair into the position Irene had requested. Soon she was balancing atop it, and thrusting her hands into the velvet draperies like a pickpocket rifling a skirt.

"Why, there's nothing here but yards of velvet, Irene," she complained, leaning forward to pummel more folds of cloth.

My warning cry died in my throat. In an instant Pink had gone over, chair, skirts, draperies and all.

Her fall had ripped a length of drapery from its rod.

I stared aghast at Pink's fallen form, but above me Irene was waxing triumphant.

"Horsehair!" she cried. "A horsehair line leading from this lighting sconce to the secret room between the draperied bow window and the room. A double set of drapes. Fairly clever. Hold the chair steady, Nell. *Steady!* And Pink! Stay exactly where you are. Do not move. I am coming directly."

Pink, tangled on the floor in petticoats, chair legs, and heavy velvet draperies, was going nowhere.

I pushed Irene's chair legs into the carpet with all my strength as she bounded down like a mountain goat and hastened to Pink's aid.

Or rather . . . she hastened to Pink's vicinity, where she stretched up her arms and commenced to pull the remaining draperies back like a demented stage manager.

"There! And there! You see what a sweet scheme it was? An entire velvet-shrouded room within a room for a confederate to hide in, and a horsehair clothesline above it all on which to 'float' all sorts of delusions from flutes to whistling spirits."

I hurried over to untangle Pink from the domestic furnishings.

The silly girl was staring up toward the ceiling as if viewing angels heard on high.

"I see it! Now I do . . . if not then, during the séance. A sil-ver . . . wire. Almost invisible."

"In the dark," Irene reminded her, "it was utterly invisible. There must have been some hook in the 'ectoplasmic' emanation, so the confederate could draw it up and make it seem to dance."

"And that is the murderer?" I asked. "The confederate hidden behind the bow window draperies?"

Irene glanced at the small chamber her efforts had unveiled. "Yes. Or perhaps no," she answered, not sounding happy. "This was an illusion gone awry. The confederate could have fled when he—or she—saw the medium had been killed."

She glanced at Pink, who was still shaking out her tangled skirts.

"So how did she die, Pink?"

"She was throttled."

"Throttled? At a table with five other persons? Throttling is not a silent process and it requires the killer to come close. Yes, it was dark, but I can't believe that no one would notice a strangler at work."

"That's just it. We saw her die. Or struggle at least. We assumed it was part of the show. I mean, mediums do moan and groan and speak in tongues and spit out spirit vapors . . . what were we to think?"

"Ah." Irene sat on the chair that had been Pink's uncertain step stool. "Her murder was accomplished in plain sight, but with the murderer out of sight. This may be a more subtle and disturbing crime than I first thought. The woman fought for her life, with help only feet away and was . . . ignored. It was brutal and cruel to the victim, as well as to witnesses who now know that they understood too late. Anyone with black gloves and a mask could have stepped behind the eerily lit medium in the dark and manipulated the murder like an unseen puppeteer. You all would have witnessed the effect, but not the means. Who would kill in such a fashion, and why?"

I could keep silent no longer. Irene and Pink seemed to dance away from what to me was the central issue. "If no one was visible standing behind her, choking her, how was she killed? And don't tell me it was a spirit guide!"

Irene looked up at Pink. "Yes, that's a good point. Was there any misty apparition of the dead? The judge?"

"There was a misty apparition," Pink said grimly. "Ectoplasm. The breath of the dead emanating from the medium's mouth. It was utterly convincing. Not just a wee trail, as one sees of cigar smoke, or even one's own breath on a frosty winter morning. It was as long as a snake and kept twisting up and up in spurts, almost like a serpent moves its coils. It made my mother shriek. I confess even I felt a chill at that abnormal substance's dance, almost like a cobra rising from its basket to the keening of a snake charmer, and don't forget that flute was floating and piping, too."

Pink turned her glance on me, something of that uncanny fear still in her expression, except it was changing into anger. "Can you guess what that ectoplasm really was, Nell?"

How could I say? The soul after death surely does not come gliding back in snakelike form to reside in the mouths of mediums.

Irene anticipated Pink. "Eggwhite-dipped cheesecloth," she said. "That soft, netlike fabric porous enough to strain something as solid as cheese, yet light and airy. Some mediums know the—art, should I call it?—of regurgitation at will. Instant ectoplasm. It's a very old trick."

Pink nodded. "Then the medium lay . . . still. Quiet. And we all realized that this was not part of the séance, but something else. I got up, and went to her. It was wrapped around her throat, that long boa of 'ectoplasm.' It was twisted and soggy and wrung so tight I couldn't unwind it, couldn't even get a finger between her neck and that . . . stuff. It was too late anyway, as Gordon quickly told me."

"A macabre story," Irene said after a pause. "Now, Pink. I have revealed the mechanics behind the séance. I have suggested who might, and might not, have been the killer. Now tell me why on earth do you think that this scene has anything to do with me? Personally?"

Pink did not answer. She asked another question instead.

"Now that you know what this murder involves and who was present, are you sure you want to know what I think?"

"Who *was* present? A group of mostly your selection, except for the medium and her unknown confederate. Why should I care who was present?"

"Are you saying that you don't recognize any of them? Not a one?"

10.

Unwelcome Baggage

How can you build on such quicksand? Their most trivial
action may mean volumes, or their most extraordinary conduct
may depend upon a hairpin or a curling tongs.
—SHERLOCK HOLMES, "THE ADVENTURE OF THE SECOND STAIN,"
SIR ARTHUR CONAN DOYLE

⊰FROM NELLIE BLY'S JOURNAL⊱

I don't quite know where my dislike of Englishmen comes
from.

It can't be from my adventures in the U.S., for the Brits
are thankfully rare on this side of the Atlantic, although I
have met a few in New York City reception halls.

I guess it's their inborn sense of superiority; that aloof,
supercilious air most of them disseminate like dandelions do
seeds.

So I stood on the wharf in New York harbor, unhappily awaiting the docking of the Atlantic steamship *Ulysses*. Much as it was
my idea and long-nursed machination, I did not welcome Sherlock Holmes to these bustling shores, except as a necessity.

In fact, I was amazed that he would come in answer to my cablegram at all, save I had used those most effective code words in his case: murder and Irene. And I had implied, a bit mendaciously, that it might be murders *plural*, a fact that might intrigue him after chasing a multiple murderer from London to Paris to Prague and beyond in the recent past. Yet I had a recent clipping in my sturdy leather handbag of a death as similarly bizarre as the one I myself had witnessed not long after. I had not yet shared it with Irene, but was saving it for Sherlock Holmes. I needed more than one freakish crime to command his demanding attention, since I couldn't manage it by myself alone, as Irene could.

Obviously, the man was intrigued by this woman who had bewitched audiences and aristocrats and criminals. And, I must add modestly, I had also used another name with perhaps even greater cachet as a lure for this quintessentially disciplined Englishman: Baron Richard von Krafft-Ebing, the man who documented maniacs.

Certainly a mere enterprising female reporter for the *New York World* would not snag the attention of the globe's first and finest and only consulting detective without the more attractive bait of Madam Adler Norton in her hip pocket.

And so it was with both faint hope and triumphant jubilation that I spied a tall erect figure, pipe firmly clenched in jaws, inching down the gangway among the usual horde of transatlantic crossers.

He looked most put out!

I couldn't help smiling at his grim demeanor as he advanced, carrying one fat tapestry bag in lieu of other baggage. Somehow I knew that was his entire kit, and that it would contain all he needed to dress as the quintessential Englishman, to nurse a pipe, or to solve a crime.

After all, his stock in trade was smoke and magnifying glasses!

I stood among a jostling crowd of greeters, watching humanity flood down the gangplank amid shouts and huzzahs.

Had he really come? Had I tempted him with enough blood and beauty under siege to stir his deficient gallantry?

Although, when I considered it, I believed Mr. Holmes's gallantry was of the mental, not of the physical kind found in that unusual Englishman, Quentin Stanhope, and the equally unusual Godfrey Norton, Irene's better half, and indeed, the ideal husband for any modern woman who was still so backward as to deign to take a husband.

I mentally viewed the Englishmen I had encountered during my European adventures: Mr. Holmes, of course, thorny, eccentric, and horribly smart in a non-fashionable way. Irene's husband Godfrey, a Daniel come to judgment among barristers, handsome and equable, if one likes that type.

Finally there was that elusive rascal Quentin Stanhope—mousy Nell Huxleigh's would-be beau, of all things!—and my favorite Englishman, being adventuresome, gallant, and somehow distant from everything but faraway lands ruled by savage men and subservient women.

I liked to imagine that had I ever been so unfortunate to be sold as a concubine in the piratical Mediterranean, I should have ended up a sultana. There is historical precedent for such a spectacular rise, and I like to think of myself as spectacularly rising, if nothing else.

I rose on my toes at the moment, seeking to peer over the sea of heads in various hats and caps, to my quarry.

He wore country clothes no doubt suitable for the deck of a steamship: a long checked coat with a short cape attached, and a plaid billed cap with ear flaps tied on top, rather silly sporting attire that only an Englishman could wear with dignity. Despite this being his maiden voyage to these shores, from what I knew, he showed no need or anxiety to find a welcoming face. Despite knowing that I would be among the welcomers, he sauntered through the madding crowd, a figure uniquely serene in his composure and keen survey of the general scene.

In fact, the great detective did not deign to notice me, though surely he must have spied me, but required me to battle my way through the crowds to seek his side.

"Mr. Holmes!"

He paused at my call, took his pipe from his lips, and waited for me to win my way forward.

"Miss Cochrane," he acknowledged me when I stood panting beside him, my hat leaning slipshod over my left temple. "I do not see Madam Adler Norton."

"She is not here. Nor would she be. She has no idea you're in New York."

"And no idea, I see, that I am here on her behalf at your behest. I fear that 'invitation' is far too bland a word for your doings, Miss Cochrane." He eyed the crowded, noisy dock with more than disapproval. "It was not your wire, nor the possible presence of Mrs. Norton that brought me here. Would you care to guess what other inducement was involved?"

Well, here I had one of the most talked-about Englishmen of the day at my fingertips, and he would have nothing to do with either fingertips or past acquaintance not forgot, or even a passing association with that paragon of song and story, Irene Adler Norton.

"Then why are you here?" I shouted over the blathering throng.

"As you deduced in your cable, Miss Cochrane, I have been thinking about Krafft-Ebing. In fact, I recently went to Germany to meet the man and report on the incredible case of the resurrected Ripper. Krafft-Ebing was quite insistent that such serial crimes are common, not an exception, and that I should investigate any instance of possible multiple murder to add to his catalog of such crimes. I agreed with Krafft-Ebing that it might be instructive. He is a man worth listening to."

"As no woman is or ever could be," I returned.

He bent his cool silvery gaze upon me. It was as icy as the mid-Atlantic when a storm is thinking about lashing out. "A few women are, or could be. Luckily, it is not my task to search out these worthy exceptions."

"Perhaps you do not need to search very far."

"Oh, that which is truly valuable is always at a distance," he replied, bending a pointed and not entirely humorless look upon myself.

I was quite certain he intended to snub me in favor of more removed females, such as Irene Adler Norton. I couldn't see why, but didn't say so.

"A man who is not willing," he went on, "to be the student of everything all his life, will never be the master of anything. So I am here to learn, and began by booking the hotel you recommended."

"Count on the humble female to know when there is no place like home," I muttered.

He pretended not to have heard me. "I would be delighted if you would join me there tonight for whatever respectable repast the house might offer. You can outline your suspicions then."

"I can't believe you're here," I said, almost mesmerized by his lofty presence.

Think what one will of the man, he is clearly expert.

"Nor can my associate, Dr. Watson."

"Dr. Watson did not come? Such a pity! I had obtained a copy of *A Study in Scarlet* and wished to discuss it with him. I have penned some accounts of my undercover work in a madhouse and also a mystery story set in Central Park right here in New York City."

Mr. Holmes regarded me as if my literary efforts had dragged me even lower in his imagination.

"I hope, unlike poor old Watson, you did not burden your accounts with sensational elements that detracted from the sheer logic and science of the cases."

"No, I fear that Dr. Watson and I have one thing in common: we like to tell a ripping good story that people will want to read.

Does he not accompany you everywhere, rather like Nell Huxleigh does Irene, to record your every movement for future publication?"

"No! Future publication means nothing to me, and I tolerate Watson's little romances because they do at least give a glimpse of the scientific method at work. Besides," he added, and I detected a very faint twinkle in his collected expression, "it is always most intriguing to have Watson wondering what I am up to. A pity that I dare not hope that Mrs. Norton is also so engaged."

"Perhaps so," I answered blithely. "If you want to reveal yourself, so be it. Irene will be quite furious with you, I imagine."

"And with you as well, no doubt. I would say that you presume, but it is useless pointing out such obvious truths to the enterprising American."

He ended this speech with a smile so shadowy that it charmed me into uncustomary silence. When Sherlock Holmes chose to be amenable, he became formidable indeed.

We made our way without further comment to the curb, where Mr. Holmes whistled a hansom up for us like a native New Yorker.

"What do you think of our Queen City?" I asked as he handed me in.

"Not so pretty as Paris and therefore a fine and festering hole for crime. Ha! These high-storied row houses look as apt a breeding ground for infamy as I have ever seen."

"We enter the city via its lowliest neighborhoods. The buildings are called tenements. They house, in conditions of untold filth and crowding, immigrant families from the world over. The poverty is unimaginable, and the variety and viciousness of the crime is as diverse as the many native tongues that wag here."

"Yet this is not the site of the bizarre murders you mentioned."

"That is farther north on the island and much more respectable, though not as gracious as Millionaires' Row up in the fifties."

"Respectability breeds boredom, at least for the student of human aberration and crime."

"Certainly Jack the Ripper plied his ghastly trade in the slums of Whitechapel and, later, the Paris underground. A pity I could not report the amazing conclusion to his bloody reign."

"Nothing is ended, Miss Cochrane, until the principal parties are dead and buried, in this case people other than his victims."

"You don't still pursue the case?"

"As I said, nothing is ended without the finality of death."

I mulled this over in silence, listening to the lulling racket of horses' hooves and street shouts all around us.

At the hotel he paid the driver to take me on to my destination and stepped out of the hansom. "Dinner at eight, shall we say?"

I could only agree, annoyed at learning so little of his plans during the ride from the docks.

"You needn't have wasted your time meeting my ship," he added, as if discerning my frustration. "I can get around quite splendidly on my own in cities the world over. I fear I have kept you from more pressing work."

"Not at all," I managed to say before the driver slapped his reins on the horse's hindquarters and my cab pulled away with a jerk.

I couldn't help feeling that I had been sent off like so much unwelcome baggage.

11.

Old Lang Syne

~∾ა⊱∾~

She suffered the penalty paid by all sensation-writers of being compelled to hazard more and more theatric feats.

—ON NELLIE BLY, WALT McDOUGALL, *NEW YORK WORLD ILLUSTRATOR,*

1889

"I cannot believe," I told Irene when we were back in our hotel room and had some privacy, "that Pink—Miss Elizabeth Jane Cochrane . . . Nellie Bly, the girl wonder— would call you from Europe on such slim pretext. As if the murder of a medium by that disgustingly unhygienic method would have anything to do with you . . . or with any mother you might or might not have had."

"I knew him, Nell."

"Him? There is no 'him' in this case! Unless you refer to the medium's absent confederate who stayed hidden after the death, most suspiciously, and whom one may suppose to have been a man. Confederates usually are."

"Tiny Tim."

"Tiny Tim? Everyone who has read Dickens knows Tiny Tim, wretched little tearjerker that he is."

Irene gazed at me, astounded. "You *are* upset, Nell, to heap such abuse on a figure of such universal sympathy. No, the Tiny Tim I knew was the strapping fellow at the séance."

"Oh, the child prodigy, although Pink didn't say at exactly what he was prodigious."

"Drumming, with great precision at unbelievable speed, from the age of two."

"Why would anyone find that to be a prodigious feat? Young children are noisy and undisciplined by nature."

"Except that Tiny Tim was as good at it as any adult. Anyway, he was quite the sensation for a while, and then, like all sensations, faded."

"And you knew this young banger on drums? Where? When?"

"Here. In this country. When I was a child."

"Oh." It was my turn to sit down and contemplate the rather dull decor of our sitting room. Perhaps that was what made me feel the city was ponderous. The hotel furniture was all rosewood and marble, burl and black walnut.

"I knew LaMar, also known as Professor Marvel, the Walking, Talking Encyclopedia, too," she added, confessing past sins like a Papist.

"When *he* was a child?"

Irene laughed as if welcoming an opportunity that might not present itself again soon. "Heavens, no! He must be in his seventies now. When *I* was a child."

"And he was at the fatal séance with this Tiny Tim who is now large? How odd."

"Too odd to suit mere coincidence, Nell."

"And why is Pink convinced that your mother is in danger?"

Irene took a deep breath and turned to face me. "I don't know. Obviously, she knows more than she's telling me. And she won't tell me as long as she hopes to startle some information from me. In fact, I dearly wish that *I* could startle some information from me! I find myself embarrassingly ignorant about far too many aspects of my past, especially before I began to seriously study singing and to work for the Pinkertons. My puzzling memory loss extends beyond my childhood into my girlhood."

"We all of us have great holes in our memories of growing up. What remains vivid is often the worst of it . . . the childish faux pas we all make."

" 'All of us' don't have a famously relentless reporter like Nellie Bly rummaging through every paper and personage of their pasts!"

"No, but Irene, there's something else that bothers you. You almost remember something, don't you? Something . . . unseemly or disturbing."

"What! Now my dear personal 'Nell' is becoming a Nellie Bly of my own? You also believe that some lurid scandal lurks in my past?"

"I believe you're right to resent a virtual stranger treating you like a, a criminal who deserves investigating. I am very disappointed in Pink, whom I took at first for a sweet and well-bred young woman even if her reputation was in shreds. Now I find out that her reputation is impeccable but she is not at all the well-meaning soul I took her for. I am almost angry enough to stop speaking to her!"

"Well, I don't want to deal with Pink again until *I* know more than I'm telling *her* . . . and that will take lashing my lame memory into better form. Until then I may unwittingly give her just the clues she's hunting for."

"What information could she want from you? For what purpose?"

"What for? For the ever-needed sensational story. I know you haven't been reading the New York newspapers since we arrived—"

"They are hardly worth the effort. Their lurid subject matter makes the *London Illustrated News* look duller than dispatches from Whitehall."

"If you had more than glanced at them you would see that Pink is but one of a throng of bold young women trying to make their marks on the journalistic world. A sensational murder case involving an expatriate opera singer might do the trick for a little while."

"She would do that, use you?"

Irene lowered her head, not meeting my eye. "I used her. I needed someone reliable, who was *not* a suspect, to help me search for you and Godfrey. When that journey was done and you were both safe, when the evildoers were found and named, our other allies prevented her from publishing a word of it. She may feel I 'owe' her a story, however she gets it."

I could say nothing. In a way, I resented that Irene had drafted Pink for my usual role, but since it was to save Godfrey and me from several fates worse than death, how could I complain of the necessity?

I couldn't even twit Irene with the fact that she had brought her present conundrum upon herself. Or that "our vaunted allies" boiled down mostly to Sherlock Holmes and his bothersome brother in the British foreign office, and the Rothschilds, of course, our sometimes employers. Powerful "allies" indeed if they turned into antagonists! No wonder Miss Pink had been effectively silenced for once. Yet I doubted that Irene agreed with them, so it wasn't her doing.

"Will you go with me, Nell?" she asked now, contrition forgotten as she drew upon what King Willie had called her "soul of steel." "I must journey back to places I hoped never to see, or think of, again. I spoke the truth. I don't have a mother. I don't know who she is—was—and I don't really care at this late date. I reared myself. I am not unhappy with the result. I resent being forced back into a past that I spent many hard years escaping. I wish no one to know a particle of it! No one has the right."

I admit to quailing in my soul before her present situation. If there were things in her past Irene wished no one to know, I did not wish to be that One. She meant too much to me in the present. I shall never forget hearing her voice in that wretched cavern after witnessing a scene of unthinkable brutality and assuming my own imminent dissolution in that abyssal evil . . . of suddenly hearing her voice, of knowing she was near, of knowing that all would be well because of her.

And here we were again, on very different ground. Irene was being forced to confront things she had tried to inter. Now she was asking me to bear burdens she wanted no one to know. It was a grave duty. I wanted to shirk it. We often blink at those who know too much about us. I never wanted to see Irene blinking at me and then looking away.

She seemed to understand how much she was asking.

Her hand rested as briefly as a butterfly's on mine. "It's all right. I can do it by myself."

"I'm sure you can." My head came up. Maybe I had a soul of—surely not of steel, yet perhaps . . . pewter?

"But I cannot let you."

12.

Of Freaks and Frauds

Indian chiefs, dancing dogs, living monkeys and dead mermaids mingle in glorious rivalry for . . . enlightened approbation. . . . But the wonder of wonders is Mons. Chabert, who eats fire with as much gusto as other of his countrymen devour frogs.

—LETTER TO *THE LONDON TIMES,* 1829

Irene spent the afternoon studying the small announcement pages in the back of the *New York World* and the *New York Herald.*

Most were miniature versions of the type-crowded playbills one saw posted on every empty alley wall and lamppost in Manhattan.

I occasionally looked over her shoulder, my eyes startled by the likes of "Mystic Marie" and her "Hypnotic Waltz," of ladies in flesh-colored tights and corsets and nothing else posing as "human light bulbs," by equestriennes and wire walkers and porcine "professors" with spectacles perched upon their snouts. Of men who shrank and stretched before one's very eyes.

"This is nothing but a freak show," I observed.

"So is most of what passes for entertainment in London, or hadn't you noticed?"

Heaven forbid that I should cast aspersions upon Irene's native land!

"Oh," I admitted, "traveling curiosity shows even visited Shropshire when I was a lass, but of course I was not allowed to patronize them. They attracted only the lowest class of people."

"Which must form the majority of the population, as such shows thrive here and abroad."

"Quality and taste are rare enough to be deeply appreciated when they prevail."

" 'Quality and taste' are not on our menu here, Nell. We must explore the other side of the footlights. Perhaps that is too sensational a task for you after our Transylvanian travails."

"Not at all," I hastened to add, realizing that I was treading on dangerous ground with Irene, though I didn't know why. "Such sideshows shall seem tame to me after what we encountered in Paris and the Carpathian mountains. I only meant that these self-advertised wonders are all likely frauds."

"That could be said of the majority of people." Irene stood, tearing a section of advertisements from the paper and folding it into a size to fit into her reticule. "Don't you agree?"

"No! Yes! Oh, I don't know what I mean, except that I didn't intend to offend you, and apparently I have. I don't say that everyone is a fraud, although more than I would like indeed are."

"And some frauds," Irene added a trifle sternly, "may prove more genuine than presumed models of respectability."

I affixed my new broad-brimmed hat to my chignon and gathered my gloves. It was better to begin our outing than to stand here arguing.

Irene accepted my accoutering as a peace offering and said no more as she also pinned on her hat and donned her gloves.

In minutes we were seated on the jolting bench of an omnibus festooned with almost as many advertising bills as passengers.

The fragrance of the stable mixed with odors from the many street hawkers' carts. Sixth Avenue was chaos. We lurched as our omnibus driver forced his lumbering vehicle past dray wagons and the carriages and hansoms it dwarfed. The edges of the cobblestones nearest the walks were mobbed with peddlers' carts and hordes of what are called street Arabs in London: ragged, dirty children selling pencils and crude messenger services, picking pockets when they could.

The combined clatter of all this lusty traffic could be heard all the way up to attic rooms on the fifth floor, I'm sure. And with the streets laid out as straight as a raceway, nothing slowed or softened the rush and noise of so many people all in a hurry to get elsewhere. With that goal I could surely sympathize!

"You are unusually quiet, Nell." Irene's voice boomed like the opera singer she was over the hubbub. "What do you think of old Gotham?"

Apparently this was a pet name for the world's rudest, roughest city.

I wasn't about to bellow out my criticisms, so I merely shrugged, grimaced, and nodded, looking as mad as my fellow travelers, I'm sure.

We departed the omnibus on a grubby street lined with marquees here and there, and with people clustered around odd windowless doors.

"Stage doors," Irene told me as we stumbled arm in arm over unmentionable effluvia to the relative safety of the sidewalk. "They wait for a favorite player to emerge after the matinee."

We paused, allowing the street's constant flow to rattle past and the pedestrians to break stride around us as if we were an awkward logjam in a river.

Irene looked around, getting her bearings. I saw that she knew this street. She inhaled deeply, unaware perhaps of the odors of foreign food that wafted from many of the peddlers' carts.

"Ah," she said, "this takes me back to Saffron Hill in London. Remember, Nell, our first rooms there?"

"Yes, but not often."

"You prefer living in France, at last?"

"I prefer living in Neuilly, which is a charming and peaceful village, and a locale scented only by peaceful country blooms."

"You will not find 'peaceful blooms' on the sidewalks of New York," she said, putting her arm through my elbow as if to protect and compel me, both at the same time.

In moments she had steered us expertly crosswise through the pedestrians, so we stood at the foot of another set of stairs, this one topped by a small wall, on which sat a single pot with a geranium plant. Shabby, of course. Even nature withered in this unnatural hothouse of a tenement they called a city.

"I haven't been here in a long time," Irene said slowly, as much to herself as to me. "I don't know what, or who, I'll find still present. Perhaps only ghosts, only spirits. Yet I must start somewhere. . . ."

She squeezed my forearm, as much to give herself courage as me, I think, and together (how could I escape such a firm or perhaps desperate grip?) we mounted the stairs and entered a door into a common hallway.

"Irene, I believe this establishment is—"

"A boardinghouse. A quite respectable, old theatrical boardinghouse."

"Irene, I have never known the words 'respectable' and 'theatrical' to sit cheek by jowl before."

"Here in New York they do, I assure you," she said sternly. "You are entering my past, my world, willingly, Nell, as a companion, not as a critic, I hope."

"A critic? I? Heaven forbid."

"I believe it did, at least once. 'Judge not lest ye be judged.'"

I was so astounded by Irene, who mentioned God about as

often as pigeons do, quoting Scripture, that I had nothing to say. The admonition was well given, and well taken. Since I had seen real sin at such close quarters during my ordeal in Paris and beyond, I found I had lost my zeal for finding it in my immediate vicinity.

Irene was admitting me into her holiest of holies, her inner sanctum, not willingly, but because for some strange reason she needed me there. So . . . I would endeavor to reserve judgment for my own private thoughts and meditations. And my diaries.

She was watching me like a policeman suspecting me of coveting a peddler's apple. I nodded my agreement, knowing that I would now have many an occasion to bite my tongue, which was not used to being harnessed. But this was foreign ground and perhaps foreign feelings would be part of the price for treading it with my oldest and dearest . . . and only . . . friend.

We moved past a pigeon-hole sort of secretary built into the wall, with numbers on the compartments and letters and newspapers jammed into them, and past a stairway leading to an upper story.

Between the stairway and the wall was a door, and on this Irene knocked as if she had a right to.

She knocked again, and finally the door was opened by . . . Mrs. Hudson, that white-coifed, white-capped brusque old Scots soul who had opened the door to 221B Baker Street on an occasion (I recalled with blushes) when I had very good reason to go snooping there. I smothered a gasp of surprise. Of course the lady was *not* Mrs. Hudson, but was much the same type. It is amazing how alike the gatekeepers of the world are, from the women who control domestic portals to the men who guard the entrances to public buildings, or those that have become public by becoming crime scenes!

"Good day to you. And who is it that I have the honor of addressin', Mrs.—?" Irene began in a voice that was tinged with an Irish brogue.

"McGillicuddy," came the answer Irene had obviously anticipated.

"Well, Mrs. McGillicuddy," Irene went on as if appearing in
the opening scene of a play, "I am a former resident of the house.
Me friend and meself are back in the city after many years and
hoped an old acquaintance of days gone by might still be in residence."

" 'Twould not be an Irish tenor you're seeking, miss?"

Irene did not correct her form of address. "Ah, ye've found
me out. 'Tis my cousin, of course. He was always musically
inclined, but to other instruments than his voice."

"The pipe and flute, then?"

"The drums."

"Drums!?"

"I don't know how long you've been livin' here, Mrs.
McGillicuddy, but he was famous for it when he was a boyo. Tiny
Tim, d'you recollect?"

Here the landlady laughed like a barker at a circus, loud and
hearty. "That was more'n twenty years gone, girl, almost longer
than you've been tripping the light fantastic yerself."

"Time flies, ma'am, and us with it. So he is no longer in residence?"

"Oh, Mr. Timothy Flynn is here, yes, but he's another kind of
drummer now. Men's furnishings, don't you know?"

"I do now," Irene said with a roguish smile I would swear was
dimpled. I had never noticed a dimple on her before! "Would he
happen to be in?"

"I don't spy on the comings and goings of my lodgers, miss,
but his room number is nine, a floor up. You, and your . . . er,
friend here are as welcome to knock as I am when the rent is due."

"More a caller cannot ask. 'Tis glad of your blessing we are,
and if Mr. Timothy is not in, perhaps I can leave my card on the
way out."

"A card is it?"

"Well, a note I would pen on some stray paper or other."

Mrs. McGillicuddy nodded like the Queen at Windsor accepting an introduction to a prominent tradesman.

On that the door closed and we began trudging up the stairs.

"Tiny Tim," I hissed in the dimness. "He was present at the fatal séance. You think he is a witness . . . or a suspect?"

"I don't know what I think yet, Nell, except that I hope that Mr. Flynn is in. We don't have time to waste, I think."

The number nine of the door had loosened on its single brass screw and now more resembled a six.

Irene raised her gloved knuckles, took a breath deep enough to deliver an aria, and knocked, sharply.

In half a minute the doorknob turned.

I sensed a door into a mysterious past swinging open, a door into secrets and shame and, if possible, murder many years later. What had Irene, the prima donna of the Imperial Opera at Warsaw, to do with drummer boys turned hawkers on the streets of New York? I might soon know more than I wished.

A tall and lanky figure was silhouetted in the light from the window beyond the door.

Once, recently, I would have questioned the propriety of two women entering a strange man's rooms. Now I only felt a fervid eagerness to learn what he knew, propriety be . . . pickled!

I walked in behind Irene, my skirt hems and hers hissing over the uncarpeted floor like serpents.

The room was humble, but homespun. I was startled to observe doilies on the chair arms and head rests. A rag rug that bespoke some weeks of woman's work lay before the fender by the small fireplace. Photos and posters were affixed to the walls. A bureau hosted cabinet portraits of a man and woman dressed in the clothing of mid-century.

I was surprised to find such an island of domestic history in this huge, rude city.

"Tim!" Irene said, surprised into using the name.

He was surprised, too. "I haven't been called aught but 'Timothy' for twenty years." He frowned his youthful brow, for he was barely thirty, and squinted at Irene as if she were a stamp in a collector's magnifying lens.

"Is it . . . little Rena? Little Rena the Ballerina? En point at the age of three?"

He spread his arms and stretched out his fingers. Irene matched his gesture and suddenly grew three inches as she lilted onto her toe-tops.

"Dear Lord, you're back! Rena the Ballerina."

"Merlinda the Mermaid."

"And such a singer. I'll never forget making a duet of your 'Clementine,' you in a checked sun bonnet and boots the size of ships. 'In a cavern, in a canyon—' "

" 'Excavatin' for a mine—' "

" 'Dwelt a miner, forty-niner—' "

" 'And his daughter, Clementine,' " Irene produced a ceiling-shaking operatic finale.

The former Tiny Tim spun a formerly flat-footed Irene under his arm, while he sang: " 'Big ole bootsies, on her tootsies, for to hold up Clementine.' "

" 'Oh, my darling,' " they chorused together, contralto and tenor. " 'Oh, my darling Clementine, Thou are lost and gone forever, dreadful sorry, Clementine.' "

The Dear Lord help me, but I could see these two as tiny children pantomiming this very schoolroom nonsense. And I couldn't help giggling. Perhaps it was hysteria.

The former Tiny Tim turned to me at once. "They loved us, the audiences. They tittered and gushed and applauded and threw bouquets of tea-roses. Then I would sit down and drum my head and hands off, and she would dance a jig to it all. We were . . . what? All of three and six."

What they reminisced about suddenly struck me full force. "You sang for your suppers, both of you, at so young an age? Why, that's indentured servitude!"

Tiny Tim descended upon me like a fairy-tale giant, a laughing boy-giant, and swept me into the same irresistible pirouette Irene had performed.

"Theater folk are fairy folk, don't you know, miss?" he said, or sang perhaps. My head was spinning too much to tell. "Small and fading fast. Magic."

He dropped my gloved hands and I stood there waiting for my head to settle.

"I'm a little drummer boy no longer," he finished, shrugging.

"Yet you still live here, where we all did," Irene pointed out.

"'Did' is right." He sat on one of his upholstered chairs, laid his pomaded hair against the antimacassar. "I'll never forget the thrill of it, being so young and so acclaimed, but it was a passing fancy. A man must do daily work for his living, and I'm no exception."

"Then no one else we knew still lives here?" Irene pressed, following him to the chair.

He sobered instantly, and the performer's mask dropped to reveal a melancholy man behind it.

"No. Not now that Sophie is dead."

"Sophie? I *remember* her. Well." Tim could hardly guess what a revelation this was for her. "Sophie lived here recently? And has just now . . . died?" Irene's voice had dropped into a soft, lower register I did not often hear, except when she was deeply touched. "I only just . . . missed . . . her?" Her plaintive tone reminded me of a fretted child.

He nodded, his head leaning back as if resting from his impetuous excursion into past and such very youthful glories.

Child prodigies, I thought, had the bitter lot of soon outliving their best days.

"Sophie," Irene was repeating as if every intonation of the name's syllables was a lost memory. "Only dead recently."

"A freakish sort of death." Timothy shook his head, his eyes still closed. "At a séance. I was there, God help me."

"Sophie!" Irene looked at me, as if demanding that I at least disbelieve what she could not avoid knowing for truth. "That . . . the dead medium we heard of . . . that was *Sophie?*"

The fact shocked her.

What shocked me was to see her so horrified.

Who was Sophie, and what had she been to Irene, or to little Rena the Ballerina, who was some father's "darling Clementine"?

13.

Smoke Rings

❧

Fire resisters, who traditionally appeared on the bills of magicians or ventriloquists, even found their way to the séance room.

—RICKY JAY, *LEARNED PIGS AND FIREPROOF WOMEN*

Who was Sophie?

"A fire resister," Irene told me in the hansom cab she had hailed to take us back to our hotel.

She herself certainly was not subscribing to fire-resisting, whatever it was, in the hansom, for she had struck another match on her clever little cigarette case. Soon the snug compartment was filled with enough smoke and sulphur to mask the departure of the Devil through the vampire trapdoor in a stage floor.

I coughed pointedly, but Irene's eyes were growing dreamy over the wisps of smoke she breathed out like an elegant dragon.

"Sophie and Salamandra," she went on. "I remember now! They were twin sisters and both fire resisters. They could walk on hot iron or coals, swallow flames, soft-cook raw eggs in the burning oil cupped in their bare palms. It was a stunning demonstration and quite outdrew the ventriloquists and prestidigitators who often shared the playbill with them."

"The only useful application of such a gift is for cooking eggs," I answered, "and I would prefer a pan-basting for my eggs, rather than someone's sweaty hand."

"Oh, there was no perspiration involved, though other liquids might have been. Certainly there was some trick to it."

"And you don't know what the trick was?"

"It was worth one's life to know too much of arcane practices then. These arts have been passed down since the Middle Ages, or even ancient times. Family livelihoods depend upon them, have for generations."

"But you knew the Salamander sisters?"

"I even saw them perform. 'Salamander' is an ancient term for a fire dragon. Sophie was always Sophie, but Salamandra was christened Amanda, I believe, and only adopted the more mysterious name when she joined the act. I'd like to discover when it became a solo attraction, and why Sophie turned to séances instead of flames."

"Does it matter?"

"It might be the reason Sophie was murdered."

"Isn't the likeliest reason a disgruntled client? She was a fraud."

"All performers are frauds, Nell. They weave artful illusions. Sophie and Salamandra wove more imaginative illusions than most, but I consider them little different from myself."

"Irene! The grand opera is a respected art form that requires its performers to perfect the human instrument of the voice to celestial levels."

"And then only to sing heavenly notes about 'rather lurid stories,' as you once put it, Nell."

"That was long ago, when we first met. I did not understand then that opera singing was the most elevated of arts."

Irene smiled upon a perfect levitating ring of smoke she had produced. "This is a skill as well, Nell. It takes practice. I must master my instrument, in this case my breath and lungs and the humble cigarette. Most people cannot do what I just did."

"And why would they want to?"

"To amaze. Amuse. Divert. Opera is no grander."

"Surely you cannot compare blowing smoke rings to the hours and years of practice a world-class operatic voice demands! You put them in yourself. I saw you lilting through endless scales on the old piano in Saffron Hill when we shared rooms there. You must not belittle your art."

"Nor should I upraise it on the backs of others. I respect the talents and the hard work of these novelty performers, Nell. I must. I grew up amongst them."

"Ah! Is this what that nasty Nellie Bly knows?"

"Pink knows. It is not so hard to trace when you look. Even Buffalo Bill recalled my Merlinda the Mermaid act. Quite a compliment from a master showman like himself."

"Merlinda? The Mermaid? I know nothing of such things. You would not take me to see Buffalo Bill's Wild West show encampment at *L'exposition universelle* in Paris, but only Pink, who now repays you by turning your past into a riddle to lay before her readers. What is this about mermaids?"

"I'd forgotten you weren't there when Colonel Cody brought it up. That was the first time my American past raised its head."

"Your American past was being an inquiry agent for the Pinkerton's."

"But before that, I was a prodigy in . . . assorted areas."

"Like Tiny Tim! That was what he was blathering about! I thought him mildly demented, to tell the truth. You actually danced some hornpipe on the stage at the age of three?"

"Sailors dance hornpipes. I jigged."

"No! You would never perform some low Hibernian jig."

"I did, and a hornpipe later, in a cunning little sailor suit."

"You were barely past a babe in arms. Who would sell you into such servitude at so early an age?"

"The mother I did not have, apparently."

This silenced me. I saw then that Pink's quest to unearth Irene's origins truly might be less of a galloping girl's reporter's ambition and more of a threat to all I thought sensible and stable in my life, and Irene's.

"Does Godfrey know?"

"Know what, Nell?"

"About mermaids, and . . . jigs?"

"No. No one knows, except those I knew then, and Pink perhaps, a bit. And now you."

"Oh, dear."

"Oh, dear what?"

"I do so hate secrets. I am not good at keeping them."

"But don't you keep a few yourself?" She smiled knowingly, yet gently enough to have me writhing in shame.

She couldn't know, of course, where the root of my secrets lay, in herself and the private papers of a physician named (so pedestrianly) Watson. But she guessed another one, with a less pedestrian name: Stanhope. Oh, to think of it is to blush and then to bite my lip and stiffen my spine. And then to despair. And anger.

"Nell." Her gloved hand tightened on my forearm. "I'm glad you're here with me. Events are forcing me back into a past I did not so much escape as fold away into a trunk in the attic of a house I never expected to return to. I could stand company."

"Events are not forcing you, Nellie Bly is."

" 'Nellie Bly' is a pseudonym, as 'Salamandra' is. It has been adapted for the presenting of mysteries to the public. It is the manifestation of an art form, or a craft, at least. I cannot condemn her, our Miss Pink, but neither need I assist her, especially not in the unraveling of my own past. We must anticipate her, Nell."

"I will truly be useful in this matter, not some burden who must be hied off to America to forget certain events in Transylvania?"

"Ah. Godfrey gave you that impression, did he?"

"He gave me the impression that the only reason he is not here is that I need a change of scenery more."

"The reason you are here," she said, her grip on my forearm tightening to painful intensity, "is that I need you more than anyone. You knew me before Godfrey did. Somehow, I feel, that you can better know me before I knew myself. Godfrey understands that without even thinking it. Which is why I married him, and why you worked for him. But he is not here now. We are."

We. I felt a flare of guilty secrets, and then a certain pride. Were we not the match of Nellie Bly and her eternal nose for news? Were we not the match of Sherlock Holmes, and his endless omniscience? Were we not friends, before either of them had darkened our doors or our doubts or our necessities?

"I will go where your past takes us," I vowed. "And try not to complain."

"That would be appreciated." Irene stamped out her cigarette on the cobblestones as we thumped down from the hansom cab in front of our hotel. "And the next place my past takes us is to the New Fourteenth Street Theater tonight, for a performance of the remarkable incendiary illusions of the incredible Salamandra."

Oh, dear.

14.

Curtains!

You know my method. It is founded on the observation of trifles.

—SHERLOCK HOLMES, "THE BOSCOMBE VALLEY MYSTERY," 1891,
SIR ARTHUR CONAN DOYLE

⊰FROM NELLIE BLY'S JOURNAL⊱

It was clear as consommé that Irene was determined to snub my reporter's investigative help, so I settled for second-best: an expedition with Sherlock Holmes to the site of the lethal séance.

When he discovered that it was within walking distance of his hotel, if one were accustomed to walking, he immediately set out.

I had to trot a bit to match his pace but he was occupied with studying the street scene all around us and never noticed my staccato pace. Or perhaps he did, and didn't care to accommodate it. Englishmen are so impossibly self-absorbed, and he worse than most!

Still, my mind could not help drafting headlines for a story:

STRIDING MANHATTAN WITH SHERLOCK HOLMES
BRITISH SLEUTH OBSERVES CRIME SCENES ON THE
STREETS OF NEW YORK

"*Tsk,*" he said of a sudden.

I scurried to come abreast and see what had spurred that disdainful syllable.

"Pickpockets are as plentiful here as anywhere." His stick pointed at a woman with her hands tucked into an affected muff of rose-strewn chiffon as she bustled down the crowded street.

In a moment the cane tip had slid through the opening of the large fluffy muff as efficiently as a letter opener through the daily mail, stopping her as thoroughly as would a sword across her path.

"A bit warm for muffs, Madam," he noted, nodding at a man she had just passed. "Sir, you may now retrieve your money clip from this lady's muff, where it no doubt caught itself during the press of pedestrians."

The woman had frozen in place the moment his cane had intercepted her. I saw a thick fold of bills appear from her cape *above* the muff.

Her gloved hand swiftly passed the money to the stunned passerby.

Only from the vantage of myself and Mr. Holmes could one notice that the lady's arms remained lost in the muff and that to return the money she had to produce a *third* hand!

This apparition disappeared as soon as the money was reclaimed and the frowning man rushed on, looking annoyed with all three of us. I frowned, recalling a fatal séance.

The woman, a perfectly respectable-appearing matron in her middle years, also glared at us and sailed on with hardly a stutter in her step, so speedy had the transaction been.

"It is not only buildings," Sherlock Holmes observed in the manner of a professor, "that use 'false fronts.'"

He was striding along again so briskly that I could barely gasp out, "There's a policeman half way down the next block. Surely—"

"None of the parties involved will want their time wasted. I can see that New York puts most metropolises to shame with its dedication to Yankee industriousness. It's no wonder, then, that the bizarre murder you mention has not become the public equivalent of the Ripper's Whitechapel depredations last autumn."

I was pleased to be able to stop and announce, like a tram car conductor, "We are here."

He spun to examine the building before us. It was an ordinary brownstone of four stories, with a half-basement.

"This was the scene of the first murder?" he inquired.

"It depends."

"The first murder that you believe is related to your inquiries into Irene Adler's past?"

"No. It is the first murder that I mentioned to her, since I had learned that there was some likelihood she had known the victim."

Pausing had made us into a resented island in the stream of pedestrians parting to rush around us. Mr. Holmes took my elbow like a proper gentleman and escorted me up the building's front steps.

"Perhaps we could discuss this indoors. The rooms of the late medium have not been rented, you say?"

"Word of the death has gone round the neighborhood. The rooms are now reputed to be haunted and no one wants to rent them."

"Haunted! I am ever amazed by the gullibility of the human mind. At such times I am tempted to believe that we are descended from apes, as Watson and Darwin would have it, and that the banana has not fallen far from the family tree."

I almost found myself laughing. "You dare to dispute the latest scientific theories of our times?"

"I dare nothing but to express my benighted opinion. Show me incontrovertible proof in a test tube and I am a convert. Spout grand theories about the content of the universe and its beings and I am bored beyond stupefaction. I am a specialist, Miss Cochrane, and also a generalist. That makes me a contradiction but it is contradiction that intrigues me, such as a spirit choking its medium, surely a form of psychic murder-suicide. The landlady expects us, you say."

"She has become quite used to my importing people to the scene."

"Had you troubled to learn anything of my methods, you would realize that you have irrevocably spoiled the site with your guided tours," he said in disgust.

He looked so put out that I half expected him to demand to be taken to the nearest boat dock.

"Only Mrs. Norton with the ever-present Miss Huxleigh," I said, "and Irene came to some astounding conclusions."

He held up his gloved hands imperiously enough to stop traffic on Broadway, which is saying something. "No more spoiling the scene, Miss Cochrane, I beg you. I am interested in no one's conclusions but my own. I must admit that these ladies previously showed some slight respect for the hidden tales to be read in a murder scene or two in Paris, but here the authorities have been all over it first as well, and unlike the London police they have not been trained by me to tread softly."

What gall! "Trained" indeed. I'd like to see him "train" a New York City policeman. Not even Tammany Hall could do it.

Despite his reservations, he nodded at the brownstone's door and I was encouraged to ring the bell.

Mrs. Titus soon answered, her apron coughing clouds of flour as she wiped her hands on it. "Why, it's Miss Nellie Bly again, this time with a gentleman. I keep hoping for lodgers, but my advertisements go unanswered. I'm thinking of turning the tables on things and advertising for a medium, though I don't like what happened to the last one on my premises. Who would you be, sir?

This is a respectable house and I expect gentlemen to give their names."

"This is," I put in quickly, "the renowned British consulting detective, Mr. Sherlock Holmes."

"Well, he's not renowned enough for me to know him from a coal scuttle, but if you say he's useful, I'll go along with it. Perhaps he'll like the look of my rooms and rent them."

By this time Mr. Holmes had tipped his hat and murmured his thanks, ignoring the rest.

So we entered and he doffed his hat for the nonce, glancing around the wide foyer with its white-tiled floor and wooden bank of boarder post boxes.

"I take it that the rooms in question," he asked Mrs. Titus, "are on the main floor behind the right bay window."

"Why, yes! Did you spy a ghost in the window, Mr. Holmes?"

"I saw that the curtains have not been pulled back in several days. There is dust on the sills that would have been disarranged by the daily act of drawing and closing them. And, of course, they are closed now. Since they are the only means of light for the front rooms, it's extremely unlikely that anyone resides there."

Mrs. Titus gave me a conspiratorial look. "Makes one shiver, doesn't it? Downright uncanny how a man from England can know so much about our New York ways on one visit."

I myself found Mr. Holmes's deductions no more than common sense, but call a woman a medium or a man a detective and people will make all sorts of wrong assumptions about them.

That fact made me wonder whether Mr. Holmes was no more of a wonder worker than the average spiritualist. Quite a joke it would be on me if I had lured a fraud to our shores.

Mr. Holmes seemed used to such skepticism, for he bowed to Mrs. Titus and offered to inspect the premises and perhaps declare them ghost-free so that she could rent them.

It was as if he had said "Open sesame."

She dredged a ring of keys from a skirt pocket beneath her apron and once again I stood on the threshold of the death chamber, my third visit.

This time I was instructed to remain there while Mr. Holmes quizzed me about the arrangement of the various people and pieces of furniture during various stages of the séance.

He then began to search high and low, a magnifying glass he had produced from a coat pocket in hand. It was like watching a party of one play some silly parlor game in search of a hidden object. Or, perhaps more vividly, it was like watching some slow, gigantic insect about its mysterious rounds.

First he crawled on his hands and knees around the entire room, examining the rugs and planking, the bottoms of the table and chairs. Then his inspections moved up the walls, recalling his recent macabre explorations of blood-spattered cellar walls in Paris.

It still infuriated me that I was silenced from announcing the deliciously gory trail and astounding solution to the new and recent Jack the Ripper murders on the Continent in the public press. From Whitechapel in the London fall of 1888, Saucy Jack had moved his bloody dalliance to the Continent, to Paris, Prague, and beyond in the spring of 1889. I could have revealed every appalling detail in the public press that employed me, the *New York World*. How Mr. Pulitzer would have rewarded a coup like that! Not that he treated me shabbily, but he was new to the ownership and determined to win the stunt reporting sweepstakes.

The gagging of Nellie Bly in this vital regard was owed to two people, two blasted Englishmen who believed they served the larger cause of their own infernal government: Sherlock Holmes and Quentin Stanhope. Sherlock Holmes I would tolerate as long as he served some purpose of my own, as now. Quentin Stanhope I would tolerate because he was a remarkably attractive gentleman, far too much so to waste on the mousy Nell Huxleigh. In a way I am as wary as she of remarkably attractive gentleman, for a different reason. My work comes before any man. In another way

I am convinced that a modern woman may have her cake and eat it, too.

But eating cake was not a pleasant thought when it came fast behind memories of blood-spattered cellar walls in Paris.

At least these walls were papered, and the only likely looking "blood" was the dye in the crimson cabbage rose.

Finally Mr. Holmes turned his attention to the bay window and the velvet draperies that sequestered it from the room.

Here he paused to eye me where I stood as patiently as any soldier at his post. "I see that you were making merry with the draperies. I presume that was during a visit after the mischief had been done at the séance."

The easy blush that had given me the childhood nickname of "Pink" suffused my face with heat. "Irene wanted me to examine the rods from a chair. I lost my balance and fell. How did you know that?"

"The scuff marks on the planks and wrinkles in the velvet are unmistakable."

"Proof that the draperies fell down recently, yes. But how did you guess that I was involved?"

"I never guess, Miss Pink; I deduce. Remember that Miss Huxleigh recorded the footprint you had left in the murder room in Paris? Another of that size leaves a perfect impression on the edge of the carpet, there. No doubt that is the last step you took, all your weight on that one foot and the drapery fabric, before the rod slipped its anchor. The rings pulled off and you fell forward into the material, which was heavy and plentiful enough to cushion your tumble. Miss Huxleigh and Madam Irene came to your rescue and you all three reinstated the draperies, but in your haste missed securing one ring on the restored rod." He held up the loose ring he had found. Wouldn't you know it was a brass one?!

I sighed heavily, not much impressed by his mastery of a simple household accident that had no bearing on the crime.

His pale eyes narrowed at the now subdued draperies. "A pity you were so clumsy. That set of curtains is the key to the entire séance and, indeed, the murder, and you managed to blur the evidence as effectively as any murderer could wish."

"All I have imported from across the Atlantic so far is criticism."

His dark brows lifted. "That is not criticism, that is fact. I deal in facts. Among them here are these: the fabrics in the room are heavy and thick, as ideal to take impressions as soft sand. When you waltzed with the falling curtains you were also waltzing with a ghost: the former presence of the man who murdered Madam Sophie."

"It was a man, then?"

"A tall man, something over six feet, with either a deformity or arthritis in at least his left hand, that was not severe enough to prevent a swift garoting. He moved so quietly in the dark because both his shoes were muffled in a sort of flannel mitten, and he wore loose clothing all in black, also a sort of flannel, for I have found the tiny pills such fabric sheds. They litter the carpet, planks and especially the velvet curtains, whose nap traps threads and other bits of lint, as soft Brie does caviar."

"He was dressed to murder unseen!"

"He was expressly and expertly dressed to deceive, and could have been the medium's accomplice and had been before this, or he would not have been so dressed. As for murder, I can't yet say what turned him to killing his partner in bogus spiritualism, although it's possible someone else substituted for him." He stopped regarding the curtains and frowned at the tiny notebook and pencil I had removed from my coat pocket, on which I was recording as many details as I could remember.

"Have you always taken notes so assiduously?

"Of course."

"Have you always worn such checked coats?"

"Well, no. This is new."

"Then so is your uncanny imitation of Miss Huxleigh. I had no idea you admired her so much."

"I don't! She is a perfect pickle of an Englishwoman and I am nothing like her."

At this he smiled slightly. "Of course not. The admirable Miss Huxleigh is an utter original. I would almost call her Bohemian, but that would offend her belief in her complete conformity to the world's opinion."

"I thought it was Irene you admired."

"You must realize that I have neither the time nor inclination for the art of admiring women."

"If you are going to waste an instant on such a pursuit, you should know that Nell, despite a few stabs at playing a useful role in life, is not a modern woman."

"Fortunately so! What is most interesting about her is that she little knows her own self. She is so stout-hearted precisely because she fears so much." He chuckled, actually chuckled, although it was an almost mechanical sound. "I shall never forget her rather touching attempts to flirt with me in one of my less prepossessing disguises once in order to save her friends. It is something Watson would have done, had he been born a woman. Loyalty"—and here he regarded me as severely as a schoolmaster—"is the most sublime of the virtues."

"I am loyal, first and foremost, to my readers."

"*Hmmm.* It is interesting that they are the most distant individuals from yourself." His glance released me as he examined the curtains again.

"How did you discern the size and condition of the man who stood behind these panels?" I asked.

"By the size of the shapeless footprints. And there is a hand print high on the drapery. The impression was deep and the fingers appear crooked, as if he clutched the cloth in a death-grip. He was nervous, very nervous for a veteran of séance manipulations, if indeed he was, so I assume that he knew from the first that murder would result."

"How do you know that he was nervous?"

He smiled again, to himself. "Velvet records the emotions of those who wear or touch it. Dampness in the fingers or palms impresses a perfect image on the nap. I learned that trick from a reluctant colleague once, or perhaps I should say a dedicated competitor."

"I thought you had no equal."

"No equal, but would-be rivals: the police, for instance, who resent their professionalism being outdone by a mere amateur." He shook his head at the scene before us. "If I were to go to the New York police and seek their suggestions on this case, which I would never do, they would no doubt regale me with Bertillon measurements of known stranglers, utterly unaware that this strangler was an amateur himself."

"Bertillon measurements?"

"A system invented early this decade by a Frenchman. It uses calipers and compasses to identify criminals through an enormous number of inane measurements of their physical bodies, including the skull, as if what is in the head is less lethal than its outward dimensions. Mostly nonsense, of course, except for identifying a man whose measurements are already recorded, and even then offers much possibility for error. Since the system is amazingly time-consuming and cumbersome, it has become the darling of police forces the world over."

"I have never heard of such a technique."

"And I hope that few will ever hear more of it in future. Now, could we but make every criminal nervous and arrange an encounter with velvet in every case, we would have an excellent scientific means to match murderers to crime scenes, as I have noticed that the minute whorls on the fingertip offer amazing variety. I believe some attempts have been made in India and Japan to systematize the phenomenon, and I intend to experiment once I am back in Baker Street with my equipment at my own fingertips.

"For now"—he eyed the curtains again—"the best course is to

investigate the shady theatrical world that supports these shoddy illusions that pass as everything from bald entertainment to something so elevated as spiritual solace by communing with the dead."

I shuddered a little. Perhaps by being stranded on the threshold I was subject to drafts. Perhaps dead spirits really did linger on this scene of mysticism and murder.

"If one really could conjure the dead," I ventured, "I imagine that your cases would provide a virtual chorus of corpses."

"The dead never frighten me, Miss Cochrane. It is what the living have done and may yet do that does."

Englishmen! Cold fish, all of them, this one particularly so. Still, now I knew that I sought a tall and lithe, yet stiffening shadow, a mature man who perhaps once had performed until arthritis had disabled him, and then had turned his talents to polite fraud, and now had killed his employer. Was this for some reason he alone knew, or for another, larger purpose that encompassed more deaths?

Whatever his story, or purpose, I sensed that the nub of it, the center, the untold history, involved the child performer who had grown up to be Irene Adler Norton.

Phineas T. Barnum and his ilk would have the public believe that his freakish featured acts—the conjoined Siamese twins, the sword swallowers, the dwarves—were suitable objects of wonder and entertainment. It struck me that such shows pandered to the worst instincts of both performer and audience, that parading disability as entertainment diminished the humanity of each, and that the attraction of the rope dancer or the fire eater—even of the water-breathing mermaid—was the ever-present possibility of violent death.

And where there was possibility, there surely would someday be consummation.

15.

Smoking Ruin

~·ꞷꞷ·~

*The vulgar gape and stare, and are fully prepossessed that the
fair heroine is by nature gifted with this extraordinary
repellent to fire. Several of this salamander tribe... may now
be seen traveling from town to town.*

—R. S. KIRBY, *WONDERFUL AND ECCENTRIC MUSEUM OR MAGAZINE
OF MEMORABLE CHARACTERS*

I had never sat in the audience at a common entertainment
before.

The New Fourteenth Street Theater felt more like a
hall than a theater. Obviously the performers had booked
it for themselves. Just as obviously, the performers and
their agents would pocket most of the profits.

Anyone could rent a hall in these days, advertise it, and sell
tickets. Not everyone would attend, but quite a few had come
forth for the performance of the sole Salamander sister. Oh, that
did sound rather fishy!

The bottoms of my boots scraped across—I bent over to look,
amazed—peanut shells. Indeed, folk all around me were either
cracking their knuckles or breaking the backs of the humble

peanut, one after another. Neither activity was exemplar of polite public behavior.

But then the playbill displayed in front of the theater was hardly polite either. I had never seen such an assemblage of elaborate capital letters and exclamation points in my life!

And all this large type, following rows of fine type, was interspersed with small illustrations of very bizarre (and tiny) people doing the oddest things with the strangest mechanisms.

Around us thronged scores of people seeking entry to this shabby array of oddities.

Irene led the way and soon we were slipping into whatever free seats we could. . . . Actually, Irene had led us far closer to the stage than I would have chosen.

Beside me, Irene was as nervous as if she herself were slated to perform, but the program allowed for no such elevated artistes as opera singers.

There was Maharajah Sing-a-poor and his flying Persian carpet direct from Ali Baba's cave. . . .

Little Dulcie and her performing pig-poodles . . .

Oh, and Salamandra the Fire-Queen, who appeared to be a solid woman in flowing robes surrounded by an aura of living flames . . .

Next to me in the audience, on the side Irene did not defend, sat a strange gentleman. Actually, he was no gentleman, for he wore a derby hat that he apparently felt no need to doff, indoors or in feminine company.

His elbows on the seat armrests nudged mine with ignorant rudeness . . . unless he was one of those pickpockets Irene had showed me on the omnibus in London years ago, who wore a false set of arms so his larcenous fingers could be at work behind them.

I leaned away as far as I could to avoid the odious and possibly thieving contact, but Irene on my other side nudged me back.

I pulled my elbows tight to my whalebone corset sides and thought of England.

Thus I remained when the "show" began, with much shrill trumpeting of instrument and voice.

The "flying carpet" was suspiciously unsupple. The "pig-poodles" oddly resembled King Charles spaniels crossed with pit bulls. I had heard the word "vaudeville" applied to such entertainments. I did not know its meaning, but the obvious origin was French and, well . . .

We sat through a mind reader who did not call upon us, and luckily so, as he would have been exposed . . . through a ventriloquist who made a flat-iron speak (it asked for a rest in the Arctic).

And then . . . Salamandra.

I admit it was an evocative name, like Sarah Bernhardt's Théodora.

As for Salamandra, I must confess that when she appeared from above the stage seated on a swing of fire I was somewhat impressed.

Slowly she was lowered as assistants laid red-hot rails on a large box-frame filled with stones.

Salamandra drained the champagne flute in her hand, yet left enough liquid to turn the glass upside down and let it weep upon the stones before her feet.

Steam hissed upward, visible and audible to every eye and ear.

I sat forward, taking care not to brush Mr. False Arms's elbows.

Irene had sat forward, too, but she was frowning.

Really, this was the most impressive . . . illusion.

The stones now glowed bright red, like the heart of an ember.

Salamandra's bare feet touched toe to the stones, and then she stood.

Yet she did not move a muscle, not even a toe.

Applause and whistles erupted, and many more peanuts also broke out from their confining shells.

Perspiration erupted on my forehead. I was rapt. I could feel the heat radiating from the insensible stones to the tender flesh of the woman's bare feet.

I wanted to look away, but could not. Her expression was serene.

She began to walk down the avenue of red-hot stones as though it were cool summer grass.

At last she stood, bare of foot, on the bare wooden stage.

I admit I expected to be further amazed.

I watched the stage erupt in flames, watched the exotic Salamandra, draped like a Roman matron, swallow flames and tread barefoot on red-hot coals and juggle fire. At last she swept her robes tight around her body, bowed to the audience, and began to strut toward the hall's curtained wings.

Only . . . a brazier in the background exploded into wings of flame as she passed. Then her entire figure was subsumed into the expanding illusion of fire and her hair lifted upward in fiery tongues, her draperies an inferno, the effect truly a human torch of excitement.

Save that Irene was standing and drawing me up with her.

"That's no illusion," she cried. "Oh, my God! Water! We must reach the stage. *Salamandra!*"

Irene bounded into the aisle like a hound after a hare.

What could I do? Remain with Mr. Derby False Arms?

I followed as fast as I could.

I was far enough behind to see Irene rush infallibly up a short set of stairs on the far left linking the auditorium with the stage.

I followed, stumbling on black-painted steps not meant to be noticed by the audience.

Now we were not audience, but . . . unwilling attraction.

Irene seized the Maharajah's flying carpet, apparently paused in mid-air in the wings.

While I gasped at the rug's revealed frame, she rushed onto the burning stage floor, her boot soles drumming an up-tempo rhythm.

"Quick, Nell!" she cried. "Roll up the carpet. Remember Cleopatra!"

I found myself stomping over red-hot coals and feeling not a thing, one end of the carpet in my gloved hands. I understood without demur her reference to Cleopatra . . . unrolled before Caesar in a rug. Such are the benefits of an English education, even if it is at the knee of an obscure country parson. . . . Irene and I rolled, not unrolled in this instance, and in smoking seconds Salamandra was crushed in our curled carpet like Turkish tobacco in one of Irene's dark Egyptian papers.

For once I was glad that I knew the arcane arts of rolling tobacco, for only smoke drifted up from the coiled carpet, and muffled cries.

"Well done!" Irene rode the roll of carpet like an equestrienne the back of a spirited Arab steed. The position was most unlady-like, but effective. She rocked back from her position of triumph. Somewhere, applause sounded, and cast peanut shells seasoned the smoky air.

Irene coughed.

"Your voice!" I complained hoarsely.

"Bother my voice! Is she . . . all right? You look, Nell. I can't."

So it was left to me to unpeel the fireproof lady, to see if she lived up to her advertisement.

I unrolled one end of the rug and saw her smoke-smudged features, wincing.

"Are you—?"

"Alive? Just barely, my dear. What has not been smoked has been smothered. I beg you, miss, free me."

This Irene and I contrived, to the audience's delighted applause. They thought our exploits a part of the show, can you credit it?

In the end we released a smudged and charred, but otherwise unharmed, Salamandra, and all three took a deep bow, myself drawn down into this ridiculous position by the fact of Salamandra's firm hand in mine, quite cool and uncooked.

The show was over, and the local fire department had been called by stage managers who had recognized an extreme departure from the show's script.

If not for Irene, and perhaps myself, Salamandra would have burned to death.

Irene stood in the wings, once her own personal sacristy, now bowed over as she tried to take smoke-free breaths.

We had been through a scene from Grand Opera, and no one here could recognize that reality except policemen and firefighters.

What chain of events had we interrupted?

A fire resister nearly killed by fire.

Her medium sister dead of a ghost.

Certainly these were not matters for Inns of Court barristers now laboring in France. Godfrey had been right to recommend my making this journey.

I had now become furious at the brutal death nearly inflicted in the public eye, in my eye.

I went to Irene, touched her hunched shoulders.

She straightened like a ventriloquist's dummy. "Nell? This is far more sinister than I imagined my past to be. Salamandra was almost killed before our eyes, as her sister died recently before other eyes. I can no longer deny it, or Pink's allegation. These crimes are somehow personal to me."

"Nonsense," said I. "This evil act was prevented. By us. You. I think we should repair to the backstage manager's office and see to . . . um . . . Madame Salamandra. She is obviously the focus of this attack, not you or your past."

Crowds made the halls, already dim and narrow and now smelling of smoke as well as pomade, into cramped alleyways.

By now, Irene had recovered her performer's instincts. She pushed and wove her way to a door barred by a large, blue-serge-clad Irish policeman.

I knew I observed an operatic confrontation: Irene, the clever village girl against the stern solid wall of authority.

"My dear sister," Irene cried in a voice to wring hearts and possibly brass buttons. "I must see her! Does she yet live?"

"And what is your name?" the policeman demanded.

"Sophie," Irene declared.

He nodded, as if recognizing a password, and stood aside.

Irene wasted no time in pushing past him, and, seizing my wrist, in drawing me with her.

The office door swung shut behind us.

Before us lay a room papered in playbills, with a desk deep in unsorted papers, and even a large mirror on one wall. Its center-piece was a woman attired in smoky cerements, looking as if she'd escaped from Hell itself.

"Salamandra?" Irene asked.

"You called yourself 'Sophie,'" the other woman said in a small, sad, and husky voice. "I heard through the door."

"Forgive me. I needed a password, like Ali Baba in the cave of the forty thieves."

Salamandra's great blue unfocused eyes fixed on me. "I was burning," she said, "quite against cue. I saw you worrying at an Oriental rug. Should I know you?"

"You should know *me!*" Irene interrupted, setting herself between me and this woman of fire so her face was plain to see.

Salamandra's eyebrows, I saw, had been singed to stubs, like a forest rubble after the fire. Her blue eyes were red-rimmed.

Irene took a deep breath.

Salamandra gazed at her. "I do not know you."

"She," I put in, "first saw the fire was real."

"The fire is always real," Salamandra admonished me, her eyes softening her tone. "But something had seared the robes I wear. Perhaps an error by the stage crew."

"Perhaps," said Irene, "an error by the person who killed your sister."

Salamandra stared at Irene. "Person? The police said she choked on the ectoplasmic matter she expelled. It was an accident in their eyes."

"It was convenient to call it an accident. Was your burning robe an 'accident' here? Tonight?"

"Such mishaps do occur, given the volatile nature of our performances."

Salamandra sank onto a chair that had turned its back on the large looking glass. Her gown was charred from neck to hip, as I saw in the mirror, so close had the flames come.

"No accidents happened," Irene said. "Not to your sister, and not to you."

"Who are you?" Salamandra stared through lashes that had been singed to a short frizz.

"I don't know," Irene said slowly, finally acknowledging that an original identity underlay all she had made of herself today, realizing and declaring it for the first time. "But I do know I used to be . . . one . . . of you," she finished with a smile.

16.

Unburnt Bridges

❦

I'm cool and determined as any salamander, ma'am, Won't you come to my wake when I go the long meander, ma'am?

—MOLLY BRANNIGAN, IRISH FOLK SONG

"One of us?"

Salamandra brushed the cinders from her hair.

"You do seem to understand more than most the . . . depth of our illusions." She glanced at me, who had been just now introduced to her. "Ah, Miss Huxleigh. Right you are to look bewildered. I may not seem to be in mourning, but I tried to go on, after Sophie's death. How could I expect an attempt on my own life? With Sophie's death . . . who is not to say the spirits spoke their wishes at last?"

"It was murder," Irene said, her tone final. "Spirits had nothing to do with it."

Salamandra regarded her. "You are a skeptic, yet you say you're one of us. We live a half-life, half believing our own notices. We are all Gypsies, aren't we? Mountebanks and illusionists, believing too much in our own duplicity. Now we are to believe in murder. And that we somehow suddenly sow death. Tell me how, so I have hope to redeem Sophie's loss."

"I don't know," Irene repeated.

"You saw me burning. People see me burning every night and pay good pence to see it again the next night. You saw . . . me perishing. And intervened. Why? How? What gift have you to penetrate our delusions?"

"I am one of you," Irene said, shrugging.

Salamandra stared at her, as if an adamant gaze would elicit truth. "And this one?"

She referred to me, and not idly.

"She is most assuredly *not* one of you," Irene said with a wry amusement, "and will not be beguiled. Nor will she allow me to be beguiled."

Salamandra took my measure, and retreated as she would not have from a red-hot needle.

"I should be seared flesh by now," she admitted. "That I am not is due to you two. Tell me what you want to know."

What an amazing conversation!

In minutes Salamandra had accepted Irene as the fully grown incarnation of the jig-dancing child known as "Rena." Salamandra reminisced with Irene about Rena and Tiny Tim. I was a mere onlooker to this reunion of long-lost fellow performers.

"I recall watching your fiery illusions from the wings," Irene admitted, "but why did Sophie give up performing with you? And what were you called when you both set the playbills on fire, so to speak?"

"Oh, we were a popular pair. Twin flames. 'Gemini Burning' we called ourselves. We traveled a good deal in those days. We were all either in town or out of town. And you . . . little Rena!

You were our doll-baby. We tended you and taught you and applauded you. Do you remember the time Sophie tried to teach you to drink arsenic?"

Irene visibly struggled to recall this appalling incident, then shook her head. "That was a long time ago. So . . . who were my parents?"

Salamandra paused to consider a matter she had not thought upon for perhaps twenty-five years. "Why . . . no one, little Rena. The child performers were pets of all the adult performers—whether any performers are adults is a question I leave to future generations to answer—unless the adults in question were curmudgeons like Rufus Pope. What an unlikeable cuss he was! Vinegar for blood. But aside from an ogre like that, you were the darling of every playbill you appeared on. And Tiny Tim, too."

"Was I always a jigger?"

"Oh dear me, no! You played the harp—"

"Harp!"

"A sweet gilded tiny one. You sang, too: *'Crying cockles and mussels, alive, alive oh,'*" Salamandra trilled with enough vibrato (what Irene called an "amateur warble") that my friend winced with almost physical pain. Vibrato, she had always said, was a symptom of an untrained voice.

"Was I Irish, then?" Irene asked a bit warily.

Salamandra did not even notice the child rearing its curly head to ask after its origins.

"Heavens, no. Or, perhaps more accurately, who knows? Such songs always went over well, especially when piped from childish lips."

Irene's deep intake of breath produced far more vibrato than she would have permitted on any stage in her next words. "Surely someone took responsibility for my comings and goings? Some . . . guardian."

"Well, you know that is funny. I never thought of it before. We show folk are a tolerant lot. We are always changing names and addresses and specialties. We just never think too much about the practicalities. All I remember, my dear, is that you were present in the theater when you were needed, and absent when you were not."

"Surely I was . . . paid for my infant capers! Who received the money?"

Again Salamandra shrugged. "All I can say is we all—with the exception of Mr. Pope—we all considered it our duty and pleasure to look out for your little head and feet backstage and onstage, and that you always did your numbers as required and were a very *untroublesome* child, acting much older than your tender years, at least in your zeal and performance, and really quite, quite too adorable for words."

Irene looked ready to explode with aggravation. She had not come all this way to learn that she had been a beautiful baby.

I intervened to keep the interview, for that was what this conversation really was, on ground that might prove rewarding.

"Are there no laws, er, Madame Salamandra, that govern the employment of such young children in such an unrespectable venue as the sensational stage?"

"Goodness no, Miss Huxleigh! Children may work as they are wanted and where their parents send them, and I hope matters are as simple and straightforward where you come from. No doubt there are bluenoses about who would sniff that a stage is a worse place to work than a shoe factory. I would stand up to any one of them to say that our labors are as light as our recompense sometimes is, that we enjoy mystifying a work-weary public and are the least-abused laborers in the nation, for we give joy and collect coins and must never toil from dawn to dusk as the factory drudges do, but trip the light fantastic every evening and at weekend matinees. And wear very pretty clothes. Who could ask for a better life, or livelihood?"

I confess that for a moment this thrilling speech had me considering converting to the fire-breathing school, although there may be some who would be so unkind—or honest—as to say that I already had.

Irene waggled her fingers at me and shook her head. I instantly understood that she considered this line of questioning fruitless, for now, at least.

"Enough of my mysterious origins," she said, waving one hand like a magician. "What we must answer here is the nature of the very odd attack on you. You are coated, of course, with fire-proofing formulas?"

This was news to me. I had no idea that one could avoid flames—perhaps even those eternal ones of Hell?—with formulas . . . except for the Ten Commandments, of course.

"Naturally." Madame Salamandra also waved a dismissive hand. "It was not my flesh that was the medium, but my form."

"Ah. Your clothes. Aren't they, too, treated in fireproof chemicals?"

"Naturally."

"And they are kept—?"

"In my dressing room. Of course."

"Of course." Irene stood. "May we see this place?"

"Certainly." Madame Salamandra gathered the blanket around her slightly charred form (reminding me of an Indian advertising a Buffalo Bill Wild West Show) and led a procession from the manager's office to deeper into the bowels of the theater.

This was not terrain unfamiliar to me, thanks to my association with a former prima donna like Irene. I soon found all the under-stage odors assaulting my senses: the potent perfume of mustache wax and crêpe hair, of oiled face paints and rouge, of spirit gum and spirits of a more powerful, and liquid, sort. . . .

Madame Salamandra's dressing room was a semi-common one for the women of the playbill. A number of costumes ranging from silly to bizarre hung from a single metal pipe.

Salamandra paused by a filmy array of pastel gowns in such colors as jonquil, pumpkin, scarlet, and crimson.

"Meant to imply flames," she noted.

"And this night you wore the—?"

"Tulip. A gay assemblage of gold and orange, with crimson panels."

Irene lifted the thin, layered muslins. "What substance would make these suggestively flammable fabrics literally so?"

Madame Salamandra fidgeted. "I can think of but one thing."

"Naphtha?" Irene offered.

"Why, yes! How did you know?"

"Apparently I absorbed much backstage lore as a babe. These muslins would not be hard to submerge into some liquid substance that encouraged flammability. They would air-dry soon. And would there be no odor or stiffness to betray such a lethal bath?"

"No. These formulas we use in the fireproof business are undetectable when dry. I see what you imply: I donned my own death when I put on my costume tonight. But who would plan such a vicious end for me, and why?"

"Whoever killed your sister," Irene replied. "As for 'why,' that is always the query first asked, and last answered."

17.

Origin of the Species

Many cases depend upon reasoning back to events of years ago—family secrets, vengeance visited even onto the second generation. In a sense the past shapes those who become victims or villains in the melodramas of my cases.

—SHERLOCK HOLMES, *GOOD NIGHT, MR. HOLMES*,
CAROLE NELSON DOUGLAS

"Irene—?" I ventured in our hansom on the way back to our hotel.

"Say no more, Nell," she warned, puffing away on one of her signature little cigars as if to offer the horse-drawn conveyance the additional advantage of steam. "I have heard more tonight than I wish to hear in half a lifetime. My own!"

"If wishes were fishes, then beggars would ride—"

"And so we do. We ride. And we beg for answers. Say no more."

"Apparently your 'half a lifetime' is what is in question."

Irene put her palms to her ears like an obstreperous child.

I admit that image gave me pause. I must remember that I was dealing with two Irenes now. One was the adult and impervious, sometimes even imperious, and well-defended one who had humbled a king and a consulting detective in the process of protecting her liberty and her integrity.

And then there was the babe barely out of arms, that mewling infant she had been in a barely remembered past . . . helpless, alone, pushed into the limelight before she even knew the word, or the words . . . Mama and Papa. She would never know them.

Although the eight years we had known each other had seen our roles and relationship shift through many changes, I had never before felt more the nanny . . . and more the ineffectual friend, the burden.

It was an odd juxtaposition that made me feel both useful and helpless.

"Oh!" Irene exclaimed after long thought. "That Nellie Bly is up to something that I do not like! Unfortunately, she is also *on* to something. There is a reason that these theater folk are marked for death, and so far the only link I can find is myself! A self I barely remember, and do not wish to."

"I can understand that. Well, I can try to understand that. I recall little of my own youthful years, yet I am sure that they were sadly predictable. I was, after all, a widowed parson's daughter in Shropshire. I suppose certain . . . sheep have had more inspiring histories. Your youthful years are not. Predictable, that is. Normally I do not advocate the unpredictable, but in your case, this may have been an advantage."

She gaped at me, and I felt strangely rewarded. "You advocate the unpredictable, Nell? The unconventional upbringing? The unanswered questions in regard to origin?"

"But need anything go unanswered? I think not. Certainly the Sage of Baker Street would not allow for such eventualities. Are we to ask for less?"

"'The Sage of Baker Street,' Nell? Surely you exaggerate, although *he* would never think so. At least that is one boon we face here. We need not worry about the peripatetic Mr. Holmes tracing us to the New World."

"He would, if I may say so, be quite out of his depth."

"As we may be."

"Never! That would be giving that self-serving Nellie Bly the upper hand, and I will never do so."

"Self-serving, or serving an audience larger than self? I admit that I am somewhat confounded, Nell. A performer, even an elevated performer like an opera singer, may touch an audience of two or three thousand at once. A New York City journalist in these days may reach an audience of two or three hundred thousand."

"One is art," I said stoutly. "The other is commerce."

"*Hmmm.* I think our modern world is blending both into a new enterprise, and also makes of death a new sensation."

"You refer to murder?"

"To murder." Irene was silent for longer than her usual wont. "I remember Sophie now. A child's memories are as tender as a violet in the snow. A flashing picture here, a remembered scene there. The little Rena who danced is mostly lost to me. I don't doubt her existence, but it is nothing to me. I remember Tiny Tim, standing beside me, and towering even then in my tiny Alice mind. In my kittenish, wide-eyed sense of wonder. He was the Big Boy. The one who went before me. And then . . . he was gone, Rena was gone. Where? Nellie Bly says I had a mother. Why is there no memory? Why is she fainter than the fireproof sisters and Tiny Tim growing large?"

"She was not ever there, Irene, as my dead mother was not there. She was utterly absent, that's all. I at least had a father to remember until I was almost twenty, and I could presume to a memory of my mother."

"I had no father," Irene declared. "Nor any mother who would accept the title. The rational conclusion is obvious. I was, like Godfrey, a complete bastard."

There was nothing I could say to this shocking declaration, except one thing: "Then who would kill to keep you so in the public record and your own mind?"

For once, my friend Irene Adler had no answer.

I could not believe that I had accomplished this wonder.

We dined quietly that night in the hotel dining room.

How accustomed I was becoming to being a woman out on my own! No one glanced askance at us, but then this was the United States and Irene had forsworn smoking after the meal at my request.

This did not prevent her from ordering a half bottle of wine with our dinner and then taking out her Russian blue-enamel cigarette case when the coffee came, to play with it. The glittering diamonds of the cover's serpentine *I* slanted across the enameled blue sea like a bright white sail.

I marveled again that she so favored a once poison-equipped object originally meant to take her life. Or did she treasure it because Sherlock Holmes had disarmed it before it could hurt her? I could not imagine any woman much treasuring what Sherlock Holmes did or did not do . . . the man was that aloof and that annoyingly cerebral, in the way of a too-smart-for-his-own-good boy, a type I had often seen in my governess days. I wondered again why boys discovered arrogance at such an early age, and why so few girls seemed to discover it at all.

Across from me, over her strong-smelling coffee, Irene laughed.

I looked up.

"I agree, Nell, Sherlock Holmes is most annoyingly arrogant."

"I said no such thing!"

"But you have always thought it."

"And how can you agree with me when I have said nothing?"

"Because your emotions were as plain upon your face as your thoughts." She picked up the case, turned it in her fingers. "It is exquisitely made, and beautiful, that is why I love it. So much in life is neither exquisite nor beautiful. Such transcendent objects remind us of the perfection we never find, in ourselves or in others. The artist who crafted this transcends my admiration of it, he even transcends the base and lethal use an enemy tried to make of it . . . transcends even the brilliant, single-sighted way one Sherlock Holmes unveiled and disarmed the corrupt purpose it had been adapted to: my own death.

"He would not appreciate this object as Keats's 'thing of beauty and a joy forever,' our Mr. Holmes." She smiled again. "Yet he much admired the cleverness of both the maker, and the one who made it into something as subtle and poisonous as a living serpent. And," she added casually, "he liked showing off to me. He is not quite all mental icewater, Nell. Almost, but not quite. And that is how he disarmed himself to me in that moment. So I see many makers in this object now. The artist. The assassin. The savior. And the survivor. Sometimes I think they exchange roles without knowing it, which makes things even more intriguing."

"It is a sinister memento of a bad time," I said.

"Yet . . . do you not keep your Gypsy boots?"

The reference startled me. It is true that a pair of colorful leather-worked boots sat at the bottom of my cupboard at Neuilly. Now that she had mentioned it, I could not for the life of me say why I had saved this unlikely souvenir of the worst time of my life. She missed nothing, my friend Irene, and sometimes I could throttle her for it.

"They are . . . folk art."

"This is"—she flourished the immensely more costly cigarette case—"aristocratic art. Both serve better as reminders of bad times, and how we overcame them, than as decorative objects."

"You are saying that decorative objects can be useful as well?"

"I am saying that they *must* be, Nell, even when they are only human."

18.

The Dictating Detective

I would give a great deal to know what inevitable stages of incident produced the likes of Irene Adler. Show me a method of forming more women so, and I would show more interest in women.

—SHERLOCK HOLMES, *GOOD NIGHT, MR. HOLMES*,

CAROLE NELSON DOUGLAS

⊰FROM THE CASE NOTES OF SHERLOCK HOLMES⊱

I have resolved to keep this record for Watson's benefit, since I was less than forthcoming about my sudden trip to the United States of America and the reasons for it. I may, or may not, ultimately show it to him.

It appears that his attempts to spin tales from some of my cases promise to become routinely published. Much as I may gently mock his literary efforts, or at least his impulse to turn the sober facts of my investigations into "thundering good tales," I bow to the inevitable.

Despite the presence of murder on Miss Nellie Bly's agenda, I am not pursuing her particular commission on these teeming shores. I have, in fact, a trifling though tasty puzzle to solve for the Astor family, which has generously sponsored my voyage. Although I was in a sense lured here by a mermaid, no siren song can lure me onto self-destructive shoals, and the wax is firmly installed in my ears.

When I encountered the American courtesan known as "Pink" in Paris, I never believed for a moment that she was what she wished to seem. Nor was I particularly surprised to find her established here in America as a newspaper reporter under the lively pseudonym of Nellie Bly.

While I had no time to waste in surmising her origins then, the small callus on the first joint of her right middle finger betrayed itself as a cradle for the pen, and not even the most ardent invitation-penning society woman builds such a callus; only a writer. Watson, in fact, is developing the beginnings of the same sign of vigorously unleashed fancy. I assume the typewriter will soon banish this telltale mark to an antique footnote. At least the eccentricities of typed lines are almost equal to the betraying individuality of handwriting.

At one time I might have considered Miss Bly the most prepossessing young woman I have ever met. Even now I can see Watson the Married Man stroking his mustache and weaving subplots of a romantic sort for his most unromantic old chambermate.

Alas, I am annoyed rather than intrigued by such naked feminine ambition, and he will no doubt twit me again for the chronic suspicion with which I regard the so-called gentler sex. You see, I do not believe *that* common delusion for a minute.

I must confess to harboring a professional curiosity about another enterprising woman, to whom the blatant is an impossibility and whose deepest ambitions remain a mystery. This is the woman whose murky history Miss Bly offered to me as the usual snare and delusion to which mortal man is supposed to surrender. I am given to understand that her vague personal history from an early age in the States is somehow involved in a bizarre murder, or several. At least Miss Nellie Bly devoutly hopes so.

No creature on earth is more secretly bloodthirsty than a lady-like woman.

Ah, Watson, old fellow! I have been forced to conceal so much from you lately, all in the cause of Queen and country, which you would never deny me. Still, it is a shabby way to treat a loyal companion. Hence, my penitence through these pages. Also, this record will help me to think. There is something about your undemanding presence, old fellow, that always puts me into the mood for intense cogitation, almost more than my pipe and shag. Even the completely irrelevant questions you ask stimulate my mind by their very banality.

So I will continue to address you here, in theory and across leagues and leagues of ocean, and thereby enter into a dialogue with myself.

I suppose I should characterize the city of New York. It is dirty, loud, bustling, and tall, Watson, buildings lurching sky-ward like mushrooms after a rain. It is just this straining for height that strikes me the most about this metropolis of nearly three millions of people.

There is also the sense that this city is all business. Everything is new and growing. There seems at first little history to celebrate. Then one realizes that the inhabitants have dragged their history behind them, as snails their shells, even as they also have left it and the Old World behind.

Everyone here appears to be an immigrant of one sort or another, and all of these immigrants, instead of being absorbed into something older and greater than they, shape the city to their own presence. New York must reflect them and support them and bow to the sheer impress of their numbers. Quite a backward way of building cities, I believe, but then this is a backward country, thus far, at least.

Nevertheless I hold great hopes for it producing new and vast and vile varieties of crime. It was in this city, I suspect, that Madam Adler Norton first found employment with the Pinkerton Detective Agency of Chicago. I confess myself eager to learn more of this trusty organization, which has created on a nation-wide scale what I founded on an individual basis: a private detective force that works outside the police apparatus, although sometimes in cooperation with it.

I find it astounding that women were welcomed to its ranks as long ago as just after the American Civil War, shortly after you and I were born, Watson! Not many women were Pinkertons, I understand, but ten or so years later, one of them was Miss Irene Adler.

My earlier pilgrimage to visit Baron von Krafft-Ebing in Germany, and my admiration for his splendid catalogue of the sort of killer he calls "lust-murderers" has, oddly enough, turned my mind to this lady.

You know that I regard her as forming a class by herself among her sex. You mistake this for infatuation when it is merely fact. Among her achievements I number her newest astonishment: recruiting Nellie Bly to her service last spring. I could barely contain this intrepid reporter from trailing me back to Whitechapel and meddling in my laying Jack the Ripper to rest for all time.

Madam Irene, at what was surely the most devastating moment of her life (unless I uncover any even more devastating moments here in New York), managed to bridle Miss Bly, turn her to her own purpose, and silence her at the spectacular end of the affair, to boot! I quote the King of Bohemia on only one subject: "What a woman!"

This does not betoken any personal interest, I should soundly advise any Watsons into whose hands my private notes may ever fall. Rather it signifies my new quest to become the Krafft-Ebing of psychological types both elevated and debased. As a solver of crimes I am most rewarded when I encounter a mind and a personality worthy of the keenest steel. Given my slight handicap in personal knowledge of the female sex, I have concluded that the proper study of this consulting detective is woman, and *the* woman is the best subject for my elucidation.

I know, Watson, that you still devoutly believe this lady to be dead, and therefore mourn the impossibility of my succumbing to her intellectual virtues, if not any other of her many more obvious charms, which you are far better suited to appreciate than I. One of my unwelcome tasks is not to disabuse you of this wrongheaded conviction until the time is right. I know you are set on telling her story with pen and paper, and it ends so much more dramatically with her plunging off a precipice, along with the train she and her new husband were taking through the Alps. I believe that storytellers of the sort you aspire to be have a weakness for endings that plunge off a precipice.

Ever the romancer, Watson! Fiction is undoubtably your métier. Mine is fact, And I shall know all the facts that are to be learned about Madam Irene's past, and likely future, before I quit this Continent.

19.

A Deeper Solemnity of Death

❧

Dr. Ferguson is a lightning autopsist and a sort of scientific Jack the Ripper.

—THE *NEW YORK WORLD*, 1889

The very next morning Irene surrendered and sent a message to Nellie Bly at the address she had given us.

She addressed it to "Miss Elizabeth J. Cochrane," to my great satisfaction.

"Need we really resort to Pink?" I asked her after the messenger boy had left, content with his fistful of American dimes.

"Yes. She is ahead of us here, though not for long, I hope. Now I know enough to bluff her into revealing what she knows to me."

" 'Bluff'? In what way do you mean that?"

"In the sense of hoodwinking with apparently greater knowledge than one actually has."

"I wonder, then, if Pink, with all her vague hints and portents, isn't already 'bluffing' us."

"You are quite right. We are all engaged on a game of 'Blind Man's Bluff,' instead of 'Blind Man's Buff.' "

"Only we are women, not men. I have played 'Blind Man's

Buff' in the schoolroom with my charges . . . and once with Quentin."

"Quentin? Did you really?"

I had not intended to refer to that remote and rather embarrassing incident, but mention of the game brought him to mind, he who played the Great Game on the harsh slopes of Eastern lands nowadays. Where had he gone after Transylvania? Where had he gone after our disastrous reunion when I had utterly failed him, and myself? I could ask myself such questions, but I feared the answers. Would we ever meet again? Perhaps not, and it was all my fault.

"Quentin," Irene repeated quietly, her amber-brown eyes as soft and sympathetic as a rabbit's, a most unusual expression for her.

But she said no more, and for that I was most grateful.

Our guest (or tormentor) knocked late that afternoon.

The room reeked of smoke, for Irene had puffed and paced, and paced and puffed throughout much of the day.

I understood that all the amazing people we had met and tales we had heard since arriving in the States were churning through her mind like clouds in a windstorm.

She was preparing for the next stage of the quest, or the battle: confronting Pink to provide the evidence of Irene's so-called "mother."

I tried to imagine what I would think or feel if someone produced a live woman and introduced her as the mother I had always thought dead.

But my reactions were not Irene's.

Irene admitted Pink, who was attired quite smartly in a city dress with a wide-brimmed hat of heliotrope velvet and pink taffeta, the whole feminine affair pinned into her chignon within an inch of its life.

I was disturbed to see that Pink had adopted my Paris habit of carrying a large, flat artist's portfolio for her papers. I discovered I was as temperamental as Irene about imitators, and was just as likely to be annoyed as flattered.

"Ladies," Pink greeted us in the brisk, businesslike manner she employed in her home city.

She sat without invitation on a side chair, the large leather portfolio almost a tabletop on her knees.

"Before you ask me the questions that are no doubt burning at the backs of your throats by now, I'd like you to read a small story of mine, from a few weeks back."

"Back?" I inquired. "You mean 'prior to now'?"

"I mean this all happened before we ever set eyes upon each other in Paris, or before we ever stared into the face of Jack the Ripper. Sensational news stories don't just occur in Whitechapel, London, or in the cellars of Paris. We have plenty of our own right here on the streets of New York City."

At this she untied the strings binding her portfolio together and drew out a still-fragrant sheet of newsprint.

"Either one of you can read it, or both would be better. Anyway, it's the incident that got me on the trail of your mother, Irene, if there is such a being."

"You mean even you are not sure?" Irene asked.

"I mean your past is as hard as a walnut on Christmas Day to crack. I don't mean to tear my fingernails raw over it, so thought you might lend me a hand if I showed you the strange trail by which your past came to my attention."

"Show away," Irene challenged, leaning back and looking amused, or worse . . . bored.

Thus it was left to me to take the ink-impregnated papers from Pink's dainty hand and skim the contents first before passing them on to Irene. I almost got the sense of a Borgia princess allowing the court taster to sample the menu first . . . but Irene was always onstage in some opera in her head, so I was very eager to swallow this intriguing information first.

What I read was a newspaper story dated toward the end of the previous May. The date was after we had met the prostitute "Pink" and before Irene had discerned her real identity as the daredevil female reporter who wrote under the *nom de guerre* of Nellie Bly.

Amazingly, it was a journalistic piece that had *not* been written by said Nellie Bly, but by a rival lady reporter. I read with deepening interest. Our Miss Pink was passing on a story she had missed while dallying with Jack the Ripper in London, and, along with us, in Paris, Prague, and points eastward.

THE EXTREMELY STRANGE CASE OF WASHINGTON
IRVING BISHOP AND THE IMAGINARY MURDER
AT THE LAMBS CLUB
by Nell Nelson
(recorded by witness testimony after the circumstances revealed)

The Lambs Club meets in a dignified white stone building in New York City, an august institution established in 1875. Along with the Players Club it is the most renowned gathering place of theatrical personages in the States, or at least in New York City. (Some are so unkind as to say that its sole purpose for being is to establish the notion that actors can be gentlemen and create a club. However, from what one hears of the revels and masques that are staged therein, sometimes with men in women's dress, it is entirely too jolly to be genteel.)

In this place has recently occurred an event more dramatic than any acted upon the stage. It has presented the public with a mystery of frightening dimensions, in that it involves the death of a dead man.

A MAESTRO INVITED TO PERFORM WONDERS

It began with a simple invitation to a wonder-worker on the 12th of May of this year, two eminent Lambs Club members, the actor-magician Henry Dixey and Sidney Drew, another actor, invited a performer of a slightly different stripe to entertain their fellows.

Mr. Washington Irving Bishop was a world-renowned mind

reader and he offered the interested Lambs Club members an effect he had performed for the Czar of Russia. First, they must choose one of their number to escort Mr. Bishop from the room. Then they must invent a murder, victim, weapon, and killer. The "murderer" was to act out the crime physically and then hide the "weapon."

This done, Mr. Bishop returned to the room with his escort, who swore that Mr. Bishop could neither hear nor see any part of the imaginary murder while absent.

Another member, who had been in the room when the pantomime had been performed, was assigned as Mr. Bishop's impromptu "assistant."

Blindfolded, Mr. Bishop grasped his assistant's wrist, asking the man to think only of the fictional "victim."

In their midst, Mr. Bishop slowly turned like a top, then began dragging his assistant through the occupants of the room, both people and furnishings. His excitement mimicked that of a hunting dog on the trail. He trembled from toe to fingertip, the veins of his forehead distended. He lurched about the room in this manner. When he stopped to point to one person . . . it was indeed the very individual chosen to play the role of "victim."

Mr. Bishop repeated the same actions to indicate the chosen "murderer" and "weapon."

Amid applause and wonder, and some discreet scoffing, Mr. Bishop was asked to provide a further demonstration of his powers. For this next stunt, Clay Green, a comedy writer and the club secretary, complied with Mr. Bishop's request to mentally choose a name in the club register. Still blindfolded, still lurching and trembling, presumably with effort, Mr. Bishop took Mr. Green in hand, located the book and even indicated the proper page. Begging Mr. Green to "concentrate," he scrawled the letters that came to him, purportedly from Mr. Green's mind, on a paper.

ᴖᴎƎƧᴎWOᴛ

Mr. Green frowned politely at the gibberish Mr. Bishop had produced. The name he had in mind was Margaret Townsend.

But when Mr. Bishop's scrawl was held up to a mirror, of course the word read "Townsend."

A SUDDEN SWOON

The crowd applauded as one, but Mr. Bishop, always an energetic, even frenetic figure, grew suddenly agitated and in a moment the great mind reader fell mindless to the floor.

Applause turned to gasps and mutters of consternation.

CONFESSION OF CATALEPSY

"Do not worry, my friends," said a portly fellow who stepped near the unconscious mentalist. "I am Dr. John Irwin. I've known Mr. Bishop for years and I am familiar with such 'swoons' as he may suffer. In fact, he is that most interesting and rare anomaly, a true cataleptic. Many today fear being buried alive, but Mr. Bishop has far more right than most to dread this awful fate. His disease inflicts without warning severe muscular rigidity, the suspensions of all sensation and an outward appearance of all life signs being extinguished."

Not long after that Mr. Bishop did indeed revive and was taken to a bed upstairs to rest. Rest was not his desire, however, and soon he insisted on repeating his last trick. He demanded that the club ledger be brought to his room and that Dr. Irwin act as his assistant.

But the famed mentalist seemed past his powers. He only located the correct page with great effort, and when he stood to determine the chosen name, he collapsed, unconscious again.

COMES THE CONSULTING PHYSICIAN

Dr. Irwin called on Dr. Charles C. Lee, who had attended the mentalist before, but by 4 A.M. the following day all his efforts to revive the fallen man had failed, and he left.

A most appalling and touching picture of the bizarre efforts to revive the dead man is available from Mr. Augustus Thomas, Mr.

Bishop's advance man, who was intercepted while strolling along Broadway by a friend who ran up, shouting, "Your star is sick at the Lambs."

Mr. Thomas sped to the scene, where he "found Bishop in a little hall bedroom on an iron cot where he had been for twelve hours, a tiny electric battery buzzing away with one electrode over his heart and the other in his right hand."

Mr. Thomas, chagrined at his famous client's circumstances and "unconscious" condition, noted the two doctors smoking in an adjacent room, worn from the watch. Mr. Thomas sat beside his most famous client, studied the handsome face of this man of thirty-three years, even though Mr. Bishop was "to all appearances dead." Then "a deeper solemnity came over his features," and Mr. Thomas summoned the absent doctors to point out the change he had witnessed.

PRONOUNCED DEAD

The two men of medicine immediately declared their patient dead. Mr. Thomas just as swiftly departed for Philadelphia to inform the dead man's family. Such is the speed of rail transport in our modern day that Mrs. Bishop was at Hawkes Funeral Parlor on Sixth Avenue later that morning, gazing upon her young and handsome husband's dead body through the glass top of a coffin.

Who can guess at the many deep feelings that crowded that poor woman's mind? In times of such utter sorrow, often the smallest detail will assume significance. Mrs. Bishop asked the attendant to comb her husband's hair. No doubt the physicians' long night of attendance had disarranged it.

A GRISLY DISCOVERY

The attendant nervously drew a comb through the dead man's hair, the eyes of his widow fresh upon him. He dropped the comb . . . and it disappeared! It had fallen, subsequent inquiry revealed, into the corpse's empty brain cavity!

At this Mrs. Bishop wailed in despair. It was all too evident that an unauthorized autopsy had already been performed upon her husband, upon a man known to suffer from catalepsy, who always carried a note—his "life guard," he used to say—explaining his condition and prohibiting an autopsy and also using ice or electrodes on his body. The note also listed the addresses of Mr. Bishop's family and lawyer, to be alerted if he ever fell into a trance.

Mrs. Bishop, in that dawning moment of horror, cried out, "They have killed my husband! Those doctors slew him for his brain."

No note was ever found, or admitted to have been found.

A MISPLACED BRAIN

The issue of Mr. Bishop's missing brain soon became a chorus. In addition to the dead man's wife crying "Murder" at the Lambs Club and Dr. Irwin's office, the mother of the deceased, Eleanor Fletcher Bishop, descended on the scene and demanded a coroner's inquest.

In no time Dr. Irwin and Dr. Lee, Dr. Ferguson and Dr. Hance, the men who had performed and witnessed the autopsy, were arrested and forced to pay bail in the princely sum of $2,000 each.

ANOTHER SHOCKING MISPLACEMENT OF AN ORGAN

For the dead man's brain was indeed found. It had not been stolen, it had been concealed . . . in his chest cavity.

At the inquest, Mrs. Eleanor Fletcher Bishop testified to her own propensities to catalepsy, and to her son's previous apparent deaths (erroneous and fortunately *not* followed by hasty autopsies). One occurred in 1873, when he was but a lad of seventeen. The doctors found no respiration, no pulse in his motionless form, and thus he was declared dead. Twelve hours later, young Mr. Bishop awoke "with a start" on the application of tincture of ammonia (which has often been known to revive many a whalebone-corseted damsel from a dead swoon).

He had been pronounced dead at least two more times, according to inquest testimony, and always had emerged from his trances none the worse for wear . . . save for the autopsy following his final and ultimately fatal swoon at the Lambs Club shortly after one of his greatest triumphs.

But weep and wail as the women would, none of their pleas and cries could change the fact that the mistakenly dead man was indeed dead for good this time, irretrievably dead, bereft of breath when he had been bereft of brain. The elder Mrs. Bishop tried to prevail upon the undertaker to chisel on his headstone epitaph: "Born May 4, 1856—Murdered May 13, 1889."

She was denied the editorial comment in the epitaph.

For despite a New York Penal Code prohibiting any dissection without permission, a jury of the late Mr. Bishop's supposed peers (although according to his advance man, Mr. Augustus Thomas, "he had no peers") released the doctors without penalty.

The senior Mrs. Bishop did not slacken her labors, appealing to Joseph Rinn, a renowned psychic investigator and long-time friend of the escapologist, Houdini. It is even rumored that she presented the case to an obscure British doctor who had written a mystery story involving poison pills.

The fact remains that the man, whether dead at the time of the autopsy or not, was certainly dead now, and so has remained since interred at Green-Wood Cemetery in New York City on May 20th last.

May he rest in peace, but this humble reporter inclines to the theory that he will not.

"Well, Pink." Irene sat back after perusing this rather lurid report when I had passed it on to her. "This case appears to be almost as outré as your recent experiences in Europe trailing the Ripper. I had no idea that they told such grisly tales in the *New*

York World. No wonder you were so dismayed that the Ripper story was too volatile to print in any land."

"The real world is grisly and I tell it as it happens."

"But what has this macabre little case to do with us?" I asked.

"Not you, Nell. Not a bit. It's Irene. When I returned home, I found that Nell Nelson, an upstart imitator of my own undercover methods most noted for a sordid 'slave girl story,' had stolen this gem right out from under me whilst I was off chasing a story Whitehall and Sherlock Holmes and half the world wants to keep me from writing. I decided to follow up on the blank spots Miss Nelson leaves in her journalistic efforts. This got me to talking to the sort of folk who put on these kind of shows and shortly thereafter I came across this!"

She withdrew a larger sheet than the newspaper from the portfolio and flourished it at us like a flag.

This example of the typesetter's art was even more emblazoned with large type in fancy faces, and words that shouted rather than whispered.

MISS MERLINDA THE MERMAID, it as good as screamed. SHE GLITTERS, SHE SLITHERS THROUGH THE SEA, THIS NYMPH OF THE ATLANTIC COAST BREATHES WATER NOT AIR, COLLECTING TREASURES FROM DAVY JONES'S LOCKER, BEWITCHING ALL WHO SEE HER WITH HER CURRENT-BLOWN LOCKS, SEA-GREEN EYES, AND SHINING SCALES.

I passed it to Irene with what I believed was damning silence.

She took the playbill, and smiled. "Quite a rare souvenir by now, I should think. This I remember. Who would think that I would become more noted for my 'shining scales' on the international opera house stages than in the theaters of New York?" Irene yawned, like a bored shark. "Is this the shocking evidence of my past you have stumbled upon, Pink? Buffalo Bill has already recalled my long-ago performance as a Denizen of the Deep. I promised him a reprise of the act at his Wild West Show in Paris before *l'Exposition universelle* closes this fall. He is even now constructing the water tank for me on a wagon, which should be an innovation. I was never a mermaid in motion before. Hardly a scandalous revelation, don't you think?"

"I recognized you at once."

At this point, I stared at the playbill she had produced as if it were a scandal sheet. The mermaid's face and hair had been hand-tinted peach and auburn, with excessively pink cheeks and lips that one would think the cool and briny deep would hardly confer upon even a mermaid without cosmetic aid. I must admit relief to see that her seaweed-long tresses and danging necklaces of shells and lost Spanish jewels quite bridged the gap between her face and the skirt of scales that sufficed to depict a mermaid's tail.

Irene certainly was far less scandalous than numerous female equestriennes, electric ladies, wire-dancers, and magician's assistants I had seen pictured in flesh-colored tights that clung to the lower limbs all the way to their, well, corset covers, and left no detail of the female form unguessed. Irene's colorful tail was the model of discretion compared to these!

And so I told Miss Pink in no uncertain terms.

"I don't care if our friend Irene disported, or disports herself, in false scales," Pink retorted. "The fact is that Mr. Bishop had a large collection of playbills upon which he . . . and our mutual friend, were featured performers."

"Odd," Irene put in, "I don't remember him."

"He, as you, was a child performer. You often appeared on the same bills. As I tried to trace the playbills missing from his assemblage, I discovered that someone was collecting these old-time souvenirs everywhere I went. The playbills were being sold to unidentified third parties, or went mysteriously missing. So as I tracked backward from Merlinda to 'Little Fanny Frawley,' the petite pistolera or sharpshooter of twelve (a clear predecessor of Annie Oakley), to tiny Rena the toe-dancer, I discovered that everyone recalled you, but no one knew where you had gone, or had come from. When asked about your parents, they blithely assumed you were everybody else's offspring."

"So that is why you assembled the cast you did for your séance: several there remembered me, and knew me, or of me, at least. Did you really expect that exercise in Spiritualism to produce any useful results?"

"Before anything came of it, it produced what you call 'murder,' didn't it?"

"And if it truly did, so much more shame on you." Irene allowed herself to look utterly unforgiving, which I had seldom seen in our eight years of association and never directed at me, thank God. Despite her . . . unusual history . . . she had a moral center that I had to respect, even if I could not understand it. It forgave deeply personal foibles but not the smallest sins against others. "What have you stirred up, Pink, in your zeal for stories and to 'unmask' me? My past was eccentric, I admit. I admit that I want it to remain my past, and forgotten, but I'm not ashamed of anything I did. Can you say the same? The medium is dead.

"She was an honest fraud," Irene added as an epitaph from a fellow showman, "and I do remember being excessively fond of her as a child, though I do not much remember being a child." Irene's revived emotions forced her to a long, forbidding silence, a condition I had never witnessed before.

"What have you done?" she said at long last. "And can anyone undo it?"

Pink crushed her hands together on her lap. "I don't know. One thing I observed from the dead man's playbills that I was able to see: the Gemini Twins were listed on them, and one of them, Sophie, was the medium who was killed. And I just noticed in the paper today an obscure notice of the death of Abyssinia, a former Egyptian dancing girl of that same era, who died bizarrely in the embrace of a former performing partner, a twenty-five-foot pet boa constrictor."

My interest perked up. Was it possible that Madame Sarah might meet a similar fate?

"I was only pursuing the truth of your ancient history, but I seem to have stumbled over a trail of recent suspicious deaths, including Bishop's, and possibly murders. I'm now convinced that Sophie's death was deliberate, yet am no closer to the identity of your mother."

"The truth will not be caught sometimes, Pink, and sometimes is not worth the price of catching. So to find a murderer, you are convinced that you must also hunt my true mother among these theatrical folk, a quest I gave up before you were born. It's an unlikely relationship. You have confused your obsession to solve the mystery of myself with the trail of a story worthy of reporting in your newspaper."

Pink's eyes lifted to challenge Irene's assertion.

"Yes," Irene went on, "by the time I was five or six, I saw that where I came from didn't matter. It was where I was going. By ten years later, Professor Marvel, the Walking, Talking Encyclopedia, had not only schooled me, but he had found me a singing teacher, and I had found my true voice. No matter what I did, I was no longer a disciple of Terpsichore, or some future Little Sure-Shot. I was a singer, and from then on my days in the amazing arts of sensational theater were numbered. I sang my way out, note by note, a 'lonely orphan girl.' "

Irene's apologia, if indeed that was what it was—an explanation for being what she had been and had become—ended on that final, cutting note. She had quoted what Elizabeth Cochrane, also known as Nellie Bly, had signed herself on the key letter to the editor that began her journalistic career. *Lonely orphan girl.*

We were all that, we three. I due to the death of my mother at my birth and my father's death before I turned twenty. Irene for having been birthed indeed as Athena, from some mysterious thought rather than a mortal man and woman who could be named. And "Nellie Bly," the creature Elizabeth Cochrane eventually created on the death of her father that left her mother and siblings unprovided for, save by her own workaday efforts.

Perhaps Irene should amend Pink's phrase to "poor brave little lonely orphan girl."

"Is it my past," Irene asked, "that you pursue? Or your own?"

"Too many of us are orphan girls," Pink said. "I pursue the social customs that make us ashamed of our origins."

"There is a difference between shame and discretion," Irene said, "and until you learn it, you will hurt other people rather than help them."

"Blame me for Madam Sophie's death, if you will. It was *your* deliberately foggy past that set me on this path."

"No. It was my deliberate decision to use you as I could to save my dear ones that made you so resentful. You are a strong young woman, Pink. You will go far. Just try not to do it on other people's pain."

"I cannot believe that you are so indifferent to the fate of your own mother! Have you no heart?"

"It is better than being all heart, and having no conscience. We owe the present, not the past."

I was utterly lost during this contretemps. Perhaps it was because I had a much more boring past than either of my companions. I sighed. Surely, the unconventional Englishman, Quentin Stanhope, had taken note of that very fact and discreetly retreated in the face of this lamentable lack.

I was a Woman With No Past, and therefore, dull. Irene, apparently, had danced, shot, and sang her way to present fame and fortune, which was sadly stalled because circumstances had forced her to become anonymous. Life was not fair.

"Miss Pink," I said, reverting to my governess mode, which was dull but effective. "You owe Irene and myself more than an apology. You owe us an explanation, so that we may undo any ill you have done."

"Not even you, Irene, can bring the medium back to life!" she burst out, truly contrite.

"No," said Irene, "but we can find out who killed her. If you are wrong, Pink, and she has no connection to me, still her death was sudden and undeserved and merits solving.

"If she died, as you think, because she was related to me, or knew who was, it was still an evil, senseless death. 'Each man's death diminishes me.' That was written by a sixteenth-century poet, a man whose life combined great self-indulgence and great holiness. You see? Nothing is ever simple, ever clear-cut. And those words are as true today as they ever were.

"Use my past as a goad, if you think you do so for the common good, Pink. But you need no fancied relationship to me or my past to make me care about Sophie's passing. In principle alone, it's an abomination that is not to be tolerated. If you are right that this murder relates to me or my past, then it is an abomination that is not to be tolerated, but it is no worse a crime to me because I might be a cause. No murder is acceptable, to any civilized person. I would still want to find who had killed her."

"Exactly," I said in my sternest tones. Then I looked at Irene. "Can we?"

"Ah, Nell," Irene said, once we were alone again in our hotel room. "Can you understand why I don't wish to solve the mystery of my mother?"

"Of course. She was no doubt a scandalous woman. I am sorry, Irene, but it is likely you share the same miserable past that Godfrey does: you were conceived in shame and secrecy, sin and error, and it is best left thus, and unsaid."

"Such conceptions are rarely that simple, Nell. If Pink is right, and she may be, my . . . secret birth could cause deaths today. That is a notion I cannot accept."

"You know, Irene"—I leaned near and whispered—"I used to think as a child, quite fancifully, of course, that perhaps I did not have a mother who perished at my birth, but was an . . . offspring of the Prince of Wales, or a Gypsy fortune-teller, who left me on the parish steps, and then I had been adopted by my kindly father."

Irene regarded me with the utmost attention during this confession, and then cackled like a hyena afterward. Like a soprano hyena, I might add.

"We are *all* foundlings, Nell, in our own imaginations! Even the child of the most fortunate birth sometimes imagines a lurid past! Pink is unearthing the capacity of the human mind to deceive itself, that's all. 'I am so much more uninteresting than everybody thinks!' the little voice speculates. Well, Nell, in your case, you are *more* interesting than anybody thinks, which is why Quentin is so taken with you."

"He is? Truly? Quentin taken with me? No."

"You know it's so, though you dare not admit it, not even to yourself. It's amazing how much we will not admit to ourselves, much less anybody else. Just as I know that Pink's quest into my past will unearth truth, though I dare not admit it. Well! There is no stopping a daredevil reporter, so we must steal the march on her. We will follow the trail she has cut through this wilderness of American antecedents."

"I don't want to know," I wailed.

"Nor do I. I was not lying. I have forgotten most of my youth, probably for good reason. Pink is forcing me to revisit it. It may not be pretty and it may not be what I wish to remember. If I have a mother who can eventually be identified and named, I despise her, Nell. There is no point in finding her, except that I may have a specific name to hate."

"Irene! She is your mother."

"Is she?"

"A mother is sacred."

"Is she?"

"She should be."

"We all should be more than we are."

"Agreed, but until we are, what are we to do next? Perhaps Godfrey should join us?"

"No! I want no one else to know of this until I understand it myself." Irene sighed deeply, and a single breath of hers could resonate to the back wall of an opera house. "I would never voluntarily stir up my own past, Nell. It's not that I'm ashamed of my theatrical origins, silly as they were. It's that I believe that the present is all that matters."

I considered what secrets an inquiry into my late mother's early life might unmask. Probably nothing, but then again . . . I preferred her to be a faint tintype in a velvet-lined case that, closed, would fit in the palm of my hand. A mother was a notion alien to me, as it must be to Irene. I could indeed sympathize with her instinct to leave well enough alone.

Unfortunately, Pink Cochrane and Nellie Bly had never done any such thing in their entire conjoined lives.

20.

The Show Must Go On

❧

*The wearing of mourning is a time-honored institution. . . .
To be sure there is no inherent quality of consolation
in the black garments themselves——they are merely a silent
but appropriate expression of grief.*

—THE DELINEATOR, 1891

Once Irene had decided to investigate her own past, there was no holding her back.

That very day we returned to Union Square on a round of revisiting the persons she now knew had shared her mostly unrecalled childhood.

This time she intended to squeeze every droplet of memory out of them.

And this time we were three again: Irene, Pink, and me.

Numbers were no match for fate, however.

At Tiny Tim's boardinghouse, we found him gone, indefinitely.

"What wonderful good fortune!" trilled Mrs. McGillicuddy in answer to our inquiry for him. "He was offered a long-term tour of the West with Balambo, the Levitating Levant. After years of not working, can you imagine that!" A frown darkened her excitement. "I will have to advertise for another tenant, of course, and Timothy was such a quiet resident . . . for a former drummer."

"Imagine that," Irene remarked tartly as we descended the brownstone's exterior stair. She caught my eye with a look that Miss Pink, busy hunting up a gurney, couldn't notice. As a "New Yorker" Pink seemed determined to show us that we were on her ground now and she knew it like no other.

I understood Irene's unspoken message: could Tiny Tim's sudden decampment be too timely to be accidental? Had he fled for some reason, or had someone seen to his swift removal from the scene?

Someone with power or money. Or both.

"Where to next?" Pink was asking impatiently at the gurney's gaping door.

"The matinee and Madame Salamandra. The New Fourteenth Street Theater and drive like the Devil!" Irene tossed this last aside to the coachman high on his seat.

Had I not read Dr. Watson's horribly biased account of Irene's first brush with Sherlock Holmes and her hasty wedding to Godfrey—with Sherlock Holmes in disguise as an impromptu witness! (something I doubt even bride and groom knew)—I would have never known that her parting instruction parodied Godfrey's command to the driver on their wedding day.

Pink, of course, thought nothing of Irene's call for speed. New York streets were so clogged with pedestrians and vehicles of every description that making time through them required the patience of a Job. No wonder New Yorkers had taken to setting steam locomotives on tracks high above the city streets, to huff and puff above the madding crowd, adding to daily reek and din. The "El" the lofty track for these demon engines was called, perhaps a shortening of the word "elevated," but I couldn't help hearing it as the Cockney version of the road to " 'ell."

Our timing was impeccable. My trusty lapel watch, recovered

from the scene of my greatest distress during our recent Paris adventure, read half past three. Surely the matinee program would be ending as we arrived, and that was indeed the case.

Pink lifted her pretty but rather straight brows as Irene immediately made for the stage door . . . where we were admitted by an old fellow in antique muttonchops who greeted Irene like the Duchess of Devonshire paying a call on Windsor Castle.

Irene always had made a point of meeting all the humble folk employed around the theater, a practice that had begun during her childhood performing career, no doubt.

"Snub a prima donna," she had told me years ago, "and she will skewer you with ugly looks for at least a fortnight. Idly overlook a stage doorman, or a dresser, or a supernumerary, and you will ever after rest as uneasy in a theater dressing room or on stage as Duncan in Macbeth's castle."

I would have put it differently: Blessed are the meek, for they will never forget someone who remembers them.

"Greetings, Mr. Fisher," Irene hailed her new friend. "Have we come in time to catch Madame Salamandra cooling her heels, and the rest of her inflammatory self, in her dressing room?"

"Certainly, madam. You missed a fine act today, though not as spectacular as the one you assisted in yesterday."

"Act?" Pink sailed through the door on a hail of arrow-sharp questions. "Why are we visiting this Madame Salamandra? A fireproof woman, I presume. And . . . Irene, you were onstage? Performing! On a variety bill? Recently? Irene? Wait!"

Irene bustled along the dim hallway paralleling the theater house's unseen length, turning at the end to take an iron spiral staircase to the lower level at a clip I, and especially Pink, were hard put to match.

I distinctly heard Pink's foot clang against the railing's tight metal curve, and would have tittered, except that my own skirts screwed into a narrow sheath and I almost tripped before I touched the cold brick floor beneath the stage.

Above I could hear muffled thumps and roars. The program was not quite finished.

Irene paused only to knock at the door we had first broached yesterday, and how she knew it from several others that lined this lower hall, I cannot say.

"Yes?" inquired a voice within.

Irene nodded at us with satisfaction to find the quarry at home.

"It's Rena the Ballerina," she caroled back.

Pink's jaw dropped. I must admit the sight was most pleasing to me, and unflattering to her.

"Come in, darling little Rena," the woman's voice cried. "I have been thinking so much of the old days since you called upon me yesterday."

Come in we did, and despite the mirrors, the three of us crowding in made the costume-cluttered dressing room seem the size of a freestanding wardrobe.

Madame rose from her chair, a fluttering vision in apricot and orange gauze, to take Irene's hands in welcome.

"The bill has changed order today, and I am to close, so I haven't much time, but sit where you can and we will chat while we may."

As Pink and I competed with piles of gauze and chiffon to find a sit-worthy surface, Irene installed herself behind Madame Salamandra at the dressing table and finished her coiffure with an expert application of pins and flame-colored silk flowers.

"You look incendiary, my dear," she told the diva of apparent self-immolation. "Did you know that our Tim left suddenly on a contract to tour the West?"

"Tiny Tim? No! Gracious. I hope he remembers his act. Who on earth would hire him?"

"Balambo."

"No! There's hope for us all."

"Speaking of hope, dare I assume that you've recalled anything more about my misspent childhood since I called yesterday?"

Madame Salamandra spun around in her chair to regard her
hairdresser. "That is a better coiffure than I have ever had, but I
must thank you most for saving my life. Dear little Rena." She
took Irene's hands again. "I realized, in afterthought, how careless
we had been in those days. We were so young! I was so young,
barely past seventeen. We seemed a family, all of us young people
who performed. We seemed sufficient unto ourselves, in our peculiar private world that we expected no one else to understand. So
we questioned nothing. You do know what I mean?"

"The young don't think," Irene said quickly, unable to keep a
note of disappointment from her voice.

"No, they don't. Nor did we. We accepted everything as it was."

Irene nodded, pulling her hands away, as if not wanting to
return to that time when questions were not asked.

I returned for an instant to my own childhood, when Shropshire and its ways seemed the bounds of the whole earth. I could
never go back there, never see it as I had so long ago. The thought
almost made me weep even as I understood that I never wanted to
return to Then and There either.

That made one almost an orphan, didn't it? From one's own
past.

"But," Madame Salamandra said, "I did remember a few trivial things after you had left."

"Trivial?" Irene asked guardedly.

Madame Salamandra sat down, facing us, her dyed crimson
hair a curly flame around her slightly age-paled features.

"I remember," she began with a heartwarming smile, this fireproof woman, her eyes only for Irene.

For a moment I was struck dumb. There was no mistaking the
fondness she had felt for the young Irene, it was there in the
warmth of her tone, the delight with which she began her tale. I
too had felt such maternal moments, spinster that I was and had
long been, with some of my young charges when I had been a
governess. There is nothing to match telling avid young faces

something that opens their eyes on the world like flower petals unfolding.

I so hoped Irene would glimpse a lost garden of youth with Madame Salamandra's next words.

The performer went on, slowly, precisely. "I remembered that although the playbill listed you as 'Rena the Ballerina,' we—all of us around the theater, curtain-raiser, opening or closing act, sweeper—we *all* were to call you 'Irene' offstage."

The spell broke, for me, when she pronounced the English name *I-reen-ie* in the vulgar American fashion, *I-reen*.

The spell did not break for Ireenie, or Ireen. "Who? Who demanded I have that name?"

"Someone I hardly recall. I was barely out of childhood myself then, you must understand. I was self-absorbed as only a child of seventeen going on adulthood could be. A woman came around, a very . . . exotic woman."

"*You* call her 'exotic'?"

Madame Salamandra smiled. "I was only a song-and-dance girl then." She hesitated. "She was a bit odd. Such eyes, like stabbing blue flames, and yet . . . her personage was . . . fading. How else can I put it? She made a great impression on me, but I always felt she was not *central* to anything. Now that I think of it again, I see that she had a great, even fierce, personal interest in you, and yet bore a deep sadness in her soul. Now that I am a woman, I pity her to the depths of my heart. But I have so little to pin my feelings on, an instinct, that's all. We all of us were either part of a large theatrical family, like Sophie and me, or solo artists, like you and Tiny Tim, orphans really, foundlings come to join our noisy troupe. We welcomed you, but we never understood you."

"Understanding," Irene said quietly, "is the last thing I have sought in life."

"Understand this," Madame Salamandra said. "That woman

cared for you; she came to see that you thrived. And you did. No child grows up on stage who is not strong."

Pink had breathed not a word during all of this.

This was too good to last, but I too felt a sense of revelation of times and personalities past, of mystery and regret, of something that resounded in every soul's life. Of growing up. And wondering. Always wondering. Maybe there was no growing up, only wondering we choose to forget about. For some reason, I suddenly thought of Quentin.

While I was thus distracted, Pink finally gathered her reporter's wits.

"Are you saying, Madame Salamandra, that Irene's mother came to the theater to check on her?"

The fireproof woman regarded Pink as if she were a cinder that had drifted down a chimney uninvited.

"I am saying that we theater folk are a family, and we play many roles. And some may be 'mother' and some may be 'child,' but we are sufficient unto each other. Miss."

Pink lowered her head and her voice. "I have been both mother and child in my own life," she said levelly, "though I am not theatrical."

Irene laughed suddenly, a sound innocent of tension. "Not theatrical! Pink, my dear Pink! You are the most theatrical of us all." She turned back to Madame Salamandra. "You remember nothing else of this woman?"

"She dressed in black."

"Mourning!"

"Or . . . practicality. I remember I thought of—You will think me foolish."

"I think no memory foolish," Irene said quickly.

"I thought of the widowed Queen of England. Queens of England were mighty high figures to young American girls at the time, you will remember . . . or maybe you will not."

"You thought of Victoria, in widow's black?" Irene pressed.

"Yes. The lady possessed great dignity. And sorrow. I chose to think of her as a dethroned Queen, appearing in our midst in disguise. She seemed to need a champion, like a knight."

"A dispossessed Queen," Irene mused.

"Dispossessed, exactly yes! She seemed to be uneasy here. I remember thinking that such a lady would be uneasy anywhere. I felt sorry for her."

"But not for me."

"You were our darling little dancer, my dear. We spoiled you and watched out for you and made you our own."

"Your own."

Madame Salamandra nodded. "I am so happy to see you again, older, wiser, and well. In the theatrical world people come and go, but they are never forgotten. And you still use the name 'Irene,' how remarkable. She got her way, that woman, for whatever reason she wanted it."

"Irene. Yes."

I saw that "Irene" was most struck by the foreordained nature of her name, she who had never knowingly accepted a foreordained future.

I saw that we all unknowingly carry the ordained wishes of others, even if we know them not. I wondered then what my dead father had truly wished for me, and what he would think of me now, and if that would change anything I thought of myself.

And I had not a single answer to all these questions.

21.

All Fall Down

Her coming has acted like the application of fire to combustible matter.

—THE SAN FRANCISCO HERALD, 1853

We left that place each musing on our own thoughts.

I knew enough of Pink's history to guess that her widowed mother and her stepfather, the deceased judge, figured formidably in them. I knew enough of myself that my parson father and my unremembered mother haunted my recall, and then I thought of Godfrey, my unrelated brother and Irene's husband, and of how much he meant to both of us for different reasons.

What Irene thought, I cannot say. I can never read her thoughts, as she can guess mine, and I often think that is why we get on so well together.

I was hardly aware that we were exiting such a scandalous place as a theater until I dimly heard a burst of applause, and then more clamor.

I put my hands to my ears. Really, this theatrical quest was most unnerving. Still the roar of the crowd penetrated my ears, and I finally realized that I was hearing not enthusiasm, but . . . screams and chaos and shouts and terrible, drawn-out howls!

Irene stopped on the street outside the theater. She clapped her hands to her temples like a touring company Medea.

"*Mein Gott im Himmel!*" she cried out in German, as if performing in a Wagnerian opera. "We have been overconfident."

She whirled to face behind us, reminding me of Lot's wife, frozen into a pillar of salt.

For an instant she stood frozen so, then she dashed back into the theater, past the ticket-taker, ignoring the stage door that had been our previous entree, storming the building like a trooper of another sort than the theatrical kind.

Pink was on her heels and I on Pink's.

Inside, catastrophe choked the air and shortly after, we inhaled the smoke. The house was shrouded with a haze beyond that generated by the men's cigars.

We pushed against the tide of fleeing patrons down the central aisle toward the stage. Flames caught at the curtains like giant, fiery hands, and a massive scrim of smoke billowed over the entire stage. I recalled a parade of theatrical fires in the newspapers, a professional risk of the limelights, apparently.

We coughed, ran, cried, wailed. It was impossible to say who did what. In an instant we knew the same thing: the identical crime had been attempted again, and this time had succeeded.

I shut my eyes against the roiling billows of smoke and pictured Madame Salamandra again amidst her flaming costumes. Naphtha! Irene had named it. Hadn't any stagehand prepared to detect it? Forestall it? Stop it?

I populated the thick haze with ghosts: a woman in black bowed down in mourning, and insisting the tiny child be called "Irene." I glimpsed a warm, living woman enveloped in flame, defying reality, recalling the past in all its soft, melting sorrow.

Could we beat it out again, the fire? Could we reverse ill fortune? Could we retrieve any part of the past that some one, some thing, was determined to forever deny Irene? And me? And Pink?

Could we keep little Rena from watching her entire world exploding in flames?

Stumbling, choking, weeping from smoke and frustration, I stubbed my toes on the dark side of the stage stairs. I reached for Madame Salamandra as I had once dreamed of my own dead mother.

And someone held me back.

Held us all back.

Firemen.

Men in boots stormed the stage, turning it into one vast drum, a tympanum. They dragged long, uncoiling serpents of canvas behind them, that spat streams of water at the theatrical flames.

They smothered flame to smoke.

Amid the smoke, Salamandra lay, ashen from her complexion to her dampened gown, bereft of breath, and of memory. Mother to us all somehow, we three. We grieved, but none more than Irene.

22.

Ashes, Ashes

⤜⧫⤐

When the building caught fire there were lions and tigers running around the streets of New York.... Firemen shot the snakes as an act of compassion as they were being incinerated in their glass cages.... A heroic fireman rescued the 400-pound fat lady by carrying her down a ladder.

—NEW YORK CITY FIRE MUSEUM EXHIBIT ON THE BARNUM & BAILEY

FIRE, DOWNTOWN MANHATTAN, 1865

Irene lit a cigarette and gazed long at the match-flame as if bidding adieu to an old friend, and then shook the lucifer out.

Her first inhalation on the cigarette resembled one, long, heartfelt sigh. Her exhalation reminded me of the macabre "ectoplasm" mediums gagged back at the gullible folk who paid to talk to or see their own dead.

"Two women," Irene said, looking around our hotel parlor, avoiding the gazes of Pink and myself. "Dead. Two sisters. Sophie and Salamandra. What do they have in common? For God's sake, what do they have in common that they should die such horrible deaths only days apart?" She finally focused on one of us: Pink. "Say it is something else other than my own poor self, please, Pink. I do implore."

The brave little newspaper girl was pale and visibly composed herself to speak. The violent death by fire at the New Fourteenth Street Theater had shaken even one who had posed as a sweatshop worker, a prostitute, and a madwoman for the sake of the all-important "story."

"They were both performers in the shadowy world of exotic phenomena," Pink said at last.

"Good," Irene encouraged.

"They were—"

"They were," I interrupted, suddenly afire with insight, "killed by the *means* of their own illusions. Ectoplasm. Fire."

"Better." Irene smiled sadly at me, both proud of my acuity, I sensed, and beyond pride. "And don't forget the odd demise of Washington Irving Bishop. He too died while performing, by the very oddity that had fashioned his early fame, catalepsy. Was there anything else similar?"

"They all performed with you, knew you," Pink riposted, a bit maliciously.

"*You* knew *them!*" I put in, not to be outdone by Pink.

"Not quite," Irene corrected both of us. "They had known me at an age so early I barely recall it."

"There is no denying it," Pink urged. "*You* are the common link."

"It would seem so," Irene agreed, darkly.

Only I who knew her could see how shaken she was by the most recent tragedy.

Each time she inhaled upon that annoying cigarette, I saw the banked fire at the ashen end of the tobacco burn bright. Each time she exhaled, I saw a thin thread of ectoplasm snaking toward the ceiling.

Death by smoke of a sort, and death by fire. What else was there? Water? And then I remembered Merlinda the Mermaid and grew very afraid.

"These are not the first deaths," Pink said, a tone of confession in her voice.

"The first death was in Eden," Irene responded, "when Cain slew his brother Abel out of jealousy. What do you mean by the first death in this case?"

"I mean—" Pink twined her fingers and turned them inside out, so her palms were facing us. I had seen the very same behavior in a schoolroom miss who had been up to something forbidden. "I had meant to tell you sooner, but then you and Nell arrived so fast on the heels of the séance death and there didn't seem to be any time—"

"There is always time for truth," Irene said. Her utterly sober demeanor offered Pink no chance to charm her way out of censure on this issue.

"Sometimes truth must be administered in small doses."

"Not with Nell and myself." Irene crushed her half-smoked cigarette in a crystal tray, then leaned forward to present her case, like Godfrey in court: steady, concentrated, impossible to ignore.

"Pink, I do understand that you feel yourself shabbily treated during our European enterprise. I even understand that a startling new story is as much life's blood to you as a new operatic score would be to me. But murder is not a parlor game, surely you saw that in Paris and beyond. You cannot afford to keep me in the dark in the name of some bizarre game of one-uppance. However these deaths may touch upon my past, no personal interest I might have exceeds my obligation as a human being to see that no more harm comes to anyone. The time is far past when you dare withhold facts or even theories from me, from us. This is much too serious a matter."

Pink cleared her throat. Her writhing fingers turned themselves to point back to herself. "I thought I saw a pattern in the earlier deaths, including one Abyssinia by snake-crushing a few weeks ago, but in truth I thought of it as an excuse."

"An excuse?!" Irene spat out the words, then waited with a patience her tone had not predicted.

"Oh, fudge it, Irene! I suppose I must confess the worst."

"The worst," I repeated faintly. I glanced at Irene. What *had* this brash young woman done now? At least we would learn the scope of the damage, and I was certain there would be damage.

Pink went on in a flood of words: "I was reminded of the related killings in Europe and Baron Krafft-Ebing's book on lust-murders, and I thought it would be interesting, story-worthy, really, to invite Europe's most notable detective to try his hand at the matter."

Irene turned to stone, and then to thunder. "You cannot mean—Pink!"

The girl swallowed, then spit out the truth in one great rush. "I wired Sherlock Holmes as well, saying that America and New York City had its own current onslaught of linked murders. Oh, what a story it will be! An Englishman on the Bowery! It will be the greatest coup since Oscar Wilde toured the States! I imagine Mr. Holmes could command a very active lecture circuit. He would be the toast of the booking agents. I must admit that my fellow citizens are wild for Englishmen with their noses in the air. I could accompany his investigations and report them daily in the *World*. The whole country would be talking about it."

Irene had stood during this recital, and the more enthusiastic Pink grew about the idea, the more Irene took on the aspect of an Amazon queen.

"Pink," she finally said, the name falling like a judgment from her lips. "You do understand that it would be quite a contest to determine which would be the more repelled and appalled by your notion and the harm it would cause: myself or Sherlock Holmes. He would no more embark on your imagined 'lecture tour' than he would climb a tree and throw coconuts on the people gathered below. Nor would I."

"You worked for the Pinkertons once. Surely they would like a connection to a case this juicy."

"We are not discussing the condition of a steak at Delmonico's," Irene answered, referring to the society restaurant that catered to all of upper-class New York, not that I thought any part of New York was upper-class at all, wealthy as portions of it may be. The Four Hundred indeed! In England we had a far shorter and more exclusive list of First Families than that!

"Besides," Irene added more softly, "the Pinkertons no longer have a Female Department and would not appreciate your attempting to join it by default. At least we can rest assured that Sherlock Holmes will hardly cross the Atlantic at your beck and call."

"No." Pink paused, looking as guilty as any of my schoolroom charges ever had. "No," she agreed sadly, "he most definitely would not."

Irene nodded her satisfaction and sat again. I sighed my relief.

I was premature, as I have so often been in my life, which is informed by expectations of civility and restraint, rather than the extremes other people will go to at the slightest excuse.

"You're quite right," Pink went on. "He responded completely negatively to all my wires . . . until I mentioned your involvement."

"What involvement? I was not even on this continent until days ago."

"I explained that the murders involved your youthful years."

"On what evidence?"

"Well, you were active on the popular theater circuit from an early age."

"That is not 'involvement,' Pink. That is coincidence. I cannot believe that Sherlock Holmes would hie across the Atlantic on testimony as flawed as yours has proven to be."

"I did not rely upon his regard for me to bring him to our doorstep. I relied upon his regard for you."

There. It was spoken, what I had known for the past year: *The*

Man harbored a deeply unwholesome admiration for my friend Irene. For my married friend Irene. I had long fought to conceal my secret evidence of such an unsuitable attachment. Now brash Nellie Bly had put it on record. Soon it would be in the newspapers, and then Godfrey would know, the whole world would know, and we would all be ruined.

Irene was not . . . unamused by this revelation.

"His 'regard for me,' dear Pink, is mere professional rivalry. I cannot see why you insist on bringing my enemies down on me when I came here on a mission of trust and a certain obligation to help you out, as you had recently helped me—" Irene finished by shrugging as wryly as a Frenchwoman, much sinned against, poor thing.

"He might actually have the insight to solve these bizarre crimes," Pink offered.

"Here. In America? An entirely different social scene? Has he not already demonstrated himself as somewhat at sea when it comes to the murders of women? I cannot see that this fact has changed; in fact, I cannot see that Sherlock Holmes is at all subject to change. Englishmen are notorious in that regard."

"And Englishwomen?" I demanded.

Her honey-brown eyes flashed me a glance bearing both humor and apology. "Pardon me, Nell, but the English are to the rectitude born, don't you think? Of course you do, and you would be right. The English are always right, is that not so?"

"Well, yes," I was forced to admit, "except when we are wrong. Which is seldom, naturally."

"You cannot fool me, Irene," Pink said hotly. "There's a thundering good story here, worthy of a dime novel practically, and this one I will have. If it agitates your snooty Continental sensibilities, Madam Norton, that is too bad, but that is what you get for embarking on a public life."

"You are so unfair, Pink!" I felt my cheeks warming to match her nickname. "It is you who embarked on a public life, though you hide behind a pseudonym. Irene merely became a performing artist, and then the public life came to her. If you possessed a gift as sublime as her voice you would not need to be stirring up matters in the public print."

" 'Clementine' sublime?" she mocked. "I saw it on a playbill."

"And what did you *write* at an age as early as that? A, B, C?"

"Enough, Nell," Irene urged me. "We are not debating callings or talents, but rather ethics, and people have been arguing that subject since the Greeks." Irene regarded our guest, our former associate, our betrayer.

"You hinge your entire campaign to lure myself—and now Sherlock Holmes, of all unlikely people—to your shores to provide fodder for your newspaper forays, on one unproven fact. That somewhere, somehow, a mother of mine is involved, is imperiled even. You have not made your case."

"Sophie and Salamandra performed with you years ago. They mothered you as best they could, to hear the late Salamandra tell it."

"That makes neither one my actual mother, and you must admit that there's no physical resemblance whatsoever. Even if I grant that they looked out for my young self in a big-sisterly way, each was barely old enough to be my mother."

Pink scowled, an expression too new to damage her fresh face, but, give her enough disappointment and time, and it would.

She untied the artist's folio and drew out a photograph, one obviously taken for journalistic purposes.

"Sophie had a trunk," Pink said. "I don't know where it's gone, or why she kept it, but it had traveled with her for some time."

The word "trunk" made us both sit up. How common trunks are, how long they are kept around after there is any immediate use for them. We both knew what buried and forgotten treasures they may hide, such as enormously valuable violins.

I recalled the treasured instrument Sherlock Holmes's visit to

Neuilly had unearthed from Irene's old trunk. What had Pink found in another such survivor of the years and lives of someone else not known to us?

We fear old trunks, and are fascinated by them, because so many are forgotten, along with what memories lie within them.

Pink smiled sadly. "She was 'born in a trunk,' Sophie said once, when I was arranging for the ill-fated séance. That's an expression in the States, among the theatrical folk, being born in a trunk. Sophie's trunk had been around so long and the surface was so scarred and scratched that she had pasted it over with travel posters and playbills of where she had been when she was younger. The entire surface was covered, these typeset papers acting as crude graffiti. Even now I could smell the faint reek of boiled animal glue. She had used whatever paper was at hand and no longer useful. It looked like something Jules Verne's Philéas Fogg had toted around the world on his one-hundred-and-eighty-day jaunt, had he the room for a whole trunk."

Pink leaned forward to hand a sepia-toned photograph to Irene.

"I had an ace *World* photographer jump through hoops until this one pasted-on letter came up close enough to read."

Irene squinted at the photograph, then rose and took it to the shaded lamp on the desk, where she squinted some more. "Nell, you are good at close-work. Decipher this for me."

I rose and approached the photograph. Penmanship twice as large as life scrawled angularly across the brownish surface, so the ink looked like dried blood. I made out each word, one by one.

"else to do."

Irene nodded at me. She had reached the same interpretation of the spidery pen scratchings. The ink seemed too dry to flow much longer, but I made out: "I leave my—"

I did not say "darling daughter Irene" aloud, but both of us took in this phrase in silence.

"to . . . kinder hands than have dealt with me. I leave my"

And there the scrap of letter, yellowed by the elderly glue dried on its underside, ended.

Irene looked at Pink. "How many 'Irenes' has the city of New York seen in the past thirty years, do you suppose?"

Pink would not be denied her "evidence."

"This scrap was stuck around the side of the lid. On the front was a playbill featuring Tiny Tim and Rena the Ballerina."

"That is proof of nothing, Pink, but your dramatic imagination. No doubt that is an advantage in the newspaper trade, where facts fly fast and loose, but in the detective business, it is even less than the ever-despised coincidence."

"Still, you have a dead mother somewhere."

"I don't doubt it. Many of us do."

"Don't you see? You were left with Sophie and Salamandra. Dixon was their last name. They were as much mother as you were going to get. And they are dead now. Both of them. Murdered. I was going through Sophie's things after her death, when I saw her trunk of many playbills again, and claimed it as a memento."

"A fine bequest, Pink, but if this letter meant anything to Sophie, she wouldn't have pasted it on the lid of a trunk, but kept it secret."

"Perhaps 'darling daughter Irene' had left the country by then. Certainly all contact had lapsed. Why didn't you keep track of the only family you had ever known as a child?"

Irene's usually piercing gaze wavered and moved toward the window. She followed it an instant later to present us with her unrevealing back as she finally spoke again.

"I told you, Pink. I forgot much about that time. Perhaps that was because I had so many more things to remember than a child in an ordinary household would. My 'family' was a constantly changing cast of 'acts,' all unique and interesting, but very transient. I had lines and songs and melodies and dance steps to remember, from earliest babyhood. Is it any wonder that I failed to remember?"

Pink Cochrane shuffled the papers and photograph back into the folio, tying the strings into dejected bows.

"Perhaps you held your breath so long in the role of Merlinda the Mermaid that all memories bubbled up to some unseen surface and burst. I see that I can expect no help whatsoever from you in deciphering your own history." She stood. "So be it. I will print whatever I find, if it is sufficiently interesting, and if it is not, according to you I shall make it up, so it *will* be interesting! Let's make a race of it, Irene, and see who finds the truth first."

Pink spun with a sharp rustle of taffeta petticoats and marched out of the room.

As soon as the heavy door swung to with a bang, Irene stared after her with the amazement of someone watching their own image misbehave in a mirror.

"Bother the girl! She is so determined to make her mark on the world that she never for a moment thinks what harm her careless revelations will cause." Irene began pacing, her own skirts rustling in ceaseless agitation. "We are forced to outthink and outrun her, or face the consequences of being declared to be what she thinks we are."

"I doubt I am included in her agenda, Irene."

"Who knows where her campaign for sensational speculation will stop? And is it possible that Sherlock Holmes leaped to accept her invitation into the contest? Would he cross the Atlantic, Nell, simply to embarrass me? Is our rivalry that petty and impassioned? I would not cross so much as a rain puddle to discommode him. Why should he bother? He did not strike me as a man who put much stake in relations, not even that highly placed brother of his."

"Why would you ask me about the possible movements and motivations of Mr. Holmes? The less I see, or think, of him the better."

"You did, Nell, finesse him into taking you into his confidence during part of our last and most murderous matter."

"I 'finessed' him into using me for a flunky! An errand girl. A magician's assistant at best."

"You learned nothing interesting during your brief association?"

"The varieties and uses of cork? How many disgusting motes a magnifying glass may find upon a cellar floor? That even a madam will stoop to subverting an official investigation?"

"Oh? Madam Portiere interfered with Mr. Holmes's investigation at the *maison de rendezvous?* I didn't know that. How so?"

By now she had sat down again and reverted to her usual pacifier, the cigarette case.

"Really, I'd rather not say. I saw a great deal during that interlude that I know I should not have, and wish to forget, forever!"

"Wishing does not make one forget, or remember," Irene said ruefully, blowing out a thin stream of smoke. I would never see a cigarette smoked in future without recalling's Pink's vivid description of the fatal ectoplasm emerging from Madam Sophie's dying throat.

"Pink was so engaged in her large family's history, and histrionics, growing up," Irene mused, "that she can't imagine a child who is born grown-up, or learning early that nothing stayed the same and was therefore worth remembering."

"In my childhood, everything stayed the same!" I burst out.

"And therefore was well worth putting behind one. The fact that Pink still lives with her mother at the ripe old age of five-and-twenty is very telling."

"I live with you!"

"But I am not your mother, nor would I wish to be."

"Would I be such a bad child?"

"Not at all. Far too good for the likes of me." Irene laughed; the distress of the past few previous minutes had evaporated with her cigarette smoke.

At times like these, I could not begrudge the habit its soothing effects.

I laughed as well. "Pink is such a, an overenthusiastic girl, Irene, like Quentin's lovely niece, Allegra. But unlike Allegra, she is dangerous because she has a public forum. She resembles one of these fanciful figures that is blown about by the wind."

"A whirligig, you mean? How apt, Nell! The entire city of New York strikes me as a whirligig. It has changed so much in less than a decade."

"Then you prefer London."

"I prefer Paris. And, in returning to Paris, as a subject of discussion, I still wish to know what bribe the madam of the *maison de rendezvous* offered our Mr. Sherlock Holmes."

As much as Irene may have wished to know (and it must have been considerably, as she had not let the dropped thread of our conversation lie unnoted for long), I did not wish to tell her.

"He is not 'ours' in any respect beyond that of a mutual nuisance," I said.

Her laughter rang out even heartier, an aria of merriment. I felt quite proud of my small success in improving her mood. None of Irene's apparent reactions could fool me after all these years of association. I knew that this unsettling exploration of her past was perhaps the most difficult journey of her life.

"She offered him money," Irene guessed.

"No."

"Introductions to Parisian men of influence."

"No."

"Escargot and goose liver paté with truffles."

"No! Irene, how can you combine such a vile roster of inedibles? It is more revolting than any atrocity we have witnessed in the past two months."

"Culinary crime can be gruesome," she admitted with a grin. "All right, Nell. I must state the unthinkable. Madam Portiere offered Mr. Holmes her own, fair, fat, grimy hand, so to speak. The madam of the house in exchange for him declaring it free of the taint of murder."

"No! Well, yes, in a way! It was worse than that."

"How could anything be worse than that?"

I pictured the blowsy madam reclining in state on her green satin chaise longue like a frog on a lilypad. "I believe—and I may have misheard, for I was most unhappy to be in her receiving room, or perhaps I should say, her parceling-out room—I believe that she offered him a . . . a brace of companions."

"A brace!? Gracious, Nell, that is the funniest thing I have heard in ages. After all, I only offered him a shabby old violin. And what did he say?"

"Very little. Would that all men could be so firm in resisting temptation. I must give him credit for that."

"Ah, but Nell, that was not temptation. The poor madam misjudged her man. You saw what will tempt him, and even then he resisted."

"The violin, you mean. You've always said he was indifferent to women."

"Not indifferent . . . something other." She smiled at me. "You must have been mortified to witness such a crass attempt at a transaction."

"I was mortified to hear human flesh bartered so casually. I thought the days of slavery were past, even in this benighted nation, but Quentin said it continues all over the globe, despite the British presence."

"Much continues despite the British presence, including yours, Nell," Irene pointed out gently. "You are right in assuming this to be a wicked world. The women in Madam Portiere's house are presumed to be there of their free will, but how free is that will when reasonable work that pays reasonable wages is so hard to find? When other women are forced into such work more directly, that is called 'white slavery.' As irritating as it is to find Nellie Bly taking my own unhappy history as subject matter for a 'story,' I must admit that she does much good in exposing the plight of 'lonely orphan girls,' as she once labeled herself. I just wish that she would leave this 'lonely orphan girl' alone!"

"Did you ever really think of yourself as a 'lonely orphan girl,' Irene?"

"Yes," she said, surprising me by her sober tone, "but that was after I left America to make my way in London. I knew no one, I was a foreigner, and the theater directors were prejudiced against Americans."

I thought back to the day Irene had rescued me, hungry and homeless, from the London streets to feed me on tea and stolen muffins. Was it possible that she had seen my plight and taken mercy because she too was alone and friendless? I had always accepted her as my guardian angel, awed by her energy, her sophistication, her American nerve, and her beauty. I had never considered that such a blessed creature may have needed me as much as I had needed her.

"If Sherlock Holmes dares to show his face on these shores," I said with renewed vigor, "I shall stab him with my hatpin until he slinks all the way back to London."

"Please, dear Nell! You don't wish to damage your very formidable hatpin! I doubt Sherlock Holmes will be such an ingenuous fool as I was to come running at our lady reporter's beck and call. A man who can resist a brace of Paris *filles de joie* is not about to fall victim to any blandishments from Nellie Bly!"

I joined in her hilarity. I don't know which was the more amusing image: Nellie Bly seducing Sherlock Holmes, or him impaled on my foot-long steel hatpin with the Venetian glass parrot finial.

I laughed until my corset stays felt like the medieval torture implement known as an Iron Maiden and my mind's ear could hear Casanova's raucous admonitions to "cut the cackle!"

"That's better," Irene said. "We'll sleep upon Miss Pink's challenge and plot our course in the morning."

23.

The Detective in Spite of Himself

~~~

*The stage lost a fine actor, even as science lost an acute
reasoner, when he became a specialist in crime.*
—DR. JOHN H. WATSON, "A SCANDAL IN BOHEMIA," 1891

SIR ARTHUR CONAN DOYLE

⊰FROM THE CASE NOTES OF SHERLOCK HOLMES⊱

The key to Miss Nellie Bly's little problem is of the simplest
sort that turns upon a single notch or two.

The murderer has left an imprint on the scene of the
first, or possibly second, crime, the strangling of the
medium. (The death of the snake charmer—Watson, are
you listening? This is meat for your hungry pen—may have been
the first, or even the death of the famous cataleptic mind reader.)

My first inquiries among assorted spiritualist mediums produced the hardly earth-shaking news that Madame Zenobia, otherwise known as Sophie Dixon, probably used an assistant, either
in disguise at the table with the genuine attendees, or hidden. No
one had any idea who such a person might be. Such employees
are plucked from the roster of unemployed performers, and come
and go with alarming rapidity. The skills involved are minimal,

although it took some sleight of hand to strangle Madame Zenobia in the presence of witnesses.

I see that telling hand print on the velvet every time I close my eyes. The height of the impression, the depth of the grip, the odd clawlike configuration where the fingertips made their mark . . . and the nails, close-clipped but still cutting into the malleable nap of the rich cloth. . . . These are all the observant detective's dream.

The only problem is finding the exact physical type that matches this indelible impression, and then discerning that person's motive.

Fortunately, I'm the unwanted recipient of all of Miss Bly's researches and theories, so well know the cast of characters, their usual settings, and their connection to the woman whose life sits at the center of these two, and possibly three, deaths so far. Irene Adler, like a Hindu god, has had many incarnations from a young age, including Rena the Ballerina . . . 'Little Fanny Frawley, the petite pistolera' . . . and the pièce de irrésistance, Merlinda the Mermaid. From these playbill phantasms, I can erect the renaissance woman you and I encountered two years ago in St. John's Wood. She is not only a superb vocalist, actress, and intellect, Watson, but also a dancer, a "sharp-shooter" as they say in the Wild West Show, and possibly a swimmer, but even more likely a phenomenon of that vocalist's skill called "breath control." In her case, it was a complete five minutes underwater in a glass aquarium. The mind boggles at what criminal pursuits such a gift could be put to use exploiting.

To find out even more about my quarry, whether it is the currently active murderer or the retired prima donna, I realize that I must haunt the theatrical boardinghouses.

I toy with various amusing disguises to deceive these masters and mistresses of illusion, and with inventing the sort of "acts" I could perform on the variety stage. I am not often offered such a large palette of investigation to work upon. Really, I don't know how you manage, Watson, to wring any excitement at all from my exceedingly staid profession. It is simply a matter of making logical choices.

I could, of course, masquerade as a sharpshooter, although I do not have the long hair apparently necessary to the role in these parts, and no time to grow it, and my disguise kit is left at home with Mrs. Hudson. At any rate, I shan't be able to prove my talents over the gravy and lumpy potatoes of American cuisine, though I could certainly spell out a serviceable B. H. P. on the landlady's flocked wallpaper if required to prove my skill. Somehow that does not have the panache of the V. R. that adorns my Baker Street lodgings. Benjamin Harrison, president, abbreviated, simply does not offer the dash and visual grace of "Victoria, Regina," much less the challenge of a perfectly balanced "V."

I do have my poker-bending trick, which always amazes you, Watson, but that is hardly enough to credibly play the role of strongman, although I could certainly find a convenient poker to distort in a boardinghouse.

Baritsu seems an Oriental martial art too refined to be appreciated by the American taste for raw fisticuffs.

I could always represent myself as a fiddler, but there is scant call for such a skill except in the orchestras, and the role I wish to play bespeaks a solo "act."

Ah. I have it. I will simply play myself and use the elementary tricks that set my dear friend Watson's jaw a-dropping. I will be an "occupation" reader, instead of the usual mental sort. "The Mind-Boggling Body Reader, Shylock . . . *hmmm*, Shakespeare."

Ha! That will be quite a lark, passing myself off as an utterly honest fraud.

24.

Not Her Cup of Cocaine

"I'm taking as a starting point, Nell, Pink's impertinent conclusions about myself. One, that I had a mother."

"Much as I find Pink impertinent, I can't argue with her conclusion in that case."

Irene was enjoying striding about the parlor, as if moving meant taking action, and perhaps it did. "Two, that my mother was American."

"I object," I said, unintentionally imitating some of Godfrey's legal opponents in Court. "Her derivation is not clear. I will posit that she lived in America at the time you were born, as it would be rather silly to have you elsewhere and then make a long, wretched Atlantic crossing simply to deposit you in a trunk near Union Square."

Irene sent me a conspiratorial smile. She much appreciated my joining in her game, and tracking down her possible mother had to be a game; otherwise it was a heartbreak.

"Two," she said, pausing in her pacing. "She lived in America . . . shall we say the East Coast? I was always given to understand that I had been born in New Jersey, Nell, which would be a good deal away from theatrical trunks in New York City's Union Square."

" 'New Jersey' has quite an English ring, of which I heartily approve. We have the Isle of Jersey, you know. Lillie Langtry was born there."

"Precisely why I could not have been. Lillie Langtry and I are utter opposites, therefore it's plain we were born on utterly opposite shores."

She was talking like the Red Queen in Alice in Wonderland, utter nonsense with utter conviction. I joined in, fancying I heard Casanova intoning "Off with their heads!" in the distance.

"Indeed," I concurred. "Lillie Langtry was the mistress of a king. You refused to be the mistress of a king. Lillie Langtry has no performing talent. You have many performing talents. Lillie Langtry sells soap. You sell . . . Worth gowns. Clearly you come from very different places."

"Clearly. On the basis of this incontestable logic we will begin searching for my mythical mother here in New York City, using as a starting clue that ridiculous scrap of a letter glued onto Madam Sophie's trunk. We will take that miserable scrawl as Gospel, Nell, and we will proceed as if it were Holy Writ. I am determined to come up with a mother of mine to present to Miss Nellie Bly. I hope she is . . . someone most unlikely. In fact, I believe that we can arrange for it to be so. I will follow the path of ludicrous logic that our friend Pink has laid out for us, and I will see that it points to a candidate so outrageous that even Pink will not dare print the supposition."

I clapped my hands. "You will build an incontrovertible case, that is—"

"That is sheer nonsense. Anything may be proved, Nell, if you stretch to do so. By the time I am through, Pink will deeply regret her expedition into my past, and hopefully refrain from bothering others with her meddling."

"You are truly angry with her," I said in a more sober tone.

"I am angry with the world of the sensational press, that will not let even the poor dead women in Whitechapel and Paris rest in peace. It is admirable that Pink has made her way so well in that world, but her zeal makes her forget the privacy that every human being is due. Since I am here . . . since we are here, we are in an admirable position to teach her that lesson."

"You don't . . . think that you really are the 'darling daughter Irene' in that letter, do you?"

"I? I assure you I must have been an infant with a lusty set of lungs that would have tried the patience of the deaf. I was no doubt, Nell, the unforeseen result of an immoral alliance between a chorus girl and some would-be man-about-town. We must be realists about that, even, or especially, you."

"Is that why you are so unlike the other women of the performing sorority, whose first role is mistress and whose stage exploits are only secondary?"

Irene sighed. "I don't know, Nell. I only know that I have a most fierce hostility toward selling myself, any part of myself, even my past."

"Then you are more nobly born than most in this day and age," I said stoutly.

She smiled at me then, a sad, tender, almost (dare I say it) maternal smile. "You have come a long way in dealing with the unpleasant facts of life, Nell. I am not sure if I am entirely happy about that. This last trial—"

"I am now less likely to believe the surface of anything, that is true," I said quickly, reassuringly. We both had so much to protect the other from now. "I should not like to be less able to deal with the realities of life than Nellie Bly."

"You mean Pink."

"I mean Nellie Bly, who goes into madhouses and sweatshops and brothels, all in the name of good, one must believe. I wish she were posing as a prostitute now, instead of plaguing you with figments of a past that matters to nobody! What is her purpose?"

Irene sat upon the upholstered chair and picked up the cigarette case. "You have asked a key question. She is terminally curious, for one. And she has a hot heart for the downtrodden."

"You and I are not downtrodden!"

"And she likes to set forces in motion . . . one antagonistic segment of society against the other. The working poor against the slumlords; the unprotected woman against the masher, the seducer. It makes for strong stories, Nell, and she is ambitious to both change the world and women's downtrodden role in it."

"Is that bad?"

"Not necessarily, but sometimes it is unmerciful."

For a moment Irene reminded me of Portia pleading the case of the merchant Antonio. I wondered why an opera had never been made of *The Merchant of Venice*; Irene would make a superb Portia . . . and then I hoped that Mr. Sherlock Holmes had not come to the same conclusion and drafted Sir Arthur Sullivan and Mr. Wilde to accomplish that very feat—*The* Man was indefatigable!

But so was I!

"We will take this search seriously, then?" I asked.

"Deadly seriously." Irene shook out her lucifer and drew thoughtfully on the lit cigarette in her hand. "However much Pink intended to draw me into an embarrassing hunt for my own American antecedents, she has involved us in a nefarious case of multiple murder. Though my youthful memories are dim, I do . . . feel very deeply about Sophie and Salamandra. And Tim.

I did know them, as much as my infant self was capable of, and I am beginning to remember even more. Pink is right that *something* is bedeviling these people from my past. So, under the . . . guise of hunting my supposed mother, we will be able to investigate the thread that connects the two sisters' terrible deaths. I believe someone who hates their professions is at work here. They were slain by their own illusions, by their own tricks, if you will, turned tables upon them. Someone clever is behind this, and someone quite mad."

I shivered a little, I couldn't help myself.

"My dear Nell!" Irene was leaning forward, wreathed in smoke like Hamlet's father's ghost. "Perhaps such a subject is too much for you after Paris and Prague and Transylvania."

"No. You misunderstand. I find myself eager to stop such madness, as we did so magnificently in Paris and Prague and Transylvania."

She eyed me skeptically, and I was much flattered. No one had ever taken me seriously enough before to suspect me of prevarication. Or boasting.

"I only hope that Sherlock Holmes is not taking Miss Pink's summons seriously," she added, settling back into her chair like an irritated dragon, with a temperamental huff of smoke.

"Oh, I doubt that," I said, although I did not. When it came to Mr. Sherlock Holmes, no one could be more skeptical than I. Clever and mad killers were exactly *The* Man's cup of tea. Or cocaine.

25.

Playing Parts

❧

*All the world's a stage, and all the men and women
merely players.*
—SHAKESPEARE, *AS YOU LIKE IT*

Once my friend Irene Adler Norton resolved to involve herself in a "case"—even if it was her own!—she was as committed to it as a diva is to an opera role.

Many mistake an operatic performer for an actor,
when, in fact, many gifted vocalists who perform in grand
opera are far from actors.

Irene explained to me once that a singer is a technician, a living
instrument. The playing of any instrument involves emotion as
well as expertise and musicality, but none of this requires acting.

Acting uses the emotions as a musician uses an instrument and
is quite a different discipline, she said. She herself was a singer-
actor. Or an actor-singer, depending on the role. Her new "closet
opera" about the wives of Henry VIII was custom-made for a
singer-actor like herself, which was why she was so excited about
the project.

Precisely why I was so *un*excited about the project: it had been initiated by Sherlock Holmes! Considering this while thinking of Irene's definitions of performance, I had to decide whether Sherlock Holmes was a detective-actor, or an actor-detective. He thrived, as Irene did, on disguise, on reshaping himself to deceive others. This was more than an exercise in vanity, although it had that aspect.

It was a certain natural defense, like the chameleon's, that permitted each of them to penetrate rungs of society that would never accept them on their apparent aspects. Thus I had seen Irene masquerading as a rather befuddled old woman, when she was the exact opposite, and Mr. Holmes as a dashing and romantic figure, when he was the utter opposite of that! Did such charades release the *actor*'s urge to play the Other to perfection? Or did it release the *detective*'s need to disguise his or her function to perform the role required?

Ah, I was what I was, and only and always what I was, neither actor nor detective. Except that I seemed to be changing anyway, although I would fool no one.

I suppose my role was to record the alterations of others, and admire or admonish, as the case demanded. I was still a governess, though my "charges" were presumed adults, and I was becoming an unreliable observer, because the act of observing had become the art of acting, even though my only role was myself.

Enough! Only Casanova could make sense of such speculations, and that was because he never made sense!

Thus the next day I found myself playing the perfect amanuensis in the cluttered rooms of Professor Marvel.

"Rena?" this elderly and rotund individual had exclaimed when Irene and I came knocking unannounced on his boarding-house door.

The area surrounding Union Square alternated theaters and

halls with boardinghouses, and in one of them Professor Marvel was waiting for us as for a cue.

"My dear Merlinda," he added, bowing to the fact of Irene's serial identities in the theatrical world. "I never forget a face."

"Or anything else, for that matter," she said, accepting his gesture of invitation to enter his rooms.

I had indeed come very far, for I no more blushed at barging into strangers' living quarters, even if they were men, than I did at mounting the steps of an omnibus.

"My goodness, you are a woman grown. Am I that old?" he added plaintively.

I studied our host (though he had offered no refreshment, which makes him *not* a host). This tall, gangly man, rather round in the middle, had an intelligent face that was also foolish. Perhaps it was the eternally raised eyebrows, the wide eyes, the slightly apologetic smile.

This was a man who would not intimidate in any arena, save that Irene had told me that he knew more than any man in the world and demonstrated that fact nightly at various theatrical houses around New York. He had also been, she said, her sole tutor.

"I heard," he said, sitting and flipping up his jacket skirts quite laboriously, "that you had abandoned us for Europe."

"I sang opera abroad," Irene said modestly. "It was my first passion."

He lifted a professorial finger. "I demur, my dear. It was your last passion. You had always sung quite exquisitely from the age of three on, but it wasn't until you were introduced to the maestro that it became clear that your voice was born to evoke bravas from the crowned heads of Europe, or even Newport. But what am I thinking of? Two lovely ladies have called. Would you like a cookie?"

I looked around the neat but shabby room, sniffed a decidedly stuffy scent, and decided I would rather eat at a public restaurant, which for me was an enormous concession.

"Thank you, no," Irene said, with that tact and swift assessment so typical of her. "I am here on a sentimental journey, to revisit the scene of my youth."

"Odd," he said with a foolish frown. "You were never a sentimental child. I don't see why you should start now."

"What was I?" Irene asked, so lightly that I realized the answer was important to her. "I admit that my early years are a blur. I seem to have been a motherless child."

From the way she intoned the words "motherless child," I sensed that she was putting them into a context I could never understand.

Professor Marvel got her meaning at once.

"Indeed you were, dear girl, which is why we all took you under our wings . . . however well our wings were suited to deal with a young and precocious creature like yourself. Sophie and Salamandra dreamed up your infant acts, for money was needed to keep you and we all earned little enough to keep ourselves in those days. Luckily, you were an amenable child, and quite versatile. Indeed, sometimes *you* kept *us*!"

"I belonged to no one? No one paid for my keep?"

"You were an independent lass from the first, and quite a pet of ours, I might add. The theatrical life is a solitary one, save for the lucky couples who enter it, like Houdini and his Bess. Yet we are a family in a larger sense, and someone was always available to take you in hand when needed."

"But why was I among you? Surely someone claimed me?"

Professor Marvel looked down at the buttons on his coat. "Do you know that my performing coat weighs forty pounds? That it contains sixty pockets filled with fifteen-thousand such bits of knowledge I have written down and can grasp in an instant? That I can answer any questions from the audience with a scrap of paper I can lay my hands upon in a split second? I am a walking encyclopedia. I know everything that a man or a woman in the audience can ask. But I cannot answer your question. Ask the women."

"They are dying. Sophie and Salamandra gone, and Abyssinia the snake charmer."

"Acts die, little Rena."

"These acts ended in murder," Irene said.

"Such tragedies, but does it matter how we die? We are old troopers and play a command performance for death when called."

"I fear that these deaths had something to do with me, with my childhood, when I performed with you all."

"And who would know to trace you through those long-forgotten years, more than two decades, my little chameleon? You yourself evolved through a half dozen stage names before the maestro took you in hand."

"The maestro? Who was he?"

"You don't remember?"

Irene passed a gloved hand in front of her face, almost brushing the extravagant brim of her hat.

We women had gone from modest perched bonnets to shadowing, wide-brimmed hats in a year or two, it seemed, and had not caught up with the latest demands of our attire. Fashion was like that, a taskmistress who ever demanded new skills and tricks.

"I don't remember." Irene sounded alarmed by her own confession. "Why have I forgotten so much of my childhood?"

"You grew up too fast." Professor Marvel bit his bloodless lip. "I didn't approve of you apprenticing that man, but the women were all for it. It was your chance to perform for the legitimate stage, they said, as if we were all illegitimate."

"No!" Irene was revolted by the old man's rejection of his own history. "I was the illegitimate one. I must have been. The wages of sin whom no one would claim."

"I paid no attention to that. Let the women worry about it. There was—"

"Was what?"

"A . . . woman who came around. Gowned in black. A widow? Now that I think of it, she showed an interest in you."

"Was she the only one?"

"No, my dear. You were adorable! The women in the audience all gathered around you, cooing like pigeons on rooftops or on those damn telephone poles that line the streets today. Of course there were none of those wires overhead when you were a lass. We kept you safe, never fear. You were our ward."

"But who gave me to you? Someone must have."

The old man shook his head. "I know everything, did you know? But I don't know that. I don't think I much cared." He smiled his foolish-wise smile. "You were a gift, as well as gifted. I can't recall that you were ever any trouble. Or if you were, the women kept it to themselves. They cherished you. Our lives don't allow much for routine domestic arrangements. You were our little orphan girl, and we made sure you never noticed it."

Irene sat back with a strange expression. "Maybe that's why I never remembered much."

"You? Not remember? There wasn't a melody or a dance step any of them could show you that you couldn't repeat exactly almost at once."

Ruefulness passed over her features like a mask. "And I remember bits of them today, now that you mention it. I meant that I seem to have forgotten the important things: whys and wherefores, even some of the whos."

"*Hmmm.* I don't know what to advise someone suffering from forgetfulness." He leaned forward suddenly, his watery blue eyes alight. "I know! Wee Wilhelmina. She was of an age with you. You often shared a bill with her and her twin sister Winifred, especially when you were younger and had not yet branched out into your array of eclectic acts, and before you began to concentrate on vocal studies. I don't know who decided that, come to reflect. One of the women, no doubt. They made our rambling lives into a semblance of order. Look up Wilhelmina. You do remember her?"

Irene shook her head, too embarrassed to voice her demur.

"I do," I put in. Her startled face snapped to view me. "I noticed the names on some of the playbills we've seen lately, along with an illustration of an impossibly wasp-waisted young woman in flesh-colored tights. At least I presume they were flesh-colored, the drawing was in black and white, of course."

Irene turned back to Professor Marvel. "Is she still performing?"

"Heavens, no! There was some dust-up even before you left the stage. Something the men didn't know about and the women wouldn't say. But I did hear later that she'd snagged herself a very wealthy man. Old Gilfoyle, titan of boxcars. Lives on Fifth Avenue and Fifty-second Street now, like all the gentry rushing to build and inhabit mansions in the city. I guess she'd remember you if you called upon her, and, being of an age with you, she might recall just those things you have forgotten."

"Wilhelmina, not Winifred," Irene repeated the name.

"Yes, Willie goes by Mina now. You were always quite the actress. I guess you could pretend to remember her well."

"Indeed," Irene agreed readily. "Especially if she wears flesh-colored tights."

Irene was unusually quiet as we walked back to our hotel. When I tasked her for being such a taciturn companion, she merely nodded.

It was only in sight of the Astor's familiar façade that she spoke. "I rummage in my memory and it is like stumbling blind through someone else's attic, Nell, dark and murky with unrecognizable shapes lurking in the shadows. I remember my life in England and hence forward as if every act and scene were recorded on stereopticon cards, but this, all these years, I can't believe I have . . . mislaid so much of my childhood."

"No doubt as you moved into the respectable theater you naturally wished to forget your vaudeville roots."

"Ah! You recognize a 'respectable theater' now. You certainly did not believe in any such thing when I met you."

"I had not seen much of the unrespectable theater until now! Compared to this, singing in a Gilbert and Sullivan operetta chorus is the next thing to joining the heavenly choir for respectability. I'm not at all amazed that you forgot the parade of improbable personalities marshaled through your childhood and youth. Nor can I imagine that any mother worthy of the name would have abandoned her offspring to such a life."

"Yet I came out of it . . . how would you describe me, Nell, when you met me?"

"Oh, intimidating! Very. Amazingly observant and quick to act. A great lady of fashion, a defender of the downtrodden, and a woman of charity and high culture . . . I mistook you for a lady of quality. Of course that was all sleight of hand, most of it. You were as poor as I, your dazzling toilette was fashioned from flea market scavenging, and your grand airs were all acting."

"I do not sound much different from the young woman who had graduated from the *Ecole de Vaudeville*. Do you know why that French word for a performance bill has come into fashion? Because it sounds more respectable!" Irene's laugh faded into a sigh. "So how was I able to so well mimic all those fine, elevated, ladylike qualities, if I came from such an environment as this?"

"I don't know, Irene. Natural intelligence, I would presume. And moving to London couldn't help but polish your manners."

"I see. I owe it all to the English."

"Perhaps I have had some small influence on you during all these years."

"And I on you also!" she riposted, her eyes glittering like the amber earrings swinging from her earlobes. "This will no doubt stand us both in good stead when we gussy ourselves up and call upon Mrs. Heywood Gilfoyle, formerly of the New Fourteenth Street Theater, at her city seat on Fifth Avenue."

She linked arms with me as we swept into the hotel lobby through the double doors the liveried doorman held wide for us.

"Gussy?" I asked weakly. It did not sound at all like a refined thing to do.

"An American expression, dear Nell, for dressing to impress. You will be hearing a good many American expressions, I fear."

Gussy. Irene was right. I did fear.

26.

No Place Like Home

On the first floor are the grand hall of tessellated marble, lined with mirrors; the three immense dining rooms ... parlors and reception-rooms. ... Other parlors on the floor above ... Fourth floor——servant's rooms in mahogany and Brussels carpet, and circular picture-gallery; the fifth floor contains a magnificent billiard room, dancing-hall, with pictures, piano, etc., and commands a fine view of Fifth Avenue.

—JAMES McCABE, *LIGHTS AND SHADOWS OF NEW YORK LIFE*, 1872

During my long association with Irene Adler I had entered, not always invited, places no humble parson's daughter would ever expect to see, including Ferrieres, the Rothschilds' sprawling country house outside Paris, Prague Castle, and Sarah Bernhardt's overstuffed Parisian parlor, which was probably the most dangerous, given its population of Big Cats and even bigger snakes.

Yet my powers of description balk at any representation of the new-built mansions that line New York's Fifth Avenue like the cliffs of Scylla and Charybdis in the Straits of Messina, which were the downfall of many an ancient Greek sailor.

Some, with their classical pediments and marble-faced fronts, more resembled museums or other massive public buildings than private residences. In amongst them crouched the sober brownstone façades of "older" homes built twenty, thirty, and forty years before. There are sheep sheds in Shropshire that are far "older" than that, yet no one makes pilgrimages to see them, as we did now.

Irene had insisted we leave early enough to capture one of the rare hansom cabs. I think she felt the more lumbering gurney was not suitable transport for calling upon a former performing peer who was now part of the highest society New York City had to offer (which could not be much, I thought with a silent sniff, if everything was so intolerably *new*!). No wonder a woman with an undistinguished—one could even say scandalous—background could now queen it over the intersection of Fifth Avenue and 52nd Street.

I had no doubt that the edifice we faced was costly beyond belief, but it was also as four-square as a prison, looming as it did five stories over the surrounding trees and more modest two-story buildings. All brownstone, it was a great architecturally undifferentiated dark stone mass pierced by enormous rounded-top windows draped in luxurious fabrics. The way the pale draperies swagged to right and left reminded me of lily-of-the-valley flowers, an oddly delicate comparison for such a formidable mansion.

The flat roof was topped with as many chimneys as a factory, thick enough to resemble stovepipe hats for giants. Some spindly-by-comparison stone finials at front and back were the only decorative relief from the severe and even foreboding architecture.

We stared at it, taken aback, for I was reminded of Jane Eyre's oppressive school, when our coachman leaned his face near the trap to take Irene's coins.

"Awesome, ain't it, ladies? The wickedest woman in New York built it, but she's long gone to her just reward, though some will say they see mysterious veiled ladies coming and going through

the side basement door to this day. There was death done within,"
he added with a leer.

"Ghosts?" I asked in all-too-obvious dismay even though I
realized that the hack driver simply wished to thrill obvious visitors to this shore with unsavory stories.

"So much the better," Irene said briskly, shutting the inside
trap door so I could hear no more ghoulish tales. "We are pursuing the ghosts of my past. I would be delighted to interrogate a
ghost from the right era, but doubt we shall encounter a one, even
from the wrong era."

Irene adjusted her pale cream gloves after we descended from
the hansom's foot-and-a-half step down, met by a liveried valet's
own white-gloved hand supporting our arrival and preventing us
from making an entrance that resembled the exit of leaping lem-
mings.

Irene, ever a master of social nuance when she wanted to be,
nodded graciously at the man without quite looking at him.

"Ah," she murmured, surveying the imposing façade. "It
reminds a bit of dear Monte, save that the stone is not white,
but . . . brown."

Save, I thought ungenerously, *that Monte Carlo is a sunny
Mediterranean city of green palms and white stone . . . and New
York is a mousy gray-brown metropolis populated by stunted trees and
foraging goats in some neighborhoods!*

"I wired Mrs. Gilfoyle yesterday. She is expecting me." At this
Irene opened her magnificent cigarette case, the diamond "I"
winking in the exceptionally broad daylight of the famous
avenue, and extracted a visiting card. It was on thick cream linen,
featuring a beautiful cursive script and was quite lovely, save that
it was written entirely in French!

I watched the valet's eyes flick respect at the blue enameled
case with its proud initial "I" of diamonds, yet blanch a bit at the
French flowing over the calling card's prim surface.

"This way, Madam Adler Norton. Madam," he added with a

bow to me, leading us up a long, broad set of steps to a pair of entry doors that would have done honor to a cathedral.

We passed through a palatial hall of tessellated marble and were ushered into a side parlor that more resembled a royal funeral parlor in terms of sober magnificence. There we were to wait.

Irene and I perched on black-satin-upholstered chairs, catching glimpses of our multiple selves reflected in the mirror-fitted and gilt-framed wainscoting.

I couldn't help blessing Monsieur Worth, the English-born founder of French couturier, for making Irene his *mannequin de ville*. This arrangement had swelled her wardrobe with the latest Worth creations, to wear for a season and return, the point being that her beauty and cachet in Paris made her a subtle walking advertisement for the "man-milliner's" priceless wares.

Today she wore the charming black lace fichu wrap that barely took any packing space and exquisitely dressed up any ensemble. It was a delicate sleeveless and ruffled tunic caught tight at the waist and ended in a peplum both front and back. Through its tracery peeked a pale Persian blue gown with brocaded hem and three-quarter-length sleeves. Her hat was black straw chosen for the fact that she could match its trim to any of the four gowns she had packed for the voyage.

I had been persuaded to don one of the unconstructed Liberty silk gowns Irene had taken the liberty of ordering for me without my knowledge in London. It could hardly compete with any Worth costume, but it was new and fashionable and I was given to understand that the society women of New York coveted anything of that nature from London and Paris. My source was Irene, of course.

"I am glad we dressed to kill," I confessed in a whisper that the room's hard surfaces turned into a small echo. "I feel as if I'm visiting Napoleon's tomb!"

"No more dead bodies on this trip, Nell, please," Irene whispered back.

"And what is this 'calling card'? You never used such a thing in Paris."

"It is an improvisation, Nell. One cannot visit a society matron like Mrs. Gilfoyle without the usual ceremonials."

"Very impressive, but I doubt she reads French! What on earth does it say?"

"It, um, gives my name and an introductory phrase, *'Les six femmes d'Henri VIII.'*"

I thought deeply to translate the three, key words. "Irene! You have had cards printed up for that loathsome closet opera foisted upon us by that dreadful detective! When on earth did you do so? There was no time before we left Paris to print such a frivolity."

"What I handed over was a sample I wrote myself on the ship on the way over. There was much time to waste."

"I must say I am impressed by your penmanship under the strains of being tossed upon the butter-churn of the Deep. It looked like the finest copperplate printing. Where did you learn such a skill?"

She shrugged. "It must have been at the New Jersey and New York 'Schools for Scandal,' the vaudeville stage. There was a woman, I now recall, who could write simultaneously with her fingers and toes and also her mouth."

"Good gracious! She couldn't have done that unless she appeared on stage *unshod*!"

"So she did. I do distinctly recall the long wands with pens attached sticking up from between her toes and fingers like reeds."

"Is there nothing people will not do on stage?"

"Nothing less than they will do offstage."

"Mesdames."

A man in evening dress, in other words, the butler, bowed from the threshold. We rose and followed him up a staircase grander than the Paris Opera's, and that is saying something to anyone who has ever traversed that ocher and russet marble-lined passage to perhaps the most elaborate performance building in the world.

When the staircase forked at the first story before a statue of some Renaissance figure, we took the right bank to another richly carpeted passage wide enough for the Cossack cavalry and Buffalo Bill's envisioned Rough Riders to perform quadrilles in.

At last we were ushered into what passed for a private chamber in this mausoleum, a sitting room. Sitting in it was a woman of about our age wearing a Worth receiving gown. I was appalled to find myself developing such a keen eye for the frivolity of fashion.

She stood to rustle forward three steps, no more. "Madam Norton?" she addressed me, thus guaranteeing my shocked silence for at least twenty seconds. During it, her eyes shifted and finally settled on Irene. "I do not know your name, but you look vaguely familiar."

"We were schoolmates," Irene said smoothly.

Confusion clouded that cool white brow with the russet hair waved richly back from it like fur from ivory.

"Indeed?" our hostess said. "I cannot contest you, for my memory of names and faces is abominable. All my friends and family know my failing, though it might seem rude to an . . . acquaintance."

We had not yet been asked to sit and we were not about to be.

Irene glided across the Aubusson carpet to perch uninvited upon a tapestry-upholstered Louis XIVth armchair.

"I should say," she said while seating herself, which required a great deal of flaunting the luxurious folds of Maison Worth around her erect figure, "that we were mates at the school of tiny thespians, rope-dancers, and assorted marvels of physical and mental oddities."

"And you are from France?" Mrs. Gilfoyle demanded, a touch of fishwife in her oh-so-cultivated drawing-room drawl, as she glanced again to me.

"Paris," Irene corrected her. "My friend Miss Huxleigh and myself were called to the States by our enterprising acquaintance, the reporter Nellie Bly."

Again that confusion rippled over our hostess's countenance and then the truly outrageous thing Irene had said finally registered on her face. Where "Irene Adler" was forgotten, the name of "Nellie Bly" made Mrs. Gilfoyle stiffen. "Nellie Bly! Such a low, common name, and not her real one either. She is one of those sensation-seeking hoydens, always exposing the ugly side of life."

"Exactly. That's why she called us here. She is currently exploring the arena in which you and I both grew up, I'm told. Surely you remember Rena the Ballerina and Merlinda the Mermaid? I seem to recall twin-sister performers called Wilhelmina and Winifred."

Mrs. Gilfoyle turned her back on us (and a lavishly laced and bowed back it was, a thoroughgoing Worth) to move as briskly as her heavy skirts would allow to the door.

"Turning tail and running," Irene murmured to me in a broad American twang. "My, my."

The woman shut the double doors with her own soft white hands, then turned to lean on them as if to hold them shut, or perhaps to hold us in, prisoners in this huge, dark, ugly house that was lined like a costly stone jewel box nevertheless in draperies of extravagant fabric. Like a jewel box, or like a coffin. *Ghosts*, I thought again.

"I am called simply 'Mina' now," our hostess said, but her tone was unfriendly. "Who are you, Madam, and what do you want?" she demanded.

"I am exactly who my card indicates: Irene Adler Norton. I admit that I don't remember you very well, but we both have changed a great deal since our youth, I imagine, and I have it on good authority that we performed at many of the same theaters, often on the same playbill."

"And now you've learned that I married well and wish to blackmail me with my past."

There was a pause. Irene put a forefinger to her chin in a stage-coy manner I had never seen before.

"Oh," said she sweetly. "I hadn't thought of that. I suppose I could, couldn't I?"

"I remember you now." Mrs. Gilfoyle pushed herself off the support of the doors and came stalking back toward us like one of Sarah Bernhardt's Big Cats, dragging a twitching train of taffeta and brocade behind her like a glamorous tail. "You were that jill-of-all-trades down the playbill from me."

Irene lifted an eyebrow. She and I had both fanned through our collection of playbills. Irene, whatever her *nom de performance*, had always been listed *above* Miss Wilhelmina Hermann.

However, Irene was not about to debate billing when she had important information to glean.

"Indeed," she said with winning modesty, "you were always above me. I do remember that. But I remember so little else, and I am on a quest to recapture what I've lost. Are you . . . a mother?" Irene put all the hearts and flowers that were in her into the last line.

"No." Mrs. Gilfoyle stopped in her tracks as if struck by a verbal bullet. "Not . . . yet."

Irene, never one to miss when she had blundered, rushed on. "Oh, my dear, I have no children myself. Yet. Nor Miss Huxleigh here, although that is to be expected. I suppose. At any rate, I have reached an age—past thirty, I confess, though a young thing like you may not be able to share my concern—when I yearn to know the mother I never did before."

Mrs. Gilfoyle, despite the blatantly inaccurate flattery as to age Irene had ladled on, grew paler and paler as Irene's heartfelt speech continued. My actress friend was skillfully plucking every heartstring within fifty feet—indeed, I thought again of my own mother lost so soon after my delivery and felt tears spring to my eyes—but everything she said, every artful pause, every human wellspring she appealed to, only worsened her case in our hostess's eyes.

While I was always willing to defer to the sterling theatrical instincts in Irene's character, I was also more than willing to step in and correct a faulty course.

"Mrs. Gilfoyle," I said, speaking up for the first time and thus capturing her attention as though I were a Sarah Bernhardt. She who speaks last is listened to first!

"Mrs. Gilfoyle, we are sorry to intrude, and, believe me, any discomfort to you is our last wish, but my dear friend has suddenly realized that she was an orphan tossed upon the stormy bosom of life. Now she belatedly yearns to know something more about the woman who must have borne her. The trail is cold, the facts . . . few. Do you remember, from that time both you and she wish to . . . *must* forget, for you both now enjoy—may I say?— sterling present lives, and my dear Irene is a noted diva on the Continent."

Here I stumbled and paused, for my last phrase had returned the icy fire to our hostess's eyes. Somehow I, too, had blundered.

"I appeal to your best nature," I said, rushing on. "Is there any information, any fact, you can impart about Irene's dear lost mother? Surely there was some hint—?"

"No." Mrs. Gilfoyle stalked toward us again like Sarah about to take poison in front of the limelights. There was that kind of dark determination in her. "I'm sorry. I can't help. I cannot help. I cannot even become a mother myself—"

This last was ripped from her like a breech-birth (which I had attended in my youth). I recognized in those few unwilled syllables an inconsolably awful, breathtaking pain.

She sank onto a chair (all indeed she could do in the convoluted gown she wore, all corsetry and spiraling draperies).

I was instantly reminded of Bernhardtian melodrama. Perhaps the French actress was so acclaimed because she touched the emotions of her age. She evoked privileged, even powerful women, who were yet denied the power of making another in their own image.

Irene had never referred to her and Godfrey's hopes for parenthood, or the lack of them. They were two supremely individual people and it was hard to imagine them fixated on something other than each other. But then, they were still newly married, and perhaps did not require an outside diversion. Unless it was a mystery, or myself. Or perhaps I was a mystery to them. And to myself.

Irene waited, then spoke softly, in a voice almost like a lullaby. "Is your own mother still alive?"

"No," the woman answered in a dead voice. "I ultimately was . . . abandoned to whomever would take me, like you."

"And you never knew of anyone, any woman, with an interest in me?"

"They were all interested in you!" she burst out, her face twisted with deep emotion. "Why do you need a mother? Why does anyone? Or need a child? But I do. Here. And now." She sighed, rested her face upon the spread fingers of one white hand. "There was," she said slowly, "a woman who came around to see us. When we were very young things. Dressed all in black. Like a widow. She rode in a coach with four white horses. Do you suppose she was our lost mother? Do you suppose we were . . . sisters?"

Her slightly sinister singsong tone sent goose bumps up my arms. I sensed a sorrow deeper than the Atlantic ocean that had tossed me upon it like a wayward seagull and I detected something more. A taunt almost.

Irene's voice softened even more in response. "No. True answers are never so symmetrical as that. And you *had* a twin sister. What more can one want? A woman in black, a black widow. I will . . . look for her. And if I find a trace of your own origins—"

"Forget them!" Mrs. Gilfoyle pushed herself upright by the

arms of her chair, shaking off her mood of a moment before as a woman might dislodge a suddenly discovered spider in her skirts. Her white-knuckled hands looked as chill and hard as alabaster on the richly colored upholstery. "Forget me. Forget your past, if you want my advice. Don't call on me again."

She finally stood on her own two feet, stiffened, and left the room, leaving the doors flung wide, like windows meant to let birds out of cages.

Irene took my elbow. "Well, we've learned that there is something to learn, I suppose. Come. Let's leave this palatial hothouse. There is a black spot on the resident rose that I don't want to catch. Remind me never to envy wealth and privilege."

"You never did," I pointed out as she hustled me down the extravagant staircase like a fairy godmother dragging Cinderella away from the ball and a certain eligible prince. I couldn't resist looking wistfully back, for . . . whom?

"Remind me to remember my own advice," she muttered as we whisked past the butler and the valet and out onto the crowded, crude New York City streets.

"Ah." Irene inhaled deeply of horse manure. "Fresh air."

27.

Small Luck

⚬⚭⚬

Thumbelina, Thumbelina, Tiny little thing
Thumbelina dance, Thumbelina sing. . . .

We returned to Professor Marvel, who professed to know everything, again.

"I am always ready to welcome lovely ladies," he said gallantly, "but I don't recall the name or identity of this woman in black. Of course the theater is full of overly dramatic women, and we veterans learn to overlook almost any eccentricity. I believe only another woman would have noticed such a visitor, and with Sophie and Salamandra gone . . . they were your stage mothers, little Irene, so much as you ever required one. You were hardly ever a child, you know, merely a small independent person. That is why it was so odd when you abruptly left the stage to study with the maestro. None of us could imagine how you kept body and soul together while you committed to developing your voice, although we did soon learn when that voice of yours took you abroad."

Irene thought for a moment. "I worked for the Pinkertons at

that time, I remember. The founder was alive then and he was eager to maintain a female detective branch. Such work suited me, for it came and went, fast and then slow, and there was plenty of time to schedule lessons between assignments."

"I imagine," he said with a twinkle, "that the detective work suited you because you were as clever as a vixen fox and a mighty fine all-around actress by then. But now who is still plying these old stages who would have been older than you, and therefore remember more than you about your own past, yet would notice this mystery woman in black? I assure you that this poor man's Queen Victoria would not normally draw much curiosity around a theater, not when we have sword-swallowers and rope dancers and all sorts of exotic women to pay attention to. Let me think."

He rose from his deep armchair and went to a bureau, from which he drew a sheaf of playbills.

"Ah, these go back a good ways, and that's what is required, something to jog the memory, even that of a world-famous mentalist. Missing mothers were hardly my onstage speciality."

He wet his forefinger as if about to test the wind, then began paging through the yellowing pile.

"*Hmmmm.* Madame DeSoto. No. Too old. Ah. The Mazeppa of Manhattan. No, that was a trick riding act and those who work with animals seldom notice mere humans coming and going. But she had a fine figure . . . a shame to bind it to a horse's back every night. And Little Dollie Doiley was too young at the time to notice anything, especially a quiet figure like a woman in black. So many wore mourning then anyway. When were you born?"

"I was told 'fifty-eight."

"And you were performing by 'sixty-two. Right in the middle of the Civil War, wasn't it, then? Though daily life went on here in New York, many a mother lost a son or husband to that bloody conflict in the South. I well recall the clusters of black that bloomed during those brutal years and only now are diminishing as those poor bereft women follow their menfolk to the grave-yard."

"Professor Marvel!" Irene admonished. "We are not here for a lesson on the futility of war, and if I searched among women who lost sons and husbands in the Civil War I should grow gray and wear black, like Mr. Whistler's mother, myself by then."

He shrugged and continued to page through the playbills.

I contemplated for a moment the American Civil War, of which I had, of course, heard, but had never regarded as a phenomenon of women in black appearing on the domestic scene and not dying out for more than two decades, long after the idea of a disunited United States seemed ludicrous. Mothers who survived to rear their children, it occurred to me, were in danger of outliving them, and that must be the saddest thing of all time.

Could the woman in black have been one of those doubly bereaved women who had lost children to illness or war or misadventure, visiting the motherless children of a theatrical troupe?

Such a woman was not necessarily the actual mother of any child in the troupe, but merely one seeking to reclaim a lost child in another guise.

"Ah!" Professor Marvel beamed foolishly at a particular playbill he had flourished from the pile. "Thumbelina. Of course! She is retired, but she had a memory like Jumbo the Elephant! Almost like myself. And she lives not far from here."

He jotted the address down on one of the many slips of paper that populated his rooms. He was a man, I realized, who thought in short bursts, which was what allowed him to remember so many trivial and arcane things.

"Thumbelina." Irene stared at the figure of a fairylike little creature in ballerina's tutu. "I remember her!"

Only I understood what a triumph this was, for while I had many recollections of my early years in Shropshire, Irene had proved herself strangely bereft of childhood particulars during her return home to New York.

I had not said anything to her, of course, but as former governess I felt a growing disquiet at the utter lack of childhood memories she demonstrated. Either the theatrical life was so chaotic that it distracted her from the usual sort of things a person would remember . . . or there was something lacking in her own makeup that prevented her from recalling what a child from the most ordinary upbringing might remember.

I had come to look upon Irene as a sort of Wonder of her world, perhaps as Sherlock Holmes was regarded in his. The Irene I knew had confidently inhabited a world that was London and Paris and major cities at points east. I had no doubt that she could have been the operatic performer of her age, had petty kings and circumstances not conspired against her. She was the consummate mistress of stage and self, and, when I had stopped being intimidated by her, I had admired and trusted her as no other.

Now that I had returned westward to the place of her origin, the wonder to me was that from such vague and eccentric and mostly forgotten roots she had grown into the magnificent bloom of a woman that she was.

Something was very wrong, I felt, and it had very little to do with lost mothers. Or perhaps I was missing something vital. It would not be the first time, for I was not a consummate mistress of anything, but I was, at least, exceedingly loyal.

By now Irene had become utterly engrossed in the search for some abiding woman in her past.

She would never admit it, and I would never make her admit it, but there is no doubt that her finger hesitated over the bell of the boardinghouse where Thumbelina resided. Irene never hesitated. It was her greatest strength, and her greatest flaw.

I made so bold as to lift my hand and push her finger down on the button.

Her eyes flicked to mine, startled. I almost never took the lead in anything. At least before Transylvania.

"Now is no time to play the indecisive schoolgirl," I explained.

"It's just that I do remember her now, Nell, and I am afraid of what we will find. She was a dwarf, enchanting to everyone while she was a child and a young woman. She must be past forty today, and—from what Professor Marvel said, and did not say—no longer well. I dread seeing what has become of her."

"The dread becomes you, but you cannot stop now."

"Why not?"

"Because she has heard the bell ring. You don't wish to abandon her as if you were a mischievous, cruel child, do you, who comes near only to run away?"

"No! Of course not. The die is cast."

"Now where did you get that—Caesar crossing the Rubicon—if you were so ill-educated as your background implies?"

"Professor Marvel? He knows everything. Perhaps I am a compilation of quick facts and that is all."

"Nonsense! You have outwitted Sherlock Holmes and the King of Bohemia, and Jack the Ripper. You are more than a compilation of 'quick facts.'" I took a deep breath that was too determined to be taken for a sigh. "Irene, I know that you stand on foreign ground that is also old to you. You mustn't let it overwhelm you. We are investigating a puzzle that happens to be your past. It need not be . . . personal."

At that she laughed. "Look at me! I'm as nervous as a schoolgirl, which is quite absurd, for it's quite obvious from my history that I never went to school."

"I disagree," I replied in my strictest governess tone. "Having met your former associates, it's clear to me that you did course work with the most eclectic and amazing scholars of your generation. Professor Marvel alone is the sum of at least fourteen Oxford dons."

"Nell! You can't mean that." She began to giggle at the very notion, but I had never been so sincere in my life.

"I have never meant anything more. Since . . . meeting Sherlock Holmes I have come to see that the ardent pursuit of knowledge, any kind of knowledge, produces more honest learning than all the rote exercises in any schoolbook. It is a fine thing to be able to quote enormous numbers of Greeks and Romans, and there is wisdom there as well as snobbery, but unless the quotes are applied to something practical in modern life, they are only so much make-work."

To this she had no answer, and thus was discovered gaping at me when her (my) ring was answered by . . . no one.

The door swung open as if by mechanical hands.

We gazed ahead, mutually stupefied, and were hardly an advertisement for either a classical or an eclectic education.

"Well, if it isn't an arguing pair of Brobdingnagians," announced a Lilliputian voice at the level of our knees.

We glanced down. A small, thickset woman in a miniature morning gown was awaiting our answer.

"Madam Thumbelina?" Irene asked.

"No madam and no longer Thumbelina," she answered in a piping but gruff voice. "What do you want?"

"You," Irene replied. "Professor Marvel—"

"What's that old fraud up to now?"

"He doesn't strike me as fraud," I put in.

"We are all frauds. I'm not Thumbelina, but Phoebe Cummings, dwarf. Who are you?"

"Irene Adler, opera singer," Irene replied as forthrightly.

"Penelope Huxleigh . . . not much of anything."

"Former opera singer," Irene amended her vocation quickly, "and Miss Huxleigh is a former governess, clerk, and typewriter girl."

"Well," said Phoebe Thumbelina Cummings, "I am a former

curiosity, and being such, am curious enough to wonder why two such accomplished ladies with such glorious pasts would call on me."

"To explore your own glorious past, of course," Irene said, "and mine. I am the former Rena the Ballerina, Merlinda the Mermaid and assorted other incarnations."

"And Miss Huxleigh here?"

"I have had no assorted other incarnations," I said quickly. "I am a parson's orphaned daughter and former employee of whosoever would employ me, alas, therefore a nobody."

"English?" Phoebe asked Irene.

"I'm afraid so."

"Oooh, I like the breed. Very ladylike. So, come in, ladies. I haven't any tea to offer, but a glass of lemonade. Rena, you say? I begin to get the picture. I get a lot of pictures. A living album, am I. I've thought of penning my memoirs."

She waddled—and there is no other way to describe her short-legged hesitating gait—down a hall in which advertising circulars had become an impromptu carpet, to a door that she stretched up to open (despite Irene's hand twitching to assist her) by herself.

We entered a doll's house, where every stick of furniture was child size and no framed playbill or painting was hung higher than our waists.

I felt like Alice after she taken the mushroom that had made her bigger in Wonderland.

"Have a seat," Phoebe suggested, a wicked glint in her eyes.

We settled on a tiny tapestried rocking chair and a miniature sofa that had our knees almost up to our chins.

Phoebe hoisted her small frame up onto a child's rocking chair, grunting like a roughrider trying to tame a bucking bronco from Buffalo Bill's Wild West Show.

I bit my lip and decided that if Phoebe could lever herself about in such obvious pain, I could certainly commune with my kneecaps without complaint.

"We'll talk first," Phoebe said abruptly.

I began to understand that she could not speak long without grunting, which made her speech seem abrupt. "Then I'll decide if you're worth the lemonade."

I understood that she referred to the effort of serving us. I myself didn't know yet if we would be "worth the lemonade."

"Do you remember me?" Irene asked gently.

Phoebe's features, which were blunt and full-sized compared to her stunted body, puckered to indicate both searching her memory, and a resentment of the effort.

"Pretty lady," she said finally, and shook her head.

"As a child," Irene amended.

Phoebe looked again, long and deep. "What child?"

"Rena the Ballerina."

"Oh, you grew! Didn't you? That's why I couldn't place you at first. We used to be of a size, you and me."

"I was the baby, though," Irene admitted, appealing to our hostess's greater age.

"Baby, yes. They took me for a baby until I was, oh, twenty. I had the longest childhood of any human on the East Coast. Then suddenly, it was over. I was 'grown,' though I hadn't added an inch. I wasn't interesting anymore. I was just a . . . freak. A dwarf. A Something. And nobody would pay me for that."

"We were all freaks," Irene offered.

Phoebe gazed at her for a long time, seeking sincerity. And found it.

"Yes, we all. Were. Freaks. Do you want some lemonade?"

"If it's not too much trouble," Irene said. And remained seated while Phoebe threw herself off her chair and waddled into an adjoining room.

I started to lift from my cramped chair, but Irene nodded a vehement "No" to me and I settled back down into that most uncomfortable of positions.

By the time Phoebe returned with a glass of lemonade in each hand my back was aching and my legs were developing those prickling tingles that will make standing again an exercise in pain and futility.

I clasped the glass and balanced it on one knee. Irene did likewise.

Phoebe pushed and manipulated herself back into her chair.

"Thank you," Irene said, sipping from the glass as if we sat on Mrs. Astor's back porch, did Mrs. Astor deign to have such a lowly American annex on her Newport castle-cum-seaside cottage.

"The city can be hot this time of year," Phoebe noted, lifting her own glass of previously poured lemonade from the tiny table at her side. "What can I do for you ladies, besides wait on you?"

The sharp comment merited a brief smile from Irene. "You can do a great deal. We came at Professor Marvel's suggestion because my memory of my youngest years is faulty."

"You grew up," Phoebe complained. "We used to be the same, only I was older. Much older, but it didn't show. Now you're a giant."

"I couldn't help myself," Irene answered.

"Nor I." Phoebe sipped her lemonade again and made a face. "I got used to being praised for being tiny and clever. Now I'm just tiny and old, and everyone could run me over in the streets in an instant and hardly even notice."

"You know how to outwit their blindness, though," Irene commented.

"I do, but I resent having to do it."

"So do I," Irene said.

For a moment Phoebe looked angry, like a spiteful child.

"The world," Irene said, "has many excuses to overlook all sorts of persons. What I was when you knew me would be ridiculed by some people who know what I supposedly am now."

"And what are you?"

Irene considered the question, then lifted her head with a smile. "I am still a performer, though I am not paid for it much anymore. I am still a student, if you understand that we learned much from our colleagues. I am still . . . a mystery to myself."

"And this one, your companion, what is she?"

Irene turned to regard me and I quailed at what her summing up of me might be, since she had been so humble with herself (for humble was not a word I would normally associate with Irene; I was perversely pleased that was the case, as my own history had condemned me to be humble).

"Nell . . . prides herself on being predictable, but her strength is in surprise. I believe that is your strength, too."

"Hmmph."

Phoebe struck me as a sour and stunted individual in more than stature, yet she grimaced a smile as she glanced from myself to Irene.

"I should hate you to your toes," she told Irene. "You grew straight and beautiful and tall, though we used to dance duets together. You dress like someone on Mrs. Astor's guest list of four hundred and yet you hunker down like a Red Man to sit on my chairs. You have a friend, and I have none—"

"No longer," Irene said, her voice suddenly as taut as a strangled violin. "I have lost my past, and am here to reclaim it, and my friends. There is something wrong. I can't remember what I should."

Phoebe glanced at me, her mud-colored eyes narrowing in alarm.

"Nothing wrong," she said gruffly, "except that you were sold young into the hands of that damned maestro."

28.

Fairy Godmothers

⌘

Thumbelina, what's the difference if you're very small?
When your heart is full of love, you're nine feet tall!

"You needn't gasp, Miss Huxleigh, I am plainspoken," Phoebe said. "I see no point in painting pansies on the truth when it is an ugly and cracked vase that will only please when it admits what it is."

She glanced at a white-faced Irene, who apparently was taking the notion of being "sold" as badly as I was.

"The others, of course," she rumbled on in her Billy Goat Gruff voice, "being the type of performers who can afford to lie to themselves, and each other, doubtless thought it was a good thing and would be shocked by my opinion. I didn't regard what happened as much better than Miss Wilhelmina running off to play from the age of fifteen with any man who wanted a peek at her garters."

"Wilhelmina," Irene repeated in as much of a daze as she ever allowed herself to be.

I knew her well, and had never seen her so off balance.

"We just saw Mina before coming here," she offered, concentrating on a subject matter far removed from her own stupefaction.

Phoebe burst out with a derisive chuckle. " 'Mina'? Is that what she's going by now? I'd heard she married far above us all, but there's many a slip between the lip and the wedding ring, and Wilhelmina made them all." She leaned toward Irene. "Don't you remember all the hush-hush about her being delicate and suffering consumption and missing so many performances? Overconsumption, that's what she suffered . . . first of spiritous liquors and then of the men who bought them for her."

"I suppose," I said weakly, "such sad stories are not unheard of in the theater."

"The Theater, miss? I wouldn't know about the Theater. We were all lowly variety performers. Freaks and oddities. How'd you like to grow up with me for a godmother, maybe small enough to be a fairy, but not pretty enough?"

She leaned so far forward in the rocking chair that I thought she'd tumble off the place she'd struggled so to sit upon. Miss Muffet on her tuffet, I thought, waiting for the spider that terrified her. Or was *she* the spider? I couldn't stop myself from leaning away from her, not repulsed by her stunted stature, but by her vehement unhappiness. I was reminded of Rumpelstiltskin from the tales, an embittered old man who liked to suck young girls dry of hope.

"Godmothers." Irene plucked one word from the diatribe and held it up before us like a jewel. "That is what I grew up among," she went on, almost dreamily. Her voice was as mellow as a solo cello, low and soothing. A soft answer turneth away wrath. It also mesmerizes and Irene had long since mastered that bizarre process.

Phoebe's tightened facial features loosened a bit. "You was a charmer, a natural little sunbeam, you was. Not a minx like Wilhelmina. . . . Still, for all her selfish ways from the time she was in baby skirts, I'd not wish upon her the fate that she found. I thought you'd escaped it." She regarded Irene sternly, but there was a suspicious sheen to her eyes before she continued.

"But then they were all for you studying The Voice with that maestro fellow, who wasn't even one of us, but too good for all of us. And then you left, and when you came back you hardly knew us, or we knew you, and finally you came back not at all and then the next we heard you had left for Europe, without a word for any of us. Moved up and forgot us, as she did, Wilhelmina, only her way was a rough one, and you used to be as upset as the rest of us about it, until you went off with the maestro and never came back yourself again."

"How old was I when this happened?"

"Not as young as she, but she was born old and knowing where the ladder out of the gutter stood. Still, she paid a pretty price for taking the wrong ladder a couple of times. A pretty price. You have children?"

The abrupt subject change startled even the unflappable Irene. "No. I don't. Not . . . yet."

"A bit old for it, aren't you?"

"Perhaps." Irene regained command of herself now that the conversation had touched on something she never permitted to be pawed in public: her personal life. "But that is my business, and my husband's."

"Caught one, did you? Wealthy and well placed?"

"Healthy and well intentioned. And he caught me."

Suddenly those small, pencil-point-sharp eyes the odd color of obsidian drilled into my face. "You look a respectable woman."

"I am a respectable woman! I am a parson's daughter."

"Parsons. We don't have much of that title here. Preacher will do. So you are satisfied that Miss Rena here has a decent husband and reputation?"

"Godfrey . . . her husband, is more than decent. He is a prince among men, wise and kind and a brilliant barrister and—"

The woman waggled her small stubby hand, so like a child's that I was tempted to clasp it to still the tantrum that was stirring in that small and mightily angry breast.

"Parsons and barristers. I don't know much about some folks, but your friend is dressed to meet a queen and I hope that she has come by that as honestly as women can these days."

"More than honestly. She struck a business deal for it. Such things are all business with her, and while I cannot condone too great an interest in the material things of life, Irene is an operatic performer and must be allowed her extravagances, especially when she is clever enough to earn them without sacrificing a scintilla of her integrity."

"*Hmmmph!*" The woman sounded annoyingly unconvinced.

"I am working," Irene put in, "as an investigator for the Pinkertons."

So much for integrity. That was a blatant lie, ladled directly atop my stirring defense of her.

"My dear Lena," Irene said, making me glance around the tiny room looking for a new person, "I am so touched that you worried, and still do, about my moral state, but I assure that I am the most indecently respectable married lady in Paris, London, and perhaps New York City. I have had a respectable career singing opera, and whatever you may think of my leaving the variety stage to apprentice in voice with the maestro, it resulted only in respectable things."

Trust Irene to realize that the woman's venom was on her behalf, not aimed at her guest.

"Is it true?" the imperious little figure demanded of me, like a dowager doll come to life.

"Of course. I would never associate with a demimondaine."

"Another foreign occupation, I take it, like parsons and bar-risters."

"Not like those at all," I said, horrified. "A demimondaine is a French expression for a woman whose respectability has been compromised by the shadows. Irene's never has. I would swear to it."

"Ain't many women who haven't been compromised by the shadows."

A silence held in the room. I reflected that I had been in many places I shouldn't have been with Irene over the years, including the presence of death at its most brutal. This was perhaps the strangest, a rooming house in New York City, the bawls from the street below coming as faint as seagulls' cries, and a dwarf sitting in a rocking chair and demanding answers like a judge.

"Thank you, Nell," the object of our argument said drily, "but I can defend my own reputation. I am, however, most interested in Mina's. I remember her vaguely, but you, Lena, as our elder, would know more frankly what became of her. I was still at an age when my elders thought it best to keep things from me, I'm sure, for I remember less of my life in those days than I do of my infancy."

"And better that you should," the woman murmured, fidgeting on her seat, not like the restless child she recalled to me, but rather like an old woman in constant pain. Perhaps she was a bit of both.

"The early days for you were suet pudding, Rena. It didn't hurt that you were the daintiest thing under a checked bonnet in vaudeville. Everyone doted upon you . . . and don't ask me where you came from, because one fine day you were there and that was that."

"Whom did I live with? Who tended me?"

"Why, you made the rounds, and whoever could best keep you did so. The first year you slept in a tray in Sophie's trunk. I believe a photograph was made of you in your makeshift bed. They even put it on the playbills. 'Little Miss Rena. Born in a trunk, a perfume tray for a pillow.'"

"They wanted to bill you as a dwarf like me for a while, you were so quick to dance and sing ahead of your age. But I kicked

up a fuss. If I had a future only as a freak, I wanted to be the one
with top billing. You would grow up . . . and grow."

"And Mina grew up with me, in the theater?"

"With you? Heavens no! There was no 'with' for Mina! She
was for herself first and last. Even when it came to her sister. It
got her in trouble, being so forward, and I'll give you credit; you
were never no trouble, nor got in any. How that annoyed Mina!
Quite infuriated her. Her face would turn scarlet, then her fists
and feet would hammer whatever—or whomever—they could."

Phoebe's wheezing chuckle quickly became a cough.

"Perhaps we're tiring you," Irene suggested. She could never
stand to hear a cough. It reminded her of times when her voice
had suffered and she couldn't perform. "We could leave and call
another day."

She sounded truly alarmed. Indeed, Lena's small thick body
had doubled over. As coughs racked it, the rocking chair swung
wildly back and forth, not a comfortable seat like Old Dobbin's
but more like a runaway horse's.

Irene and I hastened to her side, offering sips of lemonade
and pats on the back, but she soon straightened, tear tracks running willy-nilly on her cheeks and chin.

"Ah!" she dismissed it. "It's from all that sawdust for the acro-
batic acts. Where was I? Oh, yes. You wanted to know if anyone
took an interest in you as a child." She settled back, closed one
tear-swollen eye, looking rather notorious, and said, "Of course
they did, and particularly when you were not a small child any
longer, but I doubt you wish to know much about that kind of
scum."

She frowned, shut her eyes, and went on. "I saw a lot nobody
expected me to. Partly it's because I'm a dwarf, and they expect
me to be deficient in most everything. Partly it's because I'm a
dwarf and am easy to overlook, quite literally. I would have made
a good Pinkerton detective," she said, suddenly grinning at Irene.
"Oh, at first everyone would notice me, but then they'd realize

my condition and pretend not to see me. It would never occur to them that I could see—and hear—them perfectly well."

"You had an invisibility cape," Irene suggested, "only it didn't work until after you had made your grand entrance."

"Exactly! What a bright girl you always were. And you were right earlier. You did have your set of fairy godmothers, just like that Sleeping Beauty in the old story. When Mina had her troubles, they enclosed you like a wall of briars. That's why I couldn't understand why they simply turned around then and turned you over to the maestro."

I was most intrigued by this "turning over" to the "maestro," but Irene seemed least interested in that part of the story.

It never failed that what I regarded as most vital she considered most trivial, and vice versa. In fact, we should not have got on as friends at all, save we were so different that there was no point in attempting to win the other to our own vantage point.

On the other hand, what Irene accepted with the most casual disinterest was often what most deeply concerned her. It was if she feared that showing what she cared about could most destroy it. Perhaps that came from long sojourn in hostile environments . . . the inbred jealousies of the theatrical set.

I had never forgotten the sopranos who put ground glass in her rouge pot at La Scala, where Irene made her first grand opera debut as Cinderella. Instead of flaunting a lover's largesse in jewels onstage, as most of the other divas did, she had persuaded a former American client, Mr. Tiffany, to play fairy godfather by lending her a stunning diamond corsage for the performance. Could it be that the maestro was the key to the entire affair, to her past and the present murders? Oh, not at all likely! Such a notion was the feeble woolgathering of a spinster's limited imagination.

Irene had another question for our petite hostess. "Going back to my early years, did I ever have a fairy godmother from outside our theatrical set?"

"Like Mrs. Vanderbilt! Now that'd be a story! I fear not. We did have a few do-gooders about the place. That was before the Salvation Army became such a big presence. Still, those ladies were made for some kind of army. I remember one, all in black. Made me think of a nun. She came to see to the children. Had a great weakness for them, would swoop you up and rock you like a baby when you were already three years old or so. You seemed to like her. You were always pulling on her bonnet strings. She had a beautiful face, like a madonna with doll eyes, blue as cobalt glass . . . they were always giving me dolls as they thought I looked so sweet hauling around a toy as big as myself."

Irene glanced at me: again we encountered a rumor of the Woman in Black. "And do you remember a name?"

"Lord, no! We were informal around the stage life, and all of us had stage names and nicknames on top of that. Besides, she was not from the stage." Phoebe frowned, the fretful expression making her look like a grandmotherly child. "But I recall . . . she liked to take you by the hands and dance around, and she would point her toes quite professionally. She had the smallest, daintiest feet, almost like mine then."

Irene listened, enchanted. "You saw her feet?"

"Yes. She must have lifted up her hems. She was very playful with you," Phoebe nodded, smiling. "She treated you like a child, as none of the others did. She was even kind to me. I remember her bending down so gracefully, it was a like an angel leaning down from heaven, not someone thinking I was too short, or too stupid, to understand anything that happened above my head."

"I doubt much was above your head," Irene noted with a knowing smile.

Phoebe smiled back. "You're right about that. I'd have had ripe material for blackmail, had I been so inclined. People spoke in front of me as if I were the town idiot."

"And you remember nothing more about the mysterious woman in black and why she would be visiting the performers backstage and why she'd play with us, with children?"

"*Hmmmmm.*" Phoebe put a forefinger to her lip as if to prevent herself from speaking prematurely. She shook her ponderous head from side to side. "I think so little about the past. I am not fond of those days, or these even. And I saw a great deal that a child my age should not have." She looked up to regard Irene. "Our lives were amusing and hard and satisfying and frustrating. So were the lives of the women who watched over us. Sometimes they did not watch over themselves so well. Do you understand what I'm saying?"

Irene nodded soberly.

Well, I didn't! And I didn't want to ask and appear stupid, or worse, naïve. The conversation was moving into those half-spoken areas where one needed a code book to decipher the real meaning. I hated it when people talked in that veiled way in front of me, but I also understood that they talked that way to spare themselves, as well. That there were some subjects so shocking, so socially forbidden, that they could only be broached sideways, and softly.

"We were children," Irene said contemplatively. "Worldly children. Perhaps that's why I forgot so much. . . . Or perhaps not." Her voice had hardened. "We aren't children now. Tell me what you think, what you remember."

"I was abandoned as an infant."

I gasped at those harsh words, and Phoebe quirked me a smile. "I'm sorry, Miss Huxleigh. I can see you have a kind heart beneath your stern exterior, but one look at me after I slipped my mother's anchorage and it was obvious I would be crippled."

"You are not crippled!" I interjected. "You do not even use a cane."

"And I was not expected to live," she went on quietly. "I never knew my parents, or my mother, for I doubt I had a father who would have stayed around for holy matrimony, and perhaps my mother was a dwarf as well."

"Who would—?" I choked on my next thought.

"Who would what?" Phoebe asked.

"What kind of man would take advantage of a woman with such a physical disability?"

Phoebe laughed, and it was not a nice laugh. "A man who thought she would get no attention from any other man. I've seen them myself."

I kept silence after that. No matter what I had seen that defied all belief in Paris and Prague and Transylvania, the New World also offered its ancient travesties.

Phoebe leaned forward to look me hard in the eyes. "You are a good soul, Miss Huxleigh, and if I'd had you for a nanny no doubt I'd never know whereof I speak. But I didn't, and that's that."

She eyed Irene again, as an equal, perhaps as a fellow conspirator. I was not. I was still an innocent even as I kept my ears wide open for any news that would relieve me of that increasingly annoying position. I hated being always on the fringes of the discussion, always the last to know.

"There were inconveniences like ourselves," she told Irene, the two women so physically different leaning in like gossiping flowers in the same bed to hear each other's tales. Her voice lowered, so I had to lean far forward myself to hear, and then only picked up half the words.

"Inconvenience," Phoebe whispered with a certain cynical emphasis. "A way out . . . everyone knew and no one admitted . . . disappeared . . . one woman . . . notorious . . . potions . . . physician . . . baby-seller . . . savior . . . abortionist."

I had never heard that word, abortionist. I would have to ask Irene when we left.

I looked at her face. The expression was as intent and dark as I had ever seen it, except when she was enacting bloody murder on the stage. She was not acting anything now. I did not know her.

29.

The Woman in Black

⛤

*Young man, you took to your bosom the image of purity, a
thing upon which you think the stamp of God has been
printed.... Not so; Madame Restell's Preventive Powders
have counterfeited the hand writing of Nature: you have not a
medal, fresh from the mint, of sure metal; but a base,
lacquered counter, that has undergone the sweaty
contamination of a hundred palms....*

—GEORGE W. DIXON, EDITOR OF THE *NEW YORK POLYANTHOS,* 1841

"You must tell me," I said.

Irene and I had returned to the hotel in silence. She had
smoked dark cigarette after dark cigarette in the gurney on
the way back and smoked still now.

"Tell you what?"

"What that little woman was talking about. Who was the
woman in black who visited and danced with you? Why were you
two abandoned as children?"

Irene shook her head as if tossing a hat veil back from her
face. She stubbed the cigarette out in a crystal tray, then regarded
the ashes. Next she regarded me.

"I am sorry, Nell. I lead you into darker and darker coils. I wish I were you. How I do! I wish . . . I did not have to be the one to disappoint you."

"Disappoint me in what?"

"The world. Myself. My history."

"Irene, I would never be disappointed in you, no matter your history."

"You cannot know."

"No, I cannot, because no one will tell me! If I'd had known . . . things that I now know, however unhappily, I would have never . . . Quentin and I . . . it would all be so different . . . and I wish—"

"*Shhh*," Irene said, taking my hands like a nursemaid soothing a charge. "Don't wish yet. You don't know enough yet to make a sensibly extravagant wish, for all wishes should be extravagant."

She shook my hands fondly. "I will tell you a tale. It's not a fairy tale, with pixies, and lost princesses, and kindly old magicians and dwarves—"

"But Professor Marvel and Phoebe are in it?"

"Yes, and mermaids and dancing ladies."

I settled back to listen, and Irene dropped my hands.

"I hardly know where it begins, except that it must begin with me, because I am the teller of the tale. Phoebe was right. She and I were orphans of the storm. The 'storm' was what happened to women, and girls, who were mothers too soon, or not in the approved manner."

"They were not married."

"Exactly. They were mothers, or would be, but they were not married. Enter the fairy godmother."

"She helped Cinderella go to the ball."

"This fairy godmother helped Cinderella after the ball was over."

I stared at Irene, trying to appear as if I understood. "How—?"

"There were prince's wives who desperately wanted babies."

"Like poor Queen Clotilde."

"Like poor Queen Clotilde, but these wives couldn't have babies."

"That's possible?"

"Sometimes. Yet other women have babies they don't want."

I nodded. "There were cases even in our village, but no one talked about them. Openly."

Irene shrugged. "So. Between the married women who want babies, and the unmarried women who are having unwanted babies . . . who stands?"

"The fairy godmother."

Irene nodded. "She makes unwanted babies into wanted ones."

"Unwanted? Who could not want such a marvelous thing as a baby?"

"My mother, for one," Irene said, unflinching.

I should have flinched to be forced to say such a thing. My mother died having me. Surely she had wanted me. Or would she have, had she known the price? Of course not. No. No rational person would give up her life for a baby. Except a mother. I was more confused than ever, and Irene saw it.

"There is so much pain and confusion about this whole matter, having babies, or not, that it's impossible to judge. Whatever the case, Phoebe and myself were . . . found other positions."

"You make being an infant sound like being a servant."

"And what is even the most wanted, beloved infant but a servant of other people's needs and wants and confusions? Babies can't control who they're born to, or what those they're born to decide to do with them."

"I don't want to hear this." I clapped my hands over my ears, hard.

Irene tugged to pull those hands free. I heard her voice as if through earmuffs.

Yes, you do, Nell. Listen to me. I have to accept myself as the result of my history.

"So who was the woman in black? She wasn't a fairy god-mother?"

"Maybe she was, in her own eyes. Maybe she saw that Phoebe and I were . . . placed somewhere where we could forge our own futures, for we certainly had none before."

"She cared for you?"

"As our mothers could not."

"Who was she?"

"I don't know, but I must know. I must follow her trail as far as it leads, for as long as it takes. We may pass a long time on these shores, more than you expected or I would wish. Do you need to go back home?"

"Back home? You still feel only a visitor here?"

"Yes."

"As I am."

"Yes."

"You will go back home no matter what you find here?"

Irene sighed and nodded her head at one and the same time. "How can I not? Godfrey is there."

I swallowed hard and said what I thought. "And Quentin."

Irene held her hand out to me. It was a pact.

I took it, both of us charged at that moment to follow her past West to its American wellsprings, and yet both of us turning our faces away from the East and our hearts' desires.

"If only I had known you, Nell," Irene said, "when I was a child."

If only I had known you, I thought, *when I was a governess.*

30.

Perfidy in New Jersey

✦

*Nellie Bly, although neither highly educated, cultured nor
accomplished, is a woman of intellectual power, high aims, and
a pure and unblemished career.*
—SKETCH IN *THE EPOCH* MAGAZINE, 1899

We returned to the hunt the next day, and in a most annoy-ing way.

Although I was relieved there were no more visits to the bizarre souls who had performed on the vaudeville stages with the infant Irene, I cannot say that I welcomed an interlude among the record-keepers.

For a full two days Irene and I pored over the birth records of New Jersey and New York City in the years 1857 through 1859, and I never want to see another American birth certificate penned in spidery Copperplate in my life.

Finally a gray-haired clerk holding on her aquiline nose with a pince-nez and wearing a tucked shirtwaist-front as starched as her manner took pity on us.

"You are searching for a child christened Irene Adler," she asked, or perhaps, told us.

"Yes," Irene agreed warily. She had kept the object of our search very quiet.

"I couldn't help notice the years of the records you were searching. You are not the first to request such records, and only recently."

"Not the first? What a . . . coincidence. Perhaps our efforts are redundant," Irene smiled wryly. "Oh, dear, and we have come all the way from New York City, and my companion from Paris, in fact."

For once Irene's prevarications in the service of worming information out of some helpless clerk were not prevarications, but they produced results.

"Paris?" The lady regarded me dubiously. Apparently I did not look Parisian. "I fear that your search may indeed be redundant. A gentleman asked me to produce these very records only days ago."

"A gentleman?" Irene repeated still wary.

"Indeed."

"And how would I recognize this gentleman?" Irene asked in the deceptively serene tone that always put my nerves on edge.

"Very well dressed. Top hat, striped trousers, cutaway coat . . . no lounge suit for him, like the mashers wear!"

"What a relief," I put in faintly.

The lady clerk gave me a bracing nod. "Exactly! I won't have mashers at my counter. Anyway, the gentleman asked for the very same years and locations. I couldn't help but be struck by the coincidence. That and the accent."

"Accent?" Irene inquired.

The woman nodded at me as if identifying a thief. "Just like hers. Foreign."

Irene turned to regard me with great interest. " 'Foreign,' indeed. English, then?"

"I didn't ask." The woman's tone implied that neither should Irene. "The gentleman was obviously unmarried and I didn't wish to give him the wrong impression."

I considered that she had little worry on that score, but then neither did I, and I was decades younger.

"How . . . obviously unmarried?" Irene asked carefully.

"Well, he wore no ring, only a watch on a chain with some gold frippery dangling from it, the only ostentatious trinket on his person, I might add, which was how I knew that he was English. Besides the accent. Like hers."

Again Irene turned to regard me as if I were a curiosity she had never noticed before.

"Gold frippery?" she repeated. "He must be from California, then."

"Not that kind of gold. Nothing so crude as nuggets." The lady clerk snorted delicately through the thin gold nose-pieces of her pince-nez. "Foreign coins, perhaps. I didn't notice, not liking to stare at a gentleman's midsection."

I could sympathize with her reluctance.

"Perhaps an English sovereign," Irene said.

"Or a French sou," I added primly, more for Irene's benefit than the clerk's.

"I don't know what kind of coin! Or even that it was a coin. I only know that the gentleman was searching the same records you ladies have requested. Do you know him?"

"No!" I burst out.

"No," Irene said with a tiny, very French shrug. "Perhaps he knows us."

"He found nothing."

"How do you know?" Irene wondered.

"He left."

So did we.

"*Hmmmm.*" Irene became distracted as we left the officious clerk far behind us.

"It cannot be . . . *he!*"

"Oh, there is scant doubt of that. I do wonder if he indeed found nothing, or merely allowed that foolish woman to think so."

"It is not he!"

Irene stopped and turned to regard me with wonder. "Why not?"

"He does not strike me as a man who would cross oceans easily."

"Neither did you strike me as a woman who would, yet you did."

"I was atrociously ill all the way."

"Perhaps he was, too," Irene speculated with a Cheshire cat smile. Then she frowned, severely. "What would bring Sherlock Holmes to the birth registries of the New World, hunting down my history?"

I bit my tongue. Never would I reveal what I and no other knew, except that deluded Paddington doctor who cherished literary ambitions and had left a betraying manuscript carelessly lying around in a locked desk drawer: Sherlock Holmes was invulnerable to women, an admirable trait among the male sex, I must admit, and he was invulnerable to all women save one: Irene herself.

Did he indeed cherish a strong and secret fondness for my friend, he would not be overjoyed to now overhear how the news of his possible proximity affected her.

We returned to our hotel room, where she promptly lit a cigarette, brought out her petite pistol, and stalked back and forth, huffing and puffing and waving her weapon about like a fan.

"I am most disturbed to learn of that man's actual presence on these shores, Nell," she announced, as if I had not already realized (and applauded) that reaction.

"Indeed you should be," I answered, devoting myself to the tea things she had forsaken for small cigar and petite pistol.

"So Pink hinted, but she has dealt so rudely with us that I was not inclined to believe her. I will not have intruders running roughshod over my own history!"

"No, indeed, but I doubt that Mr. Holmes wears hobnail

boots. His footprints, I suspect, will be very faint. If that woman had not seen fit to remark upon him, I doubt we should have been certain of his presence."

"Exactly!" She whirled like a dervish to confront my innocent face, now absorbed in consuming some really wonderful scones and cucumber sandwiches.

"You know who is responsible for his unwanted presence on these shores?"

"Er . . . Baron von Krafft-Ebing?"

She stood as frozen as a statue. "Baron von Krafft-Ebing. Of course. You are brilliant, Nell!"

"No, no," I murmured through my tea sandwiches. "But exactly how so?"

"That must be the lure *she* used to bring him over. A series of unexplained deaths. Were there others associated with me before the medium's, and Mr. Bishop's and the snake charmer's? We'll never know unless she deigns to tell us. So she lured him with multiple murders. With that and his own unhealthy interest in my doings that has plagued him from the first. Why must that man dog my footsteps?!"

I forbore to point out that in many instances she had inadvertently done exactly that to him. I was too much relishing her tantrum on the same subject that had so often driven me to the brink of distraction.

All things come to she who waits.

Well, perhaps not all things, or people, I thought with a pang that quite ruined my girlish appetite.

31.

The Body of Evidence

~oier~

*His expression, his manner, his very soul seemed to vary with
every fresh part that he assumed.*
—DR. JOHN H. WATSON, "A SCANDAL IN BOHEMIA," 1891,
SIR ARTHUR CONAN DOYLE

⊰FROM THE CASE NOTES OF SHERLOCK HOLMES⊱

Although I am far less known outside the narrow circles of
crime than my consultant work would merit, I expect that
the continuing publication of Watson's illustrated little
stories will change all that. (From the illustrations thus far,
however, I am portrayed to resemble a mustachioed Paris
gigolo, so my worries may be premature there.)

Still, in future I may have to rely on disguise more than ever,
which is what makes a barefaced foray into the American scene
such a treat.

I simply hied myself to Macy's on Broadway and found a loud
plaid suit of rather decent quality for a reasonable price. In fact,

the louder the plaid, the lower the cost, which suited my purposes admirably.

Next, I visited boardinghouses around the Union Square theaters until I found one where the landlady knew one of the veteran performers on Miss Cochrane-Bly's list of those who had shared playbills with Madam Adler-Norton during her tender years. (Really, this fashion for women with two last names will soon get out of hand! The great violinist and mistress of the bow, Wilhelmina Norman-Neruda, has no idea what she has started.)

By suppertime I was a new resident at a 14th Street boardinghouse that seemed as tidily run as Mrs. Hudson's Baker Street establishment, and was introduced as such at dinner.

Here is where the place fell down smartly from the high standards set by Mrs. Hudson and her ever-ready menu to accommodate a detective's erratic hours.

At seven o'clock "sharp" all boarders were to be present or forfeit food for the night. This policy suited my plans admirably, for I could be assured that at least one former associate of Rena the Ballerina, Little Fanny Frawley, the petite pistolera, or the alluring Merlinda the Mermaid would be present. These American theatrical nomenclatures are worth a monograph of their own.

We were served at one long table, with eight chairs to a side and the usual head and foot. The table's center was laden with bowls and platters piled with various food stuffs, and it was every man . . . and the occasional woman . . . for himself when it came to claiming portions.

"Shakespeare, is it?" asked a cadaverously thin and tall man when I was presented to the assembly. "Shylock Shakespeare? A bit strong, don't you think?" he added while reaching an attenuated arm three chairs down the table for a platter of pork chops. "But then you're a Brit, I suppose."

"You have the advantage of me, sir," I said, referring to his reach as well as his identity.

"I'm Bill Heron, the Human Stilt."

He was certainly not one to cavil about names. "Indeed. I thought I'd try my fortune across the Atlantic."

"Fine idea," put in the portly older man who naturally took the head of the table. "That Oscar Wilde fellow set all the country talking a few years ago. You don't seem the type to wear velvet suits, though," he added, gazing politely at my obnoxious plaid.

"I'm hoping that my work stands alone."

"As do we all. I'm Phineas LaMar, better known as Professor Marvel, the Walking, Talking Encyclopedia."

Eureka!

"And what specialty is your line of work, sir?" he then asked.

"I am a generalist," I replied.

"I meant, what is your act?"

"Act? I indeed do, on occasion. Ah. I see. You mean my livelihood. You might call me a body reader."

Professor Marvel nodded sagely. "An excellent variation, somewhat akin to mine, although I suspect that, like a mind reader, you need to work with a confederate and I do not."

"You have never used a shill in the audience, Professor?"

The older man's foolish face produced a very wise smile. "If I work it right, one half of the audience is the shill for the other half, without either of them knowing it."

"Exactly what I aim for, Professor," I answered with a swift smile.

I entered the dinner-table fray and managed to spear a pork chop the Human Stilt was not quite fast enough to snag. His long face puckered into surprise. The race is not always to the best equipped, but often to the quickest study.

The woman across from me, who was girlish in dress yet matronly in form and face, winked.

I saw that I could cut quite a swath in the company, should I choose to.

"I am not coming into your country and company unprepared," I noted. "I have made a study of various acts through the years. An amazing number of performers began their careers as children. The Hermann and Dixon sisters, the, ah, novelty act of Tiny Tim and Rena the Ballerina—"

"Don't they do that in England?" the Professor asked.

I had no idea, for I prefer classical music, but fortunately he went on of his own accord.

"Ah, I remember them all well. Many are no longer performing, lost to outgrowing their attraction. I had heard . . . and you may know this, sir, that our little Rena had found a new career singing in Europe."

"England is not Europe," I said icily.

"Well, what else is it?" the blowsy female across from me asked in some dudgeon.

"An island, madam, like Manhattan."

"Manhattan is still New York City, and part of New York State, and therefore part of the United States," she said rather truculently.

"England is part of the British Isles," I answered, "including Scotland, Ireland, and Wales. We have nothing to do with Europe, except the geographical accident of being so near it, which has cost us dearly over the centuries."

Professor Marvel chuckled. "Never call an Englishman a European, Daisy dear. They won't put up with it. So, Mr. Shakespeare, have you heard of an Irene Adler in your native land? She left us rather thoroughly when she grew up and I have always wondered what she made of her career."

The wistful tone in the Professor's voice told me that La Adler had begun her conquests at a very early age indeed. I had not the heart to disappoint the old man.

"A singer of that name appeared in some of Gilbert and Sullivan's comic operas at the Savoy Theater in London, I recall. Quite beautiful. Her voice, I mean. What happened to her after I cannot say, but I heard she had deserted England for the Continent, and operetta for grand opera."

"Grand opera really! Then the maestro did not do badly by

her, after all. She was a modest little creature, when I knew her, and would not be one to blow her own horn."

He seemed about to say more, but subsided. I suspected he had seen her again recently, but she had not satisfied him to her performance history. Why should she hide her operatic triumphs in Milan, Warsaw, and Prague . . . especially as they would mean much to her former associates? Perhaps it was because circumstances had silenced her great gift these past two years, and the subject was more tender than one would suspect with such a superficially confident woman. Regrettably, I had played a role in her premature retirement.

"The rolls, Mr. Shakespeare. Please pass them," came Daisy's voice, which certainly carried across a table. It rang with the aggrieved tones of having had to repeat itself.

"Pardon me, Miss Daisy," I said, complying. "You were born in Sussex, I perceive. I admit that I was wondering how a lovely lady such as yourself who was born of English shopkeeper parents who were themselves musically inclined should find herself on the musical stage in New York City."

"Well, I'll be!" She almost dropped the basket of rolls. "I've lost my accent these thirty . . . I mean, *fifteen* years. How'd you guess?"

"Guessing has nothing to do with it, dear girl." I had immediately perceived that calling her a "dear lady" would more annoy than please her. "Your Sussex accent has vanished, except to the expert ear, save for a trace that remains on your 'r's. The 'r' is the element of speech that varies most often in regional as well as foreign language pronunciations, perhaps because, along with the 'l,' it involves the most demanding placement of the tongue. Children, obviously, have much difficulty with these two consonants when learning to speak. I have made a study of such things. For my performing career."

"I'll say!" said Miss Daisy, putting two rolls upon her plate. "But how do you come by the rest?"

"The mature development of the calluses on your otherwise elegant fingertips shows that you have played a musical instrument from a very young age, hence I infer home instruction and likely home musicales with a musically inclined family. I believe you were trained on the flute, but now use a piccolo. My assumption is not based on physical evidence but rather the unlikelihood of the flute as a popular instrument on the variety stage in America, whereas the piccolo or other such frivolous pipes fit in admirably. I have not had an opportunity to view your feet—my loss, no doubt—but I suspect that you also dance and are exceeding light upon your feet."

I did not add that her current bulk made this phenomenon all the more amusing to audiences. (Watson, you wound me when you say I am not sensitive to the female sex!)

"You were the oldest of eight children and a second mother to most of them," I went on, "so you left England before you were twenty to seek your fortune here, and have done very well."

"Eight children, how did you—?"

"I noticed, of course, that very lovely bracelet as you reached for the rolls. It features seven charms, each studded with a gemstone assigned to various months as birth stones. You are far too young to have had seven children of your own (Oh, Watson, I can be a diplomat among men!), so I read the presence of siblings very dear to you, more so than most. Ergo, you were also a mother to them, and as much as you wished to escape a responsibility-laden childhood, you miss them very much."

By now tears were dewing those plump, rouged cheeks and the others at table were murmuring, both in sympathy for Miss Daisy, who seldom indulged in maudlin emotions, I imagine, and in amazement at my "powers," which were simply the observations any acute witness would make. A pity there are so few acute witnesses, even among the police, as is all too evident when criminal cases come to trial.

I had done my night's work.

After dinner the Professor sought me out and we conversed for some time about the "old days" he had seen and that I desired to see better in my mind's eye. I, of course, learned more from him than he from me, but I was forced to drop a few more hints about his protégé's European successes. Tears in an old man's eyes are more effective than acid in extracting information. I left feeling strangely moved and rather sorry that "Shylock Shakespeare" should desert the company with no explanation.

At the door Miss Daisy had recovered from her surprise sufficiently to "buttonhole" me and suggest that she looked forward to future dinners and revelations.

I told her that I might be recalled to England at any moment due to an impending death in the family, but most appreciated meeting her.

She clasped the wrist that was adorned by the bracelet I had noticed and confessed that she was contemplating a voyage "back home" after my diagnosis of her history.

Tears in an aging woman's eyes may not extract information, but they do respect. I took her hand, the one bearing the bracelet, bowed, and kissed it.

"Oh, you Europeans are so elegant," she sighed in farewell.

It was a small sacrifice to make for Shylock Shakespeare's first and last American performance.

32.

Unjust Desserts

~∽~

The "Alaska" is a baked ice.... The nucleus of or core of the entremet is an ice cream. This is surrounded by an envelope of carefully whipped cream, which, just before the dainty dish is served, is popped in the oven, or is brought under the scorched influence of a red hot salamander.

—ENGLISHMAN GEORGE SALA ON DELMONICO'S BAKED ALASKA

IN THE 1880S

Before our terrifying adventures in Paris last spring, I would have never thought to compare my friend Irene Adler Norton to a Red Indian.

Now that I had made the acquaintance, and witnessed the tenacious trail-following abilities of Red Tomahawk—a performer in Buffalo Bill's Wild West Show that was still thrilling Frenchmen and other visitors to the current World's Fair in Paris—I concluded that there was sometimes little difference between a detective and an Indian brave on the warpath.

After stewing for some time in our hotel room in a combina-

tion of high dudgeon and cigar smoke, Irene hauled me directly
from the comforts of the Astor House to 35th Street.

When I used the expression "hauled," I mean it quite literally.
As soon as we left the hotel, she took hold of my arm, or sleeve—
either would do; indeed, I think at the moment that a pinch of
skin would have sufficed . . . thank heavens I wore my lightweight
wool coatdress—and dragged me after her like a recalcitrant child
until the accouterments on my trusty chatelaine jingled like the
keys to a madhouse.

Irene need not have bothered hastening me along, but I suppose it gave her some sense of command that was sadly lacking in
other areas at the moment. I could have told her that I would have
gladly raced like the most ungoverned hoyden in her footsteps
to watch her track down and discipline Miss Elizabeth Jane
Cochrane for the sins of deceiving us and importing to America
the one man on earth whom Irene would most resent for poking
into her private life.

Perhaps that was because Mr. Sherlock Holmes seemed to
have very little private life to poke into in turn. Or because she
regarded him as a rival. Or because she was beginning to regard
him as something else: an insistent admirer.

While she rushed me from pillar to post—or rather hansom
cab to boarding house, for that is what all of New York City seems
sometimes: street traffic and endless rows of boarding houses,
respectable or quite otherwise—I had time to bask in Pink's new
plunge in disfavor with my friend, who had been far too tolerant
to her sister American's upstart ways in Paris, in my opinion.

The same woman who had tsked at Pink's inviting her own
mother along on an investigative visit to a medium that proved
fatal—to the medium rather than the mother, thank goodness—
now was rapping like an unpaid landlord at the dear old woman's
door, demanding entry.

"Mrs. Norton! Miss Huxleigh!" The dim-sighted old creature

blinked at us in benign surprise when she answered Irene's intemperate knock with her own mild countenance. "If you seek my daughter, I'm afraid that she is out."

"Out where?"

"Dining."

"Where?"

Mrs. Cochrane's scanty eyebrows raised as much as they were capable of. "Delmonico's," she answered, pride in her daughter's achievements in her voice.

Even I understood by now that Delmonico's was the city's finest restaurant, not only for the prestigious people and clubs that patronized it, but for catering the city's most lavish social affairs. Irene remembered from her youth that when Delmonico's had catered the wedding of "Boss" Tweed's daughter, she had received forty sets of sterling silver. She had explained that Tweed was a powerful politician who had ruled New York then. I could only recall the Jack the Ripper letter that had begun with the "Americanism" of "Dear Boss," and shudder at the implications as well as the excess.

"She dines alone," Irene stated to Pink's mother, sounding as vulgarly curious as a policeman.

"Indeed no. My daughter need never dine alone, but she seldom occupies herself with the gentlemen who so persistently seek her company. She is too busy at her job. But this is a foreign gentleman, I believe, and will not stay long in this country."

"Foreign," Irene repeated. "You mean from . . . oh, say, Montenegro?"

"Oh, gracious no, from nowhere so obscure as that. She mentioned, complained really before she left, for she has a most unreasoning dislike of the nationality, I am sorry to say, Miss Huxleigh." Here she shrugged apology at me, which was a pleasant gesture few ever bothered to show me. "He is English."

"Aha!" Irene barked the word like a soprano who has found a letter proving some basso's infidelity in a grand opera. "I mean," she added in the face of Mrs. Cochrane's gentle confusion, "that we had surmised that an acquaintance of ours was in the city and would be most pleased to speak with him again."

"If you hurry to Delmonico's, you may," Mrs. Cochrane advised our by-then-departing backs.

"Irene," I objected when we had attained the street again. "You needn't keep me in constant custody like an errant schoolboy. I expect your grip to shift from my wrist to my ear at any second."

"Oh. My apologies, Nell. I am much concerned to catch the minx consorting with the enemy, that is all."

"Much as I dislike Mr. Holmes, and have never been shy of saying so, I doubt he is 'the enemy.'"

She whistled as shrilly for a cab as any masher, and, when an operatic diva whistles, the result is ear-piercing. I cringed and scanned the area for witnesses, but it was that time when everyone was hurrying home as twilight gives way to electric street lights and no one notices anything.

Three hansoms, however, had noticed Irene and her upraised hand, after that whistle.

She eyed the drivers swiftly and chose the one who wore his hat most rakishly tilted on his head. "Delmonico's and I'll pay you a dollar for every omnibus you outrun."

I gasped as I was forced to bound into the hansom after Irene, for the omnibus drivers of New York City were madmen who jousted dray wagons and even the track-running trams for precedence on the jammed streets.

The ride was a rough clattering over tram tracks thankfully absent of cars and a constant nudging of gurneys and carriages and omnibuses that we overtook like a careening barrel.

Even while I was seated, my poor chatelaine chimed like a demented clock that mistook each second for an hour or half hour worth tolling, and my teeth chattered to match the rhythm.

"Must we race so?" I asked.

"I don't want the quarry to escape. I wish to catch them red-forked."

"Why must we do so?"

She sat back so hard that the leather upholstery squeaked protest in a great cushiony sigh.

"How would you like it, Nell, if Nellie Bly and Sherlock Holmes were dining at a cosy country inn after secretly inquiring into your hidden ancestry in Shropshire?"

"I have no hidden ancestry."

"Oh, no?" Irene leaned as close as a melodrama villain and produced a stage whisper in which she emphasized every consonant like a bullet. "And what about the pig thief hanged at Tyburn."

I kept silence for a few moments. "Baron de Rothschild assured me that this unhappy forebear was left out of my family tree in the ancient Bible he gave me as gift. How do you know of it? Did he tell you?"

"Yes." She sat back smugly and flaunted the cigarette case and lucifer that she knew I detested, especially in the close quarters of a hired cab.

"He didn't! He is a man of his word."

"Well." She exhaled a bit of smugness with her cigarette smoke. "He did in one respect. I can read lips, did you know? A most handy facility for an actress or singer who must not miss an entrance cue. Sometimes orchestras will try to drown out the superior instrument, the singers."

"You understood what he whispered to me! And never said anything from that day to this?"

"I never had reason to correct your assertions before. Usually you cut truth as fine as a mouse hair."

"I'd forgotten about the pig thief," I said, "even if you had not. Irene, what will you do, anyway, if you find Pink and Mr. Holmes dining together? There is no law against such a thing."

"There is an unwritten law, Nell, that someone who masquerades as a friend, or at least an ally, should refrain from conducting secret business behind one's back."

"Granted," I said, "but I have never mistaken Elizabeth Cochrane, or Nellie Bly, or Pink, for a friend, or even an ally."

"Is it because of Quentin?" she asked quietly. Carefully. Her mad dashing urgency of the past hour was suddenly becalmed.

I didn't bother to deny her underlying assumption. "No. I mistrusted her almost as soon as we met her in Paris. Everything about her was so *convenient*. I found that implausible."

"Brava, Nell. Your instincts exceeded mine on that score. I can see, from her newshound viewpoint, that our matters and necessities cheated her of the prize she seeks as others covet gold: the glister of exposure and renown. She has not considered that finding my origins might distress me beyond words. She sees me as impervious and my personal history is like a treasure quest to her. And I suppose there is some revenge in it, revenge for my allowing her to trail along on our Ripper hunt, then preventing her from revealing the unthinkable answer to the world."

"Sherlock Holmes was as adamant about that as you, perhaps even more so."

"Yet she enlists him to delve into my past like a miner digging for gold in the West. Why would he bother? Why would he even come to America at the beck and call of a sensation-seeking reporter like herself? Unless he is . . . enamored of her!" Irene shook her head into a veil of her own created smoke. "Impossible! I have never known a man more immune to women."

I remained silent, bearing the heavy knowledge that her assessment was true . . . except possibly in her own case. I had seen the written evidence of it, and could not forget it. "To Sherlock Holmes, she was always 'the' woman."

Sometimes my ever-so-astute friend was infuriatingly blind.

With a lurch that nearly tossed us over the half-doors that enclosed us in the hansom, our driver stopped and thrust a grimy face through the trapdoor above us. "Two dollars, ma'am, and my greetings to Boss Tweed if you get to hell before me, as I'm sure you will at the rate you travel."

She passed him three coins, I saw, and smiled tersely.

We stepped out into an electric-lit fairyland on the corner of Fifth Avenue and 26th Street. The four-story restaurant occupied the corner location and featured an excessive number of striped awnings on the first three-stories of frontage.

Irene's sudden and relentless rush had ended. "We are just opposite the lower end of Union Square, Nell, where I performed so often as a child. This I recall. Why not other things?"

"Performing was like doing lessons for you. This was . . . a holiday."

"I remember standing here—I must have been . . . what, twenty?—when Edison lit up Broadway with arc lights on twenty-foot-high cast-iron posts from here to Madison Square to demonstrate the power and future of his electric lights. These very posts remain, but the lights have expanded like the stars. That spectacular event I remember as clearly as yesterday. It was astounding."

The brilliantly lit corner was astounding even today. In my natural state (that is, alone). I should never dare approach so intimidating an establishment as Delmonico's, much less pass the handsome decorative iron railings that created a barricade around the building within which summer dinners ate al fresco.

Yet Irene's bracing presence was always an "open sesame." Her stage experience allowed her to seem at home in any environment, no matter how new or strange or even supercilious.

She approached this exclusive place like an actress entering on a cue, in a persona that brooked no obstacles. Now, once again she called upon years of theatrical bluster to broach the most blue-blooded restaurant in New York without a reservation, and without reservation.

A large man in formal dress awaited our bold-faced approach at the doors. (Irene was bold-faced, I was hoping to be invisible and remain so.)

"Madam?" he inquired. "May I help you?"

Irene gazed past him, going on tiptoe, craning her neck in the most refined, delicate manner I have ever seen so unladylike a gesture essayed.

"I fear you may not help me," she said at last, turning a liquid eye and voice upon her unsuspecting prey. "For we are late, dreadfully late."

Of course telling him from the first that he could do nothing immediately gave him a prideful stake in proving her wrong.

"It was a dreadful omnibus wreck on Broadway," she went on. "Why will they drive in that breakneck fashion?"

"I can't say, madam, but do you mean that you are late for a reservation?"

"Even worse," Irene said, looking distraught enough to have lost a dear friend in the fictional omnibus collision. "We are late in meeting our friends, and the gentleman came all the way from England. I am *desolée*."

Her resorting to the French word made her into the tragedienne Rachel for a moment. Really, had I been the girl's governess I would have nipped these thespian tendencies firmly in the bud.

The maitre d', however, was more easily impressed. "From England you say?"

"Yes, have you seen him?" She glanced hastily over her shoulder at me and lowered her voice. "There has been a long separation, and my dearest friend, well, this meeting is quite crucial."

Here I almost overcame my natural reticence and shouted out my objections like a barrister before the criminal Crown Court at the Old Bailey. Irene, my dearest friend, was making me out to be a romantic interest of Sherlock Holmes! Had I not been anticipating the tart comeuppance she would shortly be giving him and our erstwhile associate Pink, I could never have held my tongue at being a party to such a travesty.

The maitre d' honored me with an inquiring, yet not unsympathetic glance. He appeared quite taken by my quiet dress and modest demeanor, for his gaze grew as kindly as a bachelor uncle's: utterly mistaken but well-meaning.

"There are several British gentlemen dining here tonight," he admitted.

"You see, Nell," Irene tossed comfortingly over her shoulder, "I told you we should find Chauncey here and nowhere else in New York." She smiled at the maitre d'. "Chauncey is a gentleman of the finest sensibilities and discernment. He is also somewhat over six feet tall and dark-haired."

"A handsome fellow?"

This gave Irene pause. "Distinguished, rather. And I rather think he is with Miss Nellie Bly."

"Oh, madam, why didn't you say so! Of course, though I should not hesitate to call him handsome," he said with a nauseating smirk in my direction.

I blushed deeply enough to merit our erstwhile friend Pink's childhood nickname myself.

"They are meeting again after a separation," Irene confided to the waiter with the beaming pride of a matchmaking maiden aunt.

That was, of course, completely true and conveyed the completely wrong impression. I have never known someone as adept at *not* lying as Irene, and yet as able at achieving the same results as lying.

"I believe I can assist," the maitre d' said. "Please follow me, ladies."

Irene did, and thus I was forced to also.

The rooms before us shone with electric lights glancing off fine china and crystal and ladies's jewels and men's spectacles.

I felt distinctly underdressed, but then again I was the lost Chauncey's country sweetheart and could be expected to be somewhat gauche, as the French so aptly say. I was in a sad state when I could only describe my situation with a French word.

Jejune, also came to me. Apparently the French had many words for awkward women and I had learned every one.

I have never dreaded a meeting as much as I did that one. Though I longed to see Pink disgraced in Irene's and her own eyes, and possibly even Sherlock Holmes's, I did not relish seeing Irene confront the one's treachery and the other's concealed admiration again.

Both struck me as dangerous, though I could not quite say why.

I saw Pink facing us at a table for four; her small beaded evening reticule lay at one empty place. Her head was tilted in that charming heliotrope velvet hat with the pink taffeta band as she gazed at the gentleman whose erect back faced us like a well-tailored wall.

How odious of Mr. Holmes to be paging through the documents of Irene's obviously irregular birth! How mean and self-serving of Pink to unleash the London bloodhound on the trail of my American friend's humble, even scandalous roots. My hands made fists inside my cotton gloves as we approached.

As bold-faced as Irene could be when she had to, I alone understood the sensitive soul of the creative artist beneath. I saw now the tiny child forced upon the stage, alone in life except for a freak show of kindly but eccentric fellow performers. However crude Pink's own upbringing with her violent stepfather, she had at least had a mother and brothers and sisters. Irene had nothing. Except me, much later. Much too late.

"I'm afraid," the maitre d' paused to tell us when we were still out of earshot of the table's occupants. Why should *he* be afraid? "I'm afraid that the party has already ordered dessert." He paused to interrogate a passing waiter whose face was as black and shiny as patent leather. "Yes. They've ordered dessert already. Baked Alaska, a speciality of the house, for the gentleman, and tutti-frutti, a fresh new ice cream confection for the lady. Would you care to join them?"

"Oh, yes," said Irene, beginning to pinch off the fingers of her finest white kid gloves with the prissy exactitude of a debutante. "I would definitely order two more tutti-fruttis for us. That will be all."

He bowed at her dismissal and we were left alone to approach our conspiring betrayers.

Pink saw us first and looked up, shocked. Then she flushed the color of her taffeta ribbon.

"My dear Pink," Irene said, "or should I say 'Scarlet'? I understand that you are employing foreign spies in the New Jersey public records department. I can't say that I'm shocked at your going behind my back. You are, after all, a conscienceless newspaper reporter who purports to be the conscience of the community while selling your acquaintances for the thrill of a headline, but I am shocked that you would attempt, and succeed, at recruiting this gentleman to your vile impertinences."

Irene's voice radiated righteous rage. I should not have liked to have been the object of her regard at that moment, but the gentleman at the table turned to face her despite the acid etching her ordinarily mellow voice.

For a moment, I felt pity even for Sherlock Holmes.

The man's head turned with the slow social arrogance I had observed in him before. I saw his profile.

No. Not his profile. Not *his* profile.

Another's.

I tried to breath in, to draw in the reality my eyes could not deny, but I had no breath. I had stopped like a clock in need of urgent rewinding.

Sounds of clinking china and crystal and sterling silver kept easy enough time all around me. Voices murmured like waves, like the endless sick-making waves of the Atlantic Ocean. I was going to be sick, I was going to, going to . . .

Irene's gloveless hand seized my wrist and her nails dug into the bare flesh between glove and sleeve until the pain made my eyes swim in saltwater . . . my own tears.

"We will leave you two to your just desserts," she said with as much loathing as I had ever heard her use onstage when a role demanded it.

She turned me with a clatter I took for the diners' silverware all around us, chiming, chiming, but then realized it was only my own suddenly spun chatelaine, given to me by Godfrey, dear Godfrey, who was so distant and whom I so wished to be near me now.

I was being propelled back along our path through the gay and glittering crowd, past waltzing waiters with trays held over their heads like shields, past eyes that glanced up at us and vanished into our wake.

33.

Desserted

~·~

She proved to be a slender woman ... clad in a dark blue cloth dress with a corsage bouquet of red roses, a somewhat stunning hat with a big gilt arrow on the side crowned a face of some regularity of feature and from under the hat to the rear projected that arrangement of women's hair technically known as the "Psyche twist."

—A "RATHER PRETTY" NELLIE BLY TESTIFYING BEFORE THE ASSEMBLY JUDICIARY COMMITTEE, *THE ALBANY ARGUS*, 1889

"I'm going to be—" I muttered.

"No, you are not," Irene insisted. "We are on solid land now, Nell, and you will not be sick. Granted, I don't like the view, but we will not give *anyone* the satisfaction of either of us being sick. We will go back to the hotel and regroup."

"Regroup." I laughed queasily. "We are hardly a group."

So swiftly had Irene retraced our steps that we were out in the overlit evening air in no time. I suddenly felt a deep sigh escaping me and I could breathe again.

"You wanted to say something to Pink," I pointed out, rather feebly.

"At this point it is best that I say nothing to anyone. Oh, Nell! Nell." She stopped to face me, her eyes shining suspiciously. "I have miscalculated so abysmally! And the worst of it is I have dragged you into this . . . maelstrom with no idea of what we really faced. If my own accursed past had not been involved, I might have seen . . . I might have spared you. I would give anything to have spared you—"

At that moment, a man overtook us.

"Nell! Irene! Nell! I don't understand. Why are you here?"

Irene rounded on Quentin Stanhope like a fishwife, but she said not a word. He stood looking back and forth from her gorgeous Medusa glare to my own evasive eyes with an air of utter confusion.

"You are right," Irene said. "We were not supposed to be here."

"If you won't stay, at least let me escort you back to your hotel."

"No. We wouldn't want your baked Alaska to melt," she said in tones as icy as the dessert's name. I admit that even in my desperate straits I felt a wistful desire to know just what a "baked Alaska" was.

"I can't let you leave like this. Let me at least find you a cab."

"We found one to get here and we can find one to leave."

"Please." He was looking at me. I looked away. "I'm quite at sea. I had no idea you were here in America. You two. At least tell me where you're staying."

Irene considered. Her cheeks held round circles of rouge that were far too obvious to be painted there by anything but strong emotion. I had never seen her so furious, and that it was on my behalf almost made me dissolve into the tears I would rather die than release.

"You may call on *me* at the Astor House," she said finally. "I may receive you."

"Irene!" He cast another, mute appealing glance at me, but dared not say my name.

The intensity of his look made me turn away, and that in turn revived Irene's anger. She grasped my forearm and drew me with her to the curbside. We walked along the sidewalks of Fifth Avenue, which thronged with fashionable, merrymaking pedestrians alongside a frothing river of vehicles and horses of every description.

"Is he—?" I asked at length.

"Gone back inside. A gentleman does not desert a lady at table."

"Does not desert . . . dessert," I added, hiccoughing and laughing and crying at once.

"Are you still going to be sick?"

"Possibly."

"If I hail a cab will that make it worse?"

"Possibly."

"What will make it better?"

"Nothing."

"Then I might as well hail a cab."

I could not object to that, so we were soon jolting back to our hotel, Irene's forearm twined around mine as if she would never let go.

"I was just so surprised," I finally said. "I thought—"

"So we both thought, but I should have known better. I am a stupid vain creature to think that Sherlock Holmes would cross a puddle in Cheapside to meddle in my puny affairs, much less the Atlantic Ocean."

"I assumed the same, and I am not vain, though I have been known to be stupid, especially lately."

"Oh, Nell, we are neither of us stupid, only angry at ourselves because we are so angry at others. I would smoke, but that would make you sicker."

"Actually, the scent of sulphur is bracing. I rather like it."

"Then I shall light lucifers until we get home."

"How often a hotel has been our home. Perhaps we travel too much."

A scratch sounded in the demidark of the hansom cab, and then the tiny flare of a flame and the sharp smell of the devil's sulphur.

"You looked like a Fury back there," I said.

"I felt like one. I don't like to be surprised, and I don't like you to be shocked, especially by other people. That is my job."

"You do it well."

"Thank you, Nell. A demanding audience drives a performer to her highest levels."

"He calls her Pink."

"So do many people. It means nothing."

"Being in New York means something."

"We are here and it means nothing yet."

"Only because you have not figured out what it means, but you will."

"Not at this rate. Nell, I am so sorry I did not anticipate this."

I was silent for a while. "But I did, you know. Oh, not this particular instance, but the general . . . situation."

To that she had no answer, this glibbest of women. We descended our cab, moved through the Astor House's crowded reception rooms and took an elevator to our floor without me even noticing how crushingly close such conveyances were. We said little more that evening, being both exhausted and disappointed, perhaps for slightly different reasons.

It was barely nine o'clock the next morning when a bellman brought up a card. Quentin's.

Irene tossed it on the nearest table and stalked to the window. I retrieved it. I didn't know that Quentin had a card. I wondered what it would say. Very little. QUENTIN STANHOPE, it read, BELGRAVE SQUARE, LONDON, ENGLAND.

"I doubt he still lives in London," I noted.

"Nor do we."

"Such an address is not on your card."

"I am not a *spy*," she hissed exactly like one of Sarah Bernhardt's pet snakes. "A spy who turns on friends."

I couldn't defend him. It was not that I wouldn't, even now, only I couldn't think of a reason.

"Did you sleep, last night?" she asked.

"Some."

She snorted, but I had no heart to correct her. "I was awake half the night myself, asking why he was here and what Pink's true game is."

"A sensational story, you said it yourself."

She turned from the windows, the wine velvet draperies resembling a stage curtain behind her. "If so, I am not the sole subject of it. I am hardly well known enough that my foggy origins should raise a stir anywhere. Pink believes a murderer stalks my past. That must be her goal, unmasking the murderer. My past is incidental."

"No one's past is incidental to their present."

Her smile was broad. " 'The past is prologue.' Antonio. Act Two, Scene One. *The Tempest.* Quite brilliantly said, Nell, although Shakespeare anticipated you by a few hundred years. Why did Henry the Eighth kill so many wives?" she asked out of the blue.

"They were inconvenient to him. And some, he claimed, were unfaithful."

"Inconvenient and unfaithful? And what is the incontrovertible proof of such behavior?"

I shrugged more casually than I felt. The incontrovertible proof was being caught in the unexpected company of the wrong person. "The evidence of one's eyes?"

"Sometimes the evidence of one's eyes is unreliable." Irene came to take Quentin's card from my unresisting fingers. "Let's have the fellow up to explain himself. You can wait in the bed-chamber."

"I suppose I should. That way you would have free rein to question him and I could . . . eavesdrop."

"Exactly."

"Eavesdropping is rather unforgivable."

"Not as unforgivable as secretly consorting."

"Indeed." I bustled away and carefully set the chamber door to remain ever so slightly ajar by stuffing a rolled-up stocking in it.

I had some time to wait, but finally a muffled knock sounded on our hall door. Muffled voices drifted across my threshold.

I pressed my ear to the opening.

". . . insanely inappropriate to call now . . ."

". . . utterly astounded," Quentin was saying. "I had no idea you were in New York."

"Why were you here yourself, then?" Irene was asking.

"Some remaining matters related to the Ripper case."

"What matters?"

"I am not at liberty to say."

"Why were you meeting with Pink?"

"She knows New York, and she invited me to do so."

"And did you visit the New Jersey records departments at her behest?"

A long pause, during which I fought against an overwhelming urge to sneeze, as one always does when it is most crucial not to.

"Yes."

"That is all the answer you have? There is no other reason why you would spend more than a week crossing an ocean merely to pry into my antecedents, or lack of them?"

"She said something about some present story of hers being related to your origins and that a foreigner wouldn't attract comment, as he might have ancestors who had emigrated here and be interested in tracing them. It seemed harmless enough, spending a few hours assisting her. She *was* asked to remain mute about the murders of the century, after all."

"And you felt no guilt about going behind my back?"

"I had no idea I was going behind your back, as you put it, because I had no idea you were on the scene yourself. Irene, she said some crimes she was considering for a story seemed to involve persons who might have known you as a child. It struck me that I would be doing both of you a favor to perform this trifling task."

"And why would you be so willing to do Miss Nellie Bly a favor?"

I held my breath.

"Because that was the price of her silence!" he burst out. "Did you think that you and Sherlock Holmes insisting on it would have much effect after she returned to New York? She buttonholed me before I left the castle and demanded that I contact her later. When I did, she called me here. If I would do as she wished, so she could procure this new and, she said, equally appalling story, she would remain silent on what had transpired in Transylvania."

"Quentin, that is blackmail."

"It is bargaining, Irene, and I am used to such secret arrangements. I never dreamed it had anything to do with you personally, believe me, or I would never have agreed to it. And even when I arrived here, she said you were purely 'peripheral' to the story."

"Peripheral!" Irene did not like that.

He laughed at her deliberately exaggerated air of wounded vanity. "Of course you are never peripheral to anything you choose to involve yourself in. And I would never had been so reckless as to accommodate Pink had I known she was flying in the face of your personal wishes. She has apparently bent both of us to her damned sensation-mongering."

I heard the scratch of a lucifer and smelled sulphur and smoke. The crisis was over. I tried frantically to think of a way to idly enter the scene. Alas, I am no actress, and could only remain frozen by the door.

"And . . . Nell?" he asked as if treading on crystal. "How did she take the voyage over? I believe this was her first oceangoing journey."

I held my breath again.

"Splendidly," Irene lied through her teeth. "Quite the sailor."

"Is she—?"

"Tending to some domestic matters in the adjoining room. Now that I'm speaking to you again, Quentin, I'll fetch her."

By the time Irene finished her sentence she was sweeping my door open in a grand stage gesture, which unfortunately nearly knocked me over.

She shut the door behind her. "Gracious, Nell! You must be nimble on your feet when you eavesdrop. Are you all right?"

I rubbed my mashed nose. "I shall have to say I have a catarrh. Oh. Now he might assume that I have been weeping! What do you think? Is he truly in your good graces again?"

"I think he is not telling me the full story, but that is a given with the spy trade. I think he means us no harm, but he may be used to deal ill with us nonetheless. And I think that if you deign to show yourself and be your charming self, we shall have him wholeheartedly in our camp."

"My last attempt to charm a gentleman to our camp was disastrous, as you recall."

Irene smiled in memory of the full ironic implications of the incident to which I referred. "No, it was embarrassing to you, but quite advantageous to the larger rescue effort underway. If you can manage to flirt with a Gypsy who speaks no English, who does not speak at all, I daresay you can do wonders with Quentin, who is much more personable, not to mention accessible."

"Flirt! With Quentin? I could not."

"Why not? Pink can."

"How odious of you to point that out, Irene! I do not need reminding how that minx does not hesitate to ingratiate herself with unsuspecting gentlemen."

"Have you not heard the American expression, 'to fight fire with fire?' You have a perfect opportunity now, and, in all honesty, I think you have the upper hand over Pink here, if you will deign to use it."

"I?"

"You." With that she whirled to my rear and pushed me out the door into our parlor. Nor did she follow immediately after me. Quentin and I were, for the moment, alone in the room.

"Nell!" He had turned from the window to greet me.

There he stood, an ordinary gentlemen in ordinary clothes, not muffled by one of his exotic disguises. He looked as he had when I had first met him a decade before in Berkley Square, where our roles were strictly assigned: I was the untried young governess and he was the mistress's dashing younger brother.

I was wrong, though. This I saw as I approached the window and the daylight revealed the seams a life in eastern wastelands had etched as finely as acid at the edges of his features. He was as I had never seen him before, clean-shaven (a state I much prefer in the modern man) and both younger and older than I remembered.

"I'm sorry if my presence in New York last night shocked you so," he said, "and now I see why you felt so upset. I've apologized to Irene for being an unwitting tool of Nellie Bly, but I must also apologize to you. I know you would resent my conspiring against your dearest friend in any way. I don't blame you in the slightest for cutting me at Delmonico's. I see now how bad things looked."

That is what he thought it was? That I had nobly snubbed him in public on my friend's behalf? That this was a mere social misunderstanding? Could he have failed to see that my distress was purely for my own selfish reasons, that I was appalled by the simple fact that he was in the company of that brash American girl? That I was a childish, jealous fool with no reason to object to his being anywhere with anyone?

While I reeled from the blessed blindness of the man, I realized that the last time we had been alone together we also had stood by a window, far away and in far different circumstances. The memory warmed my cheeks.

"You are not still angry with me?" he asked anxiously.

"No. I wasn't angry, just shocked. You met Pink midway

through our last . . . adventure, and I suppose a man of military bent who has been exiled in savage and distant lands cannot be expected to know the wiles of a woman who has made her way in such a cutthroat metropolis as New York City. Pink has always been Nellie Bly, first and foremost. A wise woman, and man, would do well to realize that."

"Then we are friends again?" He took my hand.

He had taken far more venturesome liberties when last we met, but that had ended badly. A hand seemed to bridge past and present safely and quite nicely for now. "The past is prologue," Irene had quoted so elevated a source as Shakespeare only yesterday. And a prologue implied a future.

I found myself smiling, my fingers relaxing in his easy, comradely custody.

"We have been allies far longer than even you and Irene," he added, instantly invoking our ancient pairing in a schoolroom game of Blind Man's Buff. Then I had been the blinded one.

This time I frankly blushed. He regarded this embarrassing symptom with what I could only describe as relief, and a certain satisfaction in his hazel eyes that only embarrassed me further, for I couldn't explain it, but suspected that I would be completely startled if I could.

"I am glad to see you again, Nell, and to see you smiling again. Dare I hope that I am partly responsible?"

"Perhaps. The events of last spring were earthshaking to me."

"I shouldn't wonder, but this is summer and autumn fast approaches. Perhaps we could create kinder memories here. A visit to Coney Island?"

"How long are you to stay?"

"I don't know. It depends what penance Irene has in mind for me." His smile turned wry.

"She doesn't show it, but she is horribly disturbed by this recent probing into her past. Pink"—I nearly choked on the name but still he focused only on me, on my expression, on what I might say next—"is determined to solve the mysteries she believes she has found, no matter how much it may hurt Irene. Or me."

"A newspaper reporter is like a policeman these days, forever exposing people's secrets. For myself, my calling is to preserve secrets. I will do what I can, but—"

His fingers tightened on mine, far more than convention allowed.

"You must understand, Nell. To some extent, it is my assignment to placate Nellie Bly. The Foreign Office wants not a syllable of last spring's conclusions slipping out into the public consciousness. My superiors consider Miss Bly dangerous, and I must confess that I'm glad to find her on the trail of another story now, even if it brushes too close to Irene and you. I hesitate to say what a great government might do if it considered one individual too serious a threat to world stability."

"You—" I breathed.

"No. not I. I prevent mayhem. That's why I'm here. To prove she is no threat. If that necessity should run counter to Irene's interests . . ." He shook his head. "I will do all I can to see that it doesn't, but it would be better not to let Irene know."

"Not tell Irene?"

"Do you tell Irene everything?" he asked softly.

"Almost everything."

"But not all."

The lower his tone had grown the closer his head bent over mine.

"No." I spoke even more softly, so he had to bend his head further to hear me.

At my answer he brought my hand to his lips.

I had been right! He was very good at it indeed.

The door to the bedchamber cracked open.

We turned to find Irene watching us.

34.

Inhuman Nature

⤜✥⤛

Save for her hoggish face she is perfectly formed....
This prodigy of nature is the general topic of conversation
in the metropolis.

—JOHN FAIRBURN, 1815

I slept like the dead that night, exhausted by my previous worries, dreaming I was a compass point fixed upon a hand, spinning round and round, as in a waltz.

Irene always ordered breakfast in our room when we traveled. It was frightfully extravagant, but her own highly rewarded "cases," and Godfrey's increasing Rothschild commissions, made all possible. I was finding the habit of lavish breakfasts amenable myself. The custom bowed to Irene's former theatrical life, when she stayed up until three and rose at ten, then spent an hour or so nibbling on breakfast foods and sipping cups of bitter, strong coffee sweetened with cream and sugar over the daily newspapers, railing or purring at reviews, and preparing her toilette for the day.

Even Godfrey, industrious barrister that he was, always up

with the swallows when I had worked for him years ago, had converted to Irene's luxurious habit of morning lethargy. Seeing her lounging like a lazy cat in her lace-frothed combing gown, her auburn-gold hair coiling loose and tied back with a soft chiffon bow the color of ripe peaches, I could understand why Godfrey was often loath most mornings to leave for his new office in Paris.

Today she had been busy too; half of the *New York Sun* spread over our table like a figured cloth.

"I had so dearly hoped," she said as soon as she saw me, her forefinger triumphantly spearing a column of fine print. "Just see! 'Just desserts' indeed!"

Her mood was so markedly improved that I immediately dashed over to read the cause.

DAREDEVIL DARLING

"DESSERTED" AT DELMONICO'S

ENGLISH LORD LEAVES

NELLIE BLY IN THE LURCH

TUTTI FRUTTI-FOR-ALL

"The rival newspaper to Pink's *World*, I presume," Irene announced.

"Quentin isn't an English lord!"

"To Americans every decently dressed Englishman is a lord. Quentin is certainly a gentleman, for he returned to her table. He would never let a lady languish."

"Pink, or Nellie Bly, I should say, is not a lady."

"Nor am I!" Irene said. She knew better than to declare that I was a lady, for the title must be conferred by blood in my land. "Or you, apparently. You haven't read how *we* are described in the article."

"Good heavens! We are mentioned?"

"About as accurately as Quentin."

I read through three paragraphs of exceedingly tiny type, my nose up against it so closely that I sneezed from the rank odor of fresh ink and had to turn my head away.

"A French countess! You!"

"I am from Paris," she shrugged. "I could have been a queen. I am *desolée* that these New World hack writers did not at least mistake me for a *duchesse.*" She laughed like a schoolgirl.

"And . . . 'her British secretary'?"

"They could have at least declared you an 'Honorable.' "

"I am quite happy to remain common, and, in fact, I have in the past acted as secretary to both you and Godfrey, so I am not misrepresented at all in the article."

"No? Read further."

I could see that my righteous attitude irritated Irene, as it always did, which was why I adopted it. I read further, as instructed.

"I? Slap Quentin's face!? Never. Well, perhaps had he been a schoolroom charge of mine and misbehaved so badly."

"Quite the little scandal-mongering firebrand when you travel abroad, Nell. I shall have to reconsider associating with you in future."

"It's all . . . a pack of lies."

"Of course. It's in the newspaper. I think Pink will be fulminating over this very article this morning. Perhaps she will think twice in future about considering me as a means and an opportunity for furthering her career."

"This may be amusing to you, Irene, but I doubt Pink has learned a thing."

"And you. What have you learned recently?"

I sighed as I returned her piercing gaze. "Quentin is cultivating Pink because her reporting instincts are dangerous to the Foreign Office. That is why he's here."

"That is one reason why he's here," Irene added airily, doing something that had amazed me for as long as I had known her: sipping coffee without making a face.

I could say nothing, of course.

"What did you think of his report on the birth records for New Jersey?"

"That you do not appear to have been born there, or that no sooner were you born than you were given a pseudonym."

"Either instance is provocative, since one of the very few facts I can remember from my early years is that I was born in New Jersey. As soon as I decamped to England, I was endlessly asked where I was born, as if that made any difference in America. And I always said New Jersey. I always thought I was born in New Jersey. And everybody English I met said, "Oh, and the county is named after *our* isle of Jersey, is it not?"

"And I said it was a state, which is what we have over here and they are like very large counties. And some people, usually other sopranos, were unkind enough to mention that 'Jersey' was also a breed of cow."

I was, of course, laughing into my scones at this recital, for that is exactly what I thought, and every bit of it, when I had first met Irene and heard of 'New Jersey.' And I was not even a soprano. I could not even sing a note worth listening to.

"Are we English really so dreadfully literal-minded as that?"

"With Americans, you are. After all, it's barely more than a hundred years since you were forced to turn us out the back gate and let us go our own way."

"And that way was 'up,' as I see from New York City."

"Astounding, isn't it? The pigs were still grazing on Broadway when I left, and now look at it."

"Pigs are very astute creatures," I said from my vast store of animal husbandry observations during my Shropshire youth. "I would beware of any place they rejected."

She laughed again. Somehow this breakfast, reminiscent of many such mornings at Neuilly, and repairing the misunderstanding with Quentin last night had eased both of our minds. Or, I thought, perhaps getting the better of Pink was the cause.

Either way, I felt wonderful. Irene and I were undivided allies again after our long enforced separation last spring that had compelled Irene to forge a new alliance with the stranger, Pink.

As much as the young American reminded me of Quentin's charming niece Allegra, she was no sheltered and green girl, but a headstrong woman who had supported both herself and her widowed mother on her earnings as a newspaper reporter. If such a history was admirable, it also made for someone with a self-interest stronger than any common needs of Irene and myself.

I can't say that I was sorry that Pink had proved herself to be so treacherous, only that Quentin had been a key element in that revelation.

While I was mulling over the immediate past, it soon became evident that Irene's mind was on the future, and her own mysteriously distant past.

"I will have to take your word on the indisputable intelligence of pigs," she said finally, blowing out a sinuous wreath from her post-breakfast cigarette that would from now on remind me of deadly ectoplasm. "You are, after all, the country-bred woman. It is time, I think, to visit a person Professor Marvel mentioned to me and who is quite apropos to your upbringing and also to my vaunted but perhaps false, or concealed, origins. I refer to the Pig Lady of Hoboken, New Jersey."

35.

A Sinister Surname

❧

"That blackguard Svengali!"
"That's the man! His real name is Adler; his mother was a
Polish singer."

—*TRILBY*, GEORGE DU MAURIER, 1894

Our trip to New Jersey would have been a holiday outing were not so much in question. We took a ferry, which brazenly advertised itself as the first in the United States . . . at some laughably recent date in the early part of the century. In England there are rowboats older than that lumbering ferry boat! Once across the Hudson River, we would be in the quaint hamlet of Hoboken.

"You must understand, Nell," Irene told me while we stood at the ferry boat's eastern rail to watch the tall profile of Manhattan Island slip behind us, "that some of the people who perform on the popular stage are . . . uniquely gifted. They are not merely singers and dancers."

"What you mean is that their talents tend to the peculiar, like Professor Marvel's immense grasp of trivia."

"Yes. And I also mean that a good many of them, like Thumbelina, have turned curses into talents, have made seeming marvels from what ordinarily would be considered great misfortune."

"I don't understand."

"I merely warn you that the Pig Lady, whom I remember quite clearly despite my admittedly fuzzy recollection in other matters, followed a profession she was born to, as I was to singing. Only her career was shaped by what most people would consider tragic abnormalities. The important thing to keep in mind is that she found a place in the world despite these handicaps."

"You mean that she is deformed, that she really does resemble a pig?"

"I am one who considers what people may do, or have done to them, can deform their characters in far worse ways than what nature may have done to deform their features or limbs. Anna Bryant is the kindest woman I ever knew. She never for a moment held my looks against me, which is more than I can say for some women blessed with beauty but determined to claim it all."

"You warn me so that I don't embarrass her."

"I warn you so that you don't embarrass yourself. I see now that I grew up among quite unique people and yet took their variety and odd camaraderie for granted. Children will do that. You must understand that some of them overcame enormous odds and changed handicaps into assets, however bizarre."

"How did you remain so . . . so—?"

"Ordinary? I don't know. I was in their keeping, but I wasn't theirs. And when I was about fifteen or so, I suddenly went from having a pretty and true little voice to having a Voice. I cannot tell you how that discovery changed me, and changed everything. It led *me* then, my Voice. I couldn't not use it and it told me loud and clear that it and I were no longer suitable for light entertainment."

"That is when you were 'sold' to the maestro?"

"They resented my defection to the legitimate stage, but I desperately needed a good singing tutor at that point, and was lucky enough to find the maestro. I could no longer stay up late to perform feats of breath-holding or between-act turns before the curtain. That's when I began working for the Pinkertons and studying opera every moment I could."

"And that is all the training you had? One American tutor?"

"The maestro possessed a remarkable musicianship, Nell. He was already past sixty when I began training with him, but his ear was as acute as an F-sharp, and his hands were strong and nimble on the violin. I should have been working on this level years earlier, but he had an amazing method of hastening my progress."

"And what was that?"

"You will doubt me."

"I never doubt you. Well, not often. Tell me."

"It was why my friends in the theater distrusted him so. They felt he was one of them, but had pretensions and denied their common background."

"They felt he was a fraud, but why? Surely the progress of your voice argued for his genius."

"It was his methods they distrusted." Irene stared at the long, island panorama passing before our eyes, her smile fond. "Perhaps because those methods were as eccentric as they themselves were. One's own oddities always look worse in others. The maestro had much time to make up for in my haphazard musical education, and many bad habits to cure." She turned to me with a shrug. "How do you think I learned the gentle art of mesmerism, Nell? He hypnotized me, to free my voice of my conscious control, and he taught me to do the same to myself, and, incidentally, others. It has proved a most useful skill, as you may remember from an adventure or two we have shared."

"Hypnotized you! And the results were benign?"

"Completely! I made remarkably fast progress. In fact, that is how I got my last name, I remembered during that sleepless night after Delmonico's, so there is no wonder that it can't be found in the birth records of New Jersey."

"Your last name? Adler, you mean. Are you saying it is not yours?"

"My mother, whoever she is or was, though insisting on my first name, left me no surname. The maestro named me after his own instructor in the arts of combining hypnotism and music, an oddly intense fellow he had encountered in Paris in the mid-fifties, even before I was born. This 'Adler' had quite impressed the maestro with his approach and had gone on to train one of the singing marvels of the time, a woman of absolutely no artistic background who apparently could not sing a true note before then."

"You had no such handicaps," I ventured.

"No, save for my naturally dark soprano that is not in fashion." She leaned against the railing, gazing on the intimidating profile of the city of New York as if it were becoming a phantasm beyond her reach. "So what used to be my avocation has become my mainstay."

"You mean investigating mysteries."

"Even if they concern myself." The smile faded as her thoughts darkened. "I would hate to think that the mystery of my origins has brought disaster and death to those who cared for me when I was too young to care for myself. I can easily live with having no past beyond the point I took a steamship to England. I cannot live with the possibility that these people face current danger because of me, and who I was, or was not."

"Shall you be sorry at what you find?"

"I may be, but Pink was right to summon us. I'm somehow central to these appalling murders, which seem almost staged to demand someone's attention, perhaps mine."

"Pink! What do you suppose she is up to now that our paths have separated?"

"Nothing that bodes well for our mission. Once again we wish to expose this murderer, or murderers, and yet return my long-ago friends and myself to private life. Once again Pink has been drawn into my orbit by the morbid scent of the sensational, and will find it necessary to expose my friends and my own private life to the public.

"In a way, Nell"—She eyed me with an apologetic expression I seldom saw on her face—"I am very glad Quentin is here to distract her from mischief. No doubt his government feels the same way, although it might be that I make a far better distraction for Pink, and serve us all up to expediency. However, I have had an interesting communication from him."

"You? From Quentin?"

"Indeed, but it was about you."

"Why should he write to *you* about *me*?"

She smiled roguishly. "To get back into both of our good graces. He has invited you on an outing to Coney Island."

"Through you?"

"He wished to be sure that I was still not angry with him."

"And did he not care whether I was still angry with him?"

She eyed me with what could only be considered a smirk. "Apparently he is confident that you are not."

"Perhaps I wasn't, but I am now! Why can he not write to *me* about me?"

"Nell, he is being the complete gentleman. Were your father alive, I am sure he would have written him on this matter."

"My father is not alive and you are not my parent!"

"At any rate, I myself, as your friend, would urge you to go. After all, you may discover more of what Pink is up to."

"I will not associate with Quentin merely to spy on Pink!"

"Then associate with him for yourself alone."

"I have heard about Coney Island. It teems with gamblers, and loose women and thieves, and huge numbers of people in bathing costumes. . . ."

"And spectacular hotels and fireworks and the beautiful seaside. Besides, you would be safe with Quentin anywhere, Nell." An expression crossed her face I couldn't quite read, an exceptional instance, perhaps, in which I should definitely *not* be safe with Quentin, but she was not about to voice it.

"You must go, Nell. It is an opportunity not to be missed, and there is nothing in the nature of the invitation I could object to even if I were the sternest English parent, even if I were Prince Albert himself."

The notion of Irene in men's dress as the late and inflexibly dignified Prince Albert was so ludicrous I had to laugh. And in laughing, I lost all high moral ground, and was suddenly forced to do what I most desired and dreaded in all the world: agree to see Quentin Stanhope, alone, in a strange country, at an isolated and bizarre and shiveringly notorious pleasure garden.

So my only sojourn on water that was kind to both my eyes and delicate stomach ended with dire anxieties and mad speculations that made me as internally queasy as whitecaps on the Atlantic.

I was not optimistic about visiting the Pig Lady in such an uneasy state, for I had never been adept at tolerating the abnormal, despite the intense dose of it I had faced during our last expedition to another land.

The residential streets of New Jersey were no more exotic than those of New York City. One faced a long brown and red row of four-story domiciles, most of them boarding houses, I assumed.

I absolutely thirsted for something Georgian with white pillars and pediments, but little of that vintage seemed to have survived in this new land of America, except perhaps in public buildings. I even began to long for the elaborate mansard roofs of Paris in all their rococo frivolity.

American boarding houses may have had a domestic goddess, like Mr. Holmes's cherubic Mrs. Hudson in London, but they

were not on constant duty like a Paris concierge. After consulting
a row of mailboxes in the tiny entry hall, Irene led our assault on
a set of rooms that appeared to be at the end of a long and turning unlit staircase.

"She has retired from performing, I heard," Irene whispered
back at me as we twined our way upward single file. "I don't know
why, but certainly her funds are limited. I understand the current
performers take up a collection for her needs from time to time,
for she cannot convert to ordinary work. Like poor Phoebe, the
very condition that made her an object of curiosity and pity and
employment when she was young may prevent her from supporting herself now that she is older."

I felt in my coatdress pocket for my small leather coin purse,
wondering what I could contribute. I was used to feeding the pigs
from my early youth, but not a pig-faced woman, and couldn't
think of a delicate way to do it.

I huffed out one breath after another for four tall stories,
much missing our charming cottage in Neuilly, which featured
only one staircase, and that one straight up. It seemed odd to
think of Godfrey occupying our country home alone.

We were forced to stop several steps shy of the single door
that ended the stairs. Irene rapped on the door's lower half, several
times, and then it opened perhaps a foot wide.

I expected an occupant, but no one filled the interstice, or
appeared not to until I looked down.

Another dwarf!

I was beginning to feel like Snow White.

Irene began chattering with this stunted figure until it became
clear to me that this was not the Pig Lady, but a mere child. Once
I realized that this was a species familiar to me, above all of
Irene's exotic former associates, I leapt to the fore in both conversation and position.

"Well, my dear," I said, brushing past Irene. "I know we are strangers and may seem rather frightening, but we are quite harm-less and need only to meet the lady of the house."

I was interested to see in such close, though dim, quarters that the small figure was indeed a "child" of four or five, not a dwarf at all.

My firm but friendly way with children once again produced results. Her already wide eyes grew as large as lace doilies. "Mama's working," she said.

"She is not here?" Irene asked from behind me with a sad wrench in her voice.

I realized how very important this quest had become for her, and bent to take the child's tiny fingers in my own. They curled around my first joints in a most engaging and trusting way.

"We need only a few moments with your mama," I said in a conspiratory whisper, "and my friend is a famous opera singer who may have work for her."

"Oh!" The child eyed Irene, who was still a suppliant several steps below us. She frowned and stared. "She looks like the lady in the picture above my bed. Mama said she was my guardian angel."

I smiled on such childish faith. Doubtless her mama had pinned some madonna of the advertising world above the little girl's cot. If Irene's visage served as a calling card with this tiny gatekeeper, I was not about to argue.

As the child pulled the door wide I stepped inside, Irene prac-tically climbing my skirt hems as well as the last steep stairs to enter this aerie.

I turned back to shut the door behind her and almost teetered on the threshold, so steep were the stairs leading below. I turned with trepidation, realizing that the Pig Lady and this delightful child were living in straitened circumstances.

The room we stood in was dim, but the little girl tripped through its shadowy geography as ably as a mountain goat. An inner room had a window that overlooked the street, and at that uncurtained window sat a figure on a low stool. In her lap lay piece sewing work, a man's shirt, or an apron, perhaps. White at least, and made of coarse material from which the brutal square of daylight picked out every heavy thread.

The shock of such broad daylight made a silhouette of the sitter's figure. The curve of the head blossomed into a shapeless funnel. The profile was so inhuman that I clasped the child's small hand again, more for my own sake than hers. She was used to this place and this person.

"Anna," Irene said softly.

The oversized head lifted from the work in its lap.

"See!" the child exclaimed, wresting free of my hand to cavort toward the wall. The daylight fell on a small cot . . . and the unframed print that was nailed above it. Not a print, but a play-bill (I had seen enough lately), and I recognized the subject with a start: Merlinda the Mermaid.

Somehow this tiny child had recognized Irene, a decade later and with her flowing sea-drifting locks pinned up under a hat.

"Anna," Irene repeated, softly.

The face turned toward us, and I flinched.

But I saw only the odd half-moon that surrounded it like a dark halo, some sort of bonnet or hood. Something within that vague circumference spoke.

"No one calls me by that name anymore."

Her voice was low, and mellow, and not at all hoggish.

"You said I couldn't," the child trilled. "That I must call my elders 'Mister' and "Missus' and 'Miss.' And you 'Mama.'"

The woman didn't answer her, so I caught the child's hand and lifted her up until she perched on one arm, a mite of perhaps thirty pounds. "I am a 'Miss,'" I explained. "And my friend is a 'Missus.'"

"Is not! She's a Mermaid."

"Not recently. Now she is Missus Norton."

"'Missus Norton?'" The woman at the window's voice smiled

in the shadows. "You went away to seek your singing fortune, little Rena, and have returned a married lady, is that true?"

"Well," Irene said, moving cautiously toward the window, "I have done some singing, that is true. And I've found some fortune. And I am a Missus."

The Pig Lady's hands lifted from her lap, thimble on one, needle in the other, and she clapped her palms in approval. "I am so glad to hear what became of you. Once you began to study music so seriously, you were soon lost to us."

"It was unbelievably demanding."

"All gifts are. Are you well?"

"Very."

"And your friend who has such a way with my daughter?"

I couldn't help blushing in the dark.

"Miss Huxleigh. A stalwart soul. I have been living, and working, in England, and most recently France."

The woman's sigh pushed her dark breast up and down against the bright window like a bellows.

I grew impatient, worried. This was like conversing with a silhouette, a cutout of black paper against white window. What was so horrific about the Pig Lady's face that it remained such a mystery? At first I didn't want to know, but now I did, burningly.

I began to understand what had attracted Eve to apples.

Irene had found another small stool and sat down upon it, despite the discomfort. I think it was the child's seat and I asked her, "What are you called?"

"Edith," she said in the very dignified way that the name deserved.

"What a delightful name." I sank with her onto the cot. "I am Penelope."

"Penelope! I've never heard anything so silly!"

"Perhaps I am a silly person," I suggested.

She grasped my thumb and leaned close. "I think you are! But I'm silly too. Sometimes it takes two to be silly."

And time, I thought. Silliness takes time, which is why adults so seldom enjoy it. I couldn't help wondering how often her mother had time to be silly. Or how often she had heard people jeering at her mother.

"Anna," Irene said, "I've come back because there's disturbing news. Sophie and Salamandra are dead."

The shrouded head bowed, as if struck.

Irene spoke on. "A reporter for the *World* is determined to expose me, embarrass me, for my humble beginnings."

The woman at the window laughed.

"This news cheers you?" Irene asked.

"Only in that no one would wish to expose your 'humble beginnings' unless you had a more elevated present. I am so relieved, little Rena! In some ways you were the child I thought I could never have, back then, when I was young and foolish and so . . . flawed."

"The young are always flawed," Irene said quickly.

"I more than most. When you are known as the 'Pig Lady' from a very early age, you expect nothing of life but swill and a quick trip to the butcher. I had both."

"I'm so sorry! It's the strangest thing. My memories of my childhood years are vague and intermittent—"

"Not so strange." The silhouette of the Pig Lady leaned nearer to us even as her voice became hoarse and fainter. "You came to us by dark of night, not yet the age of my Edith. Bundled up from head to foot, as if the sheriffs were after you."

"From the West? I came from the West?"

"I don't know. Here in New Jersey, the World is East across the river: New York." The strangely shaped head turned toward me. "Miss, can you take Edith to the stairs, play some game with her. Little pitchers have . . ."

"Of course," I said, feeling no umbrage at being left out, as I too often could. Edith was a charming child, and I welcomed her wiggling weight on my lap. It had been so long.

Although I was madly curious to hear the Pig Lady's story, I knew . . . hoped . . . that Irene would later tell me every last detail. In the meantime, I had a serious game of patty-cakes to play against a very skilled opponent.

The door above Edith and me suddenly cracked open. The child leaped up, crying "Mama," and vanished within. I was slower to rise, my heavy skirts and stiff corset, and my greater years, making impromptu moments hard to come by . . . except when I had been unconventionally clothed in recent captivity.

Now Irene's silhouette stood in bold relief against an interior rather than an exterior brightness.

I realized a lamp was lit, and that if I returned to the chamber I could solve the puzzle of the Pig Lady's features. I realized that I didn't wish to.

Irene came down the four or five steps that brought her back to my level.

"Poor Nell. Are you stiff?"

"Somewhat."

"A charming child."

"So children often are, before the world grabs them by the nape of the neck and shakes. That poor woman? What can she earn?"

"A pittance. A pity." Irene looked askance, as if she couldn't quite bear to be in the here and now.

"Did you learn anything?" I asked.

"Learn? More than I wanted to." She began walking down the steep stairs ahead of me, one ungloved hand grazing the dingy wall.

I followed her as fast as I could in the unlit dark.

It was madness to descend without a candle. I recalled the faint light within the rooms above, thrown by one candle, I guessed. Hence we would make do with none, even if we broke our necks over it.

In this mood, I walked into an impediment on the stairs I could barely see, solid and soft as a big sack of flour.

I moved aside and stopped until my eyes could make out the variances of shadow all around me.

My impediment was Irene! She had unexpectedly sat down and was crouched like a clot of darkness on the stairs.

I, like the spider of nursery rhyme, sat down beside her.

Was she weeping? I could not move or speak a word, for I had never seen, or heard rather, her weep.

Certainly she had never heard or seen me weep.

That was much to be recommended in a long-term associate.

Of course I didn't know what to say, and, what is worse, risked joining her in her maudlin occupation if I spoke at all.

So we sat side by side in the dark, and ignored each other.

I had more to ignore, such as sighs from the dark. Finally, I withdrew the clean linen handkerchief I carried at all times from my skirt pocket and tucked it into the general area of her hands.

She thrust it back at me, as if insulted. Perhaps I had misjudged the depth of her despair, but despair she did.

"Their situation," I finally said, "is quite desperate."

"Oh, desperate can be cured," she answered bitterly from the dark. "I can cure desperate, if they will let me. I cannot cure memory, Nell. And . . . I once was that innocent child. I thought all these exotic grown-ups around me were the sun and the moon. That they could do no wrong, suffer no wrong, feel no hurt. And if they could do and not do all this, surely I could also. They gave me my sense of self and survival, which is the greatest gift to be given. And now they pay for it! Because of me."

"Pay! How?"

"I was the mystery child imported into their midst twenty-eight years ago. They accepted me without question, and even let me go ten years ago, with good wishes and no awkward questions.

Now I return, and all my questions are awkward, and the answers are . . . lethal."

"Goodness! Were you really that important? A mere chit of a child?"

There was a shocked silence. Her voice came meek and mild from the growing blackness. "I am not the centerpiece of this story, this mystery, Nell. I know that. But, somehow, I am the *pretext*. I cannot allow once-dear lives to end in pain and chaos."

"No, of course not," I said. "Nor can I allow us to linger a moment longer in this dark stairwell. We shall have to make our way down like the blind, as it is, and I shudder to think what has attached itself to our skirts."

I pulled and prodded her like a reluctant child until she was upright again.

"It is not only their sad state that is lamentable," Irene said, her voice still low and thready. "I have finally learned the name of the woman who came to visit us children in the theater and boarding houses. It is the infamous Madame Restell, and I very much dread what that may mean."

"She cannot be very infamous, for I have never heard of her. The name sounds French," I added with a sniff, though my heart wasn't in it. "That is a recommendation only for all that is trivial."

After living so long near Paris, I fear my determination to dislike those of that nationality who had enjoyed such a long enmity with the English was becoming corrupted.

"Hardly trivial, Nell." Irene began plodding down in the dark, clinging to the wall and whatever filth it might host. "I may have forgotten much of the middle years of my childhood, but I remember that Madame Restell was loathed as 'the wickedest woman in New York.' "

"Wicked! One hardly hears that word any more. She must be a hideous old soul."

"No more. She died horribly two or three years before I left New York for the Old World, by her own hand."

By then we had reached the ground floor. The pale spill of electric lights finally allowed us to see our surroundings, and each other.

"Cobwebs!" I cried, batting at the stringy veiling that had attached itself to my hat like spidery ectoplasm.

Irene quickly brushed the threads away, using her undonned gloves as a sort of broom, but her face remained stony and distracted.

"Surely this wicked, dead woman cannot cause us hurt now," I insisted. "I am not afraid of anyone dead."

Her smile was tepid. "Then ghosts would not alarm you. Perhaps I can produce a figure that will. If Madame Restell is involved in whatever sad history has caused these vile current events, we have no time to waste in learning the worst. There is only one way to do that speedily, and that is to swallow our pride and call on Pink and all the resources that a newspaperwoman like Nellie Bly would have."

"Go begging to Pink! After that night at Delmonico's? Never!"

"Then I will handle it myself."

Irene suited deed to word by pushing through the old wooden doors and tripping down the stairs to the street to hunt up a hansom.

Well, I needs must follow, wondering if I would more dread learning about the wicked Madame Restell or confronting the treacherous Pink again.

36.

The French Conjunction

~~

Is it not but too well known that the families of the married often increase beyond [what] the happiness of those who give them birth would dictate?... Is it desirable, then, is it moral for parents to increase their families, regardless of consequences to themselves, of the well being of their offspring, when a simple, easy, healthy, and certain remedy is within our control? (Introduced by the celebrated midwife and female physician, Mrs. Restell, the grandmother of the advertiser.)

—ADVERTISEMENT, *NEW YORK SUN*, 1839

Irene sent a message to Pink's residence from the lobby of our hotel. Then we retired to our rooms to dampen and brush our abused clothing. We had packed hurriedly for a transatlantic voyage with one trunk apiece. Nothing we had brought with us was expendable.

Irene then lit and smoked a small cigar, pacing rapidly in long, carpet-swallowing strides, so as to spread the dreadful smoke even more democratically throughout the room.

I coughed diplomatically, then frantically, but she seemed deaf and blind to anything but her own dark and murky thoughts.

Finally she stopped and stubbed out the last of the cigar in a crystal tray she had imported from the bedroom dressing table.

"I suppose we must eat. The hotel dining room is respectable."

I didn't even bother to protest that it likely was not. I had to know more about this demonic woman whose very name struck terror into my usually too-brave companion.

So we adjourned to dinner, where the only smoke I had to contend with, at least while Irene was eating, was from the many gentlemen in the room puffing away on cigars the size of piccolos.

Several women were sprinkled among the tables, including a pair or two like us, who were without male escort. New York seemed a very fast city indeed.

"It was quite improper for Pink to dine alone with a man she hardly knew," I observed when the main course was but a memory, for we were both ravenous for some reason.

"Not in New York, as social customs go here, but it was more than improper for her to meet secretly with Quentin behind our backs. I won't trust her again soon."

"Then why do we need her?"

"Because my own memories of Madame Restell are quite casual, and the newspaper files record every arrest, every trial, every mudslinging exchange of letters to the editor, every death, every jail term, and finally her demise. I must know what she was doing in eighteen fifty-eight and in the immediate years afterward, when the 'lady in black' visited my troupe of child performers."

"This creature sounds wholly possessed of an utterly black heart," I said, shocked by Irene's recital of such melodrama staples as arrests, trials, jail terms, unnatural deaths and vituperative verbal duels in letters to the editor.

"There were even rumors, at the time of her suicide in the late seventies, that she had not really perished, but merely escaped the authorities to pursue her lurid career elsewhere."

"If even you speak in such condemnatory terms, this woman was a monster!"

Irene paused to light a post-dinner cigarette. I glanced around to see, with shock, that she was not the only woman in the room wielding a costly cigarette holder, although Irene's was the most exquisite of all, with its diamond-set golden serpent twining the mother-of-pearl length like a precious swirl of smoke.

She had ordered brandy, like a man. I watched every male eye pause on her figure, then register surprise and a certain uneasy envy.

She took no more note of them than she would have a dust mote.

"What was this creature?" I pressed. "A modern Medusa, whose very look could turn a man to stone? Some American femme fatale who drove men to distraction and destruction?"

"All monsters, particularly when they are women, are misunderstood. Do you wish me to confuse you, Nell? I could tell you she was a self-appointed physician, a benefactor whose name held a sacred and secret place in the hearts of many women, even as it publicly became the very emblem of brutality."

"You do confuse me!"

"And then I would tell you that she was English, not French."

"No!"

Irene smiled.

"Restell was a name she adopted because to some people, believe it or not, a French origin conveys a certain automatic respectability and cachet that few other nationalities can. If one is French, if one's wares are French, if one's training and methods are French, all civilized people suspect that they may be superior."

"You did say that Sherlock Holmes claimed a French connection through Madame Worth, née Vernet. And he certainly acts superior enough for three men, even if they are English."

"Like many on these shores, Madame Restell immigrated here. When I heard of her, she was so well established that all New York knew her trade. Some blessed her for it. Others condemned her."

"She was not just another notorious mistress, then?"

"She was no mistress but a long-married woman, and a mother."

"Then how could she have become so disgraced?"

Irene twirled the dark cigarette in its pale rococo holder between her fingers, watching a quarter inch of ash fall off and disintegrate into a dish apparently placed on the dining table for this very obnoxious act of smoking.

"I must wait, impatiently, until Pink arrives tomorrow with more solid facts about the woman than my memory."

"You seem to remember more about her than you do about your own entire childhood."

"That was because I had set aside the things of a child by then. I was training daily for the opera, auditioning for singing assignments and working for the Pinkertons. It's only my girlhood that I see through a veil, darkly. And the papers were full of her, the entire city then was intensely aware of Madame Restell, and especially a young woman of my age and . . . condition."

I was not sure to what "condition" Irene referred, only that I did not wish to inquire too deeply into it. I returned to the subject of our speculation.

I pulled the triangle of wafer impaled in the mound of my vanilla ice cream dessert and nibbled meditatively on it. This was *my* after-dinner "cigarette." It was not Delmonico's famed "baked Alaska," but it was a divinely civil sort of occupation for a parson's daughter.

This Madame Restell was a conundrum, a construction of opposites in the public mind. Yet she dallied with Irene and her young fellow and sister performers.

"She must have loved children," I said. "Are you sure she wasn't childless perhaps?"

"She had one daughter. And some thought she loved children to the point of sacrificing herself that they might live happy lives. And some thought that she hated children to the point of slaughtering them."

"Slaughter!" My ice cream suddenly tasted like sawdust. "Innocents died?"

"Innocents always die, particularly the innocents in our-selves," Irene remarked as grimly as I had ever heard her speak. Her eyes met mine, full of import. "Nell, thanks to your association with me, you have seen some of the worst excesses of the human mind and heart. I refer particularly to our last . . . crusade. I know that Parson Huxleigh would be most shocked by where I have led his only, orphan daughter."

"He was a good man, even a holy man. But country life can be harsh and he saw humanity in all its frailty as well as its strength. He did, however, wish that I would never know as much as he." I smiled ruefully. "I am finding that ignorance is not bliss, as the saying goes, but then neither is knowledge."

"No." She looked down at the white linen tablecloth, then up at me again. "I am always the instrument of your disillusionment, Nell. Believe me, I would wish it otherwise. But the world and its ugliness will intrude into every life these days. Madame Restell was a new kind of femme fatale, as you call her. She was a woman who aided other women in dealing with the mysteries, and mis-eries, of being female and human. Sometimes that involved inter-rupting the begetting of children."

"Oh. This has to do with marriage?"

"Or not."

Irene picked up her elegant holder and screwed another dark cigarette into it. Light and dark. The image resonated in my mind, as if my mind wished to concentrate on such abstractions instead of the concrete facts behind her words.

She gazed at me through a new veil of smoke, her eyes as old and regretful as the Sphinx's in Egypt.

I realized that I again had no idea of how the world really worked, and that if I should have such an idea, I would not like it. At all.

Yet I knew a certain irritated prickling: that it was unfair that

Irene . . . and Pink . . . and Quentin . . . and possibly even Sherlock Holmes! . . . should know what I did not.

Irene waited for my response. I understood that she had trusted me with the truth, and there is no greater confidence than that.

"What did Madame Restell do that merited jail and trials and imprisonment and, perhaps, if I understand what you have *not* said, martyrdom?"

"She was an abortionist, Nell. She kept babies from coming into a world where no one welcomed their presence. To do so, she offered potions and even procedures that prevented this. She was the wickedest woman in New York, and the one most secretly blessed and publicly cursed. I myself do not know how I feel about her, save that if she was indeed present in my early childhood scenery, the implications are almost more than I can bear, and, as you know, I can bear a good deal."

Children, I wondered. *Can you bear children? Were you a client of Madame Restell, a beneficiary? Or a victim?*

I understood what she meant by something, some fact, some possibility being almost more than one could bear.

"It's not so easy," Irene went on, exhaling a thin, steady stream of smoke as if it were some visible ectoplasm from her past. "Was I one she saved, her own or another's? Was there also a market in babies born, as much as in babies not born? You see? If this notorious woman showed an interest in me, who am I? Who was I *not* meant to be? Was I not meant to be, at all?"

To this I had no answer, not even a cowardly murmur.

I saw now that to solve the mystery of Irene, we would have to face the mystery of Madame Restell, who was herself a pseudonym.

And we would have to face letting Nellie Bly know far more of Irene and her past and heritage than any self-respecting person could endure.

"Pink sacrifices her present to the future," I said.

"As her past sacrificed her to the present. She was not a wanted child either, long after birth, though not before."

"You cannot be sure about yourself!"

"I am sure that I had a mother, once, and that she left me to myself."

I stretched my hand across the table toward her. She didn't move. Her cigarette still spewed a smoky spiral that vanished in the unseen air.

I spoke.

"So am I sure, and so I also was left. We are all best off mothering ourselves."

"Or each other," she conceded, snuffing out the cigarette as if it was the embodiment of both our pasts, only so much ash.

37.

No Woman Is an Island

❦

People acted precisely as if the thing to do in the water was to behave exactly contrary to the manner of behaving anywhere else.

—COMMENTATOR ON CONEY ISLAND, "SODOM BY THE SEA," 1880S

"I am not used to patronizing amusement parks," I informed Quentin in the hansom cab.

"Nor am I," he answered with gusto. "I often think that is a serious omission in my education."

We were en route to the sidewheeler steamboat that would waft us to the infamous island on the southern, seaward side of the land mass opposite Manhattan Island called Brooklyn.

"I suppose," I answered, "that I could consider Irene and my outings at the World's Fair in Paris last spring as an education."

Quentin took my hand and twined it over his forearm, which made us less companions and more of a couple. Such a gesture was utterly unnecessary within the safe confines of a hansom cab. Then again, perhaps the confines of a hansom cab were not so safe, after all.

"Please don't hark back to that terrible time, Nell," Quentin implored. "There was nothing amusing about what happened to you there."

"I had merely wanted to see the shipboard panorama building, and—"

"You see! You *do* have a taste for amusement. Tell me what about the shipboard panorama attracted you."

"Well, that was before I had traveled on a real ship across a real ocean," I said ruefully.

"Were you ill?" he asked with concern.

"Er, no. Not very. A trifle dizzy. Were *you* ill on the Atlantic passage?"

"I have been on far rougher seas in far smaller boats."

"Oh. I understand there will be a boat today."

"A steamship, but we will mostly move through sheltered waters. If you like, we could take one of the railroads across Brooklyn."

"No. I traveled by ferry recently. I wasn't even dizzy."

"If you are dizzy on the steamship, I shall hold you up."

"Oh." I was feeling dizzy already. "About the . . . attraction in Paris. The city has many of these panorama buildings and they are quite fascinating. From the outside they look like monuments. Paris is crammed with monuments; apparently sneezing is an achievement worth celebrating to Parisians."

Quentin laughed again. "And blowing one's nose worth another monument?"

"It is a lovely city in many ways," I found myself admitting. "At any rate, the panorama buildings feature scenic paintings done in a huge interior circle, so you feel surrounded by the image until you are a part of it. One such building is populated with famous Frenchmen, but the panorama at the World's Fair is quite unique. It's moored at Seine side, and is shaped like a boat." I frowned, for I never knew the difference: why was a large ferry a "boat" and a large steamer a "ship"? "A boat. Or a ship. And it rocks ever so gently on the water, and inside there's a deck with wax figures of the captain and crew and passengers, and all around is a perfectly painted harbor filled with every kind of boat and ship. It's like being right there."

"And now you have been 'right there,' only it's here in America." He patted my gloved hand on his arm. "It's so brave of you, Nell, to remember what fascinated you about the building, rather than the awful things that happened to you there. And you were very clever to unfasten your lapel watch—" His hand left mine and lifted to the very same watch once more fastened to the bodice of my gown. His forefinger lifted the small gold-cased face. "—and let it fall behind you as a clue to your abduction site."

In that moment I relived the awful terror of eluding pursuers in the bowels of the panorama building and later in the exhibition area upstairs, my heart pounding like a pump during my scuffling, otherwise silent flight, then thundering in my ears when I felt hostile hands capture me and smother my breath. . . .

I felt the very same way again, the moment Quentin mentioned unfastening something from my bosom.

It probably didn't help that Irene had insisted I wear the Liberty silk gown on this expedition, for its freedom of movement and lightness on a hot summer's day, or that she barely tightened my corset strings, since the dress was so shapeless.

The hansom jerked to a stop, and Quentin stepped out to help me alight. Soon we were waiting for a two-tiered ship, with a great wheel spewing water fixed to one side, to dock and load passengers.

We stood on a Hudson River pier in the broad and benign daylight, I like a lady of the town, with a gentleman on one arm and a parasol on the other. Both were handsome. One, because I had borrowed it from Irene, and everything she owned was exquisite. The other, because he just was, and always would be so in my eyes.

Quentin was dressed for a day of amusement, in light-colored suit and straw boater, purchased, he assured me, on the spur of the moment at Macy's department store.

"You are sure we are not too casually dressed?" I asked.

"Not in the least."

"Paris is cluttered with department stores," I mentioned for lack of anything else to say.

"Paris is sublime, but Coney Island, I am told, is astounding."

"I have heard that it can be 'rough,' as the Americans say."

"Anywhere amusing has its rough side."

"What will we do there?"

"What we feel like doing."

"And how will we know what we feel like doing?"

He bent to gaze into my face under the shadow of my blue straw hat with the yellow daisies clustered on the brim.

"You haven't much done that, have you?"

"Done what?"

"What you feel like doing."

"I was never in a position to."

My words caused his expression to sober. He straightened and gazed at our arriving boat. "Today, Nell, if there is something you notice that you feel like doing, you must say so, and we will do it."

Still, it was an order, wasn't it? I *must* do what I feel like doing. I did not point out the contradiction in his prescription to Quentin.

The journey around the west end of Brooklyn was smooth and uneventful. Uneventful to me, on water, was not feeling ill. Good. I felt like *not* feeling ill, and I was doing it! Not exactly what Quentin had in mind, I feared.

Still, we stood side by side at the railing, watching the empty green land glide by, and I daresay it was much better than the panorama building on the Seine. The huge wheel churned, the steam billowed from two big stacks above us like clouds, birds screeched and careened, the air smelled of fish and salt.

As we rounded the bay, the ocean breeze made me hold down my hat brim. Quentin took my elbow.

"There it is!" He pointed to an amazing sight.

All along the ruffling waterline extended a long, wide, curving walkway of wooden planks. The island itself was as flat as an iron, but the constructions on it made up for the lack of geographical interest.

These too were wooden buildings, but of the massive size of Orient palaces, replete with huge domed cores and fanciful cupolas, wrapped around by moats of wooden porches. I spied three of the vast, rambling structures, reminding me a bit of Brighton in England, but looking far cruder, like everything in America.

Also evident were some amazing structures: railroads that ran up and down invisible Alps . . . an iron tower far more fragile than Eiffel's Paris construction, a vertical frame of mere wire with the occasional supporting horizontal platform . . . a huge elephant with howdah on its back, big as a building, and apparently that was exactly what it was . . . a huge, moving blot of human forms edging the surf of the beach like swarming insects, people bathing in the sea and sunlight quite openly.

"Gracious! What shall we do here?"

"Mostly walk," Quentin responded, his hazel eyes crinkling in a fine netting of wrinkles that reminded me that sunny climes were to his liking. "And what you wish."

"What are those huge, rambling buildings?"

"Very elegant hotels . . . too elegant for us to dine there today, for formal dress is required."

"What shall we eat all day, then?"

"What we find."

"And that elephant structure?"

"We shall visit it and explore, if you like."

I overlooked the entire thronging scene, liking none of it, and especially the lack of all shade, save for my parasol. The one thing I did like stood beside me, and expected me to regard this outing as a treat. Well . . .

I hoisted my parasol to rest upon my shoulder as a soldier on parade in the burning sun might brace his rifle. I would do my duty and "have fun," as Irene had instructed me, and as Quentin wished.

By my lapel watch—I lifted it to read the face and felt Quentin's eyes follow my gesture—the time was just past noon. It would be a long, hot day.

First we had to disembark on the New Iron Pier, a structure as long as a train, divided into two broad walks for people coming and going. Waves lapped on either side as the sidewheeler's passengers thronged briskly through one lane—for the next debarking was expected in twenty minutes!—the men wearing light-colored straw boaters with their dark suits. (Quentin's elegant light-colored suit made him look like a very Parisian pigeon among a flock of less imaginative crows.) The women were dressed conventionally in tight corsets and dark gowns, which made my pink free-flowing Liberty silk gown seem as Parisian as Quentin's garb.

I was grateful for the lighter dress, though, by the time we reached end of the pier, where the vast turreted bulk of the Brighton Hotel greeted us.

It transpired that this section of the island was named Brighton Beach! That was no doubt in honor of England's older and more elegant seaside town popularized by the Prince Regent at the beginning of this century.

However, nothing loomed ahead of the English Brighton visitor like the Iron Tower that confronted us now.

"We can go up in it," Quentin said, following my gaze and mistaking it for awe or interest instead of horror.

"Up in it?"

"There is a steam elevator," he added enthusiastically.

"It is not so tall nor so architecturally interesting as the Eiffel Tower, why on earth should we go up in it?"

"To leave mother earth. From the top one sees all of Coney Island."

I really didn't wish to see all of Coney Island, or even this portion of it, but despite Quentin's encouragement to please myself, I was incapable of interfering with his wishes.

So we walked another great length past the endless wooden bulk of the hotel to this structure, where he paid good American money for a trip to the top. I had neglected to mention to him that elevators made me uneasy.

The car was crowded, another source of unease, but Quentin secured a post for us near the broad glass window (oh, dear!). Soon we were drawn upward like a bucket of spawning grunion in a well.

I shut my parasol and my eyes.

The top was indeed high, and the view sweeping. The flat sandy plain below was like a game board. The island constructions with their tented turrets sat on it like scattered pieces in some pattern only a chess master could decipher. Or Sherlock Holmes. I don't know why I thought of him, except that I was sure that *he* would never permit himself to ascend to such a perilous height in such a bizarre place.

However, Quentin stood behind me at the lookout's fenced edge so I could see all there was not to see. I felt quite safe despite the height and the crowding. His hands on the railing bracketed me into a windblown pocket of protection. The expanse of blue water and the bright sun finally outshone the tawdry carnival constructions. It felt quite amazing to be as high as the birds and look down on people the size of ants.

In fact, Quentin had to tap me on the shoulder to leave, as the platform was deserted and the elevator was waiting for us.

I bustled back in and soon felt my boots on terra firma again, if shifting sands and gritty boardwalk can be considered firm.

"Perhaps some lunch," Quentin suggested.

That sounded safe enough. I glanced at the gargantuan hotel.

"Not there," Quentin said. "Too stuffy. Here's Feltman's hot dog emporium."

Hot dog? I indeed hoped not!

This was another wooden wedding cake of a building topped with the ubiquitous cupola, with the name FELTMANS in great man-high letters just under it.

We joined the crowds funneling inside, and were soon seated in an airy, lattice-surrounded courtyard with a maple tree as its centerpiece. Japanese lanterns were strung like large fireflies on a high wire above us. The oom-pah-pah of German musicians blended with the noise of passing crowds and shrieks of happy bathers.

"Why . . . this is a Bohemian beer garden!" I exclaimed, gazing around the small tables of men and women being served by an array of waiters.

"So you shall feel at home," Quentin said with some delight.

No, I should not. I had certainly patronized Bohemian beer cellars with Godfrey a time or two, but purely in the pursuit of our mission, of course. So I imagined that sitting here in daylight with Quentin, not on any mission other than amusement, which I had yet to fulfill, would be respectable enough. Women's hats dotted the area like butterflies on flowers, and no one appeared to remark on who was with whom.

When Quentin ordered "Milwaukee beer" for us both, I did not demure. I was to do as I liked, I had been told by two persons close to me, and I suddenly decided, sitting there, seeing Quentin's absurd straw hat on the table and the dappled shade of the tree falling on his earnest features, that what I would most like to do was anything that would make Quentin think that I was having "fun."

The beer was served in tall glasses with handles on one side, like a transparent stein. It shone golden in the daylight. I sipped it and almost sneezed at the foamy cap tickling my nose. I laughed instead.

Quentin laughed with me. "They poured it too fast, given the press of customers."

I looked around. "I can't believe so many people come all this way just to walk and take the sea air."

"Oh, there's more to do than that," he said, "if you are up to it."

I sipped more beer. Nellie Bly, I had been told, "was up to anything." Why could I not be?

We ordered food, and I decided to try the hot dog that the restaurant was noted for, although it served a full menu. When this item arrived, I was amazed to find it was merely sausage in bread, a common peasant lunch throughout Germany and Bohemia.

All around me people plucked up this commonplace item and tucked into it as if it were a rare and hearty treat.

"No tableware?" I asked.

"None's available in the desert," Quentin said, lifting his bulky sandwich and biting.

I nibbled a bit off, glad for my caution, for the hot meat had been slathered in spicy, messy mustard. Of course mustard is an English staple, and I must say it did much to elevate the humble sausage and bread into a tastier affair, although I found it dry and had to alternate dainty bites with sips of Milwaukee beer.

"What does Milwaukee mean?" I asked Quentin when the first flush of hunger had ebbed.

"It's an Indian name adapted by a city in mid-America, the northern part."

"There's certainly a lot of America," I complained.

"Indeed. The state of Wisconsin in which Milwaukee is found is probably as large as England, and is only one of forty-one American states thus far. I doubt they're finished. It's rumored that North and South Dakota, near Wisconsin, and Montana farther west, and even Washington on the Pacific coast, will be added this year."

"Only forty-one thus far!"

"The Americans are always adding on, like grand hotels."

"We can't do that; we're surrounded by sea."

"The Americans are surrounded by sea, and by unclaimed or

insufficiently claimed land mass. Their house permits many expansions."

"How do you know these things?"

"The world is my business. Yes, I've concentrated on, and love, the East best, but I can deal with the West if I have to."

"England is only a tiny isle! That's why we have a far-flung empire," I realized.

"Thanks to our sea power in days of yore," he said, "but those days passed with Nelson. We may not have an empire much longer."

"Then what will you do?"

He sat back to consider the question, to consider me. "I don't know. What do you think I might do?"

"I have no idea. I don't think you will . . . sell hot dogs."

He laughed and waved the waiter over, indicating our empty glasses. "Would you care for dessert?"

"I don't know. Do they serve baked Alaska here?"

He blinked and drew away as if singed. "Touché. I suggest a cooling ice cream for Mademoiselle," he turned to tell the waiter, and me indirectly. He regarded me again, a bit more gingerly. "Do you mind my ordering for you?"

"Not when it is something I would like."

"*Hmmm.* We can make an appointment to have baked Alaska at Delmonico's, which is the originator and only server of the delicacy in the world, so far."

"Did *she* have it?" I sipped the new glass tankard of Milwaukee beer the waiter had placed before me, thinking of my Paris acquaintances, Buffalo Bill. And Red Tomahawk.

"No, only I. She had the tutti frutti. And my baked Alaska melted, because I had other urgent matters to attend to, so I didn't really get to it in the peak condition."

"Oh. Melted. How unfortunate."

"So we could have it, together, at Delmonico's, before you leave, if you like."

"I am supposed to do what I like. That sounds like something I would like."

"I will ask Irene if she can spare another day or two on these shores when we return."

"When do we return?" I asked casually. The day was pleasantly warm under the tree and the beer had lost its bitter, stinging taste and was quite . . . bracing and effervescent, like seltzer lemonade.

He smiled. "When you like."

So we chatted, and invented ludicrous professions for him. My lime ice cream arrived and was completely refreshing. I finished my second beer and suddenly confronted the price of my carelessness.

"I don't suppose," I finally was forced to lean inward and whisper to Quentin, "that Coney Island has . . ."

He leaned inward to hear me. "Has what, Nell?"

"Has . . . you know."

He did not know.

"Comfort stations," I finally mumbled.

"Dozens and dozens."

"It does! How very American of it," I sighed in relief. "Where?"

"Here. All along the beach. There are bathhouses, too, where people change into bathing costumes."

"I don't want one of *those*!" I then excused myself, left my parasol on the table under Quentin's guard, and found a respectable-looking woman, who directed me where needed.

The whole process was amazingly easy and even unembarrassing, perhaps aided by the strangely pleasant mood in which I felt myself, in which it seemed I could make no misstep or say anything the slightest bit wrong, and in which I need not trouble myself about all of the things I usually did.

Perhaps this salutary condition was a result of being in such safe hands as Quentin's. After all, a man who had fended off foreign and domestic spies in the wilds of Afghanistan could certainly handle any rowdy crowds on Coney Island.

Once I returned to the table, I tried to don my kid gloves again, but they were annoyingly tighter than usual and Quentin put them in his pocket. I did pick up my parasol and we ambled into the bright afternoon, he drawing my arm through his, which was quite proper because people were doing it all over the beach.

The beach. Oh, my. I couldn't help seeing a good deal of men's bare arms and lower limbs and women's too! Their bathing costumes were tight woolen affairs much resembling underclothing, and I managed to mostly look away.

Besides, Quentin was guiding me inland, to . . . the elephant hotel!

"There is horse racing at the island's other end," he told me, "but the people are rougher there, I thought you'd enjoy the sights here."

"Of course. And the elephant is an eastern creature, isn't it? Perhaps you could become an elephant trainer."

"Sometimes I feel like one," he remarked wryly. "The government moves as ponderously as an elephant and its ears seldom hear where the feet are trampling."

We ambled around the front of the building. It was shaped like a huge standing elephant with a skin of tin, the howdah on its back as high as the spire on the cupola of the sprawling hotel to its left.

"It must be twelve stories," I estimated.

In its massive front feet sat shops, a cigar emporium on one side, a diorama in the other.

"Do you care for a cigar?" I asked Quentin, feeling he was entitled to some souvenir of the day, no matter how disgusting.

"Do you care for a cigar?"

"No! Irene would."

"Shall we buy her one?"

"No! Yes! She will be so shocked."

Of course Quentin bought it and tucked it inside his breast pocket. Poor man, he was becoming a human elephant, my gloves in his pocket, Irene's cigar in his jacket. I giggled at the sheer absurdity of it.

The elephant's other leg hosted a diorama of the island. I gasped with delight when I saw it, and we immediately paid a dime each to go inside. Even though the leg's circumference was sixty feet, as the brochure boasted, the diorama was sadly lacking the artistry of the Paris panorama buildings, which I told Quentin as soon as we left.

"America is new at these things," he answered. "Give them time."

Then we climbed the spiral staircase in the elephant's rear leg to regard the few hotel rooms the edifice offered and a gift shop, where he bought me a chiffon scarf with a drawing of the elephant on it. Then it was onward and upward, until we stood looking out of the elephant's eyes on the panorama below.

"I never dreamed I'd ever be inside an elephant," I declared.

"Neither did I. Come, there's more to do."

"More?"

Quentin next escorted me to a railroad station!

"We're leaving, then," I said, surprised by the unintended disappointment in my tone. "You said there was more to do."

"This train doesn't go anywhere," he said, smiling mysteriously as he bought the tickets at ten cents apiece.

I suddenly realized that I felt like a child again, who needn't worry about what things cost, or who would take care of her or . . . anything at all. Although, as a child, I had never been to such a place as Coney Island. Was this having fun? Perhaps.

But this was a very strange railroad. The cars were open, on wooden tracks like mine trams, and we sat two abreast. As soon as we were seated I saw that we were poised at the top of long grade downward. The sign read "Switchback Railroad."

"Quentin—"

"It's an amusement ride."

"That grade doesn't look amusing in the slightest."

I remembered the deep alpine valleys I had traversed alone by train to reach Irene in Prague once. How my fingernails had cut welts into my palms with the tension! I had never told anyone.

I remembered, also, how Quentin and I had returned from Prague more recently by train, and as well as we got along during that enforced sequestering then, we were on entirely different footing now, with more wariness between us, and deeper feelings as well. Perhaps the first was because of the second.

He grinned at my serious face. "It's supposed to be fun."

"Many things that are supposed to be fun are simply dangerous," I began to answer in my governess guise, but the odd "train" pulled away from the boarding area right then and we shot down at a fearsome pace, down, down, until the tracks rose up like a mountain and we raced up the grade until momentum stopped us. There we were handed out to wait while the attendants pushed the cars to a higher point on a second track.

We boarded again—there was no other way to get back! Quentin took my hand in his, and squeezed.

Away we went, down again in a great swoop and up until the speed of that plunge again petered out.

We finally stood on our own two feet again, watching the line of eager riders shuffle forward to the sacrifice!

"That beats a gallop on an Arab stallion," Quentin pronounced.

I wouldn't know about that, but I did know that he, at least, was having fun.

"Are you game for the Ferris wheel?" he asked next.

I looked at where he gazed: a vast version of the steamship's side wheel looming against the sky, swinging cars resembling charms on some giant's bracelets, and poor benighted people sitting in them.

"Ferris wheel? That?"

"It's the biggest I've seen."

I was not reassured, but I hadn't the heart to tell him so.

Nellie Bly in a madhouse? Nell Huxleigh on a maddening Catherine wheel in the sky? Didn't they torture dead Roman Catholic saints, usually women, virgins and martyrs, on just such appliances?

"If you have any reservations, Nell—" he was saying.

And that settled it. For one day I would be a woman without any reservations, as Irene had been at Delmonico's when she had bullied her way in and we had found Pink and Quentin together.

Somehow I must be as brave as Irene, as Pink.

I gazed at the great circle in the sky. Once on, I could not get off until let off. I would have no control over anything. I would be a prisoner, only this time of my own choosing.

I nodded, and Quentin bought the tickets.

From that moment regrets nagged me like demons. *Why had I agreed to this?* Look. Other people, other couples were waiting their turns to ride, laughing. It was nothing. Or it was fun. *But I couldn't get off!* The seats were open to the air. *It was like a locked box!* Quentin would be with me. *I would still be alone!*

And then we were handed into one of the swinging boxes with a kind of bar across our laps. I pushed my reticule strings up to the crook of my elbow and braced my parasol between the bottom of the car and my hip.

Our car jerked upward, then stopped, then repeated the process until all the cars were full. We had paused, swinging pleasantly at the top of the wheel. The whole island lay visible beneath us again and I actually was coming to relish this bird's-eye view, this sense of distance and knowledge of the true proportion of things, of the world and the people in it.

Then, like the train, the wheel plunged over the edge of the world and I truly feared I would fly off it, forever, either to smash against the earth below or vanish into the sky above.

I screamed, only stopping when I saw the apparatus on the

ground level loom into focus . . . and vanish behind us . . . then we were again pointed at pure sky . . . and tumbling over the edge of the air again, as off an invisible cliff, my stomach still a half-turn behind me, my hat lifting from my head.

I clapped a hand to my hat, but thereby lost my grip on the bar and slid on the seat, almost slid out of the seat.

Quentin's arm on my shoulders clamped me back down in the seat. I caught my breath and screamed. My hat flapped like a giant blue bat before my eyes, falling . . .

He caught it and thrust it into the bottom of the car, one foot stamping the brim edge to the floor.

Again the ground rushed up at us, and again we flew away. I screamed.

Quentin clasped me tighter than I believed possible.

Over the top *yet again*, and no stop in sight!

I screamed.

And Quentin held me tighter.

I screamed again and turned my face into the dark of his shoulder.

The world turned, and us with it. I whirled, around and around. I stopped screaming. Somewhere, sometime, I began laughing. And screaming.

Because nothing horrible happened. I didn't leave my seat or the earth. The ride had a rhythm, and every time I came over the terrifying top and plunged down, I knew I was safe and I had to laugh even as I had to scream.

And finally, the pace slowed, and stopped, and we hung there swinging, then jerked down again, and swung some more.

I opened my eyes. It was still daylight, but the sun was riding low in the west. As we neared the ground I saw the shadow of our car thrown long and thin.

I had no screams left.

Quentin's grip on me eased, and my breath sighed out instead of being gulped in.

I stood up, both Quentin and the ride operator extending hands to help me out. The man handed my parasol out after me.

I stood on the gritty ground and blinked. I had screamed and screamed, as I had never done so many times during my terrifying odyssey of last spring when I could have. Then, to scream would have been to surrender. Here, it had rinsed me free of all the stored fear of that awful time. I was . . . empty. Free. Free to begin again.

Quentin kept an arm around my shoulders as he guided me away from the Ferris wheel.

"Are you all right? Was the ride too much for you?" He sounded very worried.

"Yes."

"I'm sorry. It's supposed to be fun."

"Was it for you?"

He smiled. "Yes."

"Even though I screamed like a banshee?"

"You're supposed to scream like a banshee."

"Well, if I must scream, I'd rather it be like something terrifying."

He eyed me carefully. "You're sure you're all right?"

"Remarkably all right."

"Then you're able to stay for the band and the fireworks?"

"Band?"

"Sousa."

"I've heard of him."

"And I suppose you've heard of fireworks too?" he teased me.

"Yes."

In the tepid, fading sunlight, we walked among the crowds. Quentin had forgotten to let go of me, but there were so many other . . . couples like us I hardly noticed.

We stopped once or twice at a shop. He bought a large canvas bag for "New Jersey Shore Salt Water Taffy," and a box of candy

to go in it. "For Irene," I said. As the sun went down, he put my parasol in the bag, and then he stopped and pulled the last pin from my hat and that went in the bag too.

We found a table in the twilight and sat just as John Philip Sousa's baton struck up the band. As a chill came with the dark, I felt something warm close around me and turned my head. Quentin's coat. I reached in the pockets for my abandoned gloves and donned them, then held the lapels closed and craned to see the stage.

Goodness! We couldn't see the band from where we were, though we certainly heard it. That stirring music woke up the crowd, yet I remained in a lazy dreamland, sitting here on another continent, amid strangers and stranger sights, feeling all the evil memories of the old World slipping away.

After the concert, we joined the crowd again. Their chatter and laughter and the children's happy screeches blended with the fading calls of the gulls vanishing into the night.

We managed one last walk, to the fireworks display. By then night had fallen and electric lights had turned the flat landscape into a fallen constellation of bright colors and lights.

Henry Pain's fireworks display was centered at another elaborately lit building, but it spewed far more decorative constellations into the dark sky over Brooklyn. We saw famous battles reenacted in the sky above us, rockets bursting in air, Catherine wheels spinning into the heavens as I had been so afraid that I would earlier that day. Each new explosion of red, blue, green, yellow, and bright, blinding white seemed to split the dark open and spill out shattered pieces of the rainbow. Oddly enough, a rainbow image ended the display, slowly blinking away into a few sparks in the darkness.

In silence Quentin took my arm and led me back to the Iron Pier, where our steamship and its Catherine wheel of water was ablaze with light for the journey back to Manhattan.

We stood at the rail watching the tiny lights of stars and ships both moving across the dark sea and sky. I was half asleep on my feet, but Quentin held me up. It was as if the hard cold dark box of my almost-coffin had been replaced by a warm, living box of flesh that spoke to me softly sometimes, and stroked my hair.

There was a flutter of cold air and motion as we disembarked and exchanged shipboard for a horse-drawn cab. I remember hearing the horse snort, and feeling Quentin lift me into the cab's dark interior.

In the hansom cab, Quentin leaned near to pull his coat closer around me.

"It's not half as warm as you need," he said, putting his arm around my shoulders. Though he was only clad in shirt sleeves I felt a band of warmth encircle me.

"Why is 'fun' so tiring?" I asked, only half serious.

"Because it's so hard to be ourselves most of the time."

I liked hearing the sound of his voice, distant yet close, as I was still half asleep from the sea air, so I said, "Why?"

"Because everything in society is designed to make something of us we don't really want to be."

That woke me up. "You?"

"Yes. Duty and family. I honor both, but in my own way."

"You are lucky to have found your own way."

"I paid dearly for every step of it, Nell. None of us is merely lucky."

"You? Struggled?"

"Do you think I was meant for the life I have?"

"Do you dislike it?"

He shook his head. "Never."

"A woman can't—"

"She can."

"Not me."

"Why not?"

"It's too late."

"I don't know. You know how you look just now?"

"An utter disgrace," I realized suddenly, thinking about seeing Irene, struggling to sit up, putting my bare—again!—hands to my disordered hair, neither of which were at all respectable.

He pulled my hands down. "You look exactly as you did when I saw you, in my niece's schoolroom with her friends, playing Blind Man's Buff."

"Quentin! I was a girl then. That was years ago. Besides, how can you see me at all inside this dark coach?"

"Yes, you were a girl then. That's what I saw, although you were trying so hard to play at being a governess, being only a handful of years older than your charges. And certain emotions never age. And the streetlights play like fireworks over your features every now and then. And don't you see me by flashes of light as well?"

"No. Yes. It depends."

"You never saw me then, that day I stopped by the schoolroom to greet Allegra. You were blindfolded, reaching out for some schoolgirl to identify with the tips of your fingers. You were all laughing, all you beautiful, carefree girls. You can't imagine what a sight that was for a man back from a bloody, vicious war. For a few moments, I didn't even realize you were the governess. You were one of them."

"Never! I was never a girl like that. I was not of their class, I was not carefree. I was not beautiful."

"You were to me, that day, all three."

I swallowed a tiny sob, for I would have loved to believe that fairy tale, and never knew how much until this impossible moment.

"Nell." His hands found my face, pushed the hair back. "You found me that day, with your blind fingers. You touched and traced my face, and you didn't stop, not even when your fingers found the moustache."

"I . . . don't really like mustaches. It was a game. I had to play it. And . . . I knew who you were."

"Did you?"

"Of course I had seen you at the house before. From a distance."

"Had you?"

"It was the game! I had to make sure."

"And did you?"

"I did."

"Perhaps I have to make sure too."

I was too exhausted to be puzzled, but I almost was when I heard him delve in the bag with my parasol and hat. Surely they were not needed now in the dark and out of the wind!

He withdrew something. The souvenir scarf of the elephant hotel.

"Turnabout's fair play," he said softly.

"Quentin," I objected, half understanding, half not.

He drew the silken scarf over my eyes, behind my head.

"*Quentin!*" I was back in the Paris panorama building and felt the cloth with the sickly sweet smell of chloroform cover my face, saw the endless darkness of captivity. I put my hands up to my face.

"*Shhh.* Trust me, Nell. It's eighteen-eighty and we're in the attic schoolroom on Berkley Square. Only all the girls are gone now, and it's my turn."

His hands pulled mine onto the rough sides of his face; his replaced mine on my overheated cheeks. The scarf pulled as it knotted behind my head, and then his fingertips were on my brow, light as butterfly wings, though I had never felt butterfly wings. I had never felt anything so soft.

"This is wrong," I said.

His fingers froze.

"*You* should be blindfolded! It's not a true turnabout." He laughed soft relief at my nitpicking objection. "I know, but I have to make sure," he said.

I was too confused to say anything further, and suddenly understood how he had felt, drawn into a game he was not a part of, too polite to object and then . . . captured by the mystery, the featherweight touch of alien fingers, down his brow, over his nose, cheeks, chin, lips.

I felt what he had felt that day and all fear fled. It seemed as if the sun shone on me again, and the peace of the seashore pulled at me like a tide. The terrors of my captivity completely slid away, into the future past. I was a girl again, caught in a game I didn't understand, which was so very pleasant nevertheless.

"I'd seen you too." he said. His voice broke into the bubble of sheer feeling around me.

"Where?"

"In the house. From a distance."

"Berkley Square?"

"Where do you think we are now, Nell?"

"I don't know."

His fingers stroked my throat, but his thumbs remained at the corners of my mouth.

Then his mouth was there on my mouth, and the mustache I didn't like. I could only draw in a deep, startled breath to my very core. He had kissed me before, gently and teasingly, but not like this, and I was that breathless girl on Berkley Square, who had forgotten herself and her place for a few impossibly free moments, as we kissed as we never could have then, as I never could have since then.

When it ended, and I was not sure how it had ended, I bowed my head and found my forehead tight against his slightly sandy chin.

At some moment I couldn't recall he'd removed the scarf. I had to keep my eyes squeezed closed to keep myself in the dark.

"It cannot be," I said.

He didn't answer, and I realized that I could feel the beating of his heart, that we were in a tight embrace.

"You can't! . . . Not me."

"Why not?"

"Irene is brave and beautiful. I am timorous and plain."

"You lie." And he stopped me with a kiss as fierce as any I believe that woman has felt. "Nell, you must step out of Irene's shadow. No one wants that more for you than she."

"Nellie Bly—" I said, when I could catch my breath again.

"Is a fraud. You were there first."

"I will not be easy, Quentin. I am like Sherlock Holmes in one respect. Irene said—"

"I don't want to hear about other people. I want to hear about you."

"There is no me left. I have always done what was necessary."

"This is necessary."

He kissed me again.

Someone knocked harshly on our heads, like a headache one notices has always been there, but only now has become unbearable.

The knock was *over* our heads. The hansom had stopped. We were drawn up in front of the Astor House.

"Wake up in there," the driver bellowed. "Rise and shine. We're here."

I blushed in the dark as Quentin hurriedly thrust far too many coins through the open trapdoor.

He reclaimed his jacket and picked up my bag.

I emerged, blinking in the bright electric glare outside the hotel and sure that every moment in the hansom cab showed upon my face.

The lobby was deserted but blazed with light. My eyes watered from the shock, and Quentin escorted me into the elevator and to the door to our rooms before my eyes had adjusted enough to focus on him. I was afraid to see him in the light.

Just outside the room, he paused, took my elbow.

"Nell."

He said no more. I stared into his face, his amazing face simply for the fact of being his. We knew each other with a vision beyond seeing now, but it didn't mean anything was settled. Certainly I had never been so unsettled in my life.

I tried to smile, but I heard the door to our suite cracking open and turned in a rush to make my face ready for Irene.

I sensed Quentin standing behind me with every scintilla of my being.

"A late evening," Irene observed with the smile of a fond governess welcoming her charges home. "I'm glad you two have had a chance to sample the local landmarks. Nell, come in, you must be exhausted."

Quentin handed my bag to Irene and bid us a civil good night.

Something soft drifted over my hands just as he left. The scarf.

I walked from the dim light of the hall into our rooms and under Irene's eagle eye.

My hair was windblown and half-down, my hat and parasol were in the Salt Water Taffy pavilion bag, a souvenir scarf of the Elephant Hotel was wound around my wrist and my heart, and I was shivering from the sudden chill of night now that Quentin's coat was no longer over my shoulders.

"My dear," cried Irene as she saw me plainly in the lamplight, "it's almost one in the morning. You have had a long day. Fun in too large a dose can be as wearing as not having any at all."

She drew me farther into our rooms and lifted the heavy bag to take it into my bedroom. Then she studied me.

"Your face is very . . . pink" she said.

I ignored the loathsome word. "The sun was very bright."

"You had a hat."

"The sea wind was very strong."

"You looked very tired."

"I am. There is nothing to do on Coney Island but walk and dine and see fireworks."

"But was it fun?"

"That is not exactly the word I would use for it."

"So—?"

I remembered what Quentin had said about her shadow. Irene was the least oppressive person I knew. She deserved an honest answer.

"It was crowded, noisy, full of common people and entertainments, and extremely exhilarating."

"Exhilarating."

"Very. And now I must go to bed before I fall asleep standing up, like a horse."

"Or like an elephant," she added merrily.

"Elephant?"

"Like the one on that souvenir scarf you're clutching. It's nice that you have a remembrance of your outing."

"Yes," I said, gathering my bag back into my own custody. "Good night. Oh. Irene!"

I turned back to face her, in obvious distress.

In an instant she looked terribly worried and even guilty. "What is it, Nell? What . . . happened?"

"Oh, Irene! We bought you a cigar as a souvenir, but I'm afraid it's been left in Quentin's coat!"

Relief flooded her usually unreadable features. "Then we will just have to see him again and get it," she said sweetly.

I smiled just as sweetly as I went into my room and closed the door.

38.

Babes in the Woods

*About Ann Lohman's origins only a few sketchy facts are
known, for she herself in later years had little reason to dwell
on her beginnings, while her notoriety fostered legends as
dubious as they were inconsistent.*

—THE WICKEDEST WOMAN IN NEW YORK, CLIFFORD BROWDER

We spent the morning at the city library, pursuing Madame
Restell through sere yellowed pages in which she always figured as a villain, except for her own defensive letters.

I studied a sketch of the woman who had been born
plain Ann Trow in Painswick, England, of all places!

She seemed a stout and socially solid matronly type, no femme
fatale in the French sense. But the phrase indicted a "deadly
woman," not one who simply broke men's hearts but one who
"murdered babies."

"I have never heard this word 'abortion,' before," I told Irene.

"Did a woman in your father's parish in Shropshire never lose
a baby before its birth?"

"Yes. Birth is a perilous occupation. Babies, and mothers like my own, may die at the end of birth, babies before birth, at birth, and even three or four birthdays into their own lives."

"You describe natural hazards. Madame Restell had the means, or claimed to have the means, to produce such results by unnatural means, by the aid of certain herbs, or barriers, or chemicals, or even by painful operations that disrupted the process of growing a baby."

"Why is it, Irene, that when I join you in the effort of solving some difficult criminal problem I must always learn more of the world than I am ready for?"

"Because there is so little of the real world that anyone is ready for," she answered wryly. "As these newspaper stories point out, the law has seldom meddled with the begetting of babies before the point of 'quickening.' That is the moment that the unborn babe is presumed to be capable of living and breathing on its own, when it becomes a 'person.'"

"When it is delivered into the world, and commences to breathe," I said.

"Yes. And perhaps no. No one knows when God decides such things, although many have decided they can name the exact instant. And then the law comes into it, and self-certain moral crusaders like Anthony Comstock, who are sure they know better than most what God decided when. It is clear from these articles that Comstock entrapped Madame Restell into yet another trial and possible imprisonment. In her later years, perhaps exhausted by the fight, she chose to direct her own exit from the public stage, and, as the newspapers reported, slit her throat from ear to ear with a butcher knife in the bath rather than go to prison again."

"How ghastly! A butcher knife! I can't imagine anyone managing such a brutal self-assault, much less a woman."

"From all accounts that I read at the time, and my memory may be faulty on the details, she had suddenly realized the likelihood of her conviction and at the age of sixty-seven, could no longer face incarceration in the Tombs. She had testified in court that she had not performed abortions in twelve years, but that made no difference, and few would have believed her. I agree, Nell, that the manner of death was shocking, so much so that some people believed a patient's body had been found in the tub and that she had escaped to Canada or Europe, or that wealthy clients had murdered her, fearful of being exposed at her trial. Some newspapers even had kind words for her in their obituaries, but most rejoiced in her death."

I found the entire subject very troubling. "In Shropshire, there were said to be wise women in remote places who could help a lovelorn village girl win a swain or deal with other mysterious problems. Were they these . . . abortionists?"

"Probably, when they weren't frauds. Such needs are as old as time, Nell, and such methods. Some work. Some work only to part the petitioner from her money. If you let your eye stray to these newspaper columns reporting arrests you would see a great many men accused of bastardy."

"That is so unfair! Godfrey cannot help that he was born of a mother who was not married, at least to his father."

Irene smiled. "The police are not arresting the bastards themselves, Nell, they are arresting men who got unmarried women pregnant, thus producing bastards. Although you're right. To be known as the product of an unmarried woman condemns the child as well as the mother."

"Then Madame Restell—"

"Was a heroine to many of these unhappy, desperate women. It was said even when I lived here that though she waxed rich on every daughter or wife of a wealthy family she saved from discovery and disgrace, for poor women she charged far less, and earned their equally heartfelt praise."

"So was she wicked or simply misunderstood?"

"Always the great question, Nell."

"You will not tell me what to think?"

"I don't know myself. A mother unwed is unable to hide, unable to shelter herself or her child from the greatest distress and condemnation. She is Sin Incarnate, walking, and her child is a pariah. What might anyone do to avoid such a fate?"

I couldn't answer. My father's public preaching had never addressed such scandalous subjects, and his private opinions on matters I had never even suspected existed were unimaginable to me.

I could only know for sure that neither Irene nor Godfrey deserved to be condemned for their mothers' actions, or their fathers'. It struck me that the one undeniable fact was that innocent babes paid the price in all these matters.

And I desperately did not want the "innocent babes" I knew as very dear adult human beings and my friends to be exposed for the sins of their parents.

"Must we invite Pink into this matter?" I asked.

"We must," Irene said grimly, "for she holds the keys to the past: access to the newspaper morgues, and it's there that these present murders originate. I would stake my good name on it."

I heard the sarcasm in her voice, and shriveled at her self-disdain. Irene had a good name because of every action she had taken, every talent she had cultivated. Was it to all come down to the conditions of her birth? In England, or France, yes. In America? I hoped not. I so devoutly hoped not.

39.

French Medicine

~sje~

"Madame Restell," Pink mused later that afternoon, ostentatiously opening the artist's portfolio on her knees once again to reveal piles of papers. She seemed quite smug about being invited back into the bosom of our investigation after the contretemps at Delmonico's.

The minx was even mimicking my use of an artist's folio in Paris, and also my attire of choice: a checked coatdress that bespoke a woman of business and not of frivolity.

"Was she truly wicked?" Irene asked. "Or simply unlucky?"

"Oh, you have hit the motherlode in her," Pink said. "I owe you a great deal of thanks. I was born too late to know of her long career and the chaos it caused. She is the Lucretia Borgia of America, if you ask me. And quite businesslike about it. Talk about enterprise! I can't quite figure her out."

"Perhaps," Irene suggested, "she believed in what she was doing. Allan Pinkerton, for instance, was a religious dissenter in Scotland before he immigrated to the United States. He was an advanced-thinking man, which may be why he fought for a female force against the judgment of all his male employees. They won by outliving him, but I think his philosophy will win out in the end, should we all live to glimpse it."

"If only I had been born twenty years earlier!" Pink exclaimed. "I could have gone West and recorded the Indian wars. Or . . . I don't know! I am fascinated by this Madame Restell now that you've directed my attention to her. Why are you so interested? Why do you study her?"

"Marat, dead in his bathtub in the famous painting of the excesses of the French Revolution, is immortal. Madame Restell died in a like, liquid manner, save by her own hand, yet she is forgotten in her own country. Such figures always interest me. Perhaps I see an opera in them."

"An opera! A great American opera! It has all the drama, but I doubt that an abortionist makes much of a tragic heroine."

"You are right." Irene lit another lucifer, then a fresh small cigar. "Obviously a faithless Spanish cigarette girl is a far better subject for tragedy and, thus, grand opera."

Pink frowned, suspecting that she was being satirized, but not sure how.

I smiled to see her confusion. She had decided to engage Irene hand to hand and did not understand that even Sherlock Holmes could not be sure of the outcome of such a duel.

Well, he had his Watson, and Irene had me. I may not be an educated professional woman, like a doctor, but I was as loyal as any man and not one to be swayed by sensational personal histories. At least, not lately.

So Pink produced this Madame Restell's history from her collection of newspaper clippings, and we pored over perhaps the most lurid documents I have ever seen.

I kept mostly still, although I made copious mental notes for my diaries. It was fortunate that I had apprenticed a barrister and had learned to carry a notepad in my head for later transcription.

Despite the sights and sins we had glimpsed in our springtime pursuit of Jack the Ripper, I was now seeing more than I wished of such misdeeds on the female front. I discovered that my own sex could be as cruel and bloody and merciless as any man.

"Ah, here Nell," Irene said. "You know from seeing the Jack the Ripper reports how much newspapers revel in grisly details. This article makes plain how Madame Restell died. The weapon was an eight-inch ebony-handled carving knife, very sharp, from the kitchen."

"Yet all those Ripper reports emphasized the brute strength it took cut another's throat. It would require both mental and physical power to abuse one's own."

"It says right here. The coroner found two incisions on the right side. Obviously, she hesitated, but the second slash was made with such great force that it severed the right carotid artery and both jugular veins. She must have been half-mad with desperation."

"Still . . . Someone could have come in and done it."

"And a robber would not have brought his own knife or pistol? The house had a burglar alarm, so any intruder would have triggered ringing bells throughout the place, which thronged with servants. Besides, the coroner had to remove three diamond rings and her diamond earrings from the body, and—this will shake your frugal soul, Nell—the diamond studs on her nightgown, which lay on a chair beside the bathtub."

"I am indeed shocked. That carries excess too far. And diamond studs would be very uncomfortable to roll over on during the night."

But as we read on about the decades of public argument and denouncement of Madame Restell and her works, I began to see why Irene had said that Restell's possible involvement as the woman in black in Irene's past opened untold possibilities for murder and revenge brutal enough to match the mutual wartime atrocities of the Red man and the White.

"She was quite the grande dame of New York society," Pink summed up as well as any lawyer. Her cheeks were flushed with the excitement of discovery and she looked quite . . . well, enormously attractive and youthful. (Although she was only eight years younger than I and already, at five-and-twenty, on her way to being considered a spinster rather than a marriageable miss.) I could not help picturing each of us through Quentin Stanhope's eyes, and there was no contest, save I had known him first.

My mental wanderings were interrupted by Irene's sharp glance: first to my face, than to my belt.

She obviously meant me to take notes. With the greatest of stealth, I slipped the small silver notepad cover and matching automatic pencil, another wonder of the age, from their attachments to my chatelaine.

Simply handling these objects that had been a surprise gift from Godfrey gave me a sort of tranquility. I was no Papist, but I could understand the solace of rosary beads through the fingertips, thanks to this exquisite thing of use and beauty, which was the only gift that I had from any man, save my father's steadfast support and spiritual guidance.

"I don't know how you feel about the work of such women as Madame Restell," Pink was saying, looking from Irene to me and back to Irene.

She clearly did not expect us to have the same opinion as each other, or that she held.

Silence greeted this gauntlet she had hurled down, aggravating the already tender bonds of our relationship.

Irene answered. "How did Madame Restell regard her role in society, in keeping its secrets?"

Pink rustled her papers. "I don't know. I only know how she was regarded: as either sinner or saint, and at times she looked a good bit like both." Then she eyed us. "By being what I am, a 'stunt' reporter, I have looked in the face certain realities of life from which most people avert their gaze. I have seen the factory and sweatshop girls with their one day off a week fall prey to the shallowest mashers and pay the price with disease and pregnancy and sometimes even death."

I winced at her plain speech. Her quick blue-gray gaze fastened on me.

"You see yourself as a governess still, Nell, tending to sheltered green girls from good families. Yet even they, and especially they, and their frantic parents, were clients of Madame Restell in the forties, fifties, sixties, and seventies of New York City life.

"I think back on my own family," she went on. "I think back on the judge's prodigious progeny—fourteen living children by two wives—and how custom left a mother dead before her children grew up and made second wives and second sets of siblings more common than not. My mother and her children were quite disinherited at his death, and you know the shameful consequences of our helplessness.

"The mere act of birth, once, killed your mother, Nell, and left you without brothers or sisters and ultimately an orphan."

" 'Lonely orphan girl,' " Irene quoted the signature to Pink's first and pivotal letter to the editor that had begun her journalistic career. "That is how you represented yourself, yet you still had mother and siblings."

"I had mother, yes, and siblings, but they were all children still, and someone had to take care of them. Me. I still do. Then, I was as good as alone. As Nell was. As you were, apparently."

Irene nodded, acknowledging Nellie Bly's greatest feat: surviving not only for herself, but for others.

Even I could not dislike her at that moment, despite Quentin and despite her ability to sacrifice anyone to her need to reveal what the world was really like. I wondered how many people truly wanted to know that? And how many people who lapped up other people's scandals and pains understood that they were behaving more as hyenas than humans?

There was something admirable in telling the truth at any cost, and something horrible as well.

"So," Irene asked, "was Madame Restell more sinner or saint?"

"She was arrested four times," Pink reported. "She served three prison terms. She killed herself with a butcher knife rather than face a fourth. Yet for decades she rode in her coach and four daily along Broadway, wearing silks and diamonds, flaunting her wealth."

"Four?" I asked. "Four horses?" I remembered someone at the theater saying the Woman in Black had a coach with "four white horses."

"Two bays, one chestnut, and a gray," Pink answered, consulting her papers. "She was most precise about that when one newspaper reported the horses's coloration inaccurately. Imagine splitting hairs on the color of a horse hide, yet finding no harm in seeing that babies were not born."

"There always," Irene said, "have been certain women, in the woods surrounding villages and in the alleyways of cities, who know all manner of ways, real or fraudulent, supposed to end a scandalizing pregnancy, and all pregnancies are potentially scandalous."

"Not to married women," I put in.

Irene regarded me. "Even to married women. Husbands may be gone for more than nine months, or may be ill, and still the wives wax pregnant. There is nothing more telltale than a pregnancy. No wonder women are so desperate to conceal them one way or another."

"For all the huge numbers of the men who are arrested for bastardy in New York City," Pink added, "the testimony falls upon the girl or woman involved, and they are easily labeled liars. That is why I never will marry. The men have all the advantages."

I found this news most . . . interesting. I had always considered never marrying a humiliating burden I must suffer in silence. I had not thought that it could be deemed an advantage. Irene resumed our discussion by taking up the reins, whether they lay over bay, chestnut, or gray backs.

"So Madame Restell was both wealthy and notorious, and quite bald-faced about her profession."

"Bald-faced? She advertised." Pink flourished a fan of yellowed newsprint. "I found more advertisements than actual news stories. The fact is that Madame Restell, and her husband, both misrepresented themselves as physicians, yet they seemed honestly committed to the task of advising women on the ways they might circumvent disease, pregnancy, and delivery, if the child was already conceived."

"But why would such a woman," I asked, "spend time among the variety performers at—pardon me, Irene—second-rate theatrical venues?"

"I imagine," Pink said, "that many of her clients came from that class of women." Before Irene could protest, she continued. "And the fact is that she seemed to have had a kind heart. She charged her clients according to their ability to pay, and sometimes asked nothing at all. In some cases she provided a place to stay for women whose pregnancies were too advanced to end."

"How could she know that?" I asked. "And what of the law?"

"The law often looks the other way when the wealthy are involved." Irene answered for Pink and her mound of news clippings. "What was the legal status of her business?"

Pink pursed her lips as she thought before she answered. "Difficult to say, otherwise she and her competitors would not have dared advertise so obviously. From what I read, and there are hundreds of items, abortion was not illegal if it was done before the baby 'quickened.'"

"When exactly is that?" I asked. "I have heard of the 'quick and the dead' in prayers, but what does this term mean to a woman bearing a baby?"

Irene shrugged. "Perhaps when the child first stirs in the womb. I hear that they kick sometimes.'

"Kick!" I was amazed; no, horrified. "I knew childbirth was dreadfully painful, but I had no idea the child would try to kick its way . . . er, out."

"It shifts in the womb sometimes," Irene said, looking about as enamored of this discussion as I was. "You come from a large family, Pink. What did your mother experience?"

"More than I care to say. The fact is that the term 'quickened' was as little understood then as now, which may be why the law is much more strict today. When Madame Restell slit her own throat in eighteen seventy-eight it was the end of an era." She stared down wistfully at the pile of papers in her lap. "If I'd been there, I'd have known the answers to all your questions."

I was growing impatient, and perhaps uneasy at this discussion. Such matters were best left unsaid. "Whatever the hairs that could be split over her ministrations, why was she visiting these theatrical folk?"

"Such people are presumed to be loose livers," Pink said. "Perhaps she was seeking clients."

"It sounded more like a social call," I protested.

"Well—" Pink eyed Irene rather as a common garden snake would regard the formidable cobra-slayer, Messalina the mongoose. "Other charges than providing contraception and abortion were brought against Madame Restell, not as often as the first, but often enough."

"Other charges?" I asked, not sure I'd like the answer.

"Oh, some of the women might have died from the treatment. Madame Restell and her husband were accused of chopping their bodies into pieces and smuggling them out of her building in the dark of night, along with the bodies of aborted babies."

I put my hand to my chest to keep my gorge from rising. "This is like some horrid gruesome fairy tale."

"And likely as true," Irene put in. "What other horrors did this lady stand accused of? I'm sure 'the wickedest woman in New York' was capable of more atrocities."

Irene's sardonic question helped quiet my imagination.

"Some women were purportedly too far gone to abort, so Madame Restell forced them to stay with her until the birth, then took their babies from them."

"Her answer?" Irene asked.

"In one case, she said the young woman's father had insisted she find a home for the infant, and she did."

"An atrocity indeed," Irene said, "but more indicting of the father's authority than of Madame Restell's actions."

Pink shuffled papers. "When she came to her senses the poor girl, the mother of the adopted babe, looked for years, but could never find it. Madame Restell had been requested to arrange things in that manner, and so it was done."

"Any other charges?" Irene pressed.

"That she sold unwanted babies to people who wanted them and couldn't have them."

"Is there any surviving portrait of this monster of commerce in human misery?"

Pink passed some loose pieces of faded newsprint to us without comment. Irene handed me one piece while she studied another.

I gazed upon a sketch of the she-demon, a woman of late middle years, stout and plump-faced, wearing a lace cap of the kind worn thirty years ago. She resembled a grandmother, or a landlady.

Irene's brows had arched as she studied the other likeness. I peered to see. It was the older sketch, for Madame Restell looked in the prime of life, with her hair parted in the middle to fall in sausage curls at her ears, rather resembling the poetess Elizabeth Barrett Browning, or her favorite spaniel, Flush.

Altogether a most pleasant representation, except . . . I frowned at an image like a coat of arms beneath the upper torso portrait. "What do these wings represent . . . Mercury?"

Irene leaned over the image to view it again. "I believe those are the wings of a giant bat, Nell, and the small pale thing in its claws is an infant."

"Oh!" I nearly dropped the drawing, so grotesque was its import.

"She was the most hated woman in New York of her time," Pink observed. A tight smile did not enhance her usually cheery features. "And the most beloved, especially by the most well-to-do."

"A true conundrum," Irene said casually, "but I don't see why her now-dead career has much bearing on things nowadays."

"But it's so obvious, Irene. Bearing indeed! How odd you should use that word. I believe that Madame Restell was your mother."

40.

Unwanted Mother

Restell was brought from the Tombs about noon.... She was wearing a rich black silk gown, a handsomely trimmed black velvet mantilla, and a white satin bonnet with a lace veil, but looked pale and anxious.

—TRIAL FOR PROCURING AN ABORTION, 1847

"Ridiculous!"

Irene spat out the word as a man will mouth an oath after Pink had left, but she went at once to the brandy decanter and the cigarette case.

"Pink has the mind of a P. T. Barnum!" Irene raged. "Next she will aver that Jumbo the Elephant is my mother. Why not claim I am the daughter of a mermaid and an octopus! Really, I regret the day I ever thought that a jaunt to America might—"

"Might what? Do *me* good? Admit it, Irene! You and Godfrey decided that poor Nell needed a change of scene after . . . after everything, and now see what a box of imps you have loosened on yourself. I am extremely happy to be a woman of no importance whatsoever, with no past whatsoever, since if I were not so utterly ordinary, such unpleasant surprises would be in store for me."

"You have had one very unpleasant surprise on this trip already," she reminded me, sipping from brandy glass and cigarette holder in turn.

She was more upset than she wished anyone, including herself, to know. I had only listed to my own grievances, which I had much exaggerated, to draw her attention from her own situation.

If only Godfrey were here! One thing I had not exaggerated to myself: I was terribly disturbed by Irene's uncertain past, not only by the shiftless, bizarre nature of her upbringing, but by her disturbingly vague recollection of whole years of her life. This was a woman who held every note and word from the complicated librettos of numerous grand operas in her memory. Who never failed to recall a word or deed of mine that I wished to forget. Who could speak several languages. And I was to believe that her childhood was as smudged as a few chalk traces on a blackboard?

No. Someone had wanted Irene to forget her youth, and had succeeded. And this was a sinister thought indeed.

So here was Irene, handicapped for the first time in her life by a lack of knowledge about, of all things, herself, at the mercy of the reportorial inquisition and deeply personal investigations of that untrustworthy little minx and maneater, Pink Cochrane.

Much as I deeply appreciated Irene's and Godfrey's sincere, if misdirected, concern for my welfare, I was very glad to be here in America with Irene, after all. She had never needed more looking after, and the pity was that she did not know it, she was not constituted to know it. She was used to looking out for others and therefore would be useless at looking out for herself.

However, looking out for others had formerly, if briefly, been my profession, and I was determined to resurrect it now.

Part of that welcome duty would be to see that Pink did nothing to harm Irene in any way.

Once Irene was in the grip of her usual pacifiers, I gingerly

40.

❧

began my own investigation of the apparent facts. Obviously, Pink's conclusions were sadly askew.

"Irene, I do not believe for an instant that you are that woman's daughter."

"On what grounds, Nell?"

"On the grounds that anything Pink might conclude is only so much lurid newspaper talk. However, I do find it intriguing that this woman visited your theatrical environment when you were a child. From all reports, for such a monster, she seems fond of children, although I do understand that her business included the suppression of motherhood in one way or another."

My comments stirred Irene to action, as I had known they would. She liked nothing better than explaining the seamier side of life to me, and, after my initial shock, I was beginning to find such knowledge rather interesting.

She began to page through the papers and the book Pink had left behind. "I suppose Pink would know the answer to your question, Nell."

"I do not wish to know what Pink thinks she knows. I wish to know the facts, so much as newspaper reports can be trusted for such things."

Irene dutifully bent her head to the material in search of the requested information.

Piteous! Normally I would be sent to do the tedious research, a task I had been well prepared for during my employment as Godfrey's typewriter girl. There is nothing for inspiring tedium as the documents of the law.

I found my hands had made fists and my mouth had tightened into a grim line. The last time I had endured such impotent tension I had been consigned prematurely to a coffin. But I had arisen from the apparent dead and was now finding in myself a resolve that Irene's dead past should never cause her that kind of distress.

"The husband was active in the business also," Irene said suddenly. "They were both one step up from quack practitioners, Nell, yet they espoused their work on philosophical grounds." She looked up at me, much calmer.

"These opinions to curtail childbirth are not all evil. Your own mother died of it before she could do what she most longed to: see you, tend you, rear you. Nature demands more of some women than their constitutions can survive."

"You approve of what Madame Restell practiced?"

"No, but I have seen the terrible cost that young unwed women pay, some of them even innocent of wrongdoing."

"How can that be?"

Irene's hands made vague gestures, as they often did when I asked to know more than she thought me ready for. "Nell, you know the New Testament, how an angel of the Lord—isn't that how it was put?"

"Oh, yes, I know that passage; that is what the Papists cite to justify virgin birth."

"Virgin birth. Exactly."

"But I am not Catholic."

"It doesn't matter. According to that version of the New Testament, an angel told Mary that she was pregnant by spiritual means. This can happen to girls as innocent today, except the means are devilish. They come in the guise of men they would trust, men they are told to obey, who are, in fact . . ."

"This is not possible!"

"It is, Nell. Often it is not the girl's fault. We are reared to be obedient."

"Not in your case."

Irene laughed, suddenly relieved. "Oh, Nell. You are right. Somehow, early in my education, I had the choice of being obedient or incorrigible, and I chose the latter."

"I am glad that you did, if it helped you avoid answering to the 'devils.'" I absorbed what she tried to say for a moment. "I understand your point. There are wicked men in New York too, and they might have a stake in making out Madame Restell to be a wicked woman."

Irene nodded. "If she is indeed my mother, I don't wish her to be a monster."

I didn't answer, but shifted newsprint, looking for facts. "Aha! There was only one child, a daughter, but she is accounted for, at least until the age of fourteen, when she assisted her mother. I wonder what became of her in these last eleven years? Also Monsieur Restell, who seems to have gone under another name entirely, also French. That is most suspicious."

"That is least suspicious, Nell. I remember enough of America to know that anything French was assumed to be elegant, sophisticated, and much desirable."

"And to think these citizens were once English! How far they have declined. Frankly, it is only the matter of sinning that the British cede to the French."

"Yes, the French do seem to be superior to the British in that one area. At least."

"You are trying to aggravate me, but I won't be distracted. The woman also had a brother, Joseph. And . . . remember, Madame Restell was born British. So much for your giving the French the upper hand, even in the matter of scandal and sinning."

Irene stubbed out her cigarette and sipped the last bit of brandy.

"If Madame Restell was *not* my mother, why would Pink be so eager to make her so? And if Madame Restell was not my mother, why did she linger among that minor theatrical set during the early years of my life, and then disappear afterwards until she died sixteen years later, by her own hand? If she was my mother, she was willing to leave me to my own devices for a good, long time."

"And that is why she cannot have been your mother, Irene. Anyone who knows, or knew you, would never permit you to be left to your own devices for long. That includes Godfrey and myself."

41.

The Wickedest Woman in New York

While she lived no woman was more eagerly discussed and after her death more mercilessly slandered.

—BIOGRAPHER OF ADAH ISAACS MENKEN, THE MID-NINETEENTH-
CENTURY EQUESTRIENNE MAZEPPA

We spent the rest of the day studying the news stories and pamphlets and trial book that Pink had left us much as an anarchist might lay a bomb at a target's feet, in my opinion.

We had no doubt that Pink had left them only because she had leeched every bit of useful information from them beforehand. Or what she discerned to be useful information.

By twilight our eyes had grown bleary in the lamplight. Without consulting each other, we set aside the piles of fine print.

"I still don't quite know what to make of 'the wickedest woman in New York,'" Irene admitted. "Some called her demon, some angel. She grew enormously wealthy at her trade, moving up the island from modest quarters at the bottom of Manhattan to finer quarters and finally to a mansion on Fifth Avenue to match the Astors. Although she was never accepted openly in society, the veiled wives and daughters from Mrs. Astor's guest list of four hundred elite New York City families came and went at her mansion nightly. The wealthy and powerful protected her, for she held the secrets of their hearts and hearths, yet they couldn't prevent the moral reformers from charging her in court and even sending her to prison for as much as a year.

"Even in prison her wealth and social connections made her stay far more pleasant than an average prisoner's. Her daughter followed in her footsteps, then disappeared into history, as did Madame Restell's brother Joseph. She outlived her husband, who seems to have been constant, and as much a quack doctor as she, except that their treatments were apparently effective, and that they wrote quite eloquently on their pioneer effort to educate the ignorant and prevent pain, poverty, and suffering. Then, facing yet another prison term, she suddenly slit her own throat in her bath the very morning she was due in court for sentencing, after decades of fighting all detractors in the newspaper columns. She is an enigma!"

"And so is her brief period of haunting the theaters when you were a child performer. How long do they say she did so?"

"For a year at most. Eighteen-sixty to 'sixty-one."

"The opening years of the American Civil War? Can that have some bearing?"

"Of course it can! But it was also the opening years of my life. I was given to believe that I was born in eighteen fifty-eight, so I would have been three and four when the Woman in Black visited me at the theater."

"Madame Restell was a respectable married woman, at least in her private life. She was known to have one daughter, who would have been quite a bit older than you. She certainly knew how to prevent births. I agree, how could she have been your mother?

Why would she have hidden you? She apparently hid nothing else of her private life."

Irene shook her head without speaking, then set her selection of newspapers on the desk.

"Ah, let us dine like queens tonight, Nell. Tomorrow I will take a different tack. I must find the maestro, if I can. Perhaps he can tell me more about myself, for he was instrumental in my becoming who I am today."

"I'm not sure what that would reveal about your distant past, which is where all the mysteries lie."

"I don't know either, except that music saved me. From what, I can't quite say. Once I had found my voice, I never lost myself or my memory again. I recall setting out from my boarding house each day to audition. I recall Allan Pinkerton, a remarkably liberal man on the role of women, seizing upon a diffident singing pupil as a promising private inquiry agent, as if I were a jewel plucked from a trash heap. He saw worth in me before any musical director did, and thus gave me a profession before my voice had earned me another one, and, more importantly, a confidence in myself one can only gain from going against the grain of society. And thus I come back to Madame Restell, not so different from me after all." Irene sighed, and her eyes were very bright. "I cannot ever repay Pinkerton, for he is dead these five years, and also his vision of a female force that I was a part of, but I hope that the maestro is not, and that he may give me some needed answers."

We returned, as apparently Irene had often done in her youth, to Professor Marvel.

He was playing cards in a small park near his boarding house with a set of old fellows as mellow as he. Though this was a huge, bustling city, they reminded me of the village elders in Shropshire warming the benches outside the pubs on mornings both foggy and fine.

I remember that as a child I had often sat with these benign old fellows, who taught me inappropriate card games and beguiled the time of a child who had no siblings, no mother, and a harried father.

Professor Marvel sported the side whiskers of a more gracious time and welcomed us with an offer of tea and warm intentions.

"I don't much get called upon by handsome young women," he said, winking so innocently that for a moment I became as beautiful as Irene.

"The maestro," he reminisced as we walked back to his boarding house for tea. "Quite an amazin' fellow. Been abroad, you know. Vienna and Paris and such. So he said. I never much worried whether he spoke the truth. We all said much in those days, and were young enough to believe our own lies.

"Would you like some sugar for your tea, ladies? I don't keep much about the place, except a kettle for the fire and a cannister of pekoe, and sugar cubes in my pockets at all times. Love the horses, you know. Poor burdened beasts. I walk daily down Broadway and greet them and give them a bit of sweet. I like to think my example inspires some toleration in the drivers and passengers. With my pockets full of forty pounds of answers to every question, I sometimes feel like a swaybacked old horse myself, forced to trot to the whip into eternity."

"How very kind of you," I said. "I shall remember that when I return to Paris, although the French are exceedingly horse-proud, and quite pamper them, unlike the English."

He nodded, squinting his rheumy blue eyes at the past, as Irene had requested.

"His name was Stubben. He was German and a hard taskmaster. I wanted you to study with the Italian contessa, such a warm,

gracious woman, but she returned to her warm, gracious home-
land, and there was only the maestro left. I had reservations. He
was fine dealing with automata—machines that perform like
humans—but a young, live girl who had never had a father? I had
my doubts, little Rena, but one doubt I did not have. You had a
Voice. It would be a crime not to train it. So, I sent you to the
maestro."

"It must have worked out well," Irene said, "for a singer I
became, and did quite well on the Continent. Until . . . other circumstances forced my early retirement from the operatic stage."

"Oh, my dear!" His lovely blue eyes shimmered behind the
frank tears that eighty-five years may bring. "Not using your
Voice. Surely a crime of the first water!"

"But," she said hastily, "I've just received a libretto by Oscar
Wilde and another English writer, with a score by Sir Arthur Sullivan of operetta fame, and I do intend to add it to my repertoire
for solo chamber performances."

"Ah. Sullivan. I've heard of him. And this Wilde fellow
toured the U.S. with some fanfare a few years back. Quite the
dandy I understand, but he was a hit in the Wild West. Who can
say what the modern theater will embrace. Look at Buffalo Bill!"

"We have met him," Irene said, "and I am to reprise Merlinda
for his show in Paris."

"Treats his horses well, does he?"

"And his Indians and women."

"How he treats a horse defines a man, even in these Eastern
cities. It will reflect on how he treats a woman."

Irene rolled her eyes at me as this antique philosophy came
forth. "And where might we find the maestro, if he is still about
to be found?"

"Ah! He was like me: too stubborn to die. I believe he plays
the violin at the Union Square theaters. But you must ask for
Dieter Stubben now. He has not been a 'maestro' since shortly

after you left him to make your own way in the musical world. You were his finest pupil, and he declined after that."

"One must live one's life," Irene said as we walked away from the professor's boarding house, our pockets bulging with sugar cubes.

"Of course! One must live and leave the ones we admire and love behind us, for we are young and they are old."

She paused before a poor old horse attired in a ragged straw bonnet and offered him a gloved palmful of sugar. The huge, clumsy lips snickered at her hand.

"It is odd, Nell," she said. "Not a month ago in France I discovered an old violin that is worth a fortune. Now I search in American for an old violinist. And the link is one that would be laughed off the stage. My invaluable Guarneri is one the maestro gave to me when I left America for a singing career in the Old World. He may be poverty-stricken now. I can return his violin if I find him. The student may support the teacher."

"It is a good thing that Sherlock Holmes refused your too-generous offer of the violin, then," I noted.

"I knew he would. I merely wished to see him discomfited by the offer. That was cruel of me. There is something about him that makes me wish to push him to his limits."

I recognized a certain affinity of feeling that frightened me. "He is not a likeable man."

"But he is . . . unique. A performing artist like myself should be more appreciative of that. And he plays the violin, so he has hidden depths. Perhaps I see the recluse that I would have been had circumstances not forced me to take the world by the throat and make it sing in my key."

So we spent the evening doing what I had never done before, treading the arc-lit Broadway streets, visiting theater after theater, and leaving early, studying the house orchestras, looking for a man with a violin.

If that description alone would have answered Irene's quest, I knew where to direct her: Baker Street.

But we were in New York City now, tracking her past, and all that was required was an old man with a very old violin.

The Alhambra playbill advertised dancing horses and horse-faced dancers, according to the illustrations.

We went inside, no one questioning two women buying tickets and taking seats. New York was a world away from everything I had been reared to believe.

Irene paid top dollar to get seats nearest the orchestra pit. Once seated, her corrosive glance scoured the forty or so men in penguin formal dress, all the same shabby sort.

At last, during the overture that introduced the Lippizaner stallions of Vienna, she almost leapt, like the vaunted stallions, from her seat.

"It is he! Grizzled, it is true, but the very man. Oh, poor fellow! An artiste forced to saw a fiddle for a group of performing horses."

"Noble beasts," I pointed out, forcing her to sit down and sit out the act.

The steeds were all that had been advertised. I was struck by how in all ways they served mankind, whether whipped to death in the street or trained, at the snap of a whip that never touched hide, to rear on their hind legs and dance.

It occurred to me that people also served such contradictory roles. Perhaps I had been listening too much to Nellie Bly.

At any rate, once the curtain had rung down on an interim, Irene seized my sleeve and drew me into yet another backstage maze.

The dressing rooms were loud and crowded, and the one for the orchestra was the farthest and smallest and most overpopulated.

The smell of rosin and horse hide, not to mention horse elimination, hung like a miasma over the understage cubbyholes.

Irene was not to be stopped. We surged together through the room full of men in evening dress, four mirrors among them and perhaps twenty powder puffs for their mostly bald heads.

She finally stopped at one chair. "Maestro!"

His hair was white and waved back from high temples. He was as thin as a catgut string, yet his posture was more tightly wired.

The pale eyes that regarded her were blank.

She struck her clasped fist against her breastbone, a sort of human percussion that made him blink.

"Irene Adler," she said. "I most urgently desire to speak with you."

We adjourned to Delmonico's.

The old fellow walked in like a prince, but it was clear he had not dined so well in ages. Irene ordered like a caliph, and lit cigarette after cigarette.

I kept watch.

"Irene," the old fellow murmured between courses. "I never thought I would hear you sing again."

"I have your violin. I wish to return it."

"Violin? What violin? A poor second to a human voice. Say that you still sing."

"I still sing."

"I still saw away on my lifeline. Times have changed. Did I do you a disservice, I ask myself? More escalloped potatoes? New York can be very cold. You cannot return to the past."

"Maestro."

He cringed, but ceased jumbling his thoughts together.

"I must know," she said, "why I can't remember my own past. An artist without a past is . . . nothing. I've come back to remember."

He pushed away the princely dishes. I saw an old man, hungry and ashamed. A beggar with an inferior violin. I couldn't look.

"Maestro," she pled.

I couldn't look.

"I am a fraud!" he declared. "I have not played a heartfelt piece of music since you left. You were my violin. You were my masterpiece. Yet, I cheated."

"I am a cheat?" she asked, heartbreakingly ready to accept his judgment.

"No! I! I alone." He held up his wine glass, and a waiter filled it. "My dear child."

I sensed that he had never spoken so intimately in his strange, lonely life. Was this her father, then?

"I was obsessed by music. I required an . . . heir. A legacy. Something better and bigger than I could ever be. In you I found it. Yes, I drove you. Yes, I was the stern taskmaster. Yes, I understood the sheer talent you and I had been blessed with, and it was my duty to evoke, enhance, encourage, drive you and let you leave me."

"The role you took on was harsh," she said. "You never let me be grateful, yet I understood what you did, and more so as the years passed. You had never encouraged me to acknowledge you, and I never did. Until now. Maestro."

He cringed again. "Don't call me that. You don't understand the price I paid to free you. The price I made you pay. I couldn't do it today, but I still had hope and perhaps some hubris then."

"Price?" she asked.

He sighed, swayed from side to side. "My dear Irene. What a

wonderful name, the goddess of peace, yet your history was anything but peaceful. You came to me wounded in mind and soul. I wanted and needed a voice. I had no hope of getting it after what you'd been through. One mad hope, though. I'd studied in Europe. Music, voice, a spiritual sort of technique. I'd met a man, a Solomon of musicians. He used mesmerism to free the voice from its containment. You had lost your voice when they brought you to me. They swore you had once had it, the nightingale gift. I so desperately needed to believe in nightingales. So . . . I cheated. I mesmerized you, Irene, until your voice came free of your past, like one clear note, and then I worked with that and then another note and finally you were a whole chorus of musicality. Only because I mesmerized you."

"I am an automaton?"

"No. You are what you could have been had not fate flattened all your potential."

"But . . . I can hypnotize others."

"I gave you the technique, for yourself. And for others. It was taught to me by a musical genius I met in Vienna in the fifties, before you were even born. A man called Adler. Later, known as a musical genius called Svengali, he produced the supreme soprano of the age in an unknown artist's model named Trilby. When I told you once that he was my own maestro, you took his true last name for your own, as you had none."

"I remember doing that now. Adler! So I am named for a fraud."

"A genius, though misguided, for I have followed misguided genius all my life."

Irene had drawn out her smoking apparatus again.

The maestro frowned as she drew breath through the cigarette. "That is bad for your voice."

"Not that anyone has noticed. Besides, I don't sing as frequently as I once did."

"Even worse!"

Irene turned the blue enamel case in her hand, the bediamonded initial "I" twinkling like a star.

The maestro stared at that small movement, that mote of winking light. He seemed to have lost the thread of his thoughts.

"You must tell me," she said so softly that both he and I leaned over the table to hear better, "why I had lost my voice."

"That is far better forgotten," he said, the words seemingly pulled from him like salt water taffy candy is drawn from a machine. I thought again of ectoplasm, and invisible spirits, and how we all draw into ourselves much that is unseen, yet that shapes us.

We all exhale invisible drafts of our pasts, and breathe in the future like smoke, hardly noticing it.

My own breath caught in my throat when I realized that Irene was hypnotizing the old man. It was true that she only turned the tables on him—again I thought of the mobile table at the séance, why could I not get those images out of my head? I had not even been there to see them, like Pink.

And then I understood that Irene was also calling on the dead, as much as any medium, invoking the past, asking the maestro to commune with his own lost past self, and hers.

"Why had I lost my voice? Literally lost it, couldn't speak or sing?"

"Couldn't sing," he answered at last. "Could speak, but didn't like to. They told me what had happened, and then I understood, or at least partly."

Irene exhaled a perfect O of smoke that distorted as it drifted upward, reminding me of the tormented face of a ghost at some séance in the upper air.

The maestro's weak blue eyes followed the smoke ring until it vanished. "You young women lived in a theatrical boarding house, sharing rooms and a common water closet."

"How young were we?"

"Oh . . . you were seventeen when you began studying with me, and I had already trained you for half a year. Your voice was a wonder and you had already been acclaimed on stage for it, but in musical terms you were still a little savage, with not the slightest grasp of technique. We had much more work to do."

"And we did it. I didn't leave New York until I was past twenty."

"Past twenty," he repeated dully.

Irene quietly laid the cigarette case on the snowy white linen.

All around us echoed the clatter and conversation of a wildly successful restaurant. Our table seemed encased in a bell jar of extraordinary quiet, almost as if time had stopped and begun to run backward.

A waiter hovered with the wine bottle, but Irene's swift head shake sent him skating away.

"What happened," she asked again, "when I was seventeen and living at the theatrical boarding house?"

"A tragedy. Not an unheard-of one, but a tragedy. And so close to home. Mesdames Sophie and Salamandra brought me the news when you refused to come to your daily lesson. First one, then the next. They explained that you could not sing."

"Why, why couldn't I?"

"I never understood that. Oh, I understood the shock that brought on your strange, self-imposed strangling of your greatest gift, yet I never knew why it had taken that form. It was as if you had become a nun under a vow of silence. You had always been a vibrant child, so self-possessed, so attuned to others. You had even then the air and the empathy of a great performer of the stage, who can make each audience member believe you speak and sing to him or her alone. A Patti or a Bernhardt."

"Did I?" Irene asked, truly doubting.

"And you didn't know it, which made you all the more remarkable. You didn't even see the small jealousies among the other young performers, the precocious young ladies who were prone to putting on airs about abilities that were the mere shadow of your own."

"I don't remember any of that."

"That's because I didn't want you to. I wanted you unspoiled. And once the solution to your musical muteness came to me, I realized that I could . . . repair so much more than your broken voice."

I saw alarm flash through Irene's eyes, although they never left the old man's face. She was not one to submit to "repair." Even I saw the presumption in his statement, the arrogance of the teacher, or parent, who believes his word and perceptions are law to the pupil, or child.

Irene's fingers tightened on the talisman of her cigarette case. I could visibly see her fight to avoid reacting to this last shock, to first ask the most central questions before facing any other unpleasant surprises.

"What happened to silence me? You must explain this now. A lie of omission becomes one of commission if too much time is allowed to lapse."

He then uttered the words that chill my soul, because I used to employ them myself before I knew better. "It was for your own good, every bit of it. You had been brutally confronted with the saddest fate a young girl may meet, and had to see that only by promising to serve your voice and your music and paying attention to nothing else could you avoid a similar useless, brutal end."

"Tell me!"

"It was young Winifred, though it could have been her sister. They were inseparable, as twins often are, and their mind-reading routine was truly remarkable. Lovely girls, with a mother who had retired as a wire-walker to mistress a man of business on Wall Street. Later they performed as Pansy and Petunia, and once they turned sixteen she often presented them at her parties, like dolls to be petted and admired. I believe they enhanced her hold on her gentleman friend. She was not as young as she had been."

Irene visibly winced, but he didn't notice. His eyes remained on the wreaths of blue-white smoke she sent ceilingward like some elegant Indian princess sending smoke signals.

"Why were their names changed?" she asked.

"They were called something else as children, but when they became girls they performed under Pansy and Petunia. Petunia had grown so sophisticated after her debut at her mother's affairs that she was demanding to be known simply as 'Pet.' "

Irene glanced at me, her lips tightening. "Yet we all roomed together, and performed together . . . and bathed apart. That common water closet plays a part in your story, doesn't it, Maestro?"

"How would you know? Would guess . . . remember?"

"I would deduce, my dear Maestro," she explained, quieting his wild queries. "I worked for the Pinkertons even as I concentrated on my vocal exercises for you. I became astute on two quite different fronts. 'Mystery and music,' my husband says, are my forte."

"You have a husband? He is a good man?"

"He is a great man, and a superlative barrister, and a quite charming Englishman."

"Ah." His sigh expressed relief. "You are a married lady. Then perhaps I can tell you—"

I was *not* a married lady, and perhaps he should not tell Irene anything so apparently shocking in my presence, but I was not about to miss this confession for the world! Especially after waiting so long to hear it teased out of the maestro that I'd been forced to actually sip the after-dinner wine, which was quite sweet and rather better than most wines, actually. Why had no one ever told me that wines could be other than the sour French variety?

"Tell me," Irene urged, moving her hand from the cigarette

case to his veined and arthritic-swollen hand across the table. The look she gave that sadly ruined hand before her straight, young fingers folded over it would have brought tears to a stone. "Maestro, please!"

He took a deep breath, much like an actor about to deliver an enormously long speech. Shakespeare, say, or one of the French classicists.

"My dear girl, I fear that reviving that memory will revive your awful bout of muteness. That would kill me."

"I am too recovered to relapse, Maestro. I have the libretto and music for a specially commissioned one-woman piece in which I portray the six wives of Henry the Eighth. It is a . . . series of roles any soprano would kill for. I will not lose my voice again. I am past thirty now, after all, and an expertly trained singer."

Her bow to his tutelage pushed the old man over the brink of hesitancy. "What a fine piece you speak of! I must hear it."

"You will, as soon as I have memorized it. So you see, I must have my entire memory returned to me, now that I know some of it is missing. That realization is more damaging now than anything the past might hide could ever be."

He nodded, and began speaking as if he too had been held mute, and now reveled in releasing the censored words.

"It was quite accidental. Your entering that water closet, robed and towel in hand, for what we used to call the ritual of 'the Saturday night bath.' Despite your theatrical background, you had been pampered and protected and were a sweet, innocent girl, as much as we all could see to, and we old theatrical folk knew we were your only kin and parents and took that responsibility to heart.

"Unfortunately, the twins were quickly becoming what was known as 'fast' women. I blame their mother, so you are very fortunate to have escaped such a malign influence in your own life, however much you may have missed knowing who your mother and father were, believe that."

Irene was far too canny and in control of herself to interrupt the fountain's flow now that it had come unstopped, but I saw several unnameable emotions cross her face at this speech.

"One girl, the self-named 'Pet,' it was determined later, had found herself irrevocably compromised. It pains me to speak these ugly truths to a woman I had known as a sweet and innocent girl, but you insisted. She had discovered she had been left with child, and that is the sort of condition that becomes less inescapable with every week and day.

"She had retired to the water closet, drawn a bath, laid herself down in it and slit her wrists and throat.

"When you knocked and called, as the boarders always did, there was no answer; no occupant, you thought. The door was unlocked. You entered. You saw a sea of blood and your young performing compatriot floating in it like Ophelia. I understand the bath water had run crimson, and overflowed the tub, that she was as pale as porcelain.

"You screamed, as who would not? But . . . my dear little Irene, you had a Voice. You screamed and screamed, an operatic aria of screams that woke the entire house, the neighborhood, sent people sitting up in their beds for blocks around with chills running down their spines.

"You would not stop. It was as if only Song could express your horror. And when you finally did stop, you would Sing no more.

"That is how they brought you to me, days after Pet's funeral.

"You spoke only in a whisper, when spoken to. No one could do anything with you. I was . . . at my wit's and wisdom's end. I knew that only your Voice would cure you, but how to bring it back to life? Then I remembered Adler and his mesmerism technique.

"I applied it. Slowly, surely, you recovered. You would whisper a scale. Then speak it, And finally hum it. It took patience, it took months and months, my dear. And sometimes you would stop and stare out the second-story window overlooking Union Square. . . . I finally realized that it was not enough to mesmerize you for the vocalizations alone. I instructed you to forget. To forget that awful moment you found the dead girl, to forget anything in your past that might trouble you, to forget your past and go on to a carefree and productive, and very vocal future. It worked."

He stopped like an automaton whose winding had run down, and drained a full glass of wine at one swallow. I saw a diadem of sweat beads circling his wrinkle-seamed forehead.

The telling had been as arduous as the acts he recounted.

This time when the wine waiter came around, Irene nodded, her face as pale and stiff as parchment.

My glass was refilled, the maestro's, and her own, which was only half consumed.

We none of us spoke. Later, we left together and parted ways outside, Irene seeing the old man into a cab, and taking my arm to walk the long way back to our hotel.

Not one glass at the table we left behind was anything but empty, including my own, yet I have never been so sober, and so sorry for it, in my entire life.

And I was not even in France.

42.

A Mesmerizing Experiment

~ळॐ~

With one wave of his hand over her——with one look of his eye——with a word——Svengali could turn her into the other Trilby, his Trilby——and make her do whatever he liked... you might have run a red-hot needle into her and she would not have felt it.... He had but to say "Dors!" and she suddenly became an unconscious Trilby of marble, who could produce wonderful sounds.

—GECKO, *TRILBY*, 1894,

GEORGE DU MAURIER

After pretending to sleep, I arose the next morning to find Irene still semi-sitting in our parlor, still dressed.

"What does one do, Nell," she asked, "when the people who mean you the most good have done you the worst damage?"

Well, I would obviously have to be one of those "people who mean you the most good," and hope that I did no more damage.

I sat down in an opposite chair. Irene was slumping in her seat in an inexcusable fashion, like one who had been up all night . . . or like a careless schoolgirl . . . or like Sarah Bernhardt during one of her interminable death scenes.

"You claim to have come to America to trace your origins," I said. "I suspect you came to America purely to drag me away from the Old Country and the shocks to my system its ancient evils administered. You are always thinking of others, Irene, and it has to stop."

"I? I am a prima donna!"

"You are theatrical, certainly, and have a certain flair at arranging events, but you are far too dedicated to spare your friends the heartache and shocks of . . . whatever Shakespeare said, so apparently notably. I do not see it."

"Shakespeare or my situation?"

"Either. You came here, purportedly, because you had no family, no parents, no brothers or sisters. Since we have been in New York, I have met no one but people who cared about you. You have had a multitude of mothers and fathers, Irene, and you don't need Pink to show you that."

"They smothered my past."

"They are Americans! They do not value pasts. Goodness, most of them do not go back as far as one of Buffalo Bill's Indian trackers. This is an utterly new land. I have seen that. I may not like it, but I have seen it. You have managed to leave footprints in both New World and Old. That will be the future. Forget your past. I have ancestors going back to medieval pig thieves, and I can assure you that such ties are overrated. What you have as a past is people who care for you, and that is worth any pedigree."

"But they are dead, and dying."

This I couldn't answer.

"Because of me."

"Again the prima donna!"

"Because of me. Because of something I don't know, but should have," she said quite humbly. "Because of something that was kept from me. For my own good."

"Perhaps. I've found myself quite liking these strange theatrical folk. They remind me of honest Shropshire villagers, that no one gave much accounting to, but who remain foremost in my memory when I think back to my childhood."

"I can't do that, Nell. I have a muddled memory." She rose and pressed the small smooth sun of a gold watch into my palm, as one would feed a Gypsy fortune teller coins. "I want you to mesmerize me."

"Mesmerize? I can't!"

"I am, apparently, an able subject. You have seen me work with this method. All you must do is swing the watch before my eyes until they blur, and encourage me to be peaceful in my soul. You are a parson's daughter. Such counsel should come naturally."

"I can't take that responsibility."

"There is no one else here who can."

"The maestro—"

"Has proven himself biased. He meant well. I can never blame him for that. I need someone stronger, though."

"Me?"

"Someone I truly trust."

"Irene, please!"

"Nell, please!"

And thus, at the age of two-and-thirty, an Anglican became a Mesmerist.

How foolish I felt! Rather like a woman who made a living belching cheesecloth. Yet she was dead, that woman, and I was tired of tracing the people from Irene's past, only to find them dead.

I swung the watch, back and forth. I watched her face, feeling foolish. She fixed her gaze upon that swinging watch as if it were a passing bell, tolling.

She was determined to be mesmerized. I was determined to mesmerize. This was an enterprise too much dependent on necessity.

"Irene," I said. Intoned like a church choir.

"Yes, Nell."

"I want you to watch . . . the watch."

"Yes, Nell."

"I want you to think . . . or rather, to *not* think. Imagine the . . . the . . . the mongoose Messalina."

"Yes, Nell?"

"Such a supple, smooth creature, all fur and muscle. Bright eyes and flashing teeth, like a Spanish dancer."

"A Spanish dancer?"

"Such grace and . . . passion. Like a metronome. You have heard, seen a metronome. That is the rhythm of music. Left, right, like this watch. Left, right, regular like a pendulum. Stamp, step. Dance, sing. Left, right. Like time."

"Like . . . the past."

"Like the past. Your past. Left, right."

Her eyes fixed on the watch and grew filmy. I couldn't believe my effectiveness. Then, on the brink of success, I desperately wanted to break the rhythm, deny this power, wake us both up.

Except it was working. I wracked my brain for what was needed here. Irene was suddenly at my mercy. She had put herself into my hands. I must conduct this orchestra. I must understand what mysteries needed to be unveiled.

I was both the shepherd and sheep.

"Irene."

"Yes, Nell."

How pleasant this was. "Yes, Nell" had never sounded so sweet, although, now that I heard it so easily, I realized that I much preferred "No, Nell."

I smiled. I was indeed ready to do something for another's good, because I no longer needed to cater to my own lesser needs.

"Irene, I want you to remember."

"Yes, Nell."

"It may be painful to both of us, but we will be the better for it."

"Yes, Nell."

"And first and foremost, I wish that when you wake, you will never say 'Yes, Nell' again."

"No, Nell."

"I must ask this. You have always astounded me because you have never used your beauty to win roles or men. Is that because you witnessed Pet's awful end, and saw that the wages of sin is death?"

"Not sin, but senselessness. I can condemn no one, but I can mourn those who condemn themselves. She was lovely and so uncertain. She sought false regard, and destroyed her own regard. She was doomed, for being human, and vain, and for letting someone else's regard destroy her own. So she destroyed another with herself. I see no way out of it. Was I one of these burdens worth dying for, rather than acknowledging?"

"We are none of us worth dying for, except on stage or in Scriptures. Now. You wish to remember. What happened after Pet's dreadful end? Did the police declare her death a suicide, or could it have been murder?"

"I was not told. We all wished to forget Pet and what happened to her. All those who knew me wished me to forget her fate. It was as if I had glimpsed the terrible end that awaited a girl of my history and looks and talent. Until then I had felt these gifts to be an asset. Once Pet was dead, I saw them to be liabilities. I was too easily like her, save I did not have a mother to introduce me to the circle of wealthy men in which such women seek salvation and so often find doom."

"The opera was an elevated art form. Such singers need not compromise themselves."

"Yes! That's why they all wished me to pursue that art above all others. Yet even opera singers are not proof against seduction.

Still, they are all Valkyries at heart, whether they have the voice for that role or not. The discipline is so demanding, and they aren't easily lured to the ease of immorality. Opera is hard work."

"Hard work has always stood women in good stead," I asserted. "And so has a long memory. I . . . suggest . . . command . . . you to remember what others would have you forget. You must be able to choose for yourself what you remember and forget. It may be an imprecise process, but it should be your own choice. I, Nell . . . um . . . so decree. Wake up. Have you? Did you hear anything I said? Irene? Oh . . . this is a most disconcerting process! Do say something!"

"Nell?"

"I hope so."

"It is amazing. I feel as if a wind has blown through my head."

"That sounds a most unhappy sensation."

She sat up and shook herself, claiming her watch from my slack grip.

"What did I say?" she demanded, eyeing me suspiciously.

"This and that. I believe that you'll be able to remember what you wish now. Whether you'll like it or not is another matter."

Irene shook herself into a shudder. "I will never idly mesmerize another, now that I know I have been a victim of it. You are certain that you loosed all matters that may have been bound up?"

"I tried my best. Perhaps you will recall that I noted that you have had a stout band of advocates throughout your youth. Even the maestro sought only to repair and strengthen you."

"As if I were some bruised Pinocchio! It is not pleasant to reconstruct whole years of one's youth, Nell."

"No, but it was not all a loss. Your shock at Pet's death determined your own course. You owe her your integrity."

"The cost was too high. I see it all so clearly now. Such a young girl, and no evil in her, simply . . . a desire to please her mother. Do you know, I envied her that mother? A mother who seemed like a glamorous fairy godmother who would whisk a young girl away to the balls on Fifth Avenue, where Prince Charmings wore white tie and tails, and owned whole blocks of Manhattan, and yachts, and theaters, where one might perform, if one performed well . . . I never could do that, and even if my heart had wished to, I was never quite right for the role, like my impossible-to-categorize voice."

"Thank goodness, or I would not have been here to play Mesmerist."

Irene stood, stretched, then froze in that catlike position, her face mirroring an entire spectrum of memories, then clearly a new set of speculations, and then, finally and only: horror.

She at last tore her focus from some invisible scene and met my eyes.

"Dear God in heaven. I think I see it now. I know who is dealing us all death, and I think I begin to see why."

43.

Double Death

⤙⤚

*So far Restell, superb in black silk or velvet and conveyed
aristocratically in her carriage, had maintained a remarkable
composure in court, having only on one occasion betrayed even
a hint of anxiety.*

—*THE WICKEDEST WOMAN IN NEW YORK,* CLIFFORD BROWDER

*"Why will they not let me die in my own house, and not want
to send me to prison? I have never wronged anyone!"*

—MADAME RESTELL, 67, THE NIGHT BEFORE HER TRIAL, 1878

Irene stood in the racing hansom cab, rapping on the ceiling
trapdoor with the butt of her revolver.

"Faster!" she boomed in the dark and deep soprano
voice that had carried once to the back row of the Warsaw
Imperial Opera House like a burning arrow of sheer,
splendid sound. "It's a matter of life and death."

I heard the crack of a whip as sharp as a pistol report, and
cringed for the poor horse's back, but a sudden spurt of speed
pushed Irene back down into the seat.

"They whip the air, most times," Irene said, amazingly aware of my small concern in the face of a much bigger one. "I'll pay him enough when we arrive to treat his horse like Caligula's famous equine counselor for a year, on that condition. The deaths have slowed, perhaps ended. Oh! We may be too late, Nell. An hour and eleven years too late. We may never know."

She held the pistol on her lap, one leather-gloved fist caught between her teeth, as if she did not trust herself to speak or wait the amount of time it would take for ordinary means to bear us to our goal.

"I don't understand what has galvanized you, Irene. You are like that annoying man, Holmes, three steps ahead of your own mind, and mystifying everyone around you who pays for the privilege of knowing you with eternal ignorance in the face of your enigmatic genius."

"Would that I were Sherlock Holmes! *He* would not have been so slow to discern the truth, to disarm the poison contained in the glorious outer package worthy of a czarina. There is a man in it, has always been, but if she dies . . . everything I need to know about myself dies with her. If we are too late—"

"Would contacting the authorities—?"

"Authorities! We deal with matters the 'authorities' have never been able to face. Nor most of society. *Faster! Please. Faster.*"

Our hansom careened around a corner on what seemed like two wheels. Hooves struck sparks from the cobblestones. I saw their blue fire from my window.

"We just passed Forty-eighth Street."

"Faster."

And then we came to a stop, pushed backwards and forward against the tufted leather seats smelling of tobacco and perspiration and a little vomit. A former governess well knows that aroma.

"It is worse than the Atlantic steamship," I murmured.

"Don't lose your backbone now, Nell. I need you."

She sprang out of the hansom and threw several large gold

coins up at the driver. "Treat your horse like the King of Siam, for he has raced the wind and death tonight."

The man's long face gaped longer, thanks to his open mouth, which closed shortly as he bit down on the first gold coin and nearly cracked a tooth.

"The nag's me next of kin," he cried out, but Irene was already storming the stairs to the great mansion's entry, the pistol still in plain view.

She pounded on the closed double doors with the pistol butt.

Well, I would have been hard pressed to deny her entrance so accoutered, but no one came to answer that imperious racket.

The hansom clattered away behind us at a sedate pace.

We were alone in the dark of night, on the threshold of a great house that was locked and barred.

Irene turned to regard the quiet street. It was after midnight, and this was the most respectable address in Manhattan. Only strolling policemen would prowl these elegant precincts, and Irene did not want them.

"There must be another entrance," she said, speaking more to herself than me. "Where the poor desperate women came, less observed by the passing public."

"I don't understand," I ventured to admit.

She focused on my face, as if I were a stranger. "Oh, Nell. I'm sorry. Don't you see what I only now discovered, perhaps too late? Don't you recognize this house?"

"We were here recently, to meet the one member of your theatrical set who rose to respectability in the world. Mina Gilfoyle."

"That was a week ago. That was before I had learned how I had lost my past to the wave of a hypnotist's hand. That was before I knew that this address had belonged to Madame Restell, before I saw the news stories on her death that mentioned a palatial house at Fifty-second Street and Fifth Avenue. Before I knew that she had died here in her bloody bathtub in eighteen seventy-eight."

"Oh. Good gracious! And what do you suspect?"

"That there are only coincidences in melodramas, Nell."

"Oh. And I recall now, from Pink's endless newspaper clippings, that the veiled ladies—in black, how suggestive that is now!—came and went from a more discreet door. The side of the mansion, perhaps?"

"The side, of course! She may have sent all the servants away, if what I think is happening . . . is happening. Oh, Nell, she will cheat me again, if not death itself! I cannot allow that. I owe it to my mother."

"Your mother! You know who now?"

"I know who it is *not*, and that is half the battle."

We clattered in the dark down the long brownstone steps. Only a distant electric light beamed through the quiet dark. I heard the melancholy clatter of a single hansom cab, and I feared we would walk home from this place, whatever happened.

Around the side was a servant's entrance on the street level. We barely discerned it in the dark. Arriving there, at the same instant we did, was a tall, dark figure, caped and hatted like a man who had been to the opera.

Irene stopped and leveled her pistol.

My heart simply stopped.

"I can pick the lock," a voice said. "Can you?"

"I can pick a lock, or your teeth, with a bullet," Irene answered. "Step aside."

He laughed. "I understand your urgency, Madam. Let us collaborate, just this once. It is, after all, a matter of life and death."

He bent to set metal to metal, sounding like a typist.

Sherlock Holmes!

I glanced at Irene. Her face was set and furious and . . . of two minds. "Your meddling inquiries must have alerted the miscreants. Why should I allow you entrée where my history entitles me to go, not yours?"

I put a hand on her pistol arm. "If we are too late, as you say, we could use company. Or a witness."

"Most sensible," he murmured. "Keep your pistol foremost, Madam. We broach a desperate villain."

Oh, didn't I wish that I knew what or who he meant! Or what Irene had meant all this evening? Am I doomed to be always the assistant, necessary but ignorant? I felt a sudden fellowship with one Dr. John H. Watson, abysmal fictioneer though he may be.

In moments we were inside. The floor beneath our feet was hard stone. We were in the servants' areas, kitchens and passageways, and perhaps secret passages to where the women were shown.

"Is it she?" I asked. "Madame Restell's mysterious and vanished only daughter?"

"We are all Madam Restell's daughters, but *She* is not," Irene answered. "She would not lurk in these nether regions. She believes she has surmounted the past, this place, even the woman who died here."

"And yourself as well," Sherlock Holmes added. "Let me lead, I have my own pistol, and my own theory to prove. No one here, in America, wishes to kill *me*. Yet."

Feat tightened its clutch on my chest. Did someone wish to kill Irene? Let him lead, then.

Irene hesitated.

Clever man, he knew that she would. For my sake, not her own. Never her own.

His footsteps rang up the stone stairs. We followed.

Up and up we wound, like ectoplasm in a seance room. Like so much funereal wrapping around a mummy, a dead thing that is a monument to the dead past.

Finally we reached the upper stories.

Irene defied orders, moving forward to push a bronzed door open with the long steel tongue of her pistol barrel, but Mr. Holmes stepped ahead of us both with one long stride. Irene and I followed him along a wide hall paved in marble, unusual in an upper story. We encountered no servants, when we should have stumbled over several. The house was utterly silent. Its dark and stormy history sat upon it like a stone Medusa, threatening to freeze us in this flagrant act of housebreaking.

A single heavy door, ajar, invited breeching.

Mr. Holmes pushed through the coffered mahogany and repousse surface, then Irene and I.

We were in a large, palatial bath. I sensed thick, rich rugs and a mine of gleaming silver and gilt, but could only see the chamber's centerpiece.

Steam still rose from the high waters in a deep copper tub. A woman lay there, half-submerged, far less so than Merlinda the Mermaid who had bartered her own breath against death many times.

I supposed she was naked. I supposed a naked woman in a bath should have shocked us, unrelated man and women that we were.

Instead it awed us.

And then she stirred, this corpse.

A languid hand lifted from the other side of the tub. It bore a pistol.

She lifted the hand until we saw the scarlet threads running down the wrist toward her elbow, streaking low into the water, thin as embroidery silk, slow yet certain.

"Don't move," she said, breathed. "I didn't expect company, but kept this ready for any servants who dared to defy my orders to leave." She squinted at us, as if her vision were as clouded as bathwater. "Who are you? I have so many servants . . . I don't know you all." Her expression smoothed, going from wizened to demonic in an instant. "You! My endless nightmare. I have heard you screaming in my dreams. You haunt me more than Her even."

She braced the pistol barrel on the curved edge of the bathtub.

It stared at us, that Cyclops eye of empty steel, waiting to wink death at one or more of us. She stared at Irene, saw only her, addressed only her.

"You don't remember, do you?" Her languid eyes, and now the core of the pistol stared at Irene too.

"I do remember now," Irene said softly. "I've only now learned that I was made to forget."

"Oh, could I be made to forget! Then so much would not have happened. So many wouldn't have needed to die. 'You were made to forget.' How convenient, Rena! For me, anyway." Her focus blurred and the pistol barrel swayed on its impromptu support. "Do you remember how you advised me against it all, both me and Pet? 'Don't go out walking with gentlemen in slick suits.' 'Don't believe they care for anything about you other than your compliance.' 'Don't believe you are young and beautiful, and desired for yourself alone.' "

"I don't remember saying any of that."

"But you did! Every time we were the belles of the ball at our mother's house. And do you know what was the most irritating thing? You were right."

"Right in what way?"

"They were liars, those men. They turned our heads and turned us upside down and inside out, and suddenly we realized we were ruined. Our monthlies had deserted us, and so had the men who could not resist us, as we couldn't resist them. Before we knew it, we were coming here, to this very house, not as belles of the ball but as fallen women. We 'lost' our babies here."

"You mean they were aborted," Irene said, wanting to make sure.

"How it hurt! Oh, God in heaven, *how it hurt*. That small dark room, the man with the tongs, the bit of wire.

"We came back, rinsed in the blood of the Lamb, born again, almost virgin again. We told you nothing, and yet, you knew. Do you remember what you told us? We were still two."

I watched Irene ransack her newborn memory, the memory reclaimed through the maestro's confession and my inept attempt at mesmerism.

"I had found a gentleman," the bleeding woman prodded Irene with words as well as the aim of her pistol. "He offered me wealth, protection. But you said . . ."

"I said what you didn't want to hear." Irene nodded with the abrupt surety of woman who remembers her own deeds and her own past. "I told you his offers were hollow, that there was no honor or truth in them. He merely said what was necessary to seduce a young girl."

"Even our mother urged me to the alliance. He was rich. What else was there to consider? Yet, despite all precautions, I was again with child. Children are always inconvenient, as Pet and I were for our mother, which is why she sent us to the only place unconcerned with pedigrees, the theater."

Irene seemed to absorb this statement as bitter gall. Had her mother been such a heartless pragmatist as well?

I caught my breath at my next thought. Was their mother *her* mother also?

"So you were right." Mina stirred in her shroud of clouded water, rallying her failing energy to strike at Irene with some bitterness. "He did not want children who could not be 'heirs.' I was told to rid myself of the problem, as I had done before."

"Let us help you out of the bath while we talk," Irene suggested. "The water must be lukewarm by now."

Her attempt to disarm with kindness only caused Mina to wave the pistol across all of us.

"I had 'lost' one baby. Another would be like . . . killing twins. Like Pet and myself. Madame Restell was there, as always, sympathetic but needing money for her services. I had money. For a while. His. Madame suggested a solution. We would wait until my condition was too pronounced to conceal. Then I would go to her, and she would tell him the operation had been successful, but that I was weak and ill from the aftermath. I would be sent to a secret place to recover and 'regain my figure.' In fact, there I would have my child and there it would be taken from me to be reared in some other place by other people. I was never to know where, and everything would be all right."

I blushed to think of Sherlock Holmes overhearing such intimate female matters. I glanced to him—for surely the woman in the bath had never fully registered his presence, nor mine. Her eyes and her hatred were all for Irene. He was gone! As if he had never entered the room.

In one way I was deeply relieved. Such matters were never meant for men's ears. In another, I felt abandoned, for the pistol still pointed at Irene, and the woman, although weak, was still completely mad.

"But the story has a happy ending," Mina said, reviving. Her strength was tidal, ebbing and flowing; her hatred had only one current, deep and hard and eternal. "I left that man a few months later, and found another, even wealthier, and considerably more malleable. He worshiped the ground I walked on." Her smile grew ironic. "He married me without a whimper, and wanted me to have a child."

"Don't tell me," Irene said, with the certainty of a mind reader who has received an undeniable message. "You couldn't have one."

"He wanted me to have a child. My impeccably aristocratic in-laws wanted me to have a child. *I* wanted to have a child. He took me to Europe . . . Marienbad, Baden-Baden, every spa with every sort of mineral water. I drank it like wine, I bathed in it, my skin grew wrinkled in it and still . . . nothing.

"Finally, I thought of the lost little one. I went to Madame Restell. I begged her tell me where that one had gone. By then my husband was so desperate he would have accepted any child, told any story to justify the arrival of a toddler when an infant was expected."

"But the baby was gone forever," Irene guessed.

"As if it had never been . . . what so many clients of Madame Restell desired more than anything, was what I had come to regret more than anything."

She lifted her left wrist from the cloudy bathwater, which had slowly grown pink. "Blood dissipates like a veil, doesn't it? It won't tell, it will merely trickle away into water." Her free hand touched her throat. A mixture of blood and water trailed over her chest like a necklace of pale garnets. "I only slit my wrists, north and south. I didn't slit my throat, east and west. I will fade slowly, and my finger will never leave the trigger. Should I shoot you?" she asked Irene dreamily. "You didn't make the mistakes I did, you argued against them. That is so . . . infuriating. And Madame Restell, she refused to tell me where my child had gone. She said it would have been unethical, against the good of the child, who had a new family who wanted and welcomed it. As if its own mother would not, now that she had decided she could!

"She kept a book. I know she did. I tried to make her tell me where it was, but she didn't. She had hidden it well."

"In this house?" Irene asked.

"In this house. I convinced my first husband to buy this house after her death, everyone thought for the magnificence of it, but I wanted to be able to search it at my leisure. I have probed every corner. I have looked for eleven years. The old man has died, childless, and I have remarried and kept this house and I have looked."

"How can you be sure that there was a book listing the children sent to new homes?"

"Because I found the one listing her abortion clients! Do you realize what a document like that is worth? Were one to need money? Which I never did, not again.

"I should kill you," she added apropos of nothing in her most recent discourse.

"Why?" Irene asked.

"Because you escaped it all . . . the lovers' betrayals, the humiliations, the pain, the loss, the wealthy husbands who had become only means, not ends. You never paid the price all the women who went to Madame Restell did, that my sister and I did! You went abroad and sang opera. You are wed, you said."

"Yes," Irene said uneasily, unsure what word or thought might spur that trigger finger to press death into service again.

"To whom or what?"

"A barrister."

"Only a barrister?"

"Better than a false king."

"I knew I should kill you, but then I thought there might be crueler fates."

"Why kill me? I only tried to offer you advice you now admit was good."

"I should kill you for knowing better than I, for escaping what Winnie and I ran to like fools. For all that we did wrong and you did right."

Such petty envy seemed strangely unreal in that room of nearing death . . . of double death, I realized, for this must be the very same bathtub in which Madame Restell had committed suicide.

"I hired the Pinkertons. Yes, isn't that ironic? Even there you anticipated me. I know canny inquiries are being made, and some damned English detective has been treading disturbingly close to present truths. I know my revels now are ended. It is like giving birth," she said, glancing at the water, "dying this way, except there is no pain. Only a slow ebbing of strength and will. One feels very light-headed. But this pistol is too heavy to forget, so keep your distance," she chided Irene, her attention and strength rallying again.

"You're probably in the lost book, you know. The one I couldn't find. The one that recorded children taken from their mothers. If you could find it, you might find out who your mother was. Aren't you curious?"

"Who my mother *was?*"

"Oh, she's surely dead by now, don't you think? It's been more than thirty years. Certainly she's never tried to find *you,* as I hunted my child. My daughter. And if your mother wasn't dead then, she surely is now."

Irene took an involuntary step toward her. The pistol lifted and aimed, the vague eyes behind it now black burning holes in her parchment-white face.

"What have you done?" Irene asked.

"It was that newspaper girl, coming around, prying. She only wanted to know about *you!* About our life together when we were child performers, about who our relatives were. She seemed to think *you* were somebody, can you imagine that, and that the world would be interested in your antecedents? We had no antecedents but air, my mother and sister and I, and my one living known kin, my daughter, was missing forever. I had Madame Restell's book. I knew who her clients were. Perhaps one of those was your mother, someone who had ended a first pregnancy, but had reconsidered and kept the results of a second one, yet still remained hidden. Those women of the stage, why did they raise you? Why did they never seem to question where you came from? They were mothers! Mothers who lost children one way or the other and never tried to reclaim them, as I did my daughter. So they adopted you."

Irene had moved subtly during this speech, so minutely that even I had not noticed that she had placed herself between me and the woman in the bathtub. I realized that I saw only a bent bare elbow edged in blood, and Irene's straight, cape-clad back.

I also realized that to move in any way, to draw the woman's attention to either Irene or myself any more than it was focused at the moment, would be folly.

"You killed them," Irene accused calmly, as if describing what brand of tea had been served.

"I? No. I don't kill anything but myself, or you before I go."

Silence. "Why?" Irene finally asked.

I wished I could see her face, for her voice was as emotionless as an eel.

Mina seemed to understand what question Irene wanted answered. "Maybe one of them had birthed my sister and myself. Maybe one of them had birthed *you*. I find that last notion the likeliest, the way those old biddies doted on *you*, always *you*. I decided that if my daughter could not have a mother, a mother who wanted her desperately and had searched so long and hard and fruitlessly for her, then it was deep injustice that you should find a mother after all these years. That Nellie Bly was bound and determined that she should do this very thing, for what reason I don't know. So you're half right."

"You killed them. Sophie and Salamandra. Abyssinia, first, perhaps? Simply because of who they *might* be?"

"Not so simply. They were listed in Madame Restell's book of clients."

I tried to edge around Irene, but my clothing rustled. I heard the languid water stir and watched Irene's back stiffen even more. I was doing her no favor, although what I'd do if I heard that pistol fire and saw Irene crumple, I didn't know. It would not be anything sane.

That was the worst thing about the woman in the bathtub's serene insanity. It goaded others into the same mania.

"They'd given up children, killed them in the womb, don't you see? They didn't deserve to live. You are shocked. Angry. You hate me. It's too late for any of that. What's done is done. Dead is dead. Gone is gone."

Her voice faded until I could barely decipher her words. I dread saying it, but hope flared in my heart at the possibility of her imminent death. If Irene was right, she was responsible for many innocent deaths. Yet . . . I could not quite see how.

"Maybe Madame Restell herself was your mother," Mina crooned maliciously. "There is always that possibility. You are the daughter of the wickedest woman in New York, ever."

"No," Irene said. I recognized from the firmness of her tone that she was done accepting this situation, whatever rebellion would bring. "*You* are the wickedest woman in New York, and you secretly claimed that title long ago, eleven years ago, when you killed Madame Restell yourself."

44.

Maidenhair

A bloody ending to a bloody life.
—ANDREW COMSTOCK, SECRETARY, THE SOCIETY FOR THE
PREVENTION OF VICE, CLOSING ANN LOHMAN'S FILE, 1879

I couldn't help myself.

I gasped and peered around Irene to see the face of that wretched, wicked creature killing herself by inches in the bathtub and still threatening to take someone living with her, simply because that other breathed and she herself could no longer stand to.

The dilated eyes moved to me. And so did the pistol barrel.

Unlike Irene, I was honored with a knowledge of the mother who bore me, with her name and indubitable reality. I thought how she had given her life to give me mine.

I believed I owed her something extraordinary for that extraordinary sacrifice. Her name had been Alice.

I pushed Irene aside like a sheaf of wheat at a reaping, and stepped forward to face that woman in the lethal bath, and her unhappy history and her weapon.

"No! *No, Nell!*" Irene's deep, primitive bellow was a vocal command a mastiff (or even a basso playing the Devil) would have heeded.

Unfortunately, I was nothing so powerful. I was a Shropshire lass and a parson's daughter and no one to trifle with when roused.

I stepped toward the bloody bathtub . . . and slipped on the wet tiles. As I fell a great dark spider and its entire, vast crimson web came crashing down on us all. Now I knew I was as mad as Mina. Irene had seized my elbow too late to stop my plummet, and she skidded to the floor with me in a helpless tangle.

A wave of noxious water splashed us with life's blood and some scented soap. I began to choke and almost retch, as if I were sea-borne again.

Irene pounded me on the back. "It's all right, Nell. Look!"

My soggy lashes opened to see the pistol once in Mina's death grasp, swooped up from the floor by another's hand. Who—?

I gazed up at the tub's curved copper profile. Nothing human surfaced above its lip. I thought of Merlinda the Mermaid breathing blood for the entertainment of ignorant audiences. All audiences are ignorant. That is the magic of the stage and the tragedy of life.

While I coughed and blinked, Irene pulled me to my feet.

"I could strangle you," she hissed under her breath, fondly.

"I don't believe you have any ectoplasm conveniently at hand. What was that thing?"

Before she could answer, Sherlock Holmes straightened from behind the bathtub. If he was a spider, he had caught a creature in his web. A cocoon of red velvet curtain lay on the black and white tiled floor, soaking up water and oozing an interior red.

He pulled a flaccid wrist from the imprisoning fabric and counted a pulse no one on earth would ever hear again, apparently, for he shook his head. "She was very near death all this time, but great hatred can delay the inevitable."

"How . . . how did you—?" I asked. Sputtered.

"He went exploring, Nell, when she was so focused on us." Irene glanced to the ceiling high above us and the half-moon window now bare of its curtain and framing a black avenue of night. "Are you all right?" she asked him. "That was quite a leap."

"Her hatred was finally failing with her life's blood," he answered, eyeing the bundle on the floor that lay there like a large, richly swaddled infant. "She didn't slay anyone herself, except Madame Restell."

"That's why she didn't slit her own throat!" I said. "Such sudden ends were due only an old enemy, or the 'mother' she felt had betrayed her. She had depended upon the Madame, who had served Mina's infant child as was thought best at the time. Poor mad thing." I wasn't quite sure whom I was referring to.

Irene barely listened, although she was rhythmically patting my back. "Do you have a mother, Mr. Holmes?"

"So my father told me," he answered.

"He has a brother!" I pointed, "so there must be a mother in there somewhere."

"There is always a mother there somewhere," he announced, rising to his own damp, yet imperious height. "And in this case, a plot that overarches more than thirty years." He bowed suddenly, to Irene. "I beg your pardon. Am I betraying a feminine confidence?"

"I admit to being past thirty, and relish every year of it. Vanity is sometimes useful, but it is never to be trusted in important matters. And are you vain enough to keep the things you have learned from us? I think we have earned the right to knowledge."

"Indeed you have. I will call at your hotel later. Meanwhile, I suggest you leave this place while I summon the authorities. There is sure to be a telephone in such a mansion."

Irene said nothing, but allowed him to escort us to the reception rooms below, where he left us while he returned to attend to the dead woman above.

"Quick, Nell! This mausoleum must have a library! Where? Do you think?"

"Somewhere on the first floor," I suggested, trotting after her. "What are we looking for?

"Where would one hide a book?"

"In a library."

"Ergo . . ."

We found the chamber in question, a two-story circle of waxed wood shelves and gilt spines, and began ravishing the contents for a clue. Just because a madwoman had found nothing didn't mean there was nothing to be found. We both ransacked the shelves, aware that when Sherlock Holmes returned and the dead were dealt with he would be able to devote his full attention to this same quest.

"It's no use, Nell," Irene finally said from on high, where she clung by one foot and one arm to a library ladder that seemed church-spire tall. "One would need to examine every volume and there must be several thousand here."

"How many really read, I wonder?"

"If only I could *think!*" she complained while backing down the ladder.

"I believe that we are doing well to be standing upright after that ordeal."

"Sherlock Holmes," she said bitterly when once again she was on terra firma, which in this case was a magnificent expanse of black marble, "will probably stroll into this room after we leave, pinpoint a book on the third tier and find the missing volume at once."

"Possibly, but we need to leave before the police arrive."

"So we do." She sighed theatrically and followed me out of the immense chamber to the hall. This was as long and grand as a monarch's reception room, and from it opened many elegant chambers, including an unexpected solarium, its uncurtained high, broad windows, admitting moonglow and swaths of the electric lights that surrounded the mansion.

The large exotic plants within cast sinister shadows. We paused as we passed, I feeling as if we were peeking into a nightmare version of Alice's Wonderland.

Irene seized my forearm. "Nell! What is that?"

I looked where she pointed. "An extremely overgrown maidenhair fern, I should think."

"And what does it grow out of?"

"A ... too hard to see in the dimness, but some kind of wicker basket."

"An exceptionally large wicker basket, quite large enough to contain a coiled cobra, I should think." Irene said, moving nearer as if mesmerized by the idea.

"A cobra! Not in New York City! We must leave! No time to gawk at giant houseplants!"

"With wheels," she added, sounding ecstatic. "Of course!"

I had never known Irene to take any interest in plant life, inside or out, nor what containers would hold them.

"Irene, *please!*"

By now she was rooting around beneath the arching fronds like an upper Broadway pig.

"You will ruin your gloves and one of the few gowns you have available on this trip!"

She appeared capable no longer of hearing me, much less heeding me, so I went over, determined to pull her bodily away from her bizarre new enthusiasm for ferns.

She suddenly straightened, her soiled hand hoisting a dark rectangular object.

"The lost book! I'm sure of it."

"How can you be?" Only a worm would have enjoyed the strong odor of freshly turned earth. "It's covered in oilcloth, and soil. And possibly ugly wriggling things."

Irene responded to my distaste by bringing the object to her lips and kissing it.

As I nearly gagged in horror, she laughed. "Don't you see what this container really is?"

It was a pleasure to look at something other than the filthy fruits of a potting soil. "A wicker basket. On wheels. Which is odd. It's obviously a decorative device."

"And from the design, obviously quite old, perhaps mid-century."

"Design. Oh." I had been a governess, but never a nursemaid or a nanny. "It's a perambulator."

"A very old, somewhat shabby perambulator, perhaps the very one that wheeled around Madame Restell's only daughter, later converted to a planter. And, even later, deemed a suitable receptacle in which to conceal the very private listing of clients who gave up children for adoption.

"This book has been sitting here, interred, for over a decade. Mina and no one else ever considered that a vehicle for moving infants might conceal a book of 'moved' infants."

"Gracious! Do you think Sherlock Holmes would have discovered this hiding place?"

"Never, my dear Nell, in a million years. Infants and perambulators are yet another area that is outside his bailiwick. He would certainly find the disrupted dirt worth investigating, though. Let's tidy the area like good little gardeners and whisk away our prize before we court discovery."

So we left that splendid mansion that had been the death of two women so oddly related. We left dingy but triumphant and in need of baths that had no chance of being fatal to anything but dirt.

45.

Social Secretary

~∞~

I have oysters and a brace of grouse, with something a little choice in a white wine— Watson, you have never yet recognized my abilities as a housekeeper.

—SHERLOCK HOLMES, "THE SIGN OF FOUR," 1890

SIR ARTHUR CONAN DOYLE

"Code!" Irene cried the next morning.

"Code!" I echoed.

Our victory was short-lived, for the book we had obtained, while obviously what that misdirected creature Mina had sought for so many years, was arranged into an assortment of letters and numbers that passeth understanding.

"What one person can devise, others can decipher," Irene decreed.

I was not so sure, but the debate was dropped when a page boy from the hotel knocked on our door with Sherlock Holmes's London card in hand.

"Show him up," Irene instructed, casting a quick glance around our parlor to ensure that no trace of betraying potting soil remained.

"Your nails, Nell," she said as severely as any governess.

I extended my hands. "A nail brush will erase any trace of . . . nasty natural things."

She extended her own hands to me. "Clean as a Whistler," she noted with a low vaudeville wink.

The book she slid into the desk drawer. "It is too bad we have nothing to offer Mr. Holmes."

"Not a scone or a cup of tea," I noted.

"Not a lost book or a fern frond."

And we were still laughing mischievously when his knock sounded on the door.

He himself looked quite unruffled. From his formal city dress it was impossible to imagine that he had plummeted like a bird of prey from high above to pluck a dying woman from drowning in a bathtub only the night before.

"I regret that we have nothing to offer you," Irene said, sweeping her hands around the room, "although we could adjourn for tea in the hotel dining room."

"I have, in fact," he said, "a social occasion in mind." He set his gloves in his doffed hat and lay them beside his cane on the desk near the door, right atop, as a matter of fact, the concealed book.

"Oh?" Irene sounded most intrigued. "I didn't think social occasions were something you would much care for."

"It's true that I prefer select company to grand occasions, unless they are concerts, but I think you will agree that *this* social occasion is one none of us can afford to miss."

"And what is the necessary event?"

"The post-funeral luncheon for the Dixon sisters that you will sponsor at Delmonico's restaurant this very Thursday."

"A most thoughtful notion," Irene said, "but hardly of interest to you."

"It will be of paramount interest to me, for among the guests may be the person who assisted Mrs. Gilfoyle in her murderous

mania, the person, in fact, who . . . performed . . . the earlier slay-
ings. Mrs. Gilfoyle, like too many gravely demented individuals,
was best at destroying herself, not others. She had a confederate
for that."

"A confederate," I breathed in an unintended echo.

"A confederate, as Sophie had?" Irene asked quickly.

"Indeed, and perhaps the very same one at that last séance," he
said. "May I rely upon you and Miss Huxleigh to be the host-
esses?"

"I presume you will draw up the guest list."

"With your assistance, ladies."

"Shall the murderer's identity not be obvious from the very
composition of the guest list?"

"No, Madam, that it shall not. A confession is called for in
this case, and only a confrontation with the past will aid that,
which is why I must presume upon your courtesy and also request
to be a guest."

"Why, Mr. Holmes, do you suspect that I would leave you off
such an important list?"

"No, but I am sure that Miss Huxleigh would. Now I have
things to attend to, as do you."

He turned to retrieve his things before leaving. His fingers
paused on the desk drawer, which I noticed was ever so slightly
open.

"Wait!" Irene moved so speedily that she held his hat, gloves
and cane momentary hostage at the door before he could reach it.
"What happened last night after we left?"

"I called the police, such as they are. The house remained
deserted. Apparently she had dismissed every last servant, and the
police are busily looking them up today. I told them how I discovered Mrs. Gilfoyle in her bath, dead by her own hand. I
explained who I was. You will be pleased to know that the name
of Nellie Bly gave me some credibility with the authorities. There
will be no investigation because she was a society matron and a

rich man's widow, and no scandal must taint her class. No one can doubt that the cause is suicide. Even the newspapers will hesitate to touch the story, except to echo the similar death there eleven years ago. Mrs. Gilfoyle's hand in that shall remain unrevealed. Madame Restell will still, and erroneously, be considered a suicide. It may not be fair, but it is convenient to all involved."

"You are right. Convenience rules Society: marriages of convenience, adoptions of convenience, deaths of convenience. Somehow I feel I was born to be inconvenient."

"I also, Madam," he said with a last bow, collecting and donning his property. "It is an honorable profession, perhaps the *only* honorable profession nowadays." He turned suddenly to me. "Save that of governess."

I could swear *The* Man was laughing at me.

That was impossible. He had no sense of humor whatsoever.

It is fortunate that I do have one. Sometimes.

46.

The Delectable Detective

~ole~

*I like people who have a cannibalistic streak in them and say
when they come for lunch: "I am hungry."*
—HENRI DE TOULOUSE-LAUTREC

Irene had engaged a private room at Delmonico's with no
difficulty.

Apparently she was not recognized as the disreputable
unknown who had recently caused Nellie Bly's abandon-
ment by an English lord at this very establishment.

Or perhaps she had been so identified . . . and thereby gained
cachet because of it. No doubt Delmonico's reveled in being the
talk of every tongue, whether the reason was sublime cuisine or
some succulent society scandal.

If that was the case, my friend Irene was tailor-made for their
clientele. Irene had given me to understand that Delmonico's had
been the scene of some of the most lavish events the city of New
York had ever yet witnessed, involving such legendary rascals as
"Boss" Tweed and Diamond Jim Brady.

Yet I believe that in its fifty-some years the restaurant had never seen the likes of the guest list for the memorial luncheon honoring Sophie and Salamandra, and even the unworthy Mina. Besides the invited individuals, Irene had suggested, and Sherlock Holmes had concurred, that we place a discreet notice of the event in the newspapers, mentioning the names of the honored dead. We did not expect any of Mina Gilfoyle's society friends to attend, though some performers who had known her and her long-dead sister might, and might prove enlightening.

Irene and I surveyed the dining chamber an hour before anyone was expected. It was a long rectangle paneled in rich woods that smelled faintly of the finest lemon curd, though it was no doubt a citrus polish I detected. Fans of large and exotic greenery swooned against the gleaming walnut, seemingly left behind by patient native servants just departed. Above the wainscoting, gilt-framed portraits and mirrors created an upper world as fascinating as any actual people who could gather at floor level.

I was reminded of heaven looking down on earth, or, in this case, overseeing the survivors of a very specific hell.

"This event may be partly a charade, Nell," Irene said, "but I regret that it took Sherlock Holmes to remind me that I owe these amazing people I grew up among some formal tribute, especially to those who have died at the behest of that madwoman who lived in Madame Restell's former house."

"Would you be content," I asked her, "if you found no further trace of your true parents, but only these folk?"

"I would be more than content. I would be proud. What phenomena they are! To earn a living on the stage is not easy. To turn adversity into acclamation is astounding. To adapt to every craze even more demanding. They *are* hardy, like plants that thrust through earth every spring for the simple reward of being seen and appreciated. I learned more from them than I was allowed to remember."

"I feel the same about the villagers in Shropshire. I had no mother, but I had the whole village entire. I may never see any of those people again, indeed, most of them must be dead by now, but I can never forget them. They are my soil."

"And so the adopted babies in Madame Restell's book, whoever or wherever they may be, have mother earth to grow in. Hard as it was for the actual mothers to lose them—and I can't say that I entirely agree with what happened—at least other mothers elsewhere welcomed them."

"Can you be sure their future was always benign?"

"No. But was ours, Nell? Is anyone's? I believe that meaning well goes a long way. As for those who don't mean well . . . I believe that is what retribution is for."

"Who's to say which is which?"

"Exactly." Irene gazed at the long empty table, set with delicate gilded china and silverware that blended rare woods with lavish vines of sterling silver. Exotic floral arrangements marked the length of a central runner of the richest Chinese silk and embroidery. Oil lamps gleamed on the side tables, making day into the eternal twilight of great dining. "Today I imagine that Sherlock Holmes will."

"You're willing to cede him the central role at your luncheon party?"

"I'm willing to leave to him the ugly task of naming a murderer."

"And if it is someone you knew and loved?"

"It is certain to be so, Nell, or he would not want this particular stage and this specific cast of characters present. Nor would he usurp my right here. Like it or not, my history has become a matter of crime and punishment, and I would much rather be a supernumerary at such a harsh debut than a playwright."

"Irene, I don't think I can stand the suspense. I like everyone we've met."

"Do you, Nell? Do you really?"

"Yes, of course. Although they are eccentric, still, they seemed quite warm and honest. Except—"

"Except?"

"Except for . . . Nellie Bly."

Irene's smile was relieved. "Nellie Bly is a pseudonym, Nell. She is not a real person at all."

"Whatever she is, I don't much like her," I said stoutly.

Speak of the Devil and he, or she, will appear forthwith. At least on stage, and certainly the event unfolding at Delmonico's was stage-directed, by several people.

We had arrived early, but not earlier enough than Pink to suit me. She bustled into the room with its long empty table, nattering on about Sherlock Holmes.

"Sherlock Holmes for lunch and revelation. What a red-letter day for the *World!*" She began teasing off the tips of her tight pink kid gloves as she addressed Irene and me rather like a visiting lecturer. "You do realize that this will be the first occasion that Sherlock Holmes will solve a case in public, with a member of the press present, not to mention a New York City police detective. It will be a far greater sensation than the Lambs Club death of Washington Irving Bishop just last May."

"A pity," Irene said, "that the most recent victims did not suffer from catalepsy and that there is no prayer of resurrecting them. I do hope, Pink," she added, "that the police detective will be discreet until—or if—his services are required."

"Of course he will be needed. Mr. Holmes has promised to reveal the murderer of Sophie and Salamandra, and very possibly Abyssinia, and who knows who else?"

It was clear that Pink knew nothing whatsoever of the macabre suicide we three had witnessed last night, which was the true sensation and the true solution of the case.

"Mr. Holmes should sit at the head of the table," Pink decided, standing behind the very chair, her bare hands curled proprietorially over the back strut, as if *The* Man were already in possession of the location.

She was, I admit, a vision in cream and blue-plaid voile, with a very smart ivory silk jacket decorated in blue braid like an officer's coat.

"I will sit here." She airily indicated a chair only two seats down from the great man.

"Perhaps you would care to make place cards while we await the guests," Irene suggested.

"Shan't be necessary," Pink responded with cheery seriousness, not for a moment suspecting Irene's irony. "Mr. Holmes is our anchor. Once he is properly placed to direct the proceedings we'll have nothing more to worry about."

"Except a possible killer in our midst, suddenly exposed and perhaps violent," Irene pointed out.

"Surely even a murderer would know better than to make a scene at Delmonico's!"

"I think you overestimate the social nicety of most murderers. But it is all right, Pink. I am armed, and Mr. Holmes may be as well. As surely the New York detective is. I assume he will be in the guise of some serving man until the moment he is called upon to get out the manacles. Delmonico's, in fact, may make its debut today as a target range."

"Now that would be exciting, like a Wild West shoot-out! You had best hide under the table, Nell, if any bullets start flying."

"I believe we had all better hide under the table if any shooting starts," I said. "Pink, you may be a daredevil reporter, but you are remarkably ignorant about some matters."

"We shall see who is ignorant when all is said and done here," she replied.

At that moment some of the serving staff entered the room to finish the table settings and we were forced to withdraw to the paneled walls to watch our stage being dressed for the imminent debut of its new melodrama. Pink remained center stage to order the centerpieces rearranged for some reason known only to her.

"She is becoming quite insufferable," I whispered to Irene. "She has no idea what a horrible crime we uncovered completely without her help or knowledge."

"Yet without her aid we would have never learned so much about Madame Restell," Irene answered. "She is indefatigable. She has an inbred taste for misdeeds and also a bent as strong for revealing them. That is all admirable, Nell."

"I suppose so. Were I . . . we . . . not so personally involved in these revelations, perhaps I would be more ready to applaud."

"And if Quentin were not, also," she added both gently and pointedly.

There was no answer to such a delicate barb, except to privately extract it and hope it left no scar. I doubted Quentin would appear here today, but I also doubted that he had left the shores of America or even the city of New York. Oh! That sounded so English: New York. Or New Jersey, for that matter. But such nomenclatures were deceptive. From what I had seen of these shores, there was nothing English here but past glories and associations and a few paltry place names. It was a brave new world, as the Bard had said once, and not the sort of place where I would ever be at home. I could not wait to return to the Old World, and, I was amazed to realize, to the civilities and comforts of Paris.

While I watched, a new round of waiters entered the room, these not bearing huge silver compotes of fresh fruit or tall wine stands, but . . . very elegant easels.

Amazed, I saw them place the stands around the fringes of the room, including on either side of Irene and myself by the wall.

"Is this some new liberty of Pink's?" I asked Irene.

"No, it is some new liberty of mine, for a change." She smiled as the waiters left, and then quickly returned bearing placards they distributed to the easels, one by one.

"Ah." I enumerated the placards as they were placed on the

easels. "There is Salamandra's recent playbill . . . and one, a very old one, celebrating 'Gemini Burning.' And there is Professor Marvel! And . . . Merlinda. And handsome young Washington Irving Bishop, who was a walking dead man, only no one knew it. Little Rena and Tiny Tim, the Little Drummer boy. Madame Zenobia, mistress of the mantic arts. The Pig Lady. The Great Malini!? A magician? Not one of our acquaintance?"

"No. I am importing an entire era, without prejudice."

"Oh." I leaned forward to see if the next set of female twins were Sophie and Salamandra, but they were Wilhelmina and Winifred Hermann, darling little girls with full starched skirts and curls as tight as pigs' tails.

"That is when you first knew them."

Irene nodded, then lifted her chin to indicate a new placard being settled into place on its easel.

This pair of twins were as curvaceous as circus steeds and wore flesh-colored tights beneath indecently short skirts. They clung together in coy shyness despite their bold state of undress, and the large even bolder type beneath their likeness read:

PANSY AND PETUNIA,

THE TWIN TOASTS OF FOURTEENTH STREET

THEY DANCE, THEY SING, THEY TWIST YOUR HEARTS

AROUND THEIR LITTLE FINGERS

"This memorializes the beginning of the end," I said. "The time when their paths and yours parted."

"Indeed, but first those paths conjoined in the horrible death of poor Petunia." Irene shook her head. "Some things I was perhaps better off *not* remembering."

"Have you," I asked gingerly, "in your memories recalled some facts that might possibly predict where Mr. Holmes will find his confederate?"

"Perhaps." Irene's face remained sphinxlike. "I will let Pink and Mr. Holmes direct this show."

"They cannot both do so!"

"I know, that is why I will watch. It will be most amusing."

In fact, barely had the last placard been set in place and the waiters left, then the man in question strolled through the open double doors to our private room.

His hat, gloves, and cane had been intercepted by a waiter at the door, but he kept one hand in the pocket of his soft-toned plaid suit in such a way that I suspected a firearm could lay concealed there.

After nodding at us and Miss Pink and quickly summing up the table with no great pleasure, his eyes fixed on the playbills.

Pink was still rearranging flower arrangements on the table, so he addressed her first. "Your work?" he nodded at the ring of easels surrounding the empty table."

"No. I assumed yours."

At that he smiled tightly and bowed toward us again, following the courtesy by a slow tour of each and every placard, beginning at the ones nearest the doors.

Pink cast us an impatient look, as though Irene's forethought was to be faulted for absorbing too much of the great man's time, no matter how cavalierly he regarded the display.

He stopped before us as if we were but one more placard on display: the Neuilly Sisters, internationally renowned . . . jugglers, perhaps.

"Is this to be a command performance, or a séance?" he inquired softly. "Half the artists represented are dead."

Irene was swift to answer. "I believe that you are the impresario of this luncheon, ably assisted by the energetic Pink the Wonder Tattler."

"I would prefer a singing mermaid," he muttered after glancing over his shoulder. "Or at least a reliable secretary. She expects a startling revelation in time for the morning edition, all to please her new publisher, Mr. Pulitzer."

"And will you oblige?" Irene asked sweetly.

He said nothing, merely moved on to the next playbill.

"I wish I knew," Irene whispered to me, "whether he was still making up his mind."

"Do you think so?"

But before she could answer, our first guest deposited his outerwear at the door and entered our arena.

"Professor Marvel," Irene greeted him, finally sweeping forward as the hostess she was.

He took both her hands, and kissed her cheek.

Was this a Judas kiss, I wondered, for I was now keenly suspicious of everyone we had met.

As a veteran performer on the variety stage, the professor was familiar with every sort of act, and no doubt could have stepped in to play many parts in an emergency.

My suspicions were derailed a moment later when a heavily veiled figure paused in the doorway, a dwarf standing beside it, the light at their backs making them into a sinister pair.

I rushed forward when I realized this was the unfortunate Pig person accompanied by her small daughter Edith, not Phoebe Cummings.

"Do come in," I urged, taking the little girl by the hand to encourage her mother forward.

I suspect the poor lady avoided public places. I escorted them to chairs beside Professor Marvel, who immediately greeted them warmly. He stood to seat both Edith and her mother, calling a waiter over to install a pillow on the child's chair. Soon they were chatting away like old friends, which I suppose they were.

A moment later the professor was calling for a new pillow, as Phoebe Cummings herself entered the room, attired in a checked cape coatdress that most resembled Pink's new ensemble that resembled the outfit and cap I had worn in Paris last spring. In

fact, the coat reminded me of the one Sherlock Holmes had worn
to visit us at Neuilly. Thinking of myself, Pink, and Mr. Holmes
all attired in similar checked coats quite confused me. I realized
that if Edith had been so attired, she and Phoebe would look like
twins.

Not too far away, Sherlock Holmes was aiming a battery of
questions at Professor Marvel and his "every fact at my fingertip"
technique. I was struck by the fact that they seemed to know each
other.

"My 'marvels' are the product of years of performance, my
dear sir," Professor Marvel was expounding with pleasure. "You
would be surprised at how limited any given audience's range of
questions is. I thrive on the public's lack of imagination, rather
than any miraculous skill of my own."

"It takes nimble fingers as well as a nimble mind, however,"
Mr. Holmes remonstrated.

The professor waggled chubby but knuckle-enlarged digits.
"Dexterity in both mind and matter fades with time. Luckily I
compensate in other ways. The quick quip, for instance, defers the
moment of truth just long enough, and a laughing audience feels
itself well entertained."

I doubted there would be much laughter here once the main
"act" of unmasking a murderer was underway. Speaking of
which, an utterly new performer was about to make his entrance.

The threshold hosted a man in a checked suit, his beefy form
straining at the plaid vest beneath, whom Pink rushed to greet
and install next to the chair she had chosen herself, introducing
him as "Mr. Holly."

This could only be the city police detective, and he was no
French inspector like the dandified François le Villard. I would
not be surprised to find such a man driving a hansom cab or tout-
ing horses at the racetrack. Indeed, he didn't think to remove his
bowler hat until he was halfway to the luncheon table.

While I watched this fellow eased into a place he looked most uncomfortable in occupying, Irene was escorting her own unlikely fellow to a seat opposite Pink's guest.

It was Mr. Conroy, the Pinkerton inquiry agent!

I gazed upon the two women who faced each other over their respective unhailed representatives of law and order: Pink and her policeman, Irene and her Pinkerton. They rather resembled mothers of rival debutantes jousting for pride of place for their awkward darlings at the table.

Even I had to admit that Sherlock Holmes was several cuts above these New World policemen, public and private, but then he had the inimitable advantage of being English.

He had not yet taken the seat Pink had pointed out to him, but was still roving the room, studying placards and occasionally running a disconcertingly sharp eye over the assembling guests.

Another tall figure darkened the door. I rushed to greet the maestro, who dangled a top hat from the same knobby fingers I had last seen holding a violin.

A waiter soon relieved him of hat, gloves, and cane. His tie was elegantly knotted. I was relieved to see him show some care in his dress on this formal occasion, which gave him an Old World air I had not noted before.

Irene came to claim him from me, and seated him in a place of honor on her left side, for she had taken the other end of the long table, opposite Mr. Holmes.

I was not pleased to see these two rivals thus posed, like lord and lady of the manor, but there was also something of the chess board in their placement.

Pink's mother entered thereafter. I raised my eyebrows. She had nothing to do with these matters, did she?

Here Irene certainly could not counter Mrs. Cochrane with her own candidate, as she had with the "dueling detectives."

I was not surprised to see another gentleman arrive, introduced by Pink as Mr. Gordon Evers.

This was the light-fingered acquaintance Pink had imported

to the séance to help her detect legerdemain in the doings there. With Professor Marvel also here, almost all the persons who attended that first of more than one fatal, recent performance was present.

The long table was beginning to look crowded. I quickly claimed my foreordained seat at Irene's right. Pink was in the same position at Mr. Holmes's end of the table.

Messrs. Conroy and Holly, the Pinkerton and the policeman, bracketed Mr. Holmes two seats down from his position. Clearly, Pink expected him to expose the miscreant and wanted the long arm of the law within easy reach of whoever the villain turned out to be.

I studied the table, now that it was fully occupied, myself.

Gazing upon it, I felt a sense of unease I couldn't name.

I tallied the dead women we knew of. From the theatrical world, there was the never-met Abyssinia who had endured a rather too-close encounter with her performing partner, a boa constrictor. There were the twin sisters Sophie and Salamandra, recently killed in the very performances of their acts. There was the never-met Winifred who matured into the doomed Petunia, or Pet, whose lifeless body in a bathtub had caused Irene to lose her voice. There was her twin sister Wilhelmina, also known as Mina, who had survived her twin's tragic death, yet spent anguished years trying to find the child she had given birth to in secret. Both twins had been patrons of Madame Restell's infamous contraceptive and pregnancy-terminating skills.

And then there were the sympathetic landladies and doormen we had met, passing acquaintances who yet mourned the needlessly dead.

For a moment, I wondered if Mr. Holmes would conduct a séance here! But then I realized that Irene had already summoned the dead with the device of the playbill placards.

We needed no more ghosts on the scene, we needed a murderer in the flesh!

Irene had determined one half of the equation, and had beaten Mr. Holmes to the scene of the crime . . . crimes, plural, on Fifth Avenue. One would have to credit her with that achievement.

Yet there was a missing murderer, what Mr. Holmes termed a confederate. It was indeed unlikely that Mina Gilfoyle had secreted herself at Sophie's séance to play the part of confederate-turned-murderer. It would have taken someone with more strength to strangle Sophie quickly in full view of a table of witnesses.

Strength would not be required to douse Salamandra's performing wardrobe with flammable substances, not once, but twice. Stealth, however, would be needed, and an ability to pass backstage without question.

Mina had been over ten years absent from the stage. No current doormen or stagehands would recognize her, but a woman backstage who was not a performer could not pass unnoticed. She could have gone in disguise, but that was unlikely. Mina was obsessed with cheating Irene of her heritage, the knowledge of her origins, so she wanted the Dixon sisters dead, yes, but she was rich enough to avoid the doing the murderous work herself.

As Mr. Holmes had wisely remarked, her madness was of the sort that finally turned on its possessor, not on others . . . except in motive rather than execution.

I thought again of the many personas child performers adapted as they aged. It struck me that one could get mired in a particular period, as Wilhelmina, turned Pansy, had when she allowed her envy of Irene's beauty and talent—and integrity—to fester. When her sister Petunia had died and Irene discovered the body, did she somehow blame Irene for Pet's ill fortune? Was that easier than blaming her sister, or herself? Was her vendetta against Irene a case of ancient Greek tragedy, the impulse imbedded in the tendency to "kill the messenger?"

I had many questions, but first had to put my attention to a lavish luncheon that began with cream of chestnut soup, served cold in honor of the summer season. The entree was a large fillet of fish curved like a scimitar on a bed of greens and candied apricot slices. The fish were headless, thank goodness. I cannot think why the more elegant the meal the more obviously dead creature parts the diner is forced to confront. Each fish was served in portions to several people and its entire length was covered with thin-sliced almonds arranged like fish scales. For the absent "eye," some overenthusiastic chef had sliced green olive stuffed with red pimiento into an unlikely orb. Baked onions stuffed with garlic paste and studded with cloves made an unusual vegetable course, along with a more conventional timbale of macaroni, with its rich combination of cream, eggs, chicken and ham to enhance the delicately bland fish. Desert offered ripe red islands of strawberries amid a silken creamy sea, which I enjoyed tremendously, much remarking on the unusually tasty flavor, until Irene in-formed me that the sauce had been flavored with whiskey!

It took several sips of tea to banish the uncivilized taste, which I'd fully believed was due to exotic spices, and not common spirits.

It was only when the plates and serving dishes were cleared and we were all left to our cups of tea, or coffee in some cases, that Irene rung an exquisite call to attention on her crystal water goblet with a sterling silver spoon.

She stood, lifting her wine glass as for a toast.

"I welcome our near and dear spirits to this table, those who are gone and whom we mourn and celebrate, most particularly Sophie and Salamandra Dixon, and now even more recently, Wilhelmina Hermann Gilfoyle."

First everyone lifted a glass—I made do with water—then came the buzz and clatter of neighbors interrogating neighbors.

"Wilhelmina dead too?" asked the Pig Lady's gentle voice. I had observed her eat beneath the curtain of her veil without making the sheer but opaque fabric flutter once.

A greater buzz arose. The news startled all present but Irene, myself, and Mr. Holmes.

Pink was conferring with the policeman, who could only shrug and seemed loath to interrupt his avid consumption of whiskeyed strawberries to attend to the postprandial speechifying.

"What is this new death?" Pink finally asked Irene directly, and a bit sharply.

For answer, Irene waved a hand at the poster of Pansy and Petunia. "The last of the twins. It's ironic that Sophie and Salamandra were twins as well."

"Another set of twins? With one set dead only days ago? When and where did this Pansy or Petunia die?"

"Last night," Irene answered calmly, ignoring the gasps that stirred the table. "At home."

"And was it foul play?"

"I doubt any charges will be filed."

"And her sister died too? Where and when?"

"Winifred, also known as Petunia, died in town here, perhaps sixteen or seventeen years ago."

"That long?" Pink cogitated visibly. A death that old did not fit into her scheme of some contemporary maniac killing possible candidates for Irene's mother. "How old was Petunia?"

"Perhaps sixteen or seventeen."

Pink sat quietly and unhappily calculating. In no way could a woman who would be thirty-two or -four today be considered a candidate for Irene's mother. Nor could her twin sister who had just died last night.

"Perhaps," came Sherlock Holmes's high but commanding voice, "these people attending the luncheon need to better understand why the loss of Mrs. Gilfoyle surprises Miss Nellie Bly so much."

An even greater buzz expanded as our luncheon companions realized an infamous reporter was in our midst.

Pink flashed Mr. Holmes a look of pure impatience, as if he

were quite ruining her lofty plans through a bit of pompous British stupidity. Oh, how I hoped she was wrong, even if that meant that I would have to accept Mr. Holmes as being right, at least in this one instance! Better the devil you don't know very well than the one you have clutched to your bosom in more innocent days, although no devils are to be recommended as bosom companions, even temporarily.

"Mrs. Norton," he went on. "Most of those at this table knew you well years ago, during your days as a child performer. Perhaps you would care to inform them of the mysteries that have brought you back to the shores of America."

"The first mystery," Irene said, "is Nellie Bly, who seems to have taken more interest in my history and origins than even I might have."

Every eye focused on the professional snoop at our table.

"She told me that she was convinced that I had a mother I had never known in the States, and that someone was trying to kill her."

"So that is what brought you back!" Professor Marvel exclaimed, nodding. "Didn't you realize that some of us would have told you about any parents they knew you had?"

"I did indeed. That's why I was extremely skeptical of her claim."

The next voice came from behind the Pig Lady's veil, which remained eerily unmoving despite the breath that must be wafting across it. If she wished to give séances, I have no doubt she would be most uncannily successful at it!

"Was the death of Sophie an indication that she might be your mother? And Salamandra also? That's quite impossible."

"Someone might not have known that," Irene said. "And why is it impossible?"

The Pig Lady's veil turned left and then right as she inspected both sides of the table. "I cannot speak of that in this company." The veil lowered as she presumably glanced down to little Edith at her side.

"Nell, perhaps you could take Edith for a walk outside."

"No."

"No?"

"I do not wish to leave at this critical point. I might be required to . . . to testify."

"I'll walk the child," Professor Marvel offered jovially, tossing his napkin to the tabletop in preparation for rising.

"I think not," Mr. Holmes said, rather ominously. He sent a sudden smile Mrs. McGillicuddy's way. "Could you, madam? A few minutes should suffice, I think."

She was already leaning across the table toward Edith opposite her. "Now, dearie, they're getting all grown-up and boring after eating. Let's go see something more interestin'."

The child was happy to oblige the jolly landlady, and the two went off hand in hand like the Walrus and the Carpenter, with less lethal results, one would hope.

"I hesitate to speak plainly even now," the Pig Lady's soft voice said.

That very reluctance installed a hush over the table as everyone kept quiet, leaned inward, and strove to learn the secret.

"This event, after all," she went on, "honors their lives as well as mourns their deaths. Please do not make me speak ill of them."

"I don't think you could," Irene said. "They were warm-hearted women who were dear to all of us here, second mothers to me, although I can't accept either one of them for my actual mother, unless you tell me differently. I must admit that I had thought I had set aside all notion, need, and care for a mother years ago. Yet seeing you all again, my foster family of the theater, has made me eager to find what was lost, if it can be had."

There was no doubting Irene's simple sincerity. Her old associates eyes brightened and blinked.

The Pig Lady's eyes were not visible, but her voice resumed, and she said what she had feared to say before. "I know neither Sophie or Salamandra could be your mother, Rena, because they were young girls when you were born. Even then it would have been possible, and they could have concealed it, for desperate young girls can accomplish amazing feats of directing attention away from what would normally be obvious conditions, especially in such a transient profession as ours. As a matter of fact, both *could* have been your mother, for both had been in the family way before you were born. Girls can be taken sad advantage of, and are often so innocent they don't even know why it happens."

Irene had sat back down in shock at these revelations. The women's sordid history did not surprise her, I am sorry to say, so much as the fact that not one, but two of them had been with child at a time just before she was born.

"Then either one *could* have—" she began, appalled to think that she may have just missed seeing the one again, and certainly had missed recognizing the other for her mother. . . .

"No." The Pig Lady's voice was loud and firm. "Both were 'in trouble.' They visited a 'woman doctor' who claimed to help them, and no children resulted."

"Madame Restell!" Irene exclaimed. "But there could have been future occasions—"

"No. They had learned their lessons, and, later, when they married, they discovered they could no longer do what they were so loath to do just a few years earlier. It was why both were no longer with their husbands, and had not been for years."

"Both unable to have children?" Irene sounded extremely doubtful.

"They were twins," Sherlock Holmes reminded her, and the table. "It could be they suffered the same adverse effects. I understand that sort of illegal surgery is quite crude."

Irene's eyebrows went up, even as she didn't argue with his conclusions. She was no doubt thinking what I was: that Sherlock Holmes had grown increasingly knowledgeable about hidden female matters since consulting with Professor Krafft-Ebing.

"Then"—Irene was sounding more appalled by the moment—

"were their deaths a mistake? Because they were *mistaken* for my possible mother, each of them? Why would anyone be so set upon killing a mother I had never known?"

"You forget," Sherlock Holmes put in, rather gently for one of his bent, I thought. "As a young performer you engendered a great deal of jealousy. Jealousy motivated the Bible's first murder; because of it Cain killed Abel. I seldom see a case of pure jealousy, one that does not involve the romantic relationship between man and woman, which is the most puzzling motive of all. It lies in the heart and perception of the murderer, which is often invisible, and incomprehensible, to the larger world."

Irene sat thunderstruck and silent. I remember her referring to the same Biblical crime when talking to Pink not long ago. Yet she had forgotten her own lesson. This fact was a disturbing reminder of all she had been made to "forget" when last in this country.

"Madam Abyssinia," Sherlock Holmes was saying to the larger table, ignoring Irene now as I wished he would ignore her now and forever. "I believe she was what is called a snake charmer in the trade. She also was slain by the means of her profession, a boa constrictor of apparently unusual length, strength, and size. Is this true?"

"She was not one of our particular theatrical set," Professor Marvel said after a silence indicated no one else would answer his question.

"She did share a bill occasionally, in the old days," the Pig Lady offered.

"She only died in June," the maestro put in morosely. "I knew her," he added with a smile that was both apologetic and bereft, "better than most." He drew patterns on the heavily padded damask tablecloth with the nails of his right hand. I noticed again his arthritis-mangled joints and wondered that he could play the violin at all. "She died childless, as I will. But"—his final words were muttered—"she had seen Madame Restell, years and years ago."

"That is the connection!" Irene's voice rang out. "Not *me*. Madame Restell! I am beside the point."

"I doubt that, madam," Sherlock Holmes was too hasty, in my opinion, to respond.

His comment brought a thin smile to Irene's tense lips.

"Madame Restell," he echoed. "Madam Norton is correct. I have searched for an element in common to these deaths, and only Madame Restell will serve, though she has been dead herself these eleven years. The problem is the matter of the person who wished these women dead, and the person who actually accomplished it. I believe that they are not one and the same—in fact, I found a tall man's hand print on the curtains of the fatal séance room, a misshapen man's hand—yet how seldom two people share the same mania. Almost never."

"Almost?" Irene asked.

"It is time," Mr. Holmes said, "to be frank with your friends, and all seated at this table are your friends, are they not? Or, at least, they are friends of the dead women we memorialize, for whom we attempt to seek justice. The dual nature of this case struck me from the first, and the more I learned of it, the more it rang double chimes. Not one pair of twins, but two. Events of eleven or more years ago, and fresh events of today, all resulting in death. The confusing search for a mother, which has instead found many who were *not* mothers, whether they could not or would not be.

"It is time to reveal one side of the coin, though many here would hush the matter: Mina Gilfoyle died by her own hand. Hers was the twisted mind that demanded these most recent deaths, as it had demanded another death years ago. She had lost two children to that vaunted savior of women's reputations, Madame Restell. One was prevented from entering the world, and young Mina in fact welcomed this release at the time. The other was borne, and born, and sent to another woman. This apparently face-saving arrangement an older Mina came to regret, only to find that she was forever barred from changing her mind, not only by Madame Restell, but by her then-husband. The child was alive, but gone. Later, a second husband would have given anything for a child she could no longer provide. This is when the secrets of her past, and its long-concealed petty jealousies, combined to turn lethal.

"For her sister, Petunia, too, had been a casualty of undoing the results of seduction. She had died by her own hand, hardly older than a child herself, because, I suspect, Madame Restell had been resorted to and told the young girl she was too close to delivery to undo the deed. So, Petunia chose death rather than disgrace, a not uncommon outcome even now.

"Having later suffered her own follies and losses, the surviving twin grew slowly mad. She hunted the daughter she'd lost and hated the woman who had survived missing a mother, her unsuspecting rival, Rena the Ballerina."

He pronounced that last title with suspicious relish.

Irene ignored the references to herself. "But what," she asked, "made Mina resort to murder so late in the story?"

"Two things." Sherlock Holmes produced a briarwood pipe from his pocket and proceeded to light it.

While he did so, every breath in the room was held. Once the old pipe was puffing away, tendrils of smoke drifted like baby's breath over the pink lilies in the floral arrangement near his seat. His slight smile acknowledged his awareness of the almost tangible curiosity and suspense also wreathing the chamber and everyone in it.

"First was the bizarre passing only last May of Washington Irving Bishop, the cataleptic alleged to have been accidentally done to death by a series of careless medical mistakes. This was the story that Miss Nellie Bly so resented occurring while she was otherwise engaged in Europe. It was exactly the sort of story she would have ridden into the ground like a Wild West horse, and so she looked into it anyway when she returned to New York at the end of June.

"The second event was the same Miss Nellie Bly's stumbling

over old playbills among Mr. Bishop's effects that surprised her with evidence of her European acquaintance's New York City past. Miss Bly's newspaper, the *New York World*, has been recently acquired by a new publisher intent on making news, not just reporting it. Miss Bly was determined to show Mr. Joseph Pulitzer that she was his man. Er, woman. She was sure that the death of Mr. Bishop was exceedingly odd, and that the circumstances offered much opportunity for misdeeds.

"And she was right."

Here Pink sat back with a satisfied sigh, crossing her arms across her chest like the most blatant hoyden.

While I sent a glare Pink's way, Irene kept her gaze on Sherlock Holmes.

He paused to take a long indulgence of his pipe. When he next spoke, the words came out on puffs of blue smoke.

"And she was wrong."

Now Irene shot Pink a look, but only for a moment.

"Bizarre as the events surrounding Mr. Bishop's premature death were, they served to inspire a mad pair of like minds. The notion of disposing of performers while they were literally 'in the act,' occurred to them then.

"As for the motive and for why it cropped up at this point, I will have to ask Mrs. Norton some telling questions, if she will answer."

"I will answer what I can," Irene said cautiously, wary of his hidden motives.

"I take you back, madam, to that day of all days you don't wish to remember. To that day for which the maestro ultimately gave up his Guarneri violin to forget, for he gave it to you in penance for taking your memory even while saving your voice, is that not so, Maestro?"

The old man's long white hair fell over his face as he nodded agreement and shame.

"A magnificent atonement, sir," Mr. Holmes said. "I have

played it recently, only for a few moments. That, I think"—here he glanced at Irene—"caused the first stirring of what would lead to her long dormant memories reviving."

She looked surprised at his claiming credit for first touching the strings of her long-buried memories, and would have objected, but his narrative drove on mercilessly, and her moment was gone.

"You found this young girl dead in the bathtub," he told her. "You both were of an age. She was a sister performer. She had cut her wrists almost up to the elbows with a razor—"

"How did you know that?"

He shrugged, shook his head. "You screamed. The shock. The horror of all that bloody bathwater. Can you deny any of this?"

"No."

"But you can remember it now?"

She glanced at me, a faint, weary triumph beneath the reviving horror. *He doesn't know, Nell*, she thought at me. *For all he can deduce about the dead girl years ago, he doesn't* know *that we have released my memory.*

"I can try," she said.

"I know you found this girl. I know it shocked you into screams, and then silence. What I wish to know is who found you?"

"What?"

"Your screams, an entire aria of screams I understand, must have alerted someone. Who came first. Who found you at the side of the dead girl?"

Irene blinked and looked to the array of paintings above us, as if hoping some artist might have painted the scene. Or perhaps she was consulting heaven, a rare occupation for her.

Her glance came back to the luncheon table, and flicked over all the men sitting there.

They were all tall, I realized . . . Professor Marvel, the mae-stro, even the policeman and the Pinkerton, both of them old enough to have been involved in Madame Restell's trials, arrest, imprisonments and, finally, death.

And the hand print Mr. Holmes had alluded to finding in the séance room: twisted. As were Professor Marvel's and the maestro's, with the arthritis of age.

"It was a theatrical boarding house," Irene recalled slowly, even as she spoke. "We most of us lived there, together. The professor. The maestro. The Pig Lady."

A woman! who but a woman would have understood Mina's pain? The Pig Lady, as we had seen, knew the hidden, shameful history of every woman in the troupe. What troubled female would not have confided in the nunlike, veiled figure denied normal human intercourse of every kind?

I was instantly glad little Edith was cavorting in the park outside with Mrs. McGillicuddy. Poor child, yet another daughter of scandal!

"Who found you?" Mr. Holmes insisted, like a barrister at the bar. For a moment he almost reminded me of Godfrey.

Perhaps that odd fact shook Irene loose from the fog of her manipulated memory.

"Tim," she said, certain as a witness in the box. "Tiny Tim found me."

We all held our conjoined breaths, not knowing what this meant, but realizing it was what Mr. Holmes had required.

He himself exhaled an endless stream of blue smoke.

"In all this search for mothers," he said, "there has been no talk of fathers."

Irene clapped a hand to her mouth, then removed it to speak. "So it wasn't necessarily the men in their mother's shadowed social circles who seduced the Hermann twins. I'd assumed, we all assumed . . . easier to blame those shallow swells of turning a young girl's head and deserting her than one of our own?"

"A backstage romance," Professor Marvel diagnosed with a sad smile. "So common that sometimes it doesn't even come to mind. I confess that we mostly worried about the fast crowd that adopted Pet and Pansy like pretty little lapdogs, thanks to their heedless mother. We never thought of young love. Puppy love." He glanced at Irene. "It must have been that, at that age. There was innocence in it."

Irene put her spread fingers to one side of her face, like a mentalist pretending to consult inner powers. In her instance, she was conjuring freshets of insight from the well of memory.

"Pet died, but Pansy, her twin, lived. Tim had nothing left. From a distance, he consecrated himself to Pansy, even as she repeated her sister's mistakes . . . and became Mina."

"And when Mina," I said, surprising everybody by speaking at all, "now lost in despair and fury, learned that you, her youthful rival in her own mind, were alive and performing well in Europe and that Nellie Bly was delving into the past to find your mother . . . she resolved to forbid you the family connection she had lost in losing her daughter."

"And she punished women like herself," Irene added, "women who had consulted Madame Restell."

"But why would Tiny Tim help her?" I asked.

"Perhaps," said Sherlock Holmes, "we should ask him."

Everyone at the table stared at each other. Tiny Tim was not here. He had left suddenly on a recent engagement in the West. So he had told his landlady. Who would have thought his "recent engagement" was murder?

"Quick, Conroy!" Mr. Holmes cried sharply. "The wine waiter!"

I have never seen a portly man in a checked suit move as fast. His chair fell over as he dashed toward the sideboard. On the table's other side Pink's police detective also threw politeness to the winds and kicked over his chair to assist his unofficial compatriot.

In a minute a tall young man in black-and-white waiter's dress was pinioned against a Restoration sideboard.

I had not seen this man's face during the entire luncheon, but

I had noticed his knotted hands as he filled the glasses . . . *and had averted my eyes from his face so as not to embarrass him for his affliction.*

As perfect a disguise as the Pig Lady's! Disability makes one invisible, as Phoebe Cummings, professional dwarf, had told us. And so also she and the Pig Lady had been spared, because they had never needed to consult Madame Restell.

The two lawmen pushed Tim to the table, forcing his crooked hands as flat as possible on the linens. The hands of a strangler, and an arsonist, and who knew what else.

"Of course," Irene said. "Look at his knuckles! I still thought of him as the raw-boned young man I last knew when we met again, and thought nothing of his knobby joints. Arthritis, it was, showing up early, nothing a drummer can overcome. He didn't simply outgrow the theatrical life, he was *forced* to retire. Nor was there any 'recent engagement.' He merely needed to disappear once he knew Nellie Bly and I were hunting Sophie's killer. So what was his motive?" she asked Mr. Holmes.

Nellie Bly answered for him, stepping forward boldly. "The killer can't be Tim. I sat next to him at the séance. We held hands the entire time. I heard him swallow nervously next to me as well, the entire time." She eyed Mr. Holmes, who was looking only slightly surprised. "You have the wrong man."

He did not need to defend himself; Irene did it for him.

"Pink, beware," she warned. "You reveal your ignorance. People hold hands at séances only because the use of medium confederates had become so well known that measures had to be taken to prove tampering impossible. And such measures always result in ways to overcome them. False hands."

"I'm not a fool! I know about false hands. I could feel the nervous dampness from his hands seeping through my gloves."

"A clever touch," Mr. Holmes said. "The false hand would be shaped like a shell, hollow, so the manipulator could withdraw his own hand and be about his work in the dark. A damp cloth over the false hand would reinforce the impression that Mr. Flynn was still sitting there doing various tricks to assist in the tableside illusions, and provide a nice distraction from what he was actually doing while the medium's moans snared everyone's attention."

"And the swallowing sound?"

"A repetitive sound that a drummer could easily rig some mechanical device under the table to produce. Had you told me your impressions earlier I would have identified him sooner. Tiny Tim had been a stage performer since an early age. Why would he be nervous at a private séance? His disability was not too hampering for this kind of work, and Sophie Dixon would have been happy to employ a former associate having bad luck, especially one she had been fond of when he was a child. How was she to know the hidden history that allowed him to be corrupted to another's purpose?"

"But," Pink said stubbornly, "how could he have left a handprint on the curtain then?"

"When setting up the evening's musical effects," Mr. Holmes said promptly. "Only this evening he also installed an additional horse-hair line. This one held the 'ectoplasm' up in the air as he was busy looping the lower portion of it around Miss Dixon's throat. The eerie light on her features was caused by oil of phosphor and a concealed lamp beam aimed only at her face. Such brightness fools the human eye into seeing a deeper blackness around it. Her neck was not illuminated, and he had donned a hood with eyeholes along with black gloves. He was one with the dark. I have taken the precaution of visiting his landlady with the police and abstracting these very items from his furnished room, along with a flute and a supply of horse-tail hair. You must remember that he was used to moving unheard and unseen in the séance room, and that Miss Dixon's usual cries and moans disguised her own death struggle, which was swift. His hands are misshapen, but strong, and I imagine he is used to pain when moving them."

Pink moved back to her place, silenced for once, but not for long, I thought.

"Why come here today?" Irene asked. "Hubris?"

"No. Sorrow."

Irene considered that reply for a moment, for while she had discerned Mina's role in the recent deaths, the woman's confederate had remained a mystery.

"Do you think he did her bidding because he had always worshiped Mina from afar?" she asked.

"Yes," Mr. Holmes said, "to please her. News of her death devastated him." Mr. Holmes studied the vacant-eyed young man whose sunken face looked suddenly as prematurely old as his twisted hands. "This event was in her honor. It was the first public tribute he could pay to the *two* women who had captured his soul. And, consider this," he said, turning to Irene. "Finding Petunia's dead body almost ended your singing career. You literally lost your voice. Think what he experienced, finding you screaming over the body of his dead love, who had killed herself because of the shame they shared. He began to go mad from that awful instant. It took Mina much longer, but she still had hopes for her future then."

The young man writhed in the iron custody of the two beefy New York lawmen.

"You know nothing of it," he said contemptuously to Sherlock Holmes. His next words were for Irene. "And you needn't discuss me in the third person, Rena, as if I were no longer here."

She immediately responded. "I'm sorry. Sometimes the answer to a crime is so hard to face that it makes the criminal into a nonentity. I did know you from our earliest years, Tim. Why would you kill for Mina?"

"I didn't kill for *her*. I killed for Pet, and myself, and maybe for Mina finally, because there was no one else left."

He shook his head as Messrs. Conroy and Holly drew him upright and then pulled his hands behind his back to apply the manacles. He groaned as his joints were twisted into the unnatural position.

"Can't you manacle his hands in front?" Irene asked, seeing to his obvious agony. "Surely he can't escape you both."

Tim grimaced his relief as the men loosed their hold and brought his wrists forward as the heavy iron bonds were snapped shut around them.

Mr. Holmes seconded the decision. "Now that Mina is dead, he won't run. In fact, I should watch his cell for an attempt on his own life."

"You've got that right," Tim told Mr. Holmes. "There's been little to live for since Pet destroyed herself, and our child with her."

"Ever since then?" Irene cried, amazed. "All those years? That was thirteen or fourteen years ago."

"The blink of an eye to me. Why shouldn't my life revolve around Pet's death ever after? You screamed yourself silent at the sight of her dead body, and she was only a sister performer to you. She was my . . . love."

"Why didn't you two elope then?" Irene demanded in frustration, growing as upset as he now that they examined the single horror they shared yet had never discussed. "No one need have died then, not even the baby."

"Her mother needed the novelty of both girls, the 'twins,' to flaunt before her upper-crust gentlemen friends. That woman's life was built on charm, and hers were fading."

"So she sold her daughters into the most sordid sort of society?"

"Can't blame the girls," Tim muttered. "They were young, like you and me. And they found the high life tempting. Pet and me, we shouldn't have done what we done, but it was more honest than anything she encountered on Fifth Avenue. And . . . a rich old man was set on actually marrying her. Her mother wanted that. Part of Pet even wanted that. She didn't ask me for nothing. She didn't tell me how bad she felt, wanting and not wanting the baby we made. Didn't ask me. I wanted it. I wanted her. Mina said that when Madame Restell told Pet she was too far gone to stop or undo, she didn't talk to no one. Just went home and stopped it herself. Stopped herself."

Irene put a hand on his bound forearm. "I'm so sorry, Tim. She would have been better off with you."

"Not to her mind, at that terrible moment, anyway."

"So why didn't you move on and forget?" Sherlock Holmes asked, eyeing Tim as if he were a very interesting and talkative bug.

He obviously didn't know the first thing about losing true loves! But . . . did I? I blushed, grateful that no one regarded me during this inquisition. Even Pink chose to remain silent, and take notes, as Tim's story emerged under Irene's sympathetic prodding.

"Once Pet had died like that—" Tim shook his head. His hair was lank and fine. He still seemed a tall, gangly boy, not a killer or a madman. "I couldn't help it. The only person who grieved as hard as I did was her twin, Wilhelmina. Pansy, Mina, whatever she called herself, we'd been together since toddlerhood." He glanced at Irene. "You were off with the maestro singing scales, and once you got your voice back you seemed to forget all about what had happened to Pet, or what was happening to Mina and me. So we made a pair of it."

Irene bit her lip brutally. I could see the self-blame forming in her mind, when it was not her fault that the maestro's mesmerism had blurred the painful past for her, separating her from her theatrical family at such a crucial time. Their ignorance of her own sorrow and unnatural evolution made them think she'd escaped their pain somehow, that she had spurned them. It made Mina hate her with even more than girlish envy, for there was no one else to blame for Pet's death but Tim, perhaps, and their own mother, for certain.

"We became allies," Tim said. "She looked just like Pet. Exactly. Sometimes, much later, she'd let me—"

Everyone in the room had become an audience to this long-delayed denouement. Not one of the theater folk here spoke, or breathed. All had borne witness, but had never understood what they saw.

No one asked what Mina had let Tim do.

Even I thought I understood. Mina had been the living likeness of his dead love. Mina too had consulted Madame Restell and come away once with a mourned lost baby and a second time with a living child forsworn and then frantically wished back. Finally she had faced the fact of having no child at all.

Once started though, Tim couldn't stop.

"Mina let me . . . The old man wanted an heir and she couldn't oblige him. She let me . . . but it wasn't the same. Nothing happened. In a way I was glad. It was as if Pet had never had her . . . problem. But it changed Mina. She knew the difficulty lay in herself now and maybe because of what she'd done with Madame Restell before, 'cuz Pet and me, we managed it. Then that reporter . . . *her!*"

He pointed at Pink, who looked up from her notes, her heart obviously in her throat.

"She started it all, poking around after Mr. Bishop's death. Asking questions about his death, asking about Rena . . . Merlinda. You." He looked back at Irene as if not recognizing her. "You were gone. For so long. And then you came back, and Pet . . . Pansy . . . uh, Mina. She was even more frantic. It was as if you were the person who had taken everything from her, although she had more than most. I don't know. She told me the women we knew, the girls who were just a few years older than we were, they were all 'graduates' of Madame Restell's and they'd told Pet, advised Pet, to see that murderous woman and then they told her . . . when that didn't help, they told her that hot baths . . . and she died in a hot bath, and it didn't help, didn't help Pet, or me. Or anybody. So they deserved to die. They'd gone on and Pet hadn't. Don't you see? Mina did. And I did what Mina wanted. It was all I had left of Pet."

A silence held as years of unsuspected anguish and sin and twisted vengeance lay revealed in all its sordid madness.

I felt exhausted, as if I had sat through a very long Greek tragedy I only half understood.

Pink finally stood and came over to join us.

"I was right," she said, "there was a story here, and this one I can report, every last bit of it."

Sherlock Holmes, Irene, and myself exchanged an unwelcome, but conspiratory, glance.

The truly sensational story, the truth about the death of Madame Restell, her murder, would never become public.

Sherlock Holmes moved away, taking his annoying pipe with him, as he left to acquaint the police with the final facts in the case. The pathetic Tiny Tim was taken away as well, Pink was off after him, hot on the trail of crime and punishment and journalistic fame.

That left Irene and me gazing together at an unspoken truth we alone shared: the birth book of the notorious abortionist, Madame Restell, the wickedest woman in New York.

I truly believed now that she had a rival for that title, albeit it a very recently dead one.

Irene glanced around the elegant table, which had fallen into silence.

"We still owe our lost friends tribute," she told them. "They would be very happy to see us all together and to share our reunion. I know I am."

"Even Mina?" Phoebe asked gruffly. Everyone glanced at the commotion as Mrs. McGillicuddy returned to install Edith onto the pillowed chair next to Phoebe. Apparently the departing group had suggested the child could rejoin the company. The two who sat side by side—middle-aged dwarf and child—looked like odd sisters bracketed by the Pig Lady and the professor. I was sure that Phoebe, Edith, and her mother would be looked after by their fellow performers, now sobered by the loss of Sophie and Salamandra.

No one answered Phoebe's question. From report, Mina had been headstrong and selfish as a young girl, earning no friends. Those same petty and childish flaws had turned lethal when tragedy struck her sister and herself.

"We can toast small Wilhelmina and her sister Winifred, at least," Irene said after consideration. "And Tiny Tim, the little drummer boy." She held up a wine glass. "And let us toast each other, our shared pasts, and our unknown futures. And . . . I would like to salute one mystery that may never be solved, the Lady in Black who came to be kind to all of us orphaned theatrical children, and aren't we all theatrical orphans, whatever our ages, unless we band together?"

"Hear, hear," they cried, glasses and hopes raised.

Even I drank a hearty toast to their happier and reunited future after surviving such shocking losses of people and beliefs from their past.

47.

Women in Black

~~~

She was an illegitimate child, and early deserted by her mother. She had talents and decided to make use of them to get on in the world.... She had some money, $300 of which she left to the Magdalen Society, the remainder, after paying off just debts, is to go to charitable objects.

—*THE NEW YORK HERALD*, 1861

Green-Wood Cemetery is a short ferry ride south from the very tip of Manhattan Island across New York harbor to North Brooklyn. A brief carriage drive bypasses the busy piers of Upper New York Bay to arrive at an earthly paradise of rolling hills. From there one can overlook the distant ships on the bay and is in turn overlooked by wheeling seagulls with white angel's wings whose haunting cries evoke the lost and the gone.

My experience of graveyards is not extensive, as I have had few relatives to see interred. My father lies with my unremembered mother past a small lych-gate beside his Shropshire church. Both church and headstones are made of gray stone, which looks sober against the green growth of spring and summer, and grim during autumn and winter.

I have seen London's great Gothic Westminster Abbey and its indoor Poet's Corner, where one can trod on the final resting place of some of the greatest names in English letters and history. I have visited Pere La Chaise cemetery in Paris, an old, vast assemblage of monuments to many famous names, which reminds one of a cathedral in the open air. I have visited, twice, under perilous conditions, the ancient Jewish cemetery in Prague, where generations lie twelve-deep atop each other like residents in some afterlife tenement, the short, skewed headstones a sad, visible comment upon the press of urban life, and the constrictions of ghetto death.

But if I could choose before I die where I would finally rest for eternity, I believe that I would desert country and continent, and ask to be laid down in Green-Wood cemetery in Brooklyn, U.S.A.

It comes as close to paradise as any place on earth I have seen, even though, like all cemeteries, saints and sinners lie side by side, and only Judgment Day can truly say which is which.

It's impossible to visit a cemetery without contemplation. It was impossible that late summer day, so warm and sunny that the seagulls sparkled as if they had just risen to the air from the white marble monuments below, to avoid considering one's own demise.

We had hired an open carriage at the dock, for the weather was so fine we had purchased black parasols at Macy's department store for our outing. Despite the weather, we wore black. Watching the two bay horses that drew us, I recalled Madame Restell's famous four-horse-drawn equipage that was the talk of Broadway. Now, no one remembered her.

Irene ordered our bowler-hatted driver to pause before we passed through the Gothic gatehouse on the avenue opposite 25th Street.

It was odd to encounter such citified things as streets and avenues when we were about to enter a City of the Dead. The gatehouse offered two pointed-arch openings, one to come by and one to go by. With its three stone spires it looked like the very top of some massive European cathedral, cut off and set down at ground level. To either side stretched one-story wings that had the steep gables and dignified air of a churchyard manse.

Irene left the carriage to enter one of the side buildings, and returned in a few minutes with a folded paper. Several unfoldings revealed the map of a magnificent park full of circling drives that wound through groves and past ponds and streams and places bearing names like Hyacinth Lake and Vista Hill.

"No wonder we need a map," I said when I saw the sheer scope of the place. "Where are we going?"

Irene pointed to a site far into the maze of roads and monuments.

She showed the same spot to our driver, who tipped his hat as she mounted the carriage seat again. We kept the map open over our laps. The driver knew the way, so we could observe our progress.

This felt a bit like a treasure hunt in heaven. Over every rise stood a handsome grove of trees in formal array. Small white-marble mausoleums crowned each hill and lofty white plinths lay scattered about like pieces from several gigantic chess sets.

"I have never seen a cemetery that has so little gloom about it," I commented. "Perhaps I shouldn't approve, but it is enormously comforting. One can almost hear the dead murmuring along with the breeze through the trees."

"A much more honest 'ectoplasm' than the kind produced at a séance," Irene agreed, spinning her parasol handle so its reflected shade made a kind of monotone rainbow over her features. "If I indeed had a mother who is dead, I could not wish for a better place for her to be buried."

"Since you doubt Madame Restell was your mother, why are we making this pilgrimage to her grave?"

"I cannot be certain, can I? And besides, the poor woman was marked for eternity as a suicide when she actually had been murdered. She did not die in cowardice or despair, but faithful to her beliefs, however true or false, and to her client's privacy, to the end. I want *someone* who knows the truth about her death to stand over her at last."

"Pink would have been happy to join us."

"And equally happy to write a sensational story about Madame Restell and Mina for the *World* to see and gossip about again. No. I say let her rest in peace. No one knew better than Madame Restell that she was born to be misunderstood. Being a murder victim would not restore her reputation. She will always be known as 'the wickedest woman in New York.' "

I said nothing, for I didn't feel qualified to judge. This was unusual for me, who had been reared to believe in certain absolutes, but it is the beginning of true peace on earth, I had discovered, and one will not find peace in death unless one first sues for it in life.

"Do you regret that we answered Pink's call to New York?" I asked after several pleasant minutes of mutual silence.

"No. I have met some people I used to know well, have perhaps saved some of them from perishing, and mostly I have become reacquainted with a lost part of myself. Now you know my humble and eccentric beginnings. Do you regret learning that?"

"Not at all! Like Pink, I may become one to see great opportunity in other people's misfortunes. Perhaps I shall write a sensational novel, *Ten Days in a Vaudeville Theater.*"

Irene playfully jousted parasols with me. "You will do no such thing, or I will reveal the pig thief in your past."

"Heavens! Then I am silenced forever."

And so we were laughing when the driver drew our carriage to a stop by a small rise sectioned into squares by hedges and trees.

It struck me that two laughing women *not* in need of her services would be a fine set of final visitors for the late Madame Restell, for I doubted anyone visited her grave.

We ambled up the hill, weaving our way among monuments tall and modest. The sun warmed without overheating us. Irene and I had not shared such a pleasant, unhurried, *unpursued* time together in ages.

"Here," she said finally, stopping in front of a headstone.

How odd it was to read the inscription: ANN TROW LOHMAN MAY 6, 1811–APRIL 1, 1878. "Madame Restell" and all her works judged both good and bad had vanished. No mention here of a fiend or murderer or "bat" woman or a freethinker or a martyr.

"How many people still would be alive," I remarked, "if that one child had not been given for adoption with no trace of to whom or where."

"Such things have been done that way for hundreds of years, and still are today. An unwed mother forfeits her child, and all knowledge of its disposition." Irene stared down at the headstone. "I don't doubt for a moment that she knew where the child had gone. However she is judged, she did what she believed best, whether it was preventing or ending a pregnancy, or arranging a child adoption that could never be undone."

"You mean that she refused to tell, with a butcher knife to her neck?"

Irene nodded slowly. "I believe so, Nell. A woman who would drive out daily in broad daylight when even grateful clients denied using her twilight services was not about to kowtow to the cutting edge of a blade if she believed it was for the child's good."

"How awful! Did she guess that such a death would label her a coward and a suicide?"

"She never thought of herself, or history, only the present. She must have been accustomed to handling hysterical women, and men. She was not one to back down."

"I will pray that she was as right as she believed herself to be."

I bent my head and did so, while Irene waited. I don't think she prayed, but she felt great sorrow at the waste of lives we had witnessed these past two weeks, including that of this woman's murderer, who herself was a true suicide now.

"How ironic," I said when I lifted my head to the glorious day again. "Wilhelmina's madness led her to actually enact the self-inflicted death that had wrongly been assigned to her victim. Poetic justice, don't you think?"

"Murder is an ironic occupation, at best," said a familiar voice behind us.

I whirled to face Sherlock Holmes. Irene did nothing of the sort.

He had followed us up the hill, and stood on the incline, top hat in hand, the wind actually stirring that smooth dark hair of his as well as lifting the tail of his cutaway city suit. His formal dress amid all this lushly cultivated countryside reminded me of an undertaker. Perhaps it was an apt comparison for a detective.

When Irene kept her back to him he came abreast of us to gaze down on the last words said about Madame Restell.

"Both murderer and victim," he noted, "evaded answering to a court of law. And perhaps such crimes as they stood accused of should be judged in other than earthly courts. Madam."

Irene regarded him at last.

He held a folded paper out to her.

"There is another headstone here that I believe you would be obliged to visit. Like this one, the writing etched on the marble's surface is but a small hint of the true story that lies beneath."

Irene's lips parted with surprise.

"We have played at being opponents across half of Europe, Madam," he observed. "Now we both stand in a New World—a brave New World my friend Watson would imagine I know nothing of—with a vast unsettled continent yawning around us.

"Regard this map. Regard the name penciled beside that headstone."

"Mrs. Eliza Gilbert. The name means nothing to me."

"Neither did it to her, I think. It might merit tracing to its origins, however."

"Mrs. Eliza Gilbert is dead. I am not. You apparently know what that name means, but won't say more."

"You have often complained that I meddle in your private business. So the meaning here is all yours, should you choose to pursue it."

"And you will not help?"

"I will," I heard myself saying.

Irene turned to me with a blinding smile. She eyed Mr. Holmes again. "I have my Watson, it seems."

He shrugged. "I could wager my Watson against yours."

"It is not a contest."

"All life is a contest." He shrugged again. "There are other matters to attend to here, including the arcane matter of the Astor chess board. Our paths may yet cross again."

"I can't decide whether to regard that as a threat or a promise."

"It is a possibility, which is what I deal in, and what awaits me now."

He bowed to us, donned his top hat again, and began walking over the uneven ground, suspiciously soft in some places, to the curving driveway.

"What makes him think we will linger here, in this cemetery or this country?" I asked.

"One always lingers when contemplating death." Irene's attention had deserted Madame Restell's headstone and was now focused on the map. "This other monument is only . . . across that road and overlooking the section centered around the white marble pool, here."

"You aren't going to actually follow his advice?"

"Of course not, Nell. What I will do is accept his challenge. Come! We are not about to be stopped by one more puzzling headstone. The dead may be 'but sleeping,' yet I don't expect any of them to wake up."

I followed, grumbling as my boot heels wavered on the thick grass.

Like all predicted short walks, this one proved to be a greater distance that it looked but at last we found the headstone in question.

"Not an insignificant monument," Irene noted when I caught up to her, "but neither is it rich or showy. What does that tell us?"

I agreed that the stone was modest. An arch-topped rectangle perhaps two or three feet high sat atop two stepped pedestals. The deceased's name was deeply incised into a horizontal band in dignified capital letters: ELIZA GILBERT. Such an ordinary, even modest name. Above the decorative frieze which blazoned the name from side to side of the headstone was the simple title, also capitalized, but incised in more delicate lettering, MRS.

"The form of address is improper," I pointed out. "If she was indeed a 'Mrs.,' she should be identified fully by her husband's name, say Mrs. William Gilbert, with her own given name, Eliza, shown in parentheses."

"Are you saying, Nell, that this headstone memorializes a divorced woman?"

"Quite possibly. That is not utterly unheard of these days. Consider Pink's mother, for instance."

Irene nodded. "And such few clues lie below that plain name:

DIED

JAN. 17, 1861

AGE 42

"Not a terribly young age to have perished in such a harsh country as this, and that was at the beginning of their savage civil war."

Irene bent to brush a twig off the headstone's second step.

"An epitaph is such a terse, stingy summary of a life. It quite makes one wonder."

"How? Someone survived to bury her respectably. What else more is wanted?

"A great deal more information about Mrs. Eliza Gilbert, and Sherlock Holmes knows part of it already."

"Why won't he tell us, then?"

"Because I made a such great clamor about how much I resented him prying into my private history. So he has issued a challenge."

"To investigate this maybe-Mrs. Eliza Gilbert? I should think you'd resent even more his setting you on a cryptic path with no guidance. You don't seriously think Eliza Gilbert is your mother?"

"I know now that Madame Restell is not, which is quite a relief. Her motives may have been noble and kind, or not anything of the sort, but I really don't care to be the unacknowledged daughter of 'the wickedest woman in New York.'"

"This Eliza person may be 'the wickedest woman in Brooklyn,' for all you know, or even worse!"

"Then again she may be better than anyone knows or thinks. We face a week-long transatlantic buffeting were we to return right now, Nell."

I grew green-faced at the very notion. The gently rolling hills around us seemed to shimmer with motion: endless, wretched motion.

"Or," Irene said, "we can stay a bit longer, pick up the stone gauntlet thrown down in Green-Wood Cemetery by Sherlock Holmes, and endeavor to discover who this lady was, and why anyone might think she had some connection to me."

"I have never heard of her," I admitted, pleased that we were at least dealing with a modest, forgotten soul, rather like my own dead mother. It would do Irene good to contemplate obscure origins, as most of us must.

"Eliza Gilbert," Irene read the stone again. "A good name,

solid and trustworthy. I do believe that I would take an 'Eliza Gilbert' on faith.

"I agree. It sounds, in fact, British."

"Do you think so? Many in this land are of that descent, even Madame Restell. Could this woman have been another? Could I have had an English mother?" Irene gazed fondly down at the headstone, around whose occupant she was already busy building a character and a history, as an actor envisioning a part.

I gazed benignly on Mrs. Eliza Gilbert too.

Now at last we could inter the harrowing histories of Madame Restell and her murderer as our attention moved to another woman who had died at a time far distant from this, 1861, when Irene would have been . . . oh . . . three or four. When she had first appeared as a stage orphan, in fact. A very telling fact.

Bless Eliza Gilbert, whoever she may be! I thought. She already had become the closing curtain on a dark tragedy. I was ready for a new curtain to open in our quest, perhaps this time on a warm, sentimental family drama.

Even if she had been divorced, Mrs. Eliza Gilbert could in no way rival Madame Restell for maternal horror. Could she?

Coda

❧

*Hundreds of fashionable folk quaked when they learned
Comstock had taken hold of her. They dreaded that when she
found herself driven to the wall, abandoned by friends who
were afraid to help her, there would be State's evidence given
about their affairs, and all the skeletons in the closets would be
brought out to public view.*

—A NEW YORK NEWSPAPER ON MADAME RESTELL'S ARREST, 1878

After more than a decade of reading, studying, and arranging
the diaries of Penelope Huxleigh into seven published volumes so
far, I have been struck by how many ancillary materials I am finding bundled with the actual diaries as the years progress.

I'm beginning to suspect that a previous scholar had found
Miss Huxleigh's diaries and had integrated them with supporting
materials much more readily available at a much earlier time.

The most exciting "find" introduced in this volume are three
extracts from case notes that Sherlock Holmes apparently kept
but never shared with anyone, not even Dr. Watson. These fragments demonstrate, as the published Holmesian material so
amply does, that Dr. Watson was the better chronicler of the
detective's adventures. Holmes himself might cavil at his physician friend's "unscientific" approach to story telling, but there is
no doubt that the good doctor was a more compelling writer.

As usual, my research has proved the portrayal of the personalities and facts in the Huxleigh accounts correct, in so far as they do not involve matters intentionally kept secret, such as Mina's murder of Madame Restell. It is a pity the Victorian Age deemed so many matters of normal life worthy of concealment. On the other hand, such habits make the Huxleigh diaries an exciting and enlightening window on the hidden aspects of life then.

Mr. Washington Irving Bishop did indeed perish in the outré manner described in Nell Nelson's mostly accurate report of his Lambs Club appearance. Madame Restell did indeed service both high society and low in these delicate matters, as depicted by Miss Huxleigh, for much of the middle of the nineteenth century. She was the most noted and notorious of two or three Manhattan abortionists who advertised publicly despite police and court prosecution.

Certainly this New York episode casts fascinating insight into Irene Adler's early years and mysterious origins.

Where it will all lead only the unpublished volumes of Miss Huxleigh's epic diaries and my assiduous future studies will reveal.

—Fiona Witherspoon, Ph.D., A.I.A.*
November 5, 2002

*Advocates of Irene Adler

Selected Bibliography

Belford, Barbara. *Bram Stoker*. New York: Alfred A. Knopf, 1996.

Browder, Clifford. *The Wickedest Woman in New York*. Hamden, Conn.: Archon Books, 1988.

Bunson, Matthew E. *Encyclopedia Sherlockiana*. New York: Macmillan, 1994.

Burrows, Edwin G., and Mike Wallace. *Gotham: A History of New York City to 1898*. New York: Oxford University Press, 1999.

Coleman, Elizabeth Ann. *The Opulent Era*. New York: Brooklyn Museum, 1989.

Crow, Duncan. *The Victorian Woman*. London: Cox & Wyman, 1971.

Doyle, Arthur Conan. *The Complete Works of Sherlock Holmes*. Various editions.

Du Maurier, George. *Trilby.* New York: Oxford University Press, 1999.

Homberger, Eric, with Alice Hudson. *The Historical Atlas of New York City: A Visual Celebration of Nearly 400 Years of New York City's History.* New York: Henry Holt, 1994.

Jackson, Kenneth T., editor. *The Encyclopedia of New York City.* New Haven and London: Yale University, 1995.

Jay, Ricky. *Learned Pigs & Fireproof Women: A History of Unique, Eccentric & Amazing Entertainers.* London: Robert Hale, 1987.

Keller, Allan. *Scandalous Lady: The Life and Times of Madame Restell, New York's Most Notorious Abortionist.* New York: Atheneum, 1981.

Krafft-Ebing, Richard von. *Psychopathia Sexualis.* London: Velvet Publications, 1997.

Kroeger, Brooke. *Nellie Bly: Daredevil, Reporter, Feminist.* New York: Times Books, 1994.

Mackay, James. *Allan Pinkerton: The Eye Who Never Slept.* Edinburgh, Scotland: Mainstream Publishing Co., 1996.

Femme Fatale

A Reader's Guide

"Perhaps it has taken until the end of this century for an author like Douglas to be able to imagine a female protagonist who could be called 'the' woman by Sherlock Holmes."

—GROUNDS FOR MURDER, 1991

To encourage the reading and discussion of Carole Nelson Douglas's acclaimed novels examining the Victorian world from the viewpoint of one of the most mysterious women in literature, the following descriptions and discussion topics are offered. The author interview, biography, and bibliography will aid discussion as well.

Set in 1880–1890 London, Paris, Prague, Monaco, and most recently New York City, the Irene Adler novels reinvent the only woman to have outwitted Sherlock Holmes as the complex and compelling protagonist of her own stories. Douglas's portrayal of "this remarkable heroine and her keen perspective on the male society in which she must make her independent way," noted *The New York Times*, recasts her "not as a loose-living adventuress but a woman ahead of her time." In Douglas's hands, the fascinating but sketchy American prima donna from "A Scandal in Bohemia" becomes an aspiring opera singer moonlighting as a private inquiry agent. When events force her from the stage into the art of detection, Adler's exploits rival those of Sherlock Holmes himself as she crosses paths and swords with the day's leading creative and political figures while sleuthing among the Bad and the Beautiful of Belle Epoque Europe.

Critics praise the novels' rich period detail, numerous historical characters, original perspective, wit, and "welcome window on things Victorian."

"The private and public escapades of Irene Adler Norton [are] as erratic and unexpected and brilliant as the character herself," noted *Mystery Scene* of *Another Scandal in Bohemia* (formerly

Irene's Last Waltz), "a long and complex jeu d'esprit, simultaneously modeling itself on and critiquing Doylesque novels of ratiocination coupled with emotional distancing. Here is Sherlock Holmes in skirts, but as a detective with an artistic temperament and the passion to match, with the intellect to penetrate to the heart of a crime and the heart to show compassion for the intellect behind it."

⊰ABOUT THIS BOOK⊱

Femme Fatale, the seventh Irene Adler novel, opens in the Paris in the late summer of 1889. The series's main characters are all trying to recover from the previous spring's hunt for Jack the Ripper. The notorious Whitechapel killer of 1888 had decamped to the Continent for more mayhem. But the rival investigators who forged uneasy alliances during that dangerous time—Sherlock Holmes, Irene Adler and friends, and the enterprising American newspaper reporter, Nellie Bly—will be forced into action together again.

Irene Adler's husband, English barrister Godfrey Norton, has established an office in Paris, leaving Irene and her longtime companion, British spinster Nell Huxleigh, alone at their country cottage in Neuilly-sur Seine (a present-day suburb of Paris). First Sherlock Holmes calls at Neuilly to collect a promised translation of a murderous diary related to the Ripper case. Nell, who has read an unpublished manuscript of Dr. Watson's version of the first Adler/Holmes encounter, "A Scandal in Bohemia," loathes and fears Holmes because she knows that "to him" Irene "is always *the* woman."

Then Nellie Bly reaches out from America with tantalizing talk of murder and Irene's mother to draw Irene, Nell, and Sherlock Holmes to America. There Irene will confront aspects of her unremembered past and origins and there they confront murders new, and old.

⊰ FOR DISCUSSION ⊱
Related to Femme Fatale

1. Motherhood, or not, is a major element in this novel. It's often been noted that protagonists in genre fiction like mystery traditionally don't have parents, or very visible parents, or children. Why do you think parents and children might encumber such characters? Certainly Holmes and Watson were parentless as far as readers were concerned. Are there other favorite detectives you can think of who are singularly alone in the world? What kind of parents would you imagine Miss Marple to have had? Nero Wolfe? Is the environment in which the young Irene grew up surprising to you? The only facts Doyle gave about her were that she had been born in New Jersey, was therefore American, and had sung grand opera. What history would you invent for her, instead of this one? Why did the author choose this milieu?

2. Three women with varying personalities and goals are involved in tracing Irene's history. Sometimes they cooperate and sometimes they compete, as is also the case with all three in relation to Sherlock Holmes as well. What characteristics do you admire in each of the three women? What do you not like? Motherhood, and avoiding it, are major elements of the plot and theme. Were you surprised that the nineteenth century had publicly known abortionists? How does the controversy today differ from the issues at stake over a hundred years ago? The character most capable of evolving over the course of the novels is Nell Huxleigh. Does she change in this novel, and does your opinion of her change as well? How does your opinion of Nellie Bly change? She plays an entirely different part in this novel. *The Drood Review of Mystery* observed of *Chapel Noir*: "Douglas wants . . . women fully informed about and capable of action on the mean streets of the their world." How does *Femme Fatale* contribute to this goal?

3. New York City has always been a major American setting for fiction. Did anything about the depiction of it in this book surprise you? How many elements did you glimpse in their infancy then that have become staples of American life now? For instance, Joseph Pulitzer was just entering the newspaper business then, but he would leave a permanent mark, with the awards given in his name today the most prestigious in the country. How much can history teach us? Can history change our opinions of our own times? Do you like to read historical novels for the facts of the time period or the attitudes, and how much do you think you can trust such evocations in fiction? Often, historical novelists say, they're challenged on the accuracy of facts that are absolutely true, but "seem" too modern for people of today. Are you encouraged to do more reading about the historical periods you encounter in novels?

4. The Spiritualism movement was very strong in the mid-to-late nineteenth century. Do you think people were more gullible then than they are now? Sir Arthur Conan Doyle became convinced that mediums could contact the dead and even believed in "fairies" photographed in a garden by two young girls who had manipulated the photos. What would lead a physician by training who created the eminently logical Holmes to such a change in viewpoint? Mesmerism is also a factor in these novels, including Irene Adler taking her last name from a little-known reference about a famous fictional mesmerist, Svengali. Trilby, the eponymous heroine of the George du Maurier (father of Daphne) novel that features Svengali, was hypnotized by him to sing beautifully although she was tone deaf. He married her and forced her to tour as a singer. *The Phantom of the Opera* by Frenchman Gaston Leroux arrived in 1911, more than a decade after de Maurier's *Trilby*, and was far less popular at the time. It too featured a "monster" training a helpless young woman to sing. Why, besides the ever-popular Beauty and the Beast parallels, did this theme of women forced

to sing by taskmasters create two immortal characters, both of them men and villains?

5. Sherlock Holmes has been resurrected as a character by countless writers since Doyle's death in 1930, but by very few women. Some writers say that he is a very hard character to change, that even Doyle did better with stories in which Holmes was not too dominant. How is Holmes's character growing in this series? Which aspects of Holmes as you first encountered him in fiction or film do you feel are immutable, and which allow for change? Does his associating with these particular characters, the three women, two of them liberated American women, throw any different light on his character? There are three Englishmen who are important in the novels: Irene's husband, Godfrey, Holmes, and Quentin Stanhope. How do these men differ from Holmes and each other? How do they all relate to the three women, and how is that different with each man?

6. Douglas has said she likes to work on the "large canvas" of series fiction. What kind of character development does that approach permit? Do you like it? Has television recommitted viewers/readers to the kind of multi-volume storytelling common in the nineteenth century, or is the attention span of the twentieth century too short? Is long-term, committed reading becoming a lost art?

For discussion of the Irene Adler series

1. Douglas mentions other authors, many of them women, who have reinvented major female characters or minor characters from classic literary or genre novels to reevaluate culture then and now. Can you think of such works in the field of fantasy or historical novels? General literature? What about the recent copyright contest over *The Wind Done Gone*, Alice Randall's reimagining of *Gone with the Wind* events and characters from the African-American slaves' viewpoints? Could the novel's important social points have been made as effectively without referencing the classic work generally familiar to most people? What other works have

attained the mythic status that might make possible such socially conscious reinventions? What works would you revisit or rewrite?

2. Religion and morality are underlying issues in the novels, including the time's anti-Semitism. This is an element absent from the Holmes stories. How is this issue brought out and how do Nell's strictly conventional views affect those around her? Why does she take on a moral watchdog role yet remain both disapproving and fascinated by Irene's pragmatic philosophy? Why is Irene (and also most readers) so fond of her despite her limited opinions?

3. Douglas chose to blend humor with adventurous plots. Do comic characters and situations satirize the times, or soften them? Is humor a more effective form of social criticism than rhetoric? What other writers and novelists use this technique, besides George Bernard Shaw and Mark Twain?

4. The novels also present a continuing tension between New World and Old World, America and England and the Continent, artist-tradesman and aristocrat, as well as woman and man. Which characters reflect which camps? How does the tension show itself?

5. *Chapel Noir* makes several references to *Dracula* through the presence of Bram Stoker some six years before the novel actually was published. Stoker is also a continuing character in other Adler novels. Various literary figures appear in the Adler novels, including Oscar Wilde, and most of these historical characters knew each other. Why was this period so rich in writers who founded much modern genre fiction, like Doyle and Stoker? The late nineteenth century produced not only *Dracula* and Doyle's Holmes stories and the surviving dinosaurs of *The Lost World*, but *Trilby* and Svengali, *The Phantom of the Opera*, *The Prisoner of Zenda*, Dr. Jekyll and Mr. Hyde, among the earliest and most lasting works of science fiction, political intrigue, mystery, and horror. How does Douglas pay homage to this tradition in the plots, characters, and details of the Adler novels?

✜AN INTERVIEW WITH
CAROLE NELSON DOUGLAS✜

Q: *You were the first woman to write about the Sherlock Holmes world from the viewpoint of one of Arthur Conan Doyle's women characters, and only the second woman to write a Holmes-related novel at all. Why?*

A: Most of my fiction ideas stem from my role as social observer in my first career, journalism. One day I looked at the mystery field and realized that all post-Doyle Sherlockian novels were written by men. I had loved the stories as a child and thought it was high time for a woman to examine the subject from a female point of view.

Q: *So there was "the woman," Irene Adler, the only woman to outwit Holmes, waiting for you.*

A: She seems the most obvious candidate, but I bypassed her for that very reason to look at other women in what is called the Holmes Canon. Eventually I came back to "A Scandal in Bohemia." Rereading it, I realized that male writers had all taken Irene Adler at face value as the King of Bohemia's jilted mistress, but the story doesn't support that. As the only woman in the Canon who stirred a hint of romantic interest in the aloof Holmes, Irene Adler had to be more than this beautiful but amoral "Victorian vamp." Once I saw that I could validly interpret her as a gifted and serious performing artist, I had my protagonist.

Q: *It was that simple?*

A: It was that complex. I felt that any deeper psychological exploration of this character still had to adhere to Doyle's story, both literally and in regard to the author's own feeling toward the character. That's how I ended up having to explain that operatic impossibility, a contralto prima donna. It's been great fun justifying Doyle's error by finding operatic roles Irene could conceivably sing. My Irene Adler is as intelligent, self-sufficient, and serious about her professional and personal integrity as Sherlock Holmes, and far too independent to be anyone's mistress but her own. She also moonlights as an inquiry agent while building her performing career. In many ways they are flip sides of the same coin: her profession, music, is his hobby. His profession, detection, is her secondary career. Her adventures intertwine with Holmes's, but she is definitely her own woman in these novels.

Q: *How did Doyle feel toward the character of Irene Adler?*

A: I believe that Holmes and Watson expressed two sides of Dr. Doyle: Watson, the medical and scientific man, also the staunch upholder of British convention; Holmes, the creative and bohemian writer, fascinated by the criminal and the bizarre. Doyle wrote classic stories of horror and science fiction as well as hefty historical novels set in the age of chivalry. His mixed feelings of attraction to and fear of a liberated, artistic woman like Irene Adler led him to "kill" her as soon as he created her. Watson states she is dead at the beginning of the story that introduces her. Irene was literally too hot for Doyle as well as Holmes to handle. She also debuted (and exited) in the first Holmes-Watson story Doyle ever wrote. Perhaps Doyle wanted to establish an unattainable woman to excuse Holmes remaining a bachelor and aloof from matters of the heart. What he did was to create a fascinatingly unrealized character for generations of readers.

Q: *Do your protagonists represent a split personality as well?*

A: Yes, one even more sociologically interesting than the Holmes-Watson split because it embodies the evolving roles of women in the late nineteenth century. As a larger-than-life heroine, Irene is "up to anything." Her biographer, Penelope "Nell" Huxleigh, however, is the very model of traditional Victorian womanhood. Together they provide a seriocomic point-counterpoint on women's restricted roles then and now. Narrator Nell is the character who "grows" most during the series as the unconventional Irene forces her to see herself and her times in a broader perspective. This is something women writers have been doing in the past two decades: revisiting classic literary terrain and bringing the sketchy women characters into full-bodied prominence.

Q: *What of "the husband," Godfrey Norton?*

A: In my novels, Irene's husband, Godfrey Norton, is more than the "tall, dark, and dashing barrister" Doyle gave her. I made him the son of a woman wronged by England's then female-punitive divorce law, so he is a "supporting" character in every sense of the word. These novels are that rare bird in literature: female "buddy" books. Godfrey fulfills the useful, decorative, and faithful role so often played by women and wives in fiction and real life. Sherlockians anxious to unite Adler and Holmes have tried to oust Godfrey. William S. Baring-Gould even depicted him as a wife-beater in order to promote a later assignation with Holmes that produced Nero Wolfe! That is such an unbelievable violation of a strong female character's psychology. That scenario would make Irene Adler a two-time loser in her choice of men and a masochist to boot. My protagonist is a world away from that notion and a wonderful vehicle for subtle but sharp feminist comment.

Q: *Did you give her any attributes not found in the Doyle story?*

A: I gave her one of Holmes's bad habits. She smokes "little cigars." Smoking was an act of rebellion for women then. And because Doyle shows her sometimes donning male dress to go unhampered into public places, I gave her "a wicked little revolver" to carry. When Doyle put her in male disguise at the end of his story, I doubt he was thinking of the modern psychosexual ramifications of cross-dressing.

Q: *Essentially, you have changed Irene Adler from an ornamental woman to a working woman.*

A: My Irene is more a rival than a romantic interest for Holmes, yes. She is not a logical detective in the same mold as he, but is as gifted in her intuitive way. Nor is her opera-singing a convenient profession for a beauty of the day, but a passionate vocation that was taken from her by the King of Bohemia's autocratic attitude toward women, forcing her to occupy herself with detection. Although Doyle's Irene is beautiful, well dressed, and clever, my Irene demands that she be taken seriously despite these feminine attributes. Now we call it "Grrrrl power."

I like to write "against" conventions that are no longer true, or were never true. This is the thread that runs through all my fiction: my dissatisfaction with the portrayal of women in literary and popular fiction—then and even now. This begins with *Amberleigh*—my postfeminist mainstream version of the Gothic-revival popular novels of the 1960s and 1970s—and continues with Irene Adler today. I'm interested in women as survivors. Men also interest me of necessity, men strong enough to escape cultural blinders to become equal partners to strong women.

Q: *How do you research these books?*

A: From a lifetime of reading English literature and a theatrical background that educated me on the clothing, culture, customs, and speech of various historical periods. I was reading Oscar Wilde plays when I was eight years old. My mother's book club meant that I cut my teeth on Eliot, Balzac, Kipling, Poe, poetry, Greek mythology, Hawthorne, the Brontes, Dumas, and Dickens.

In doing research, I have a fortunate facility of using every nugget I find, or of finding that every little fascinating nugget works itself into the story. Perhaps that's because good journalists must be ingenious in using every fact available to make a story as complete and accurate as possible under deadline conditions. Often the smallest mustard seed of research swells into an entire tree of plot. The corpse on the dining-room table of Bram Stoker, author of *Dracula*, was too macabre to resist and spurred the entire plot of the second Adler novel, *The Adventuress* (formerly *Good Morning, Irene*). Stoker rescued a drowning man from the Thames and carried him home for revival efforts, but it was too late.

Besides using my own extensive library on this period, I've borrowed from my local library all sorts of arcane books they don't even know they have because no one ever checks them out. The Internet aids greatly with the specific fact. I've also visited London and Paris to research the books, a great hardship, but worth it. I also must visit Las Vegas periodically for my contemporary-set Midnight Louie mystery series. No sacrifice is too great.

Q: *You've written fantasy and science fiction novels, why did you turn to mystery?*

A: All novels are fantasy and all novels are mystery in the largest sense. Although mystery was often an element in my early novels, when I evolved the Irene Adler idea, I considered it simply a novel. *Good Night, Mr. Holmes* was almost on the shelves before I realized it would be "categorized" as a mystery. So Irene is utterly a product of my mind and times, not of the marketplace, though I always believed that the concept was timely and necessary.

About the Author

‑‑‑

"Highly eclectic writer and literary adventuress, Douglas is as concerned about genre equality as she is about gender equity," writes Jo Ellyn Clarey in *The Drood Review of Mystery*.

Carole Nelson Douglas is a journalist-turned-novelist whose writing in both fields has been a finalist for, or received, fifty awards. A literary chameleon, she has always explored the roles of women in society, first in daily newspaper reporting, then in numerous novels ranging from fantasy and science fiction to mainstream fiction.

She currently writes two mystery series. The Victorian Irene Adler series examines the role of women in the late nineteenth century through the adventures of the only woman to outwit Sherlock Holmes, an American diva/detective. The contemporary-yet-Runyonesque Midnight Louie series contrasts the realistic crime-solving activities and personal issues of four main human characters with the interjected first-person feline viewpoint of a black alley cat PI, who satirizes the role of the rogue male in crime and popular fiction. ("Although Douglas has a wicked sense of humor," Clarey writes, "her energetic sense of justice is well balanced and her fictional mockery is never nasty.")

Douglas, born in Everett, Washington, grew up in St. Paul, Minnesota, and emigrated with her husband to Fort Worth, Texas, trading Snowbelt for Sunbelt and journalism for fiction. At the College of St. Catherine in St. Paul she earned degrees in English literature and speech and theater, with a minor in philosophy, and was a finalist (along with groundbreaking mystery novelist, Marcia Muller) in *Vogue* magazine's Prix de Paris writing competition (won earlier by Jacqueline Bouvier Kennedy Onassis).

Chapel Noir resumed the enormously well received Irene Adler series after a seven-year hiatus and with its sequel, *Castle Rouge*, comprises the Jack the Ripper duology within the overall series. The first Adler novel, *Good Night, Mr. Holmes*, won American Mystery and *Romantic Times* magazine awards and was a *New York Times* Notable Book of the Year. The reissued edition of *Good Morning, Irene* will be released as *The Adventuress* in January 2004.

E-mail: ireneadler@catwriter.com

Web site: www.catwriter.com